Tender Mercies

A Novel

by

Roman Bystrianyk

November, 2025

This novel is a work of fiction. Real historical events and figures appear, but the central narrative and the majority of its characters are imaginary. The author has taken creative liberties with chronology, dialogue, and specific incidents for dramatic effect. Where real historical figures speak, their words are imagined by the author unless otherwise attributed in the back matter. All other characters and incidents are fictitious, and any resemblance to actual persons, living or dead, is entirely coincidental.

The historical photographs, quotations, and references in the back matter are used for educational and contextual purposes under fair use. All sources are credited where possible. The author makes no claim to own the copyright of these archival materials.

ISBN: 979-8-9869363-8-3

Published in the United States of America

First Edition: November 2025

Edited by: Jessica Shiever
Cover Design: Salome Mumford,
www.salomemumford.com

To every reader navigating through their own storms in search of a meaningful life—may you discover that the journey itself is made beautiful by the adventure, the friends you encounter, and the love you give and receive.

It was the best of times, it was the worst of times, it was the age of wisdom, it was the age of foolishness, it was the epoch of belief, it was the epoch of incredulity, it was the season of Light, it was the season of Darkness, it was the spring of hope, it was the winter of despair, we had everything before us, we had nothing before us, we were all going direct to Heaven, we were all going direct the other way.

—Charles Dickens, *A Tale of Two Cities*, 1859

Milestones Along the Journey

Author's Note

The greatest thing a human soul ever does in this world is to see something, and tell what it saw in a plain way. Hundreds of people can talk for one who can think, but thousands can think for one who can see. To see clearly is poetry, prophecy, and religion,—all in one.
—John Ruskin, *Modern Painters: Volume III*, 1856

*T*he idea for this novel came to me while I was discussing history, drawing on my earlier books, *Dissolving Illusions* and *Moving Back from Midnight*. As I spoke, a realization dawned—one that now seems glaringly obvious: many find history books dry, dense, and challenging to digest. I realized that a novel could be a far more compelling vehicle to the past—a way to make history not just informative, but vivid, entertaining, and deeply human.

Moreover, my research had uncovered countless fascinating historical fragments that didn't fit into my previous nonfiction works. These hidden gems, rich with narrative potential, were too compelling to leave in my archives. So, I chose to weave them into a novel, breathing life into them through story in the hope that they would resonate on a deeper, more intimate level.

This book is set during the late Industrial Revolution in England, a period of tremendous upheaval. It's easy to conjure romantic images of men in top hats, women in elegant gowns, and horse-drawn carriages, but the reality was far more complex—and often far harsher. Many events in this story may surprise or even shock you. History is not always what we've been led to believe, and this book pulls back the curtain on a world as fascinating as it is unsettling.

At the heart of this tale is Victoria, a woman of upper-class standing in the waning years of 1870s London, navigating a society as elegant as it is unforgiving. When her life is upended, she is thrust into harsh realities she had only glimpsed from a distance. Stripped of comfort and illusion, Victoria must learn to stand on her own. Her journey through hardship becomes a crucible, forging a courage and resilience she never knew she possessed and transforming her from a survivor into a protector.

Victoria's story is a testament to the strength of the human spirit. As she confronts injustice, she becomes a beacon of hope, demonstrating that even in the darkest times, we can find the strength to persevere. *Tender Mercies* is more than a historical novel; it is a story of self-discovery, resilience, and the enduring power of love and friendship. It is a tale that will keep you on the edge of your seat, leaving you not only breathless with suspense but also inspired and hopeful.

While grounded in real historical events, *Tender Mercies* remains a work of fiction. I've taken creative liberties to serve the narrative—shifting certain events or blending details to enhance the narrative. For instance, although a specific incident may not have occurred in a particular hospital, it did happen elsewhere during that tumultuous era.

For readers eager to delve deeper, I've included a section of fully referenced quotes and photographs that served as the foundation for key elements of the narrative.

Author's Remarks

These are designed to satisfy curiosity, verify the veracity of the story, and perhaps ignite a passion for the past.

In a world where personal freedoms often feel threatened, Victoria's journey is a powerful reminder that one individual can make a profound difference. This is not merely a story about the past; it is a call to action, a celebration of the human spirit's capacity to rise above adversity. Step into the world of *Tender Mercies*, where history and fiction intertwine in a tale that is as heart-rending as it is unforgettable. Let Victoria's courage inspire you, a reminder that even in the darkest times, hope and humanity can light the way forward.

1. The Dream

All that we see or seem is but a dream within a dream.
—Edgar Allan Poe, *A Dream Within a Dream*, 1849

Sunlight flickered and sparkled on the surface of the gently flowing brook, casting a whimsical dance of light that seemed practically magical. Victoria stood at the water's edge, the hem of her light blue cotton dress gathered in her hands, her grip gentle yet firm, the fabric soft and worn from countless washings.

She looked down at her bare feet, pale and dainty, slightly submerged in the shimmering, crystal-clear water. The coolness sent a shiver up her legs, but it was a welcome sensation, a fleeting escape from the heat of the summer day. The water bubbled and frothed around her ankles, tickling her skin, while the pebbles and sand beneath her feet shifted with each tentative step. She dug her toes deeper, savoring the gritty texture of the riverbed as if grounding herself in the moment.

She smiled, tilting her face toward the sun, feeling its warmth seep into her skin like a gentle embrace. A light wind stirred the air, carrying with it the subtle scents of wildflowers and damp moss. It tousled her long, auburn hair, sending strands dancing across her face and along the back of her neck. Across the stream, the meadow stretched out in a sea of green, the grass swaying in unison with the scattered trees that dotted the landscape. Oak,

1

ash, and silver birch trees stood like silent sentinels, their branches weaving together in a canopy of whispers. One ancient oak, gnarled and majestic, towered above the rest, its roots clawing into the earth as if anchoring the very soul of the forest.

Victoria breathed in deeply, filling her lungs with the sweet, earthy essence of summer. She closed her eyes, bathing in the sunlight, letting the symphony of the forest envelop her—the distant trill of birdsong, the rustle of leaves, the gentle gurgle of the water. A stray lock of hair, warmed to a coppery glow by the sun, brushed against her cheek. In this moment, she wasn't a collection of features to be judged, but simply a part of the landscape, unobserved and free.

When she opened her eyes, she craned her neck to gaze at the vast expanse of blue sky above. Clouds drifted lazily, their shapes shifting and morphing like dreams taking form. Each one seemed to carry a promise, a whisper of hope for a life beyond the confines of her reality. She envied them their freedom. A breeze swept across the water, rippling its surface, and for the briefest moment, she imagined herself dissolving into it—weightless, untethered.

A sudden ache tightened in her chest, sharp and insistent. She jostled her head slightly, her hair sweeping across her shoulders, feeling a pang of longing so sharp it nearly stole her breath. Here, by the creek, she could pretend that she too was unshackled, that her world was not confined by duty and expectation. For just an instant, she could breathe.

A woman's voice called from beyond the trees, distant but insistent. "Victoria!"

She flinched. The sound cut through the peace like a blade, sharp and unrelenting.

"Victoria!" The second call was closer, gruff, and commanding. It yanked her from her reverie. She gasped softly, her breath catching as the coolness of the brook gave way to an oppressive, stale warmth. The final note of birdsong vanished, replaced by the clatter of dishes and the light hum of conversation. Her hand instinctively reached for something—solid ground, an anchor—but found nothing.

She blinked, the tranquil scene dissolving like mist in the morning sun. The creek, the meadow, the venerable oak—they faded like a dream at dawn, leaving her stranded in the dim glow of her mother-in-law's dining room. No longer standing in sun-dappled water, she now sat rigid at the polished mahogany table. The scent of damp earth and wildflowers was gone, supplanted by roasted meats, boiled vegetables, and the syrupy perfume of propriety tightening around her like a noose. Fresh air and grass gave way to the stale hush of reality. The weight of her corset pressed against her ribs once more, her bare feet encased in rigid leather boots. The murmuring brook faded, overtaken by the sharp clink of silverware on delicate porcelain.

Her heart sank. The daydream extinguished.

"Yes, Annabelle... Ma'am?" she replied, her voice tinged with reluctance. Her hands instinctively smoothed the fabric of her dress as if to erase any trace of her fantasy.

Annabelle pursed her lips, disapproval etched into every refined line of her face. "You didn't hear a word I was saying."

The Dream

Victoria blinked again, forcing herself into the rigid expectations of the present.

The dining room was a testament to the opulence of the Victorian upper class, though its grandeur felt stifling rather than inviting. The hardwood table was set with fine Wedgwood china, each plate adorned with delicate blue patterns of pastoral scenes. Silver cutlery gleamed under the flickering light of the brass chandelier, its crystals casting prisms of light onto the brilliantly bright Paris Green walls—a color so fashionable it was said to be found in every respectable home, despite the whispers of its arsenic-laden toxicity.

The heavy drapes, woven with intricate damask patterns, were drawn against the evening chill, their tasseled edges brushing against the floor. A sideboard stood against one wall, its surface bearing an ornate candelabra and a decanter of claret, the deep red liquid catching the light like a jewel. It was all so precise, so carefully arranged—so utterly suffocating.

Her own pale, tense face stared back from the mirrored sheen of the dining table surface. The entire indulgent ensemble felt like a weight designed to press her deeper into the maw of her chair.

As Victoria glanced at the unyielding curtains, she felt a sudden urge to throw them open, to let in the night air and the stars beyond. But she remained still, her hands clasped tightly in her lap, the weight of obligation pressing down on her.

The meal itself was a display of Victorian excess—a tureen of turtle soup, its savory aroma mingling with the rich, gamey scent of roasted pheasant and buttered asparagus. A dish of boiled potatoes, glistening with melted butter and garnished with parsley, sat beside a platter of braised carrots and turnips. The bread, freshly baked and still warm, was served with a pat of golden butter stamped with an intricate floral design. Yet, despite the table groaning under the weight of abundance, Victoria felt as though she were chewing on stale biscuits.

"Of course, Ma'am," Victoria murmured, her voice barely above a whisper, her hands clutched tightly in her lap to still their trembling.

Annabelle let out an exasperated huff, her lips pursed in disapproval. "See, Simon, this is what I'm talking about. She often drifts off to God knows where. You could have done much better. If only you had listened to me and marri—"

"Mama, not again," Simon cut in, his voice weary but firm, a note of finality in his tone.

Victoria's body tensed, her thoughts drifting before she grudgingly snapped herself back to the present. Her gaze flicked to Mary, the housemaid, who stood silently by the sideboard, her fingers interlaced tightly in front of her. The young woman's face was a mask of quiet efficiency, but Victoria could see the tension in her shoulders, the slight tremor in her fingers.

As a child, Victoria dreamed of traveling to far-off lands and having adventures. But those dreams had been buried under layers of duty and decorum, leaving only the faintest echo of who she once was—of who she imagined she would be.

Annabelle's nostrils flared slightly, her sharp eyes narrowing as her bejeweled fingers—adorned with rings of gold and precious stones—drew taut around her fork. Despite her years, her face bore only a few wrinkles, the most prominent being the fine lines at the corners of her eyes—eyes that were as piercing as they were commanding, a frostbitten blue that seemed to see through pretense. Her white and grey hair was scraped back into a ruthlessly tight bun, each pearl-tipped pin seeming to enforce its imposing order. She paused deliberately, her imposing gaze sweeping the room like a hawk surveying its domain.

"I am just saying you had much better selections than—"

Simon's square jaw stiffened, and his broad forehead furrowed with irritation. Like his mother, Simon's eyes were a striking deep blue, framed by thick, dark brows that added intensity to his already commanding look. He ran a hand through his carefully groomed hair, a gesture of frustration that momentarily disrupted its perfect waves. In his fine clothes, with his solid, handsome frame, he looked every inch the master of the house, yet in this moment, it seemed to Victoria that perhaps he was just another well-dressed hostage at the table.

"Yes, I am quite aware of your thoughts on the matter," Simon cut her off, his tone firm and clipped, leaving no room for further argument.

Victoria sat rigidly, her cheeks flushed with a mixture of embarrassment and resentment. She kept her gaze fixed on her plate, the roasted vegetables and slices of meat suddenly even more unappetizing. The flickering candle-light cast a soft glow on her face, highlighting the discom-fort etched into her features—the tightness around her mouth, the muted crease between her brows, the light moisture on her upper lip. She pressed her lips together to still their faint tremor and focused on her breathing, on the steady rise and fall of her chest, willing herself to remain calm. She felt like a porcelain doll on display, fragile and voiceless.

6

Annabelle's eyes narrowed, her disapproval palpable. "I just want what's best for you, Simon. We must maintain appearances. We can't..."

"And as the head of this household, I have chosen what's best for me, Mama," Simon interrupted, his voice unwavering, though his eyes flicked briefly to Victoria as if seeking her silent approval. Simon's hand brushed against Victoria's under the table, a fleeting gesture of solidarity. His touch was tender, a stark contrast to the cold disapproval radiating from his mother.

Victoria felt a surge of gratitude toward her husband, his support a small beacon of hope in an otherwise smothering atmosphere. She stole a glance at him, yet he didn't appear to notice, his attention firmly fixed on his mother.

"She is a fine and sturdy woman who is quite pleasing to the eye," Simon said matter-of-factly, without so much as a glance back in Victoria's direction.

Victoria's cheeks reddened as gratitude became laced with something bitter by the sting of his words—*a fine and sturdy woman who is quite pleasing to the eye*. The phrase echoed in her mind, a stark reminder of how little she meant to him beyond her physical appearance and ability to fulfill her duties. Her father had always said she was pretty and would make any man happy by having his children. His children. Is that all she was worth? A fine and sturdy woman. Sturdy—as if she were a cow, a horse, or a piece of furniture. As if her worth began and ended with her physical form and ability to bear children. A dull ache settled in her stomach.

Annabelle's lips curled into a sneer. "Pleasing to the eye? Is that how you make your decisions? Superficialities?"

7

The Dream

Victoria's stomach twisted, her nails pressing into the fabric of her skirt. Annabelle's words were a constant reminder of her inadequacy, a refrain she had grown all too familiar with.

"Mama! I am tired of this repetitive conversation. Let's simply enjoy our dinner."

The room fell into a strained silence, broken only by the soft crackle of the candles. Victoria took a measured breath, her thoughts slipping back to the brook, the sun-dappled water, and the gentle breeze. It was a small solace, a momentary escape from the oppressive weight of her reality.

"Victoria, dear," Annabelle's voice broke the silence, softer now but still edged with criticism. "You must understand. I only wish for you to be more present and more attentive. You must attend to your household duties with diligence. To look respectable is to be respectable."

"Yes, Ma'am," Victoria replied, her voice steady but devoid of warmth.

Annabelle sighed with resignation. "Very well. Let us continue with dinner." Annabelle's eyes flicked to the portrait above the mantel, a younger version of herself staring back with the same watchful stare. For a moment, her expression softened, a crack of vulnerability breaking through her icy demeanor.

As the conversation shifted to more mundane topics, Victoria allowed herself to relax slightly, though the strain in the room remained thick enough to cut with a blade. She glanced at Simon, who offered her a faint, reassuring smile, though his focus quickly returned to his mother.

As they spoke, Victoria barely registered Annabelle's or Simon's words. Annabelle suggested something about replacing candles with more modern gas lamps, but

Victoria caught only fragments of her words, muffled and distant, as though she were submerged in deep water, struggling to surface.

Dinner continued, the clinking of cutlery against fine china and the muted murmurs of conversation filling the air. Victoria picked at her food, her thoughts a whirlwind of emotions—bitterness, yearning, and a quiet determination to find a way to reclaim some semblance of the freedom glimpsed in her dream.

"Simon, have you given any thought to the upcoming charity ball?" Annabelle asked, her tone light but expectant.

"Yes, Mama. Victoria and I will be attending," Simon answered, casting a quick glance at his wife.

Victoria nodded, offering a polite smile. "I am looking forward to it," she added, though her heart wasn't in it. The charity ball, like so many other social obligations, felt like a performance, a role she had to play to maintain appearances.

"Good. It's important for us to be seen supporting such causes," Annabelle remarked, her eyes briefly softening. "And Victoria, dear, you will need a new dress for the occasion—something that befits your... status."

"Of course, Ma'am," Victoria acknowledged, her voice even but devoid of enthusiasm.

Annabelle's scrutiny was relentless, and Victoria knew that nothing less than perfection would satisfy her. She took a sip of water, hoping to quell the growing unease in her stomach. As the evening wore on, Victoria's mind wandered back once again to the stream, to the simplicity and peace it represented. It was a passing reprieve, yet she clung to it with quiet desperation.

Mary, the housemaid, wore the uniform of her station: a plain black dress with a white apron tied neatly at her waist, its starched edges rustling softly as she moved. Her cap, perched precariously, framed a square face that was young but weary, her cheeks flushed from the heat of the kitchen. She moved with the quiet efficiency of someone accustomed to being unseen, her eyes downcast as she cleared the table with practiced hands. The muted scent of lye soap and coal smoke clung to her, a reminder of the endless labor that kept households like this one running smoothly.

The conversations halted again, the only sounds the clatter of dishes and the servants' quick, almost imperceptible breaths. Once the table was cleared, dessert plates and silverware were placed in front of each of them. Finally, the apple charlotte was brought out and set in the center of the table alongside a pitcher of rich custard. The dessert, favored for its simplicity and elegance, was a masterpiece of Victorian culinary art. Its golden crust, baked to glistening perfection, encased a filling of spiced apples and currants, the aroma of cinnamon and sugar wafting through the room. The dish was a symbol of domesticity and refinement, yet its presence tonight felt like a reproach—a reminder of the expectations Victoria could never quite meet.

With a displeased look, Annabelle stared at the center of the table. "I was expecting trifle."

A flicker of displeasure crossed Simon's face, but he knew his mother's tirades well. Resigned, he remained silent.

Mary's hands trembled slightly as she stepped back, her gaze lowered. She shot a nervous glance at Victoria, hesitating before speaking. She stammered, "S-sorry, Ma'am. We did not have any strawberries."

Despite the splendor of the dessert before her, Annabelle's voice was sharp, her tone carrying the weight of someone accustomed to having her every whim catered to. "Trifle is the proper dessert for a dinner of this caliber," she continued, her eyes narrowing as she surveyed the table. "Strawberries may be out of season, but surely the kitchen could have managed something more fitting. I am sorely tempted to dismiss the cook altogether—such incompetence is intolerable." She added, "The Harrowbys served a proper trifle at their last dinner. I will not have us appear... lacking."

Victoria felt a pang of sympathy for the young woman. She often chatted with Mary in the kitchen, finding solace in their brief, stolen moments of camaraderie. Annabelle, however, treated the servants as little more than objects, a fact that Victoria found both infuriating and heartbreaking. Victoria clenched her hands into fists beneath the table, her fingernails biting into her thighs as she fought to suppress frustration.

"Servants are here to serve and not to cavort with," Annabelle had once admonished Victoria when she was caught talking and laughing with Mary. To Victoria, the so-called servants were far more pleasant company than an indifferent mother-in-law.

Annabelle's expression darkened further. "I see," she intoned icily. "It seems the staff is incapable of managing even the simplest tasks. Perhaps I need to reconsider my choices in the kitchen."

The servant's face flushed with shame, but she remained silent, hands clasped tightly in front, her eyes fixed on the floorboards she'd scrubbed that morning.

The Dream

Victoria longed to intervene, to offer a word of comfort, but she knew better than to challenge Annabelle in front of others.

Annabelle cast a withering glance at Victoria, a slight shake of her head betraying her disapproval. "Lost in fantasies instead of ensuring the servants do their work."

The room remained still and quiet for a few moments.

Sensing the increasing unease, Simon interjected, "Mama, the apple charlotte looks delightful. I'm sure it will be delicious."

Annabelle's eyes flicked to her son, her lips pressed into a thin line. "I suppose it will have to do," she responded curtly, her tone making it clear that she was far from satisfied.

Victoria forced a polite smile as she lifted her fork, but her mind was elsewhere, slipping away back to the brook, to the wind in the trees, to the dream that had felt more real—more hers—than anything in this house ever would. She tightened her hands in her lap, pressing her fingers into her palms as if trying to hold onto the feeling of water slipping through her fingers.

2. Chamber of Solitude

The despotism of custom is everywhere the standing hindrance to human advancement, being in unceasing antagonism to that disposition to aim at something better than customary, which is called, according to circumstances, the spirit of liberty, or that of progress or improvement.
—John Stuart Mill, *On Liberty*, 1859

Victoria was able to excuse herself to retire to the bedroom early that night, pleading a headache—a convenient excuse that no one questioned. She was grateful that no one objected; perhaps they were relieved to see her go, sparing themselves the awkwardness of her lingering presence at the table. As soon as she was out of sight, she gathered her skirts in one hand and bolted up the staircase, her boots striking the well-worn wooden steps with a rhythmic clatter that echoed through the quiet house.

The third step from the top, as always, groaned softly underfoot, a mournful sound that reverberated through the stillness—a sound so familiar it felt like an old, unwelcome friend—her creaking sentinel. She bounded up the last two steps, turned left, and rushed down the carpeted hallway, her footsteps muffled now by the thick, floral-patterned runner that stretched the length of the corridor.

Chamber of Solitude

A single gas sconce dimly lit the hallway, its flickering flame casting wavering phantom shapes on the wallpaper, making the faded, deep burgundy color seem to shift and breathe. The air smelled subtly of beeswax and lavender—the specter of the housemaid's labors, a world away from the dinner table's heavy aromas.

Victoria's room was at the end of the hall, its heavy oak door standing like a sentry between her and the world outside. She grasped the brass doorknob, its surface cool and slightly tarnished, and turned it with a soft click. The door shuddered slightly as she pushed it open, as if reluctant to grant her entry.

She stepped inside and closed the door behind her, leaning against it for a moment as she let out a long, trembling sigh. The room was a sanctuary, a space that bore the pale imprint of her personality amidst the otherwise oppressive grandeur of the house. A four-poster bed dominated the center of the room; its dark wooden frame draped with heavy velvet curtains in a deep green hue. A small writing desk stood near the window, its surface cluttered with sheets of half-finished poems and letters, a bottle of ink, and a quill resting on a well-worn groove. A gentle gust stirred the lace curtains at the window, carrying the distant scent of the garden below—a promise of a world beyond.

Victoria crossed the room to the window, her skirt rustling softly against the Persian rug that covered the floor, its intricate patterns muted under the dim light. Her forehead pressed against the cool glass as she gazed out at the moonlit garden, its silvery light casting an ethereal glow over the neatly trimmed hedges and blooming flowers. The solitude of the room was a balm, a stark contrast to the stifling atmosphere of the dining room, where every word and gesture felt scrutinized. Here, she could breathe. Here, she could almost forget the weight of expectations that pressed down like a leaden cloak—well, almost.

Victoria hurried to the dressing table, fingers quivering as she reached behind to loosen the ties of her day dress. The intricate knots, tightened that morning by her lady's maid, resisted at first, but she persisted, tugging impatiently until the fabric began to give way. The bodice sagged, and she wriggled out of the confining garment, letting it slip from her shoulders and pool carelessly on the floor in a heap of blue cotton and lace.

Next came the corset, the true prison of her day. She twisted her arm behind her back, fumbling with the laces that cinched her waist into an unnatural hourglass form. Each tug felt like a small victory, the tension in her ribs easing as the jailer loosened its tight grip. Finally, she pulled it over her head and tossed it aside, the stiff boning and fabric landing with a muffled *thump* on the rug.

For the first time since morning, she took a deep, unrestricted breath, her lungs expanding fully as the cool air filled her chest. She closed her eyes, savoring the sensation, her hands resting lightly on her ribcage as if to reassure herself that she was free, if only for a moment. The relief was palpable, a brief escape from the suffocating expectations that defined her days, a brief taste of the liberty she so desperately craved.

Exhausted, she stumbled backward and sank onto the bed, the mattress dipping beneath her weight. The bedframe, carved from dark walnut and adorned with exquisite scrollwork, creaked softly in protest, a familiar, groaning complaint that was the only welcome she ever received in this room.

She leaned forward to tackle her boots, her fingers working quickly to loosen laces that had been tightly secured hours earlier. Each boot came off with a slight struggle, dropping them unceremoniously to the floor, where they landed with a satisfying *clunk*. The sound echoed in the quiet room, a small rebellion against the silence that so often stifled her.

She peeled off her stockings, the fine silk damp and clinging to her skin after the long day. The muted scent of sweat and leather lingered in the air, a reminder of the hours spent in stifling politeness, of smiles forced and words carefully measured. Looking down, she wiggled her toes and scrutinized them, noticing the slightly chipped nails and a bit of dirt embedded beneath them. They were a far cry from the delicate, polished feet expected of a lady of her station—so alive and free when submerged in the cool, bubbling brook of her imagination earlier that day. A mixture of irritation and resignation twisted her features as she huffed out a breath and fell backward onto the bed, her body sinking into the mattress.

She lay back against the pillows in nothing but her chemise, the thin silk clinging to her skin, her hair spilling out in a tangled auburn cascade, curls splayed across her forehead like a fiery halo. Above her, the heavy velvet curtains of the canopy bed, embroidered with gold thread, seemed to close in around her, a suffocating reminder of the opulence that felt more like a gilded cage than a home.

Her eyes scanned the room's contents: a hardwood wardrobe stood against one wall, its surface polished to a mirror-like sheen, while a porcelain washbasin and pitcher sat on the dressing table, ready for her morning ablutions. A small bookcase in the corner held a collection of novels and poetry, their spines worn from repeated reading—her only solace in a world that demanded so much and gave so little.

But for now, in this moment, she was alone—truly, blissfully alone, and that was enough. The weight of her duties, the sharpness of Annabelle's scorn, and the emptiness of Simon's indifference faded into the background, like phantoms retreating from the light, replaced by the simple pleasure of breathing freely. She closed her eyes and let the silence envelop her, a rare and precious respite from the life she had been born into.

Worn out by the day's events, she drifted off for a few heartbeats—or perhaps longer—only to be awakened by the thud of horse hooves against the compacted stone of the road, the carriage's wheels crunching softly as it passed by the window. The sound, sharp and insistent, pulled her from the edge of sleep. She fluttered her lashes groggily, her mind struggling to orient itself. The room, bathed in the light silver glow of moonlight, seemed to hold its breath as she stirred.

Dropping her bare feet to the floor, she felt the coolness of the polished wood beneath them, a stark contrast to the warmth of the bed and a jolt of reality that grounded her. She rose and tiptoed across the room, her steps dampened by the thick Persian rug, until she reached the bookcase nestled in the corner, its richly grained frame gleaming dimly in the low light. The glass-paned doors of the bookcase held rows of leatherbound volumes, their spines embossed with gilt lettering that caught the pale light like whispers of muffled secrets.

But Victoria's destination was not the neatly arranged rows of books on display. Instead, she knelt and reached around to the back of the bottom shelf, her fingers brushing against the smooth wood until they found the hidden gap.

From this secret nook, she extracted a small, leather-bound book, its cover worn from frequent handling. She paused, holding her breath, and listened carefully for any sound from the hallway—a protest on the stairs, the subtle rustle of skirts, or the telltale groan of the third step, her ever-vigilant sentinel. But there was nothing, only the distant, relentless ticking of the grandfather clock in the hall below.

Reassured, she walked to her writing table, a delicate piece of furniture with slender legs, and placed the leatherbound book onto the chaotic surface. She opened it to the page marked by a thin red silk ribbon; its edges frayed from years of use. The pages, filled with her neat, sloping handwriting, seemed to glow softly in the dim light of the candle lit earlier. Here, in this private journal, she could pour out her thoughts and dreams, free from the prying eyes of her mother-in-law or the indifferent gaze of her husband. It was her sanctuary, a place where she could be herself, if only on paper, where the yoke of propriety dissolved into the freedom of ink on parchment.

Today dragged on endlessly. Only my visit to Mabel brought a flicker of joy—a rare escape from this suffocating life. She has a way of making me feel as though I am more than just a wife, more than just a daughter-in-law—more than the sum of my duties. When we laugh together, I feel alive, as though the weight of this life is momentarily lifted. It is so dreadfully hard to leave her company and return to this... this mausoleum of expectations.

She paused, her writing tool hovering above the page, and dipped it into the inkwell, the deep black liquid clinging to the nib. Her thoughts swirled like the ink in the well, restless and unfocused. She tapped the quill lightly against the edge of the glass, her brow furrowing. The faint *clink* of the quill's shaft against glass punctuated her restless, uncertain thoughts.

I hope Simon's business ventures succeed soon, so we might—

She stopped, the pen unsteady in her hand. The words felt hollow, even as she wrote them. *Would I ever truly be free of Annabelle's disapproval?* The question lingered, unanswerable, like a shadow she could not shake. But even if Simon's business ventures succeeded and they moved to their own home, what did she truly hope for? A grander house, with more rooms to fill with silence? More servants, their eyes always watching, their whispers always judging? A higher standing in society, where the expectations would only grow heavier, the scrutiny more suffocating? None of it mattered if it meant remaining trapped in this opulent prison, where every breath felt measured, every step watched, and every word weighed for decorum —a life lived in perpetual performance.

She huffed, setting the quill down carefully on the ink-stained blotter, and turned her gaze to the window. Outside, the sky was darkening, the last traces of daylight fading into a deep indigo. The dim glow of gas lamps from the street below cast long, wavering forms across the room, their softly glowing light a poor substitute for the warmth she craved. Somewhere beyond the glass, beyond the confines of this house and this life, there was a world where she might breathe freely, where she might laugh without fear of reproach, where she might simply be— unburdened and unbound. But for now, that world felt as distant as the stars beginning to pierce the evening sky.

Her thoughts shifted to an angry reflection, sharp and unrelenting. Annabelle. The name alone was enough to sour her mood, its syllables sharp as a knife against her already frayed nerves. She picked up the quill again, dipping it into the black fluid, the viscous liquid clinging to the nib like a shadow. She tapped the quill's tip against the glass, each sharp *tap* a tiny release of her pent-up frustration. Pursing her lips, she attacked the paper with a tinge of spiteful glee, the pen scratching furiously across the page.

It is beyond my comprehension how someone could become as dour and judgmental as Annabelle. I am convinced that if she ever smiled—truly smiled—her face would crack and shatter like a porcelain doll, falling to the floor in a thousand brittle pieces.

Victoria laid the quill down, a small, satisfied smile playing at the corners of her lips, the subtle curve of her mouth a rare, delicious crack in the porcelain mask she so often wore. She pictured the scene in her mind: Annabelle's stern expression crumbling, her haughty demeanor reduced to broken fragments on the polished floor. The image was so absurd, so delightfully irreverent, that she couldn't help but giggle to herself, the sound soft and muffled in the quiet of the room, a momentary burst of joy that felt almost illicit. It was a rare moment of levity, a small rebellion against the woman who seemed determined to control every aspect of her life.

The third stair sentinel sounded its familiar groan, a clarion call that shattered the trance of Victoria's amusement. Blood roared in her ears as a flicker of panic surged through her, her pulse quickening—frantic, like the flutter of a caged bird. She quickly blew across the freshly inked page, the acrid scent of iron gall ink lingering in the air as she urged it to dry by flapping her hand over the pages, the motion frantic yet precise. With swift, practiced movements, she shut her journal—her heresy—and dashed to the bookcase. Her fingers fumbled momentarily with the other volumes, her breath coming in short, shallow gasps before she deftly slid her private musings into its secret hiding place at the back of the bottom shelf, its worn cover disappearing into the shadows.

Once the book was safely concealed, she spun on her heels and hurried across the room, her exposed toes sinking into the plush pile of the woven carpet. In one fluid motion, she leaped onto the bed and landed with a soft thump, settling upright against the headboard with composed calm. She had executed this maneuver countless times before, her body moving through the steps with unconscious, flawless grace.

With a final, almost theatrical flourish, she grabbed the copy of *Great Expectations* that lay carefully tucked beneath her pillow, flipped it open to the page marked by a silky blue ribbon, and began to read—or at least pretended to.

Her eyes scanned the page, though the words blurred together in her haste. It was only then that she realized, with a stab of unease, that the book was upside down. She quickly righted it, her cheeks flushing with embarrassment, and fixed her attention on the text just as the door to the bedroom groaned open, the sound slow and deliberate, like the turning of a skeleton key in a prison lock. Her heart pounded in her chest, each beat echoing in her ears as she fought to maintain her composure.

As the door swung wider, a cold draft swept into the room, carrying with it the faint scent of beeswax and the sulfurous tang of the gas lamps from the hallway. Victoria's breath hitched as she realized, with another jolt of panic, that she was still clad in her undergarment, the thin silk hardly appropriate for receiving visitors—or, worse, her mother-in-law. With one swift motion, she tugged the plush, patterned comforter higher up on her body, its heavy fabric pooling around her waist. The thick quilt, embroidered with intricate floral motifs in shades of deep green and gold, was a wedding gift from Annabelle herself, a fact that now felt bitterly ironic.

She kept her eyes fixed on the page, her fingers tightening around the edges of *Great Expectations* as though it were a lifeline. The charade was precarious, but she had no other choice. She forced her breathing to be steady, her expression to soften into one of serene concentration as if she had been engrossed in Dickens' prose for hours. Yet, beneath the surface, her mind raced, calculating every possible outcome of this moment. Would Annabelle notice the slight tremor in her hands? The slight unevenness of her breath? Or would the dim light of the candle on her bedside table be enough to conceal her deception?

The door creaked again, louder this time, and Victoria braced herself for the inevitable. But it was not Annabelle who entered—it was Simon. He stepped into the room, closing the door softly behind him, his movements weary and deliberate. Victoria breathed an audible sigh of relief, the tension in her shoulders easing as she realized the immediate danger had passed. Of course, she thought *Annabelle, despite being a tyrant, would have at least knocked.* The thought was almost amusing, though it did little to dispel the lingering unease.

Simon looked worn out, his broad shoulders slightly slumped and his usually immaculate cravat loosened at the neck, its crisp folds now undone. His dark hair was disheveled as though he had been repeatedly running his fingers through the strands in frustration, the locks falling haphazardly across his forehead. He glanced at her, his deep blue eyes narrowing slightly as he noticed her gasp of relief. A slight frown creased his brow, and he tilted his head, studying her with a mixture of curiosity and concern.

"Victoria," he began, his voice low and measured, "is everything all right? You look as though you've seen a ghost."

She forced a smile, though it felt brittle on her lips, her fingers tightening around the edges of *Great Expectations*, the leather binding cool and familiar beneath her touch. She sought to steady her voice, though it wavered slightly as she spoke. "I'm fine, Simon. Just... lost in my book, that's all." She paused, her eyes flicking down to the open page, and she pointed to it with a slight, almost silly smile, hoping to mask her unease. "Dickens," she added as if the name alone might explain her nervous look—or excuse it.

Simon's frown deepened, but he said nothing, his gaze lingering on her for an instant longer before he turned away. He crossed the room to the wardrobe, his boots clicking softly against the wooden floor, and began to unbutton his waistcoat with practiced ease, his movements mechanical, as though his mind were elsewhere.

Victoria watched him out of the corner of her eye, her mind racing. She had grown accustomed to his indifference, but tonight, there was something different in his demeanor—something she couldn't quite place. Was it exhaustion? Or something more?

"Victoria," he started, then stopped, his voice trailing off as though he were searching for the right words, each one weighed and discarded before it could fully form. He brushed his fingers through his disheveled hair, the gesture betraying his frustration. When he spoke again, his tone was firm, almost accusatory. "Must you provoke Mother so often? She means well, even if her manner is... stern. She is entirely right in her observations. You drift off, lost in your own musings, and neglect your duties. She provides the roof over our heads, and I have no desire to spar with her daily over your... shortcomings."

He paused, his scrutiny sharp and unyielding, as though his words were icy daggers aimed directly at her soul. Victoria frowned, her cheeks flushing with a mixture of shame and resentment, the heat of humiliation warring with the cold sting of injustice. She lowered her eyes, unable to meet his stare, and nodded quietly in acquiescence, her silence a fragile shield against his disapproval.

Simon turned away; his movements brisk as he began to change into his night attire. He shrugged off his waistcoat and draped it over the back of a chair, then unfastened the buttons of his shirt with practiced efficiency. "Your duties are slight in comparison to mine," he continued, his voice carrying a note of condescension, each word dripping with unspoken superiority. "You must

24

keep the household staff in order and ensure they perform their tasks properly. Do you understand?"

"Yes, Simon," she responded meekly, the words tasting bitter on her tongue. She clutched the edge of Dickens, her knuckles whitening as she fought to keep her composure.

He climbed into bed, the mattress dipping beneath his weight, and then noticed she was still clad in her undergarments. His brow furrowed, and he let out an exasperated sigh. "Why aren't you already changed? For heaven's sake, Victoria, what have you been doing up here?" His tone was sharp, tinged with irritation, as though her mere presence were an inconvenience.

Without a word, Victoria slid out of bed and stepped behind the changing screen, a tall, freestanding partition adorned with delicate floral patterns. She pulled her chemise over her head, the fabric whispering against her skin as it fell soundlessly to the floor. She reached for her nightgown, a modest garment of white cotton trimmed with lace, and slipped it over her head, letting it cascade down her body. The cool fabric settled around her, a stark contrast to the warmth of the bed she had just left.

Silently, she returned to bed, her movements careful so as not to disturb Simon. He blew out the candle on his nightstand, the flame extinguished with a soft hiss, and rolled onto his side, his back to her. Victoria watched him for a wistful moment, the rise and fall of his shoulders steady and unbothered. She caught the hint of his cologne —a lingering trace of sandalwood and citrus—and her hand twitched, as if to reach out to him. But she pulled back, stopping herself, the gesture aborted before it could betray her longing. Instead, she reached over to blow out her own candle. The room was plunged into darkness, save for the wan glow of the gas lamps outside, their light casting ghostly patterns on the walls. She lay on her back, staring at the ceiling, where the shadow of the window frame shifted slightly as the street lamps wavered in the night breeze.

Her eyes remained wide open; her mind too restless for sleep. She knew she ought to feel grateful for the blessings of her life—a fine house, a respectable husband, a position in society—yet, it all felt meaningless, like a beautifully wrapped gift with nothing but a hollow echo inside. Simon was a good man, by all accounts; any woman would—or should—be content with such good fortune. But contentment eluded her, slipping through her fingers like sand, each grain a reminder of the life she had dreamed of but could never grasp.

Her thoughts drifted to her father, as they often did in moments like these. Since his death when she was a young lady, she had clung to the idea of stability, of having a strong man in her life to anchor her. She remembered the day the telegram had arrived, its crisp paper and stark words forever etched into her memory. Her mother had read it aloud, her voice devoid of emotion, as though she were reciting a list of chores rather than the news of her husband's death.

TO: LADY BARRINGTON

WITH DEEPEST REGRET TO INFORM YOU THAT LIEUTENANT JAMES REGINALD BARRINGTON, 24TH REGIMENT OF FOOT, SUFFERED A FATAL ACCIDENT WHILE ON PATROL NEAR LUCKNOW, INDIA. WHILE ATTEMPTING TO MOUNT A TROOP ELEPHANT, THE ANIMAL WAS STARTLED AND REACTED

VIOLENTLY, CAUSING HIM TO BE THROWN AND FATALLY INJURED. THE WAR OFFICE EXTENDS ITS PROFOUND SYMPATHY FOR YOUR LOSS.

Her mother had simply folded the telegram and placed it into a desk drawer without a second thought, her face a mask of stoic indifference. But Victoria had retrieved it later, and over the weeks that followed, she had read it again and again, the words engraving themselves into her mind, each repetition deepening the wound.

At first, she had wept quietly, mourning bitterly the loss of the man she had seen as her rock. But as time passed, her grief had been tinged with a strange, bitter irony. Her father, a decorated officer, had met his end not in glorious battle but in a farcical accident involving an elephant in a place called Lucknow. The absurdity of it haunted her, a cruel joke she could never quite reconcile.

Simon was not the source of strength her father had been, but he was a fine man, held in high regard, trustworthy, and respected in society. Yet, after just a year of marriage, Victoria felt little more than a dutiful affection for him, a pale imitation of the love she had once imagined. Their life together was a series of obligations, each day blending into the next with monotonous predictability.

But as the sleepless moments slowly passed, her thoughts shifted. She started to think that perhaps Simon was right; she needed to focus on her duties, to stop drifting into daydreams and idle fancies. If she could only discipline her mind, if she could only be the wife he expected her to be, perhaps things would improve. Perhaps she would find some measure of contentment.

She continued to stare at the ceiling, the feeble glow of the street lamps casting shifting patterns above her. Tomorrow, she resolved, she would be better. She would rise early, oversee the household staff with diligence, and ensure everything ran smoothly. She would be attentive, composed, and unwavering in her efforts to make Simon happy. With that final thought, she closed her eyes, the weight of her resolve settling over her like a heavy blanket. Somewhere in the house, a clock struck the hour, its chime echoing like a warning she couldn't quite decipher. Sleep came slowly, but when it did, it was fitful yet deep.

3. A Nightmare's Grin

*In the depth of every heart, there is a tomb and a dungeon,
though the lights, the music, and revelry above may cause
us to forget their existence, and the buried ones, or
prisoners whom they hide.*
—Nathaniel Hawthorne, *The Haunted Mind*, 1835

Victoria looked into her father's sparkling eyes, his face lit by a grin so wide it seemed to stretch beyond the bounds of his features, as if his joy could eclipse even the sun. Sweat beaded on his forehead, and the cork lining of his pith helmet was dark with dampness. The jungle air felt like a wet wool blanket pressed against her face.

Her father was bouncing up and down, his laughter mingling with the surrounding cacophony. The chattering of monkeys, the distant calls of unseen birds, and the rustle of foliage in the humid breeze created a symphony of the wild that seemed both alive and untamed.

Suddenly, Victoria realized where she was: perched precariously atop an elephant, its massive form undulating beneath them as it lumbered through the jungle, each step a rhythmic tremor that reverberated through her bones. Her heart leapt into her throat as she tried to cry out, to warn her father of the danger she somehow knew was coming. But he only grinned wider, his eyes crinkling with bliss, as though the world were a grand adventure and nothing could possibly go wrong.

Then, without warning, the elephant let out a deafening trumpet, its massive body lurching violently. Victoria felt herself thrown into the air, her stomach dropping as the ground rushed up to meet her, the world spinning in a blur of blue, green, and brown. Her father, still grinning, seemed to hang in the air for a moment, his arms outstretched as though embracing the fall.

"Viiicctoorriiaaaaaa!" he cried, his voice stretching into a slow cry that lingered in the air even as the jungle blurred around her—his yell the last sound to reach her before silence swallowed everything.

Victoria woke with a silent jolt, her eyes snapping open, her breath catching in her throat as her heart raced, each beat a painful thump. She lay still for a quivering moment, her eyes wide in the darkness, until the familiar shapes of her bedroom came into focus, the heavy mahogany furniture and ornate wallpaper anchoring her in reality. Simon slept soundly beside her, his steady breathing a quiet counterpoint to her own shallow gasps. The faint light from the gas lamps outside threw shifting shapes against the walls, making the familiar patterns of the wallpaper and drapes seem strange and unfamiliar for an instant.

She twisted her mouth into a slight scowl, more irritated than frightened. This nightmare—her father's grinning face, the elephant's violent lurch, the slow-motion fall—had visited her yet again, a relentless specter that refused to be banished. It was always the same, always vivid, and always left her with a persistent disquiet. She sighed softly, pushing the memory aside, and swung her feet onto the floor, the chilled planks sending a slight shiver up her legs.

Quietly, she crossed the room and stepped behind the changing screen, its floral-patterned fabric offering a semblance of privacy. She lifted the hinged top of the commode, the slight moan of the wood barely audible, and gathered her white nightgown, bunching it at her side. After relieving herself, she reached for a soft cloth from the small stack kept nearby. She used it to clean herself, then dropped it into the chamber pot at the bottom of the commode, where it would wait for the servant who came each morning—a silent accomplice to the night's private rituals. She closed the lid gently, careful not to disturb Simon, and let her nightgown fall back into place, the hem brushing the tops of her feet, the fabric cool against her skin.

As she padded back to bed, her thoughts drifted to the latest gossip she had overheard at a recent tea party. A precious few homes in Leinster Square, it was said, were being fitted with water closets—an expensive and laborious undertaking but one that promised unimaginable convenience, a modern luxury that seemed almost fantastical in its elegance. The idea of such innovation fascinated her, a glimpse of a future where even the most mundane tasks could be transformed into something effortless and refined.

Sliding back under the thick comforter, she welcomed its warmth, the heavy fabric a cocoon against the cool night. The early September evening carried the taste of a breeze through the slightly open window, the first hint of autumn's approach, a whisper of change in the air. The bed felt like a sanctuary against the encroaching chill, a refuge from the world outside and the thoughts that plagued her within. She lay on her back, staring at the ceiling where the street lamps continued to cast dancing shadows.

Her thoughts wandered back to her father. Of course, she knew why his death haunted her so. He had been the only person who truly cared for her, who saw her as more than a dutiful daughter or a respectable wife—a person, not a part. His absence left a void that no one—not her mother, not Simon, not Annabelle, not even Mabel—could fill. In a world that demanded stoicism from women, her grief felt like a solitary burden, one she carried in silence, a weight that pressed on her chest even in the quietest moments.

As she lay there, her gaze fixed on the ceiling, her thoughts drifting further away, she felt the weight of exhaustion pulling at her, a heavy tide dragging her toward sleep. The rhythmic rise and fall of Simon's breathing, the swoosh of the curtains in the night breeze, and the distant crunch of a carriage rolling over the compacted stone of the road lulled her into a dreamless slumber.

4. Chicken Soup

Do all the good you can, and make as little fuss about it as possible.
—Charles Dickens, *The Letters of Charles Dickens*, 1850

The morning sun filtered through the lace curtains, casting flickering patterns across Victoria's face—a golden reminder of the world beyond her walls. She squinted against the insistent morning light, an unwelcome intrusion into her slumber.

For a bittersweet instant, her mind drifted, escaping to the babbling country brook and the peace it promised—a place where she could breathe freely, far from the demands of daily life. But she quickly pushed the thought aside, her resolve hardening. Today, she would be better. Today, she would meet her duties without complaint, no matter how heavy they felt.

With a determined sigh, she swung her legs over the edge of the bed, her bare feet meeting the cool, polished wooden floor. She padded softly across the room to the washstand, where the porcelain basin and matching pitcher stood ready, their surfaces gleaming faintly in the early morning light. She gave the bell cord a firm pull, ringing a bell in the servants' quarters below—a clear summons for the maid. Not waiting for her arrival, Victoria lifted the pitcher, its weight steady in her hands, and poured water into the basin. The cool liquid flowed in a smooth, glistening stream, its surface undulating as it met the porcelain. A few drops escaped, glittering for a second before vanishing back into the basin.

She dipped a soft white facecloth into the water, its fabric absorbing the coolness as she wrung it out with practiced ease. Pressing the cloth to her face, she felt the refreshing chill wash away the lingering haze of sleep; the sensation was invigorating, a small but welcome ritual to begin her day. She patted her skin dry with a linen towel, its edges embroidered with wispy floral patterns—a touch of elegance even in the most mundane of tasks. Setting the towel aside, she heard a soft but unmistakable knock at the door.

"Come," Victoria uttered, her voice barely above a whisper, mindful of Simon, who was just starting to stir in the bed.

The door opened quietly, and Clara, the housemaid, entered the room, her presence as unobtrusive as a shadow. She carried an armful of Victoria's clothes, everything freshly pressed and carrying the faint, clean scent of lavender. Clara moved with the quiet efficiency of someone accustomed to the rhythms of the household, her footsteps soft against the wooden floor, the hushed creak of the boards, the only sound betraying her movement.

"Good morning, Ma'am," Clara said, her voice clear and crisp, yet hushed out of respect for the early hour; her words carried a note of deference that came naturally after years of service.

"Good morning, Clara," Victoria replied, her tone equally quiet, though her voice carried a warmth. She glanced at Simon, who was beginning to shift under the covers, his muffled grunt a sign that he was not yet fully awake, and added, "Let's make haste, please."

Chicken Soup

"Yes, Ma'am," Clara nodded, her hands already busy laying out the garments on the dressing screen, her movements precise and practiced.

Victoria stepped behind the screen, the floral-patterned fabric creating a thin veil of privacy. She shed her nightgown, folding it neatly and placing it on a nearby chair before slipping into the fresh chemise that Clara handed her. Next, she stepped into a pair of drawers, the lightweight fabric settling comfortably around her waist. Clara waited patiently; her hands poised to assist with the next layer.

The corset came next, its stiff boning and intricate laces a familiar yet daunting sight. Clara guided it over Victoria's head, the fabric brushing against her under-garment as it settled around her chest and waist. With practiced ease, Clara adjusted the corset into place and then began to tighten the laces, pulling with a series of firm, steady tugs. The familiar pressure closed around Victoria's ribs—a constriction that was the price of propriety. Once again, the jailer exerted his relentless grip.

Next came the petticoat, its layers of crisp cotton rustling softly as Clara helped Victoria step into it. The petticoat provided the necessary volume and structure for her skirt, a modest yet essential foundation for her attire. Over this, Clara assisted her into a plain pale blue cotton day dress, its high neckline and long sleeves designed for practicality rather than ornamentation. The dress was well-suited for managing the household; its simple cut allowed for ease of movement while still maintaining a respectable appearance.

Once dressed, Victoria sat down on the edge of the changing chair near the screen, its upholstered seat worn but comfortable. Clara picked up a silver-handled hair-

35

brush from the dressing table and began to brush Victoria's auburn hair with smooth, even strokes. The rhythmic motion was soothing, and Victoria closed her eyes for a moment of quiet, savoring the brief respite. When her hair was free of tangles, Clara gathered it into a neat ponytail, securing it with a bright blue ribbon that matched the hue of her dress.

With her hair in place, Victoria turned her attention to her feet. She reached for a pair of silk stockings, their fine fabric cool and smooth against her skin as she carefully rolled them up her legs. Finally, she slipped on a pair of brown leather shoes, their soles worn from use but still in good condition. The shoes were sensible and sturdy, designed for the demands of a busy household, yet they retained a touch of elegance that suited her station.

Victoria stood, smoothing the dress down with both hands as she turned to examine her reflection in the full-length mirror. She tilted her head, giving the ponytail a slight, testing swing, which prompted a brief smile of approval to touch her lips. For a fleeting instant, she felt a glimmer of satisfaction—today, she would be the picture of efficiency and grace.

Her eyes shifted to the bed, and her smile faltered. Simon was not there. He must have risen quietly, dressed, and left the room without her notice. Victoria exhaled deeply, a soft "damn" escaping her lips under her breath. *Had she overslept again? Or was he simply determined to outpace her at every turn?* She had hoped to be downstairs at the dining table before him to prove her readiness and commitment to the day ahead. But there was no use dwelling on it. She straightened her shoulders and moved toward the door, her resolve firm. *No matter*, she thought to herself. *I'm going to make this day perfect.*

"Thank you," Victoria said briskly as she exited the bedroom, her tone carrying a note of determination. Clara was already gathering Victoria's clothing from the previous day, her movements efficient and unobtrusive as she prepared them for cleaning later that day.

"Of course, Ma'am," Clara replied quietly, her voice respectful and subdued. She gave a small nod before continuing her task, her hands deftly folding the garments as Victoria's footsteps echoed down the hallway.

When Victoria arrived at the dining room, Simon was already seated at the head of the table, partaking in a modest breakfast of sausage and poached eggs. A teacup filled with Earl Grey steamed gently beside his plate, its bergamot aroma wafting through the air—a scent Victoria recognized immediately. He was dressed for business in a dark, tailored suit and a stark white cravat. Every detail was precise, an armor of decorum.

Victoria pulled out her chair and sat down quickly, smoothing her skirts as she did so. Annabelle's absence was immediately noticeable and surprising; it was her custom to rise before dawn, and she was almost always at the table first.

"Good morning," Victoria began, her voice steady but tinged with a hint of hesitation. "I apologize. I had hoped to be at the table to greet you."

Simon looked up from his plate, a forkful of sausage poised midway to his mouth. He shook his head slightly, causing his short, dark curls to sway, and set the fork down. Wiping his mouth with a linen napkin, he finished chewing before replying, "No, that's quite all right. I intended to eat quickly and be on my way." He paused, pulling a gold pocket watch from his vest and checking the time with a practiced flick of his wrist. "I have a meeting in forty-five minutes in Islington. As I mentioned, it's a rather important one."

"Certainly," Victoria said in her matter-of-fact tone. She glanced at Annabelle's empty seat, her curiosity piqued. "Where is your mother?"

"Mother isn't feeling well, so she's staying in her room," Simon responded, his tone matter-of-fact as he cut into a piece of sausage.

"Oh. Should I fetch the doc—" Victoria began, her voice tinged with concern.

Simon waved his hand dismissively, interrupting her. "No. Mother doesn't care for doctors. She prefers to manage these things herself."

"Oh..." Victoria trailed off, her brow furrowing in mild perplexity. She halted, unsure whether to press the matter further.

Simon dabbed his mouth with his napkin and set it aside, his expression softening slightly as he explained. "Mother is fifty-eight, and she's rarely ill. She has her own remedies—special teas, broths, and such. She swears by them, and I daresay they've served her well thus far."

Victoria paused, slightly pursing her lips, and pondered a time with Annabelle. She couldn't recall a time Annabelle hadn't been active and well. With a quiet, reflective "hmm," she thought that even though Annabelle was often an unpleasant woman, she was quite vigorous for her age.

Simon continued, punctuating his instructions with bites of sausage and sips of warm tea. "Make sure dinner is perfect. Have the table set for an additional two gentlemen..." He paused, reflecting for a moment, then amended his statement. "No, make that four—just in case Mr. Wilby brings some more associates along."

Victoria opened her mouth to reply, but Simon pressed on without waiting. "Ensure everything is flawless. The dinner must be extraordinary. And have the best bottle of port on the table as well."

Again, Victoria started to speak, but Simon waved her off without looking at her. "And make sure you're dressed in your finest gown. Mother may not join us tonight, but the dinner will proceed as planned."

Victoria sat quietly, her hands folded in her lap, waiting to ensure Simon had finished. When it was clear he had no further instructions, she replied, "Of course. I promise to make this as special an event as I can muster." She finished her statement with a broad, reassuring smile, though her eyes betrayed a trace of apprehension.

Simon returned her smile with a curt, tentative one of his own, scrutinizing her as though he were unsure whether she was truly capable of meeting his expectations. After a moment, he seemed satisfied. "Good. I will see you this evening." With that, he flipped open his pocket watch, its gold casing catching the light, and rose from the table.

Clara, ever attentive, stood ready with Simon's dark wool coat and top hat. She held the coat open as he slipped into it with ease before donning the hat. Without another word, he strode briskly to the front door and exited, the sound of his footsteps fading as he made his way to the waiting carriage. The noise of the bustling morning—hurried footsteps, the clatter of hooves, and the rumble of carriages—momentarily invaded the relative quiet of the house, only to fade as Clara closed the thick wooden door behind Simon. The heavy oak panel muffled the sounds of the outside world, restoring the relative stillness of the household.

Victoria sat for a contemplative moment, her fingers resting lightly on the edge of the table, as she wondered whether she was truly up to the task Simon had set. The weight of her duties pressed on her, but she took a deep breath, steadying herself. *I must not falter*, she thought. With renewed resolve, she pushed herself from the table and strode briskly down the corridor toward the kitchen.

As she approached, the air grew warmer, and the mingling scents of baking bread, simmering broth, and roasting meat swirled around her, creating the unmistakable essence of the heart of the household. The rhythmic clatter of pots and pans, the crackle of the hearth fire, and the low murmur of voices grew louder with each step.

She pushed through the kitchen door, and the full force of the room's activity greeted her. The heat from the hearth pressed against her skin like an invisible hand, and the mingling scents of rosemary and browning meat made her stomach growl despite her nerves. The cooking staff moved with practiced efficiency, their hands busy with chopping, stirring, and kneading. The kitchen was alive with purpose, a symphony of sights, sounds, and smells that spoke of the day's labor already well underway.

They all looked up as Victoria entered, their voices blending into a familiar, perfunctory, and slightly out of sync chorus: "Good morning, Ma'am." Gaston, the cook, stood at the wooden worktable, his knife moving swiftly as he chopped shallots, garlic, and onions for the Madeira wine sauce that would accompany the veal cutlets. A pile of wild mushrooms sat nearby, their earthy aroma mingling with the sharp tang of the freshly cut vegetables, ready to be added to the dish.

Alice and Maggie, the kitchen maids, moved with a well-worn rhythm, their black uniforms already dampened with the heat of their labor. They darted between crates and shelves, checking supplies and extracting ingredients in preparation for the day's meals. The air was thick with the scent of herbs, spices, and the faint smokiness of the hearth fire.

The kitchen hearth blazed brightly, its flames licking at the heavy iron pot that simmered above. Steam rose in gentle curls from the pot, carrying the rich, savory scent of a broth or stew already in progress.

Victoria reviewed the written list hung on the kitchen wall, her eyes scanning the neatly penned inventory of ingredients. The crates and kitchen tables were laden with fresh provisions: oysters glistening in their shells, plump salmon fillets, tender cuts of veal, and a trussed pheasant ready for roasting. Bowls of lemons, grapes, figs, plums, and raspberries added a burst of color, while bundles of assorted herbs—parsley, thyme, and rosemary—filled the air with their earthy fragrance. Everything appeared fresh and of the highest quality, but a few key items were still missing: the Stilton and Wensleydale cheeses, French bread, and, of course, Champagne and flowers.

Victoria knew the household staff was seasoned and efficient, but the importance of this business dinner demanded her direct oversight. She turned to the assembled kitchen staff, her voice calm but firm. "Tonight is a special dinner, as I am sure you are all aware. Are we prepared to acquire the cheeses, loaves of bread, and Champagne today?"

Maggie, a short and stout woman with hair streaked with black and grey like pepper, replied in a quiet but confident tone, "Yes, Ma'am. The bread will be delivered this morning. I'll go out myself to acquire the cheeses from *Stilton and Cheddar Provisions*. A few bottles of

Champagne were delivered yesterday afternoon and are stored in the cellar. The florist will arrive by noon with a variety of arrangements for your approval. Once you've chosen, the florist will arrange them in the dining room, Ma'am."

Victoria nodded in approval, "Excellent," as her attention turned to the unusual smell wafting from pots simmering over the fire in the hearth. Her nose crinkled as she peered into the cast-iron pots, attempting to identify the contents. One contained chicken with carrots, onions, garlic, and various plants, which Victoria didn't recognize. The other smaller pot held a mixture of various flowers and other botanicals.

Pointing at the pots and looking at Gaston, she asked, "What is in these pots?"

As he continued chopping mushrooms, he responded without looking up, "Those are for Mrs. Pembroke. They are her own recipes, which she has us make when she is unwell. The larger pot is a restorative broth, and the smaller one is a tisane made from chamomile, elderflower, lavender, and other ingredients."

Victoria hesitated for a moment, her gaze lingering on the steaming pots. The thought of Annabelle, unwell and alone in her room, tugged at her conscience—if only slightly. Though it was customary for the maids to handle such tasks, Victoria felt a sudden urge to attend to Annabelle herself. Perhaps it was the weight of her responsibilities pressing on her, or perhaps it was a desire to prove herself capable of more than just overseeing the household. Whatever the reason, she turned to Gaston and said, "I'll take these to her myself. Please prepare a tray."

Gaston raised an eyebrow, let out a deep breath, but nodded, quickly assembling a tray with a bowl of the restorative broth, a cup of the fragrant tisane, and a small plate of plain biscuits. "She'll appreciate the broth first, Ma'am," he advised. "The tisane is best taken afterward while it's still warm."

Victoria nodded, lifting the tray carefully. The warmth of the broth seeped through the ceramic bowl, a comforting contrast to the coolness of the hallway as she made her way to Annabelle's room. The house was quiet, save for the soft creak of floorboards beneath her feet and the distant hum of activity from the kitchen. The hallway stretched before her, its walls lined with dark wood panels that gleamed faintly in the pale morning light filtering through the tall, narrow windows. Portraits of stern-faced ancestors watched her progress, their eyes seeming to follow her as she walked. As she approached Annabelle's door, she paused, balancing the tray with one hand and knocking softly.

"Come in," came Annabelle's voice, low but steady.

Victoria eased the door open and stepped inside. The room was a sanctuary of quiet elegance, bathed in soft, filtered light that spilled through the heavy lace curtains. The air carried a faint scent of lavender and beeswax, mingling with the sharper tang of the chicken broth and the herbs from the tisane on the tray. Annabelle lay propped up against a mound of pillows, her face pale but her expression sharp and alert, like an eagle perched in its nest. Her eyes narrowed slightly as she saw Victoria enter, though she quickly masked her surprise with a polite nod. "Victoria," she remarked, her tone cool but not unkind. "I wasn't expecting you."

"I thought I'd bring these to you myself," Victoria replied, setting the tray down on the bedside table. She gestured to the bowl of broth and the cup of tisane.

"Gaston says the broth will help restore your strength, and the tisane should soothe your nerves."

Annabelle eyed the tray with a measured scrutiny. "Yes, indeed. I've been using these recipes since I was a girl," she said, though her tone lacked warmth. "Though I suppose you wouldn't know much about such things, would you? Modern women seem to prefer their remedies in little glass bottles from the apothecary."

She reached for the bowl of broth, her movements deliberate and steady despite her obvious fatigue. Victoria instinctively moved to assist her, but Annabelle held up a hand, stopping her mid-motion. "I'm perfectly capable, thank you," she declared firmly, her voice leaving no room for argument.

Victoria withdrew her hand, clasping it behind her back. "Naturally," she said, her tone neutral. She stood awkwardly for a moment, unsure whether to stay or leave. Annabelle's independence was well-known, but Victoria had hoped her gesture might bridge the distance between them, even if only slightly. Instead, the air in the room felt heavy with unspoken tension.

Annabelle took a slow sip of the broth. Her expression softened slightly, revealing a hint of gratitude as she tasted it. "You've been busy with the dinner preparations," she remarked soon after, her tone measured. "I trust everything is in order?"

"Yes," Victoria responded, grateful for the opening. "Maggie is handling the cheeses, and the florist will be here by noon. The kitchen is running smoothly."

Annabelle nodded, eyeing the bowl as she stirred the broth absently. "Simon is out on his business, I assume?" she asked, her tone casual but pointed.

"Yes," Victoria responded, surprised by the question. "He mentioned he would return in time for the dinner."

"Of course," Annabelle noted, her voice tinged with a hint of something Victoria couldn't quite place—approval, perhaps, or simply acknowledgment. "He's always been thorough in his work." She took another sip of the broth. "Though it does leave you with much to manage on your own."

Victoria hesitated, unsure whether the comment was meant as a slight or a simple observation. "I don't mind," she said carefully. "The household staff is very capable, and I'm learning more every day."

Annabelle's lips twitched in what might have been the ghost of a smile, though it didn't reach her eyes. "I'm sure you are," she remarked, her tone polite but distant. "Though one wonders how much learning is required to oversee a household. It's not exactly alchemy, is it?" She set the bowl down on the tray, leaving the tisane untouched. "The dinner is important. Simon has high expectations for these events."

"I'm aware," Victoria assured, her voice steady. "I've been overseeing the preparations closely. Everything is on schedule."

Annabelle glanced at her, her sharp eyes appraising. "Good," she said. "It's a reflection of the household, after all. And of you."

Victoria felt the weight of the words, though she couldn't tell if they were meant as encouragement or a reminder of the stakes. "I'll ensure everything is perfect," she pledged.

Annabelle studied her for a moment, then leaned back against her pillows, her energy seeming to wane. "Thank you for bringing this yourself," she added, her tone initially neutral, but then shifted to one of muted appreciation. "It was... unexpected."

Victoria nodded, sensing the conversation was drawing to a close. "Of course," she offered. "Is there anything else you need?"

Annabelle shook her head, her eyes already closing. "No, I think I'll rest now. You may go." As Victoria turned to leave, Annabelle added in her often-critical tone, "And do try to stay focused, my dear. We wouldn't want you wandering off like an old donkey meandering through the fog, now, would we?"

Victoria hesitated for a shuddering moment, her palm tightening on the doorknob. The sting of the comment lingered, but she forced herself to smile politely. "I'll keep that in mind," she managed to say. *Though perhaps a donkey would at least be shown some kindness*, she thought bitterly. She closed the door softly behind her and leaned against it, releasing a breath she didn't realize she'd been holding. The long hallway ahead seemed to watch her, its silence feeling less like peace and more like judgment.

A *thank you*. It was so paltry a thing to cling to, yet she found her hope closing around it anyway, a single dull penny in an otherwise empty purse. Victoria straightened her shoulders and took a deep breath, refocusing on the tasks ahead. The dinner was her priority now, and she was determined to show her worth—not just to Annabelle and Simon, but to herself.

5. The Deal

A dinner lubricates business.
—Lord William Stowell

*T*he clang of cutlery on fine china and the cacophony of voices, punctuated by occasional bursts of laughter, filled the dining room. The softly glowing light from the brass chandelier above danced across the polished silverware and the delicate crystal glasses. Each glass was etched with criss-crossed diamond patterns that began at the stem and gradually faded toward the rim, catching the candlelight in a mesmerizing prismatic display. The glasses were filled and refilled with Warre's finest deep burgundy port, their contents leaving a trail of stains on the once-pristine silk tablecloth. The chaotic splashes of wine and remnants of earlier courses—scraps of bread, smears of sauce, and scattered crumbs—gave the table the appearance of having survived a minor brawl rather than a formal dinner.

At either end of the table stood two crystal vases filled with a variety of exotic orchids and adorned with cascading ferns. The flowers, imported from distant hothouses, stood in stark contrast to the disarray below, their vibrant blooms and lush greenery serving as a silent rebuke to the turmoil of the feast. Their impossible perfection was a potent reminder of the wealth that had funded this entire, chaotic display.

The Deal

By all accounts, the dinner was a resounding success. Mr. Wilby—who, defying decorum, insisted on being called James—seemed particularly delighted with the veal cutlets à la financière, helping himself to several portions and forgoing the boiled capon with oyster sauce that followed. He was an older gentleman, his black hair streaked with silver, his pug nose adorned with a long, equally peppered mustache that twitched with every hearty guffaw. His portly frame, accentuated by a well-tailored but straining waistcoat, spoke of a man who took great pleasure in the culinary arts.

His associate, Mr. Samuels, was a younger man with rumpled, dirty-blond hair and a lean build. He spent most of the evening in quiet observation, nodding in agreement at appropriate moments and chortling along with Mr. Wilby's animated anecdotes. The third member of their party, a man with the peculiar name of Mr. Greenbowl, was thin and reserved, with short black hair and an air of meticulous precision. He spoke little, interjecting only to clarify a point or confirm a detail before dipping his pen into a portable inkwell and carefully recording the evening's agreements in a leatherbound journal. His presence added an undercurrent of formality to the otherwise lively gathering.

Simon's mother was still convalescing, so she was presumably resting, but according to reports from the household staff, she was recovering quite quickly and had even taken a short stroll in the garden earlier that day.

Simon was unusually jovial and often burst into laughter with Mr. Wilby. His usual reserved demeanor had softened, and he seemed genuinely at ease, a rare sight for those who knew him well.

Victoria had arrived at the dinner transformed. Her royal purple silk dress whispered with every movement, and the sapphire pendant at her throat—Simon's engagement gift—flashed like a cool blue eye, capturing the attention of the room. She was every inch the elegant hostess, a role she had poured herself into for this night.

Mary and Clara cleared the table, gliding like shadows as they removed the remnants of the feast; their movements so smooth they might have been ghosts tidying a battlefield. As they worked, Clara exchanged a knowing glance with Mary, her eyebrows lifting slightly as if to say, These men are in no state to discuss business. Mary responded with a barely perceptible shrug, her lips pressed into a thin line.

The bottle of claret and the glasses remained as the men continued to drink and laugh. Mr. Wilby—James—launched into an anecdote about convincing a merchant in India to sell his tea and other goods at a ridiculously low price, declaring with a chuckle that the man had "the brains of a coconut." For some reason, this sent Mr. Wilby into fits of laughter, his head tossing back as he roared, a trickle of claret escaping the corners of his mouth and staining his already well-worn peppered whiskers.

"Victoria," Mr. Wilby began, having already established an overfamiliarity by using her first name without invitation, "have you ever been to India?"

"No, Mr. Wilby… I mean, James," she quickly corrected herself, accommodating his insistence on informality, though it made her skin prickle with discomfort. She turned her eyes to Simon, hoping for a modicum of support, but he was too busy refilling his glass to notice.

"You need to go. It's an amazing, beautiful place. The colors, the smells, the chaos—it's like nothing you've ever seen. I will have to arrange that trip for you," he proclaimed, his tone suggesting it was already decided.

Not knowing how to respond, Victoria looked to Simon, who was so thoroughly inebriated from the port and overindulgence in food that he seemed barely aware of the conversation. "I... that's a very kind offer, thank you," she finished, her voice trailing off awkwardly as she searched for a way to deflect the attention. She reached for her glass of champagne, the cool crystal offering a momentary distraction. Although Victoria only had a slight understanding of the deal that had been struck—something to do with importing teas and exporting munitions and other arms—she knew to keep things as jovial as possible, even if it meant enduring a bit of unseemliness.

As if on cue, Mary and Clara returned with crystal serving bowls of plum pudding drizzled with brandy sauce and a large platter of cheeses, accompanied by fresh grapes, figs, and cashews. As they set the dishes down, Mr. Wilby continued to leer at Victoria, his stare so intense it made her cheeks burn with unease. It felt as though he were slowly peeling back the layers of her composure, probing her very thoughts, making the fine silk of her dress feel as thin as tissue paper. She wondered if he could sense her growing unease, or if he simply enjoyed watching her squirm.

"James," she ventured awkwardly, hoping to break the unnerving spell, "how long have you been in... this... business?"

Breaking eye contact, Mr. Wilby launched into a monologue about himself, which Victoria noticed he enjoyed almost as much as breathing. He spoke of his early days as a merchant, his rise to prominence, and the many deals he had brokered across continents. Yet, beneath his bravado, Victoria detected a hint of something darker—a ruthlessness that made her shiver despite the room's warmth.

Relieved that the uncomfortable moment had passed, she reached to take a few grapes and some cheese onto her plate, popping a piece of creamy yet tangy Stilton into her mouth. While Mr. Wilby continued to prattle on about himself, Victoria glanced at Simon and saw how he seemed utterly captivated by the man's self-aggrandizing tales.

As everyone sampled the pudding and gorged on cheese, grapes, and nuts, Clara placed a delicate champagne glass before each person and filled them one by one. The bubbles rose in a lively, chaotic dance, catching the candlelight as they raced to the surface.

Grabbing his glass with his pudgy hand, Mr. Wilby raised it high, prompting the others to follow suit. "To a deal that will make us wealthy beyond imagining!" he pronounced, his voice booming with confidence.

"Hear, hear!" everyone agreed, their glasses coming together in a sharp, celebratory *clink*.

6. Solace in Sisterhood

Friendship is certainly the finest balm for the pangs of disappointed love.
—Jane Austen, *Northanger Abbey*, 1817

*A*fter Simon's successful dinner deal, the days of September drifted by with a languid monotony, each blending into the next until they finally gave way to October's crisp, golden hues. The tedium of her daily routine and the stifling demands of societal protocol began to erode Victoria's resolve to remain fully present in her role as mistress of the household. Increasingly—if only for fleeting moments—she found herself retreating to the sanctuary of her private thoughts, a far-off natural oasis of solitude where she could momentarily escape the weight of her responsibilities.

While Annabelle controlled the purse strings, Victoria's domain was the endless cycle of daily management: planning meals that were both economical and impressive, supervising the maids, and ensuring every surface gleamed. Even her weekly charity work at the *Seven Sisters for Sobriety* felt less like a respite and more like another item on a suffocatingly long list. She per-formed her duties with diligence, but with each passing day, the allure of escape grew ever stronger.

Solace in Sisterhood

Preoccupied with his burgeoning business affairs, Simon paid little attention to her, his absences and emotional distance only deepening the monotony of her days. The once-vibrant connection between them seemed to fade with each passing week, leaving Victoria feeling increasingly isolated. Determined to break the cycle of tedium, she resolved that today, once the household was in perfect order, she would pay a long-overdue visit to Mabel. Her dear friend's lively company and unfiltered conversation promised a welcome reprieve from the stifling routine that had come to define her life.

Mabel had been Victoria's friend ever since they met at the *Young Ladies' Academy* several years earlier. They hit it off immediately and became quite close over their years at the finishing school. A few years older than Victoria, Mabel was a strikingly beautiful woman with long, light brown hair, often styled in intricate braids or flowing waves. Her eyes were a deep, captivating green, with a soft, inviting smile that radiated charm and approachability. At the Academy, they were inseparable, and Victoria cherished Mabel's light-hearted nature and quick wit, which always brought a sense of joy and levity to even the most tedious days.

In the early afternoon, Mary helped her into her boots, buttoned her coat over her modest cotton day dress, and opened the front door. Victoria had heard that today was particularly foggy, and the sight that greeted her confirmed it. She quickly pressed the white handkerchief she carried to her mouth and nose, squinting as she turned left and began walking along the dusty, uneven macadamized roadside, where the crushed stone surface sent up a fine grit with every passing carriage. The thick, reddish-yellow haze hung heavily in the air, reducing visibility to mere feet. The street lamps were barely visible, their light glowing faintly and wavering like candles behind thick, frosted glass. People and carriages seemed to materialize out of the suffocating pea-soup fog, only to vanish just as quickly into the same murky oblivion.

Through the deep haze, she also saw the ever-present crossing sweepers, those industrious figures who shuttled between people and carriages to scoop up the waste dropped by the numerous horses that passed by. The veritable army of crossing sweepers, composed mainly of young boys in their early teens, kept the streets in Kensington remarkably clear of the mud, although how they managed this during a gloom so dense was nothing short of miraculous.

Victoria often saw a particular boy, whom she recognized by his short, thin frame and distinctive green cap, which featured a short white pigeon feather on the side. His face and clothes were begrimed with soot and filth, a testament to the grime of his daily labor. His tools were a short broom and a small shovel, which he used to deposit the filth into large pails scattered along the way. They both noticed each other, and the boy stopped momentarily, took off his cap, and bowed, "Good day, Miss," he greeted with a grin missing a few teeth. Victoria, coughing slightly into her handkerchief, handed him a penny. "Good day, Sir," she returned with a twinkle of amusement. With their familiar ritual complete, Victoria continued down the side of the road.

Despite the handkerchief shielding her nose and mouth, the tiny, oily black particles of soot began to clog her nostrils, making each breath uncomfortable and labored. Still, Mabel's house was only a few blocks away, and

Victoria pressed on, though halfway there, she began questioning the wisdom of venturing out on such a day.

"Pshaw," she muttered to herself, "it's not that bad. I can certainly make it that far." She craned her neck, looking upward to see any evidence of the sun, but there was none—only the endless rows of smokestacks belching smoke, their plumes merging into the unrelenting, suffocating black lungs of progress.

Pushing through the acrid stench of coal smoke and the oppressive, otherworldly atmosphere, Victoria's mind wandered back to the summer evening when she and Simon had first met. It had been at the annual Midsummer Ball, held in the grand assembly rooms of Bath, where gaslights flickered like stars and the air was perfumed with the scent of roses and beeswax candles. Simon, a young man of modest means but boundless ambition, had caught her eye across the room. She could almost feel the thrill of his gaze finding hers across the crowded room, the warmth of his hand on her waist as they danced. They whirled every set that night, their conversation flowing as effortlessly as the waltz they shared. He had been all ambition and charm, and she had been convinced the universe itself had orchestrated their meeting.

Now, that magic seemed as distant and unreachable as the sun hidden behind the smog-choked sky. The connection they once shared had faded, much like the carriages and pedestrians who materialized briefly in the haze only to vanish again, swallowed by the murky mist. Victoria's chest tightened as she walked, not only from the soot-laden air but from the weight of her longing for what once was.

With a final *clunk-clunk* of her boots hitting the road, she arrived at the door adorned with the gold number 86.

Victoria gave the door knocker a brisk one-two *clink-clink* and waited. After a moment, the door opened, and Victoria quickly slipped inside, the smog left behind as Samantha, the housemaid, closed the door behind her. Samantha quietly helped Victoria with her coat, saying, "Good day, Miss. Terrible fog today."

Looking around to see who was about and sensing no one, Victoria gave Samantha a gentle hug. "Yes, it's terrible. Nice to see you again."

Samantha smiled gently. "Yes. It's nice to see you again as well, Miss."

Victoria turned her attention to her boots with a bit of a scowl, her lips pursed in mild frustration. "Unfortunately, I didn't dodge all the horse muck and other hazards today," she remarked, her tone a mix of resignation and wry humor.

Samantha chuckled lightly, her laughter soft and deferential. "Hazards of London streets, of course, Miss," she said as she knelt to assist Victoria in taking off her boots, her hands moving with the experienced rhythm of someone accustomed to such tasks. "We will have these cleaned up before you leave."

"Thank you, Samantha," Victoria offered softly, her voice carrying a note of genuine appreciation.

Victoria coughed and hacked a few times, trying to clear the soot from her throat. She spat a speck of blackened phlegm into her handkerchief, grimacing at the sight. "Hrmm... can you let Mabel know—"

Before she could finish, Mabel turned the corner and shrieked with delight, "Victoria!"

The two embraced each other in a long, heartfelt hug.

"It's been two long weeks, right?" Mabel added.

"Twenty days, exactly," Victoria countered with a slight frown. "And yes, too long."

Already in motion, Mabel took Victoria by the hand. "Let's go to the parlor. We have a lot to catch up on." Glancing past Victoria, she called out, "Samantha, please bring us some peppermint tea." Pausing momentarily, a devilish grin spread across her face as she added, "Victoria has a fog in her throat." Both ladies chuckled lightly at the remark, and without waiting for confirmation, Mabel tugged Victoria into the parlor, where they quickly settled onto the floral-printed chintz sofa.

Facing Victoria, Mabel tilted her head back, her nose slightly turned up, and adopted a mockingly deeper voice. "How is the mother of the house? Still as indifferent as always?" She ended her teasing with a mischievous smirk.

Victoria bubbled with mirth, feeling free and happy in Mabel's company. "More or less the same, although after I brought her some soup and tea when she was sick the other week, she seemed a bit less... umm... rigid."

Mabel giggled, her smile broadening. "Really? Maybe the old crone will actually smile one day."

Both ladies laughed as Samantha entered, bearing a tray with a steaming white porcelain teapot decorated with dainty blue flowers, matching teacups, a small jar of honey, and a dish of sliced lemons. Samantha set the tray down on the table in front of the sofa and poured the steamy brew into each cup, adding a slice of lemon.

"Is that all, Ma'am?" Samantha asked.

"Yes. Thank you, Samantha," Mabel replied gratefully.

Victoria added a spoonful of honey to her tea and took a grateful sip. "And how is Terrance?"

Mabel gently rolled her eyes and let out a breath. "Oh, off on another military excursion to who knows where. He left two weeks ago, and who knows when he'll be back. Such is the life of a military man's wife." She paused, then asked, "And Simon?"

Victoria sighed slightly. "He might as well be away on some campaign. I see him, but a thousand miles of silence stretches between us. We hardly talk. He's deeply involved in his business. Such is the life of a businessman's wife."

Both women smiled and laughed, finding solace in their shared experiences.

Suddenly excited, Mabel exclaimed, "You must see what I got for the charity ball. You'll be so jealous!" Taking Victoria by the hand, she led her up the ornate stairs and into her bedroom. The room Victoria had seen a few times before was twice as large as hers and Simon's and far more richly decorated. By the window stood a bust adorned with an elegant bonnet. Mabel took the hat off the bust and placed it on her head, pursing her lips and striking a pose with her palms on her hips.

The bonnet was a confection of deep burgundy velvet; its crown wreathed in an aigrette of impossibly delicate white feathers that shivered with her every move. It was tied with a lavish pink silk bow and studded with silk roses.

Victoria managed an "Oh my," her eyes wide with wonder as she stared at the stunning headdress. "This must have cost... well, a fortune."

"It was a gift from my husband before he departed," Mabel said with a wide smirk. "Such, as they say, is the life of a military man's wife," she added with a light chuckle. She removed the bonnet, placed it back upon the bust, and traced the delicate white feathers with her fingertips. "They say these are worth more, ounce for ounce, than gold. Can you imagine? Utter madness." She hesitated, then glanced up hopefully, her eyes wide. "Are you still going to the charity ball? Please, say you are. I cannot attend without my husband—unless, of course, I go with the two of you."

"Of course, you will come with us," Victoria affirmed with a smile. "Simon won't mind." She leaned in and added in a faux whisper, "Besides, it will help keep the whole affair from being too dreadfully boring." Then, mimicking the mockingly deep voice Mabel had used earlier, she added, "And of course, the mother of the house will no doubt be attending as well."

"Oh, wonderful!" Mabel exclaimed, clapping her hands together with exaggerated delight. "Maybe we'll finally get a chance to see her smile."

7. Whispers in the Waltz

Man's love is of man's life a thing apart, 'Tis woman's whole existence.
—Lord Byron, *Don Juan*, 1819

Simon flicked open his pocket watch, its polished gold casing catching the light of the gas lamps as he studied the hands moving with quiet precision. "The carriage should be here momentarily," he announced to Annabelle and Victoria, his tone firm yet composed. Simon was dressed in the tailored dark wool suit he had worn during that pivotal business dinner weeks earlier, its crisp lines and fine fabric a testament to his status and meticulous attention to detail. Annabelle, meanwhile, was dressed in her old but elegant light lavender gown, its flowing silhouette softened by years of wear yet still exuding timeless grace. Her new bonnet was a lavish affair of lavender and gold, its brim sparkling with a delicate fringe of pearls. Both wore white cotton gloves, an essential accessory for an event of such importance, their pristine whiteness adding a final touch of refinement to their ensembles.

Victoria stood beside them, transformed, resplendent in her new dress. Her gown was a blaze of bronze and scarlet, the colors shifting like flickers in a fire with every move she made. A large scarlet ribbon cinched her waist, its extravagant bow a declaration of boldness she rarely allowed herself. Her yellow bonnet, studded with pearls and silver, was tied with ribbons of scarlet and gold that cascaded down her back. She was a vision of vibrant, almost rebellious elegance.

Clara helped Simon into his finely tailored coat and adjusted his top hat, its polished surface gleaming in the dim light of the foyer. She then assisted Annabelle and Victoria with their evening shawls, gossamer wraps of silk and lace that added a touch of sophistication to their outfits.

Opening the front door, they stepped into the clear evening air and were greeted by the sight of the large coach. It was an elegant machine of gleaming black lacquer, its polished surfaces reflecting the glow of the gas lamps and casting pale reflections off the shallow puddles on the smooth, well-worn road. Two majestic white horses, impossibly pristine against the soot-stained city, stood patiently in their harnesses, their breath creating plumes in the cool air. A driver, seated at the front, held their reins with practiced ease.

The footman, dressed in a crisp uniform with brass buttons and white gloves, stood ready to escort them into the carriage. He opened the door with a flourish and, with a gloved hand, carefully helped the two ladies into the plush, royal purple velvet interior, ensuring their gowns were properly arranged and free from wrinkles. Simon followed, stepping into the carriage with ease. Once seated, he leaned forward and instructed the driver, "Make a second stop at number 86, if you please."

The carriage lurched forward, its wheels growling and rumbling along the smooth road, the occupants jostling slightly as they settled into their seats. In short order, the carriage arrived at its second stop, and the footman lent a hand to help Mabel enter.

"Good evening," Mabel said with a broad, infectious smile as she took her seat beside Annabelle. Annabelle nodded politely, while both Victoria and Simon responded with a chorus of "Good evening," their voices mingling in the confined space of the carriage. As the vehicle lurched forward once more, Mabel added quite jovially, "What a beautiful evening. We are quite fortunate to have such good weather tonight."

Victoria answered with a smile, "Yes, it's truly lovely. I'm so delighted the weather is so pleasant." Annabelle, however, sat with a thin-lipped and silent expression, her face unreadable. Mabel and Victoria exchanged a glance, their eyes twinkling, their faint smiles betraying their shared amusement.

As the carriage rolled through the maze of streets, Victoria peered out the window, her reflection flickering in the glass. The city's gas lamps cast a golden glow, their flames wavering in the glass and painting dancing patterns of light across her face. She felt a mix of excitement and trepidation, unsure what the evening would bring.

After several minutes, the carriage arrived at its destination. The footman opened the door and helped the ladies descend with grace, ensuring their gowns remained unruffled. Simon followed last, his presence commanding as he stepped onto the cobblestones. They stood at the bottom of the grand marble steps of the Mayfair Estate, the imposing façade of the building illuminated by the gilded shimmer of lanterns. Simon took Victoria by the hand while two doormen, impeccably dressed in livery, escorted Annabelle and Mabel up the steps, their polished boots clicking against the stone.

Two doormen opened the grand front doors of the estate, and the muffled sounds of conversation, the soft shuffle of feet, and the lilting melodies of the small orchestra playing *The Blue Danube* spilled out into the night, a tantalizing preview of the evening's splendor.

Stepping into the hall, the magnificence of the event was immediately palpable. Overhead, a galaxy of crystal chandeliers set the parquet floor ablaze with reflected light. The air itself seemed to shimmer, thick with the scent of beeswax and perfume and the harmonious swell of the orchestra. It was an atmosphere of all-encompassing, almost dizzying opulence.

Most of the gentlemen were finely dressed, their attire mirroring Simon's tailored dark wool suit, with only slight variations in cut and fabric. The women, however, were a kaleidoscope of colors, their gowns shimmering in various shades of blue, yellow, green, and lavender. Among them, Mabel stood out in her ruffled pink gown, its delicate fabric accented with bold red trimmings that added a touch of drama to her ensemble. Her pink ribboned bonnet, adorned with trembling white aigrettes, finished the look, their constant subtle motion lending an extra dash of sophistication and life to her appearance.

The group crossed the polished rosewood floor to the back of the hall, where circular tables draped in fine white linen tablecloths awaited. Each table was set with a centerpiece of fresh flowers, their vibrant hues contrasting beautifully with the pristine table settings. Small white china dishes, delicately edged with gold, were arranged alongside elegantly etched silverware and crystal glasses that caught the light from the chandeliers above, their facets glinting like stars. Some guests were already seated, their postures relaxed yet refined, while others milled about the room, their voices blending into a low hum of lively conversation.

Simon led the group toward the table where Mr. Wilby and Mr. Samuels were already seated, accompanied by two other gentlemen unfamiliar to Victoria. The men were imbibing a fine burgundy port, their glasses half-empty as they leaned in, engrossed in a spirited debate.

"Naturally, these new electric street lights will change London's character... and not for the better!" Mr. Wilby proclaimed with a tone of absolute certainty, his bushy eyebrows knitting together in disapproval.

"It's progress!" one of the other gentlemen countered with equal conviction, his voice rising slightly above the din of the room. "It will replace those gas lamps that too often sputter and go out, leaving the streets in darkness!"

"Poppycock!" Mr. Wilby retorted sharply, his voice carrying a note of indignation as he leaned forward, his port sloshing slightly in his glass. "Gas lamps have served us well for decades. These electric contraptions are nothing but a passing fancy!"

The approaching group snapped the two fervent debaters from their heated discussion. They rose to their feet, their intense expressions shifting into polite smiles in strict adherence to Victorian etiquette. Mr. Wilby, his port glass still in hand, and his companion, whose face remained flushed from the argument, now stood as a picture of civility.

Simon, ever the gentleman, stepped forward and pulled out the chairs for each of the ladies in succession. First, he guided Annabelle to her seat, her light lavender gown rustling softly as she settled into the chair. Next, he assisted Victoria, her scarlet and bronze ensemble catching the light as she gracefully took her place. Finally, he turned to Mabel, her pink and red ruffled gown swaying gently as she sat, her headpiece's aigrettes bobbing with the motion.

Once the ladies were seated, Simon took his own place at the table and, with a polite nod to the men, said, "Gentlemen, I trust everyone is having a fine evening." His tone was warm yet formal, a perfect balance of cordiality and propriety.

After several perfunctory and polite exchanges of "Good Evening," Mr. Wilby and his opponent quickly returned to their lively debate over the merits of electric versus gas streetlights. The table fell silent as all present listened intently to the rapid-fire exchange, their heads turning like spectators at a tennis match as the arguments volleyed back and forth. The debate raged on until, at last, Mr. Wilby's opponent conceded—more out of exhaustion than agreement, it seemed, having realized that Mr. Wilby would never relent until he emerged victorious.

"Right so!" Mr. Wilby pronounced triumphantly, his voice ringing with smug assurance as he leaned back in his chair, a self-satisfied smile playing on his lips. Without missing a beat, he launched into another impassioned argument, this time about the importance of the pending war in Afghanistan and how, with "The Jewel in the Crown"—referring to India—the British Empire would not only expand but endure for at least another hundred years. His previous opponent, still recovering from the streetlamp debate, opened his mouth to respond, his expression a mix of amusement and exasperation, when suddenly the musicians ceased playing.

A delicate clinking of glasses echoed through the hall, cutting through the hum of conversation and drawing the attention of all present. The room fell silent, every eye turning toward the source of the sound as anticipation filled the air. A tall, thin gentleman with jet-black hair, a short mustache that merged seamlessly into a short beard, all peppered with streaks of white and gray, stood at the center of the ballroom. He held a crystal glass in one hand, tapping it briskly with a silver spoon—*clink, clink, clink*—until the room was utterly still.

"Ladies and gentlemen," he boomed, his voice carrying effortlessly across the grand hall. "Thank you for attending this most important charity ball. For those who are not acquainted with me, allow me to introduce myself. I am Dr. Gideon Ashford, director of a most vital institution—The Royal Earlswood Hospital, located in Redhill. There, we house and treat people with a variety of disabilities and many of our unfortunate fellow citizens who suffer from maladies of the mind, providing them with care and protection while safeguarding the public from harm. I am also frequently consulted by the nearby Royal Surrey County Hospital, where the finest in modern medical care is delivered."

He paused, allowing his words to settle over the audience like a heavy cloak, before continuing. "Now, to further the mission of this esteemed institution, we are opening a children's wing at the hospital. This new wing will provide the very best care for our young citizens, ensuring their health and well-being. The hospital will maintain the strictest modern sanitation practices, employ the most advanced medications, and ensure that vaccinations and revaccinations are administered promptly, especially when smallpox is afoot. Dr. Jenner, a true philanthropist who worked tirelessly for the betterment of mankind, bestowed upon us this blessing nearly three-quarters of a century ago—"

At this, Annabelle, who had remained silent for most of the evening, let out a soft huff and muttered just loud enough to be heard at their table, "Pompous blowhard."

Victoria switched her focus to Annabelle, her forehead crinkling in surprise at the unexpected comment. Yet, no one else at the table seemed to hear—or, if they did, they chose to pretend otherwise.

Unaware of the quiet interruption, Dr. Ashford pressed on.

"—As an aside, I urge you to ensure your newborns are vaccinated by three months of age. It is, after all, the law of the land. A few small scratches by a doctor's lancet, and your child—and the community—are protected." He paused again, letting the weight of his words sink in, before concluding, "In any event, your generous donations will help complete the construction of this children's wing, which is already well underway. I thank you, and the children of the Empire thank you." He punctuated his speech by lifting his glass high in the air, his voice ringing out with finality, "Hear, hear! Now, please, enjoy your evening."

A round of applause filled the room, the sound swelling like a wave as Dr. Ashford stepped away from the center of the ballroom. He made his way toward a group of gentlemen, their heads nodding in approval as they greeted him with respectful smiles and murmured congratulations.

The musicians resumed their enchanting performance, filling the grand ballroom with the lilting sounds of *Tales from the Vienna Woods*. The waltz, a dance of elegance and grace, swept through the room as couples glided across the polished floor, their movements synchronized with the rhythm of Johann Strauss II's timeless melody. The chandeliers above cast a warm, golden glow, their crystals refracting light like glimmering fireflies, while the rustle of silk and satin gowns added a soft whisper to the music.

Simon, ever the dutiful son, rose from his chair with a quiet confidence. He extended his hand to his mother, Annabelle, his voice gentle yet firm. "Mother, may I have the honor of this dance?" Annabelle's eyes softened with gratitude, a faint blush coloring her cheeks as she placed her gloved hand in his. "Of course, my dear," she replied, her voice tinged with emotion. Together, they moved toward the dance floor, their steps blending seamlessly with the other couples who swayed and twirled in perfect harmony.

Not far away, Mr. Wilby, ever the picture of Victorian propriety in his impeccably tailored tailcoat and white gloves, rose from his seat. With a practiced elegance, he extended his hand toward Victoria, his voice carrying a note of formality. "Victoria, would you do me the honor— "

Victoria's lips pursed, her expression one of mild reproach. She interrupted him with a tone that was both firm and measured. "Mr. Wilby, I must insist you address me as Mrs. Pembroke. Moreover, it would be most improper for you to ask me to dance without first seeking my husband's permission."

Mr. Wilby, undeterred and with a hint of amusement in his eyes, quickly interjected. "Mrs. Pembroke, I assure you, I have already sought your husband's blessing, and he has graciously granted it." His hand remained outstretched, steady and patient, as if to emphasize his sincerity.

Victoria hesitated, her lips pursed and brow furrowing slightly as she processed his words. After a brief pause, her expression softened, and a polite smile graced her lips. "Of course, Mr. Wilby," she said, her voice now lukewarm with acceptance. She placed her hand in his, allowing him to guide her to the dance floor.

As they joined the swirling throng of dancers, Victoria couldn't shake the unsettling sensation that Mr. Wilby's stare was piercing right through her. His eyes held a strange, almost voracious intensity, reminiscent of how he had scrutinized her weeks ago during that business dinner. It was as though he were probing her very soul, his dissecting inspection both unnerving and inescapable. Her heart quickened, and a slight sheen of perspiration formed on her brow, despite the cool air of the ballroom. A peculiar feeling washed over her—one she couldn't quite define but instinctively recognized. It was the sensation of being hunted, a prey caught in the gaze of a predator.

As they spun across the floor, Victoria's eyes darted across the room, searching for Simon. She spotted Annabelle seated at their table, her expression serene as she sipped her tea, but Simon was nowhere to be seen. Her pulse quickened, and a knot of unease tightened in her chest. To her dismay, Mr. Wilby's smile seemed to widen, as if he could sense her growing distress. The music swelled around them, but the waltz, once elegant and joyful, now felt like a trap.

As Mr. Wilby's vulturine attention bore into her, Victoria couldn't help but wonder where Simon had gone. His absence felt deliberate, as though he had abandoned her to this man's unsettling scrutiny. *Was this part of some unspoken agreement between them?* The thought sent a shiver down her spine.

As the dance was ending, Mr. Wilby's hand lingered on hers a moment too long. "You are a remarkable woman, Mrs. Pembroke," he said, his voice low, his eyes penetrating further. "I do hope we'll have the chance to... converse further."

Thankfully, the final notes of *Tales from the Vienna Woods* echoed through the ballroom, bringing the dance to an end. Victoria seized the opportunity to step back, breaking contact with Mr. Wilby in a manner that was perhaps more abrupt than polite.

"Thank you for the waltz," she murmured breathlessly, her voice barely audible over the fading music. Without waiting for a response, she turned and hurried toward the table, her heart still pounding in her ears. She could still feel his unnerving, intense stare on her back as she retreated across the dance floor.

As she navigated the crowded room, her vision began to blur. The vibrant gowns and tailcoats of the guests melted into a chaotic swirl of colors; their faces indistinguishable. Her panic mounted, and the once-familiar ballroom now felt like a labyrinth. Just as she felt her composure slipping, a firm yet gentle hand grasped her shoulder.

"Victoria," came Mabel's voice, soft but filled with concern. Her friend's gloved hand steadied her, and Victoria turned to meet Mabel's worried stare. "Are you alright? What happened?"

Victoria let out a series of gasping breaths, her chest rising and falling rapidly as she struggled to steady herself. When she realized it was Mabel standing before her, a wave of relief washed over her. Mabel's familiar face, framed by soft curls and a look of genuine concern, was a comforting anchor in the sea of her panic. Without a word,

Mabel guided Victoria back to her chair, her touch firm yet gentle. She helped her sit, then reached for a glass of water, pressing it into Victoria's trembling hands. "Here, drink this," Mabel urged softly.

Victoria took a few sips, the cool water soothing her parched throat. Mabel knelt beside her, her gloved hands tightly clasping Victoria's, as though trying to transfer some of her own calm into her friend. "Victoria, tell me truly—are you alright?" Mabel's voice was low but insistent, her eyes searching Victoria's face for answers.

Victoria nodded, though her breathing was still uneven. "Yes, I... I think I just got winded. The dance was more vigorous than I expected." She forced a small, unconvincing smile, hoping to reassure Mabel. But as her eyes swept across the ballroom once more, her anxiety resurfaced.

Mabel leaned closer, her voice a whisper. "You look as though you've seen a ghost. Was it Mr. Wilby? That man has a way of making one feel... exposed."

Victoria nodded, grateful for Mabel's intuition.

The crowd swirled with laughter and movement, but Simon was conspicuously absent. Her brow furrowed, and she turned back to Mabel, her voice tinged with worry. "Where is Simon? Have you seen him?"

Mabel rose gracefully from her seat, her eyes scanning the bustling ballroom. She tilted her head slightly, her expression thoughtful as she searched for any sign of Simon. "Hmm... I don't see him," she murmured, her voice tinged with mild concern. "But I'm sure he just stepped out for a moment. He'll be back shortly, I'm certain of it." She gave Victoria's shoulder a reassuring squeeze before sitting back down, though her gaze lingered on the crowd, as if silently willing Simon to reappear.

Victoria sat quietly at the table, her hands clasped tightly in her lap. The din of the evening whirled around her—laughter, chatter, and the occasional burst of applause for the orchestra—but it all felt distant, as though she were observing the scene from behind a pane of thick glass. Her mind raced, replaying the unsettling encounter with Mr. Wilby. She tried to convince herself it had been her imagination, a trick of the candlelight, or the fatigue of the evening. But deep in her heart, she knew better. The intensity of his stare, the way his smile had widened as her apprehension grew—it had been real. Too real.

Just as her thoughts threatened to overwhelm her, Simon materialized at the table as if conjured from the air itself. He offered his hand, his expression polite but distant, as though his mind were elsewhere. Without a word, Victoria took his hand, her movements automatic, and allowed him to lead her to the dance floor. As they stepped into the rhythm of the music, she noticed the orchestra was playing a slower, more melancholic piece—one she didn't recognize. Its haunting melody seemed to echo the disquiet in her heart.

They danced as they had countless times before, their steps practiced and precise. Yet something felt different. Simon's focus was distant, his attention seemingly elsewhere, as though the dance were merely an obligation to fulfill. Victoria studied his face, searching for the warmth and connection that had once been so natural between them. Finding none, she leaned in slightly and whispered, her voice barely perceptible over the music, "Did you grant Mr. Wilby permission to dance with me?"

Simon's eyes met hers, and for a moment, it felt as though he truly saw her—perhaps for the first time in a long while. "Naturally," he responded coolly, his tone matter-of-fact. "He's my good business partner, after all."

"Of course," Victoria whispered back, her voice soft but laced with resignation. She forced a small smile, though it did little to dispel the growing unease in her chest.

Simon's eyes drifted over her shoulder, as if he was scanning the room for something—or someone. His hand felt cold in hers, and his responses were clipped, as though his mind were miles away.

The rest of the evening passed in a blur for Victoria. She moved through the motions of polite conversation and obligatory dances, but her mind remained preoccupied. A sense of foreboding lingered at the edges of her thoughts, like a specter she couldn't quite shake. Something was amiss—she was certain of it—but the nature of it eluded her. As the night wore on, the ballroom's glittering lights and lively music seemed to fade into a distant hum, leaving her alone with her quiet, unspoken fears.

8. Innocence Unraveled

When sorrows come, they come not single spies, but in battalions.
—William Shakespeare, *Hamlet*, Act 4, Scene 7

ictoria sat quietly near the window at her small writing desk, the mid-morning light streaming through the glass, casting a soft, golden glow across her face. The desk was orderly, with sheets of parchment neatly tied together and a quill resting idly beside a fresh bottle of ink, its stopper still firmly in place. She gazed out the window, her thoughts adrift, as the sunlight danced across her features, illuminating the faint shadows beneath her eyes, the only visible evidence of her restless night.

Still clad in her nightgown, she absentmindedly sipped at the steaming cup of tea Clara had delivered moments ago. The blend, a special concoction Annabelle had introduced a few weeks prior, was a soothing mix of chamomile, elderflower, lavender, and a hint of honey and lemon. Its delicate aroma and comforting warmth were a small but welcome solace.

The previous evening's event, which had promised to be a delightful and joyous occasion, had instead left her unsettled and weary. After returning home, Victoria had spent hours tossing and turning in bed, her mind replaying the evening's events in a relentless loop. It was not until the early hours of the morning, when the first gleam of dawn began to creep through the curtains, that she finally drifted into a fitful sleep. Her rest was short-lived, however, as she awoke with a start from a disturbing dream, its details already slipping from her memory like water through her fingers. She reached out instinctively for Simon, only to find his side of the bed cold and empty. The sun's rays streaming into the room told her it was far later than her usual rising hour.

Moments after she pulled the bell cord to summon Clara, the maid appeared, her expression one of gentle concern. "Ma'am, you're not feeling well, are you?" Clara had observed, her voice soft and sympathetic. "Perhaps you should rest a bit longer this morning. Shall I bring you something to help settle your nerves?" It was then that Victoria, recalling the calming tea Annabelle had been drinking weeks ago, requested the same blend. Clara had nodded and rushed off to prepare it, returning shortly with the fragrant brew.

Now, as Victoria sat by the window, the tea's soothing warmth began to ease the tension in her chest, though her mind remained clouded with the persistent unease of the night before. The silence of the room, broken only by the occasional rustle of leaves outside the window, offered a brief respite from the whirlwind of emotions that had plagued her since the event. But a deep discomfort remained, a cold knot in her stomach that the tea could not unravel.

Taking a deep breath, Victoria reached for her leatherbound journal, its cover worn smooth from repetitive use. She held the thin red silk ribbon that marked her place, the delicate fabric slipping through her fingers like a whisper. Flipping to the next blank page, she paused for a moment, her gaze lingering on the pristine paper as if waiting for the right words to reveal themselves. The weak scent of ink and aged paper filled the air, a familiar comfort that grounded her in the moment.

She grasped the long white feather quill, its shaft cool and smooth against her fingertips, and uncorked the glass inkwell with a gentle *pop*. The rich, dark writing fluid shimmered faintly in the morning light. Dipping the writing tool into the well, she watched as the tip glistened with ink, then tapped it lightly against the rim to remove the excess. The rhythmic *tap-tap-tap* echoed softly in the quiet room, a prelude to the act of creation.

With a hand steadied by years of practice—honed in the meticulous penmanship lessons of her finishing school —she began to write. The pen glided across the page, its movements fluid and deliberate, each stroke of ink forming elegant, looping letters. The scratch of the nib against the parchment was a soothing sound, a quiet counterpoint to the whirl of thoughts in her mind. As the words began to flow, she felt the weight of the previous night's events slowly lift, the act of writing offering a rare and cherished comfort.

The occurrences and revelations of last night were profoundly disturbing. Mr. Wilby's penetrating and lurid stare was unlike anything I have ever experienced before. It felt as though his gaze reached into the very depths of my soul, leaving me exposed and vulnerable. What could it all mean? He has always struck me as pompous, yes, but even at the business dinner, his eyes never held such lewdness—no, such imposing

domination. That was the feeling,
unmistakable and chilling.

Pausing momentarily, Victoria set the pen down and took a deep breath, her chest rising and falling as she steadied herself. She dipped the quill into the inkwell once more, the tip glistening with fresh ink, and resumed writing, her hand moving with deliberate precision.

But was it all my imagination? Yet there is
another, darker possibility. One that strikes
a deeper dread. Mother suffered from
melancholy after Father's death, and she
never recovered. She remains confined at the
Royal Earlswood Hospital, a shadow of the
woman she once was. Am I doomed to the
same fate? Is this the beginning of some
inherited madness, or perhaps hysteria? The
very idea fills me with dread.

She paused again, her pen hovering above the page as if suspended by her uncertainty. Then, with a firm resolve, she pressed the nib to the parchment once more.

No! I know what I felt. It was real.

Simon, too, was distant—so absent, so empty.
Even after he reappeared, it was as though
he were a stranger. I feel so lost, so adrift in
this sea of uncertainty. What am I to do?

The words spilled onto the page, each a reflection of her inner turmoil. As she wrote, the weight of her emotions seemed to transfer from her heart to the parchment, leaving her both drained and strangely relieved. Yet, the questions remained—unanswered and haunting—like ghosts lingering at the edges of her mind.

Blowing gently over the freshly inked pages, Victoria watched as the words glistened briefly before drying into permanence. She left the journal open momentarily, the muted scent of ink mingling with the crisp morning air. After half a minute, satisfied that her thoughts had dried and her confessions sealed, she closed the journal with a soft thud. The red silk ribbon slipped back into place, a silent warden guarding her private reflections.

After replacing her journal in its secret sanctuary, Victoria settled back into her chair, the weight of her thoughts momentarily eased. She reached for her teacup, the porcelain warm against her fingertips, and took a slow, deliberate sip. The soothing blend seemed to work its magic, calming her frayed nerves. She wondered idly if it was the tea, the act of writing, or perhaps a combination of both that had brought her this sense of quiet relief. Yet, even as the tension in her chest began to dissipate, a lingering question remained: *What should I do?*

As if in answer to her unspoken thoughts, a sharp knock echoed through the room, its crisp rap reverberating against the walls and jolting her from her trance. The sound was firm and deliberate, commanding her attention. Victoria's eyes darted toward the door, her teacup pausing mid-air, her heart skipping a beat as she called out, "Come in." Her voice, though steady, carried a hint of curiosity. At the same time, she couldn't help but wonder why the third stair sentinel—the creaky step that always announced visitors with its telltale groan—had remained silent. In a household where even the floors seemed to whisper secrets, the absence of its familiar warning stirred a flicker of trepidation in her chest. *Had it failed, or had I just been inattentive?*

The door groaned softly as it opened, and Annabelle stepped into the room, pausing just inside the threshold. Her presence was as composed as ever, her light green day dress rustling faintly as she moved. "I heard you were not feeling well," she remarked, her voice carrying a tone of gentle concern.

Victoria looked up from her teacup, her expression softening. "I am feeling quite a bit better, thank you," she answered, her voice tinged with a hint of weariness.

Annabelle's scrutiny drifted to the teacup in Victoria's hands, and a small, knowing smile touched her lips. "I see you requested the tea I use. I'm sure that has helped," she remarked, her tone warm and perceptive.

Victoria hesitated, unsure of how to respond. The silence between them stretched momentarily, filled only by the soft ticking of the grandfather clock on the first floor.

Annabelle advanced further into the room. "You shouldn't let a man such as Mr. Wilby influence you so, my dear," she said, her voice calm but firm, as though she were imparting a well-considered piece of wisdom.

Victoria's cheeks flushed with embarrassment, the color rising swiftly as she realized Annabelle had noticed her apprehension. She had not expected her thoughts to be so easily read, nor for Annabelle to address them so directly. Struggling to find the right words, she remained silent, her fingers tightening slightly around the delicate handle of her teacup. She took another sip, the warm liquid offering a brief distraction from her discomfort.

Annabelle watched her momentarily, her expression a blend of mild sympathy and quiet resolve. Then, without another word, she turned and glided toward the window, her hands clasped lightly in front of her. The sunlight streaming through the glass caught the pearls on her bonnet, making them shimmer like dew on grass. "The world is full of men like Mr. Wilby," she remarked softly, her voice softer now, almost contemplative. "You must understand, my dear, that we live in a man's world. Men crave three things above all else—money, power, and women. Some only want power, some only money, some are complete lechers who want only women, but usually, it's a mix of the three. And if you wish to survive in it, you must be stronger than they are."

Pausing a moment to look at Victoria, she promptly returned her gaze to the window and continued, "As you know, I was not happy with Simon's decision to wed you. The other choice was a woman closer to his age—more composed, more disciplined, less inclined to have her head in the clouds. You, being so much younger, seemed a complete mismatch for Simon at the time." She paused, her eyes narrowing slightly as if recalling the past. "However, you have slowly become more responsible and mature. I believe that now you have some potential."

Victoria sat at the writing desk, her fingers resting lightly on the edge, her expression one of stunned silence. She had not expected such candidness from Annabelle, nor the faint note of approval in her tone. Yet, she remained still, her thoughts swirling as she absorbed the words.

Annabelle let out a light snicker, the sound breaking the tension in the room. She turned toward Victoria, her eyes sharp but not unkind. "I know you think I'm an old shrew," she said, her lips curving into a wry smile. She waved her index finger from side to side, as if to silence any protest before it could begin. "You don't need to deny it. Perhaps I have become just that, with all that I have endured. I doubt you would truly understand."

Victoria's animosity toward Annabelle began to dissolve, replaced by a hint of understanding. There was a vulnerability in Annabelle's words, a hint of shared pain that Victoria had not noticed before. "Well...," she began quietly, her voice faltering as she struggled to find the proper response.

Annabelle pursed her lips, her expression softening. "You, my dear, are stronger than you realize," she asserted, her tone firm but not harsh. "You can take on life's many hardships, or you will lose yourself." She stared intently at Victoria, her look piercing yet oddly comforting. "I know of your family tragedies. We all have them. It's the story of everyone." She paused, her voice dropping slightly. "Speaking of which, have you recently visited your poor mother?"

Victoria shook her head, a sadness clouding her features. "No," she admitted quietly. "Not since August. I was refused a visit again. They told me she didn't want visitors—or wasn't fit for them."

"As you know," Victoria began, "my mother slowly descended into madness sometime after her husband—my father—died in India." She paused, her fingers tightening around the delicate handle of her teacup as if seeking solace in its warmth. "It was not sudden, but gradual, like the fading of daylight into dusk."

Annabelle took a slight breath, her eyes never leaving Victoria's. "You should make a point of it and go to see your mother," she urged gently, her voice steady and resolute. "Family is everything. Be strong, and don't take no for an answer. These institutions—places like The Royal Earlswood—are quick to turn away visitors, claiming it's for the patient's comfort or safety. But I've found that persistence often yields results. A well-placed word, a firm hand, or even a discreetly offered coin can open doors that others would prefer remain shut."

She paused, her look softening ever so slightly. "Your mother may not be the woman you remember, but she is still your mother. And you, my dear, are her daughter. Duty and love demand that you see her, no matter how difficult it may be. The world is unkind to women who falter, and even more so to those who are forgotten. Do not let her become one of the forgotten."

Annabelle's voice carried the weight of experience, as though she spoke not only of Victoria's mother but of countless others who had been cast aside by society. "I know it is not easy," she continued, her tone gentler now. "But strength is not the absence of fear or sorrow—it is the will to act despite them. You must go to her, Victoria. If not for her sake, then for your own. There is a peace that comes from knowing you have done all you can, even when the outcome is beyond your control."

A heavy silence permeated the room as Annabelle gauged Victoria's reaction, her sharp eyes studying the younger woman's face. Victoria, for her part, sat motionless, her mind racing as she tried to assimilate all that Annabelle had revealed. The events of the previous night—Mr. Wilby's unsettling gaze, Simon's distant demeanor, and the whirlwind of emotions that had followed—and now thoughts of her mother—flashed through her mind like scenes from a troubling dream.

"Thank you," Victoria finally uttered, her voice trembling slightly, as if the words themselves carried the weight of her unspoken fears. Then, with a sincere smile, she added, "Your words—your advice—mean more to me than I can express." She paused, her eyes dropping to her hands, which were clasped tightly in her lap. "I've spent so long trying to bury the past, to pretend it doesn't haunt me. But you're right—I owe it to her and to myself to face it."

Annabelle's expression softened, a trace of empathy illuminating her weathered features. She reached out, placing a reassuring hand on Victoria's shoulder, her touch firm yet gentle, as though imparting both comfort and resolve. Then, as if suddenly aware of the vulnerability she had revealed, she pulled back her hand, her demeanor shifting subtly, her face settling into a more composed, almost stoic mask. "My dear," she began, her voice now carrying a measured tone, "I only wish to see you stand firm, not with your head lost in the ether, but with your feet planted firmly on the ground. Strength lies not in idle dreams but in the courage to face what lies before you."

After a short moment of silence, Victoria hesitated, then ventured, "Might I ask you something, Annabelle?"

Annabelle simply nodded, her hands clasped neatly in front, her posture as unyielding as a statue, betraying none of the emotion that glimmered beneath the surface.

"Why did you call Dr. Ashford a—" Victoria began.

"—Pompous blowhard?" Annabelle finished deftly, her lips curling into a slight, wry smile. "Ah, yes. I suppose that requires some explanation." She paused, her expression darkening, a shadow passing over her features like a cloud obscuring the sun. "It's a long story," she trailed off, her voice tinged with reluctance, as though the mere act of recalling it pained her.

Victoria sat quietly; her curiosity piqued, but unsure whether to press further. She watched Annabelle closely, noting the subtle tightening of her jaw and the way her fingers twitched ever so slightly against her skirt.

Annabelle turned back to the window, her look distant and contemplative. The sunlight streaming through the glass caught the thin lines on her face, etching her sorrow into sharp relief. "When I was a young girl—no more than ten years old—the speckled menace—smallpox—made its appearance at our country estate," she began, each word carefully chosen, as though she were recounting a tale she had long tried to forget.

"A man arrived one day," she continued, her tone hardening, "clad in fine clothes and carrying a medical bag that gleamed as if it held the answers to all our prayers. He assured us he could protect us from the menace. I remember what he looked like as if it were yesterday."

Her eyes lifted slightly, as if searching for answers in the clouds drifting across the sky. "He promised my mother it would be simple, that we would hardly notice anything. He said we could even play about the room the whole time." Her voice grew tighter, a brittle edge of bitterness creeping in. "He proceeded to scratch our arms and rub some material into the wounds. One by one—me, my sister, and my brother."

A scowl crossed her face, mingling anger and grief in equal measure. "My brother died a miserable death after twelve weeks of suffering. My sister was never quite the same afterward. She withered away and died the following year of consumption." Annabelle's voice faltered, and she took a deep breath before continuing, as though steadying herself against the tide of memory. "As for me? I survived, no worse for the wear... I survived," she repeated, her tone heavy with guilt. She paused, then added with an ironic, hollow laugh, "And as if to mock his efforts, the following year, I caught smallpox anyway. So yes, a pompous blow-hard."

She turned back toward Victoria, her expression a mixture of defiance and sorrow, as though daring the younger woman to pity her. The room fell silent once more. The weight of her words settled between them, a raw and terrible truth that explained so much about the woman Annabelle had become.

9. The Road to Redhill

A railroad is like a lie—you have to keep building it to make it stand.
—Mark Twain, *Adventures of Huckleberry Finn*, 1884

*V*ictoria had finally received a telegram from The Royal Earlswood Hospital the previous week. Its brief, formal lines confirmed that she could visit her mother, Sarah Jane Barrington, on November 19th. The message, stamped with the sanatorium's official seal, had been delivered by a young telegraph boy in a crisp uniform, his breath visible in the chilly autumn air as he handed her the slip of paper.

TELEGRAM

Received: 12 November 1878

FROM: THE ROYAL EARLSWOOD HOSPITAL, REDHILL, SURREY

TO: MRS. VICTORIA PEMBROKE, HOLLAND ROAD, KENSINGTON, LONDON

MRS. SARAH JANE BARRINGTON APPROVED FOR VISITATION STOP

DATE: 19 NOVEMBER 1878 STOP

TIME: 11 AM STOP

PLEASE PRESENT THIS TELEGRAM UPON ARRIVAL STOP

The journey from their home on Holland Road in Kensington, London, to the hospital in Redhill, Surrey, was one she had made before—a two-to-three-hour trip by carriage and train. Though familiar, the journey was never easy, fraught as it was with memories of her mother's decline and the sterile, imposing atmosphere of the institution. This time, however, she felt a glimmer of relief, for Mabel had agreed to accompany her. Mabel's lively presence and unwavering support would make the trip more bearable, and Victoria was grateful not to face it alone.

It was a cold November morning in London, the kind where a brisk breeze cut through the air, making the chill all the more biting. Victoria and Mabel departed early, their carriage rolling swiftly over the newly macadamized road, a luxury that felt at odds with the grim nature of their errand. The rhythmic clatter of hooves filled the silence, and the pale glow of gas lamps along the streets flickered as they passed, throwing fleeting shadows across the carriage interior. Both women were preoccupied with reflections of the journey ahead, and the early hour lent a subdued air to their conversation.

By the time they reached London Waterloo Station, the sun had begun to rise, washing the bustling scene in a soft, golden light. The station was alive with activity: steam hissed from locomotives, porters darted to and fro with luggage, and throngs of passengers—gentlemen in top hats and overcoats, ladies in traveling dresses— moved about with purpose. The chilly air turned their breath into visible puffs, and the sound of hurried footsteps and distant whistles filled the air.

Both ladies were dressed appropriately for the journey. Victoria wore a practical yet elegant traveling dress of deep green wool, paired with sturdy boots and a thick coat trimmed with fur at the collar and cuffs. Mabel, ever the picture of practicality, had chosen a dark blue ensemble, her coat buttoned snugly against the cold. Woolen gloves and bonnets completed their attire, though the sharp November air still nipped at their cheeks, turning them a rosy hue. As they stepped from the carriage, Victoria pulled her coat tighter, grateful for the warmth of Mabel's reassuring presence beside her.

Once inside the station, they navigated the bustling crowds, their boots clicking against the well-worn stone floors. Porters rushed past with trolleys piled high with luggage, and the sharp whistle of steam engines echoed through the cavernous space. They boarded the train bound for Redhill Station, its lacquered wooden carriages gleaming under the station's gas lamps—a familiar sight that cast a warm, wavering luminescence. Finding their seats in the first-class compartment, they settled into the plush velvet seats, the familiar scents of coal smoke and varnished wood doing little to dispel the chill of the morning.

As they pulled away from the platform, the rhythmic chug of the locomotive and the gentle sway of the carriage lulled them into a contemplative silence. Outside the window, the city gradually gave way to the frost-kissed countryside, the fields and hedgerows glistening in the pale morning light. Victoria stared out at the thin silver, her thoughts circling the impending visit with her mother, while Mabel sat beside her, a steady and reassuring presence. Once the train ride was well underway, Mabel leaned slightly forward, her voice was soft but filled with genuine concern as she asked, "How long has it been since you last saw your mother?"

Victoria hesitated, her eyes fixing on the countryside passing by outside the window. After a moment, she replied, her voice tinged with guilt, "Over three years." She paused, her fingers tightening around the edge of her woolen gloves. "Each time I came unannounced, they told me she couldn't be seen—sometimes because she was unwell, other times because she wasn't fit for visitors. That's why I made sure to send a telegram in advance this time. I couldn't bear to be turned away again."

Mabel nodded, her expression thoughtful. "It's a shame they make it so difficult for families to visit," she said, her tone sympathetic. "But I'm glad you persisted. She'll be so pleased to see you."

Victoria offered a slight smile, though her eyes remained clouded with worry. "I hope so," she said, the words fragile and thin. "I just hope she recognizes me."

A long-suppressed memory bubbled to the surface of Victoria's consciousness. She was a child in the country with her mother and father, the three of them sprawled on a red-and-white checkered cloth spread over the lush grass of a sun-drenched field. Nearby, a small brook babbled softly, its gentle splashing blending with the rustle of leaves in the warm breeze. A well-used wicker picnic basket sat in the middle, its lid slightly ajar, revealing the lunch mother had packed.

They laughed as they ate sandwiches, the kind her mother always made with thick slices of bread and fillings that seemed to taste better outdoors. Ever the storyteller, her father recounted outlandish tales of his imaginary exploits, dramatically wielding a humble vegetable as though it were a sword.

"And then," he proclaimed, his voice booming with mock seriousness, "I faced the fearsome beast with nothing but... a carrot!" He thrust it into the air, mimicking a duel with an invisible foe, while Victoria and her mother dissolved into laughter, their joy echoing across the field.

It was a day like many others. Happy. Perfect. The thought caused her eyes to well up as she stared unseeing out the window, the present moment dissolving into the bittersweet haze of the past. Tears blurred her vision, but she made no move to wipe them away, allowing the memory to linger, fragile and precious, like the sunlight filtering through the glass.

Both women looked out at the cold pastoral country-side passing by the windows, the fields sheened with frost, catching the frail winter sun. As Victoria stared out the window, her mind drifted to her last visit to the hospital three years ago. Her mother had been seated in a sunlit room, her hands trembling as she clutched a faded photograph of Victoria as a child. Sarah Jane's eyes had been distant, her voice hollow as she breathed, "You look so much like her."

Victoria had reached out to touch her mother's hand, but Sarah Jane recoiled, her eyes wide with fear. "Like who, Mother?" Victoria had asked gently, but Sarah Jane only shook her head, her eyes locked on some unseen point beyond the window. The memory lingered now, a sharp ache in Victoria's chest, the hurt intensifying with every turn of the wheels that brought the imposing gates of Earlswood nearer.

With every mile the train devoured, Victoria's thoughts increasingly lingered on her mother, the weight of the impending visit pressing heavily on her heart. Sensing her friend's discomfort, Mabel kindly steered the conversation toward lighter topics, hoping to ease the tension. Mabel broke the quiet with a gentle inquiry, "And how are things with Dear Annabelle these days?"

Victoria, still looking out the window, allowed a slight smile to touch her lips. "Better than I ever imagined," she admitted. "She's shared some of her life stories with me—some quite shocking." She paused, her voice lowering slightly. "Her sister's husband—"

Mabel interjected, her tone teasing but kind, "Your aunt."

Victoria chuckled lightly. "I know. I'm not completely soft in the head. Yes, Aunt Bernice." She leaned back in her seat, her expression turning thoughtful. "Anyway... my uncle by marriage—this was many years ago—was apparently notorious for his indiscretions. Aunt Bernice was none too pleased about it, so she took matters into her own hands. She began administering small doses of arsenic, which some call inheritance powder."

Mabel's eyes widened, her jaw dropping slightly. "Your aunt poisoned her husband?"

Victoria nodded gently, her tone matter-of-fact. "And quite successfully, it appears. After several months, he died a miserable and painful death. He was buried, and that was the end of it... Or so it would have seemed."

Mabel leaned forward, her curiosity piqued, and Victoria mirrored her movement, their heads drawing closer. "Except," Victoria continued, her voice sinking to a low, ominous note, "over the years, suspicions grew that Uncle So-and-So had been murdered. Eventually, an inquest was called, and his body was exhumed." She paused for effect, her eyes locking with Mabel's. "They found he looked exactly the same as the day he was buried—perfectly preserved, thanks to the arsenic."

Mabel gasped, her hand flying to her mouth. "Good heavens!"

Victoria nodded solemnly. "The court ruled it was murder. Aunt Bernice was found guilty and, shortly thereafter, hanged for her crimes."

"What a dreadfully macabre tale," Mabel uttered in a low, uneasy tone. "And Annabelle shared this with you?"

"She did," Victoria replied, her tone thoughtful. "I think she wanted me to understand that life isn't always as simple as it seems—and that sometimes, people do desperate things when they feel trapped."

Mabel leaned back into her seat, shrugging and twisting her mouth. "So, it would seem," she remarked. After a momentary pause, she added, "And Simon?"

Victoria continued to contemplate the lonely countryside, a slight sigh escaping her lips. "The same. Very busy and distant..." She turned to Mabel, her expression softening. "And you? Is Terrance back yet?"

Mabel folded her hands neatly in her lap, her demeanor composed but tinged with wistfulness. "I received a telegram a few days ago. My husband won't be returning until spring—off on some extended campaign in India, or so I'm told." She lifted her chin slightly, then mimicked a small march with her fingers. "Off doing Her Majesty's business," she added with a wry smile.

Victoria twisted her face in puzzlement, her brow furrowing. "Will he even recognize you when he returns? I mean... how do you do it? You're always so cheerful, and your marriage... it seems to work."

Mabel smiled gently, her eyes crinkling at the corners. "When he is home, we are quite close. And when he is not, I have a great deal to be grateful for." She leaned forward slightly, a playful glint in her eye as she confided, "Besides, we are actually quite outrageous in our bedroom adventures."

She paused, watching Victoria's reaction with amusement. Victoria's cheeks flushed a deep crimson, her eyes widening in fascination. "Oh my," she breathed, her voice hushed with scandalized intrigue. "Do tell."

Straightening up and pursing her lips, Mabel shook her head slightly from side to side. "In public, we are prim and proper, as is expected," she said, her demure tone contradicted by a spark of pure impishness in her eyes. Then, leaning in, she confided in a voice rich with secrecy, "But behind closed doors, there is passion, playfulness, and exploration. When he returns from a long trip, he is... quite eager to ...reconnect."

Smiling devilishly, Mabel leaned even closer to Victoria, her words a thread of delicious scandal. "Especially when he returns from a long trip. There's a hunger in him that cannot be tamed. He lingers over me with his lips for hours, savoring every moment, before finally claiming what is his. By the end, we are both utterly spent and gloriously content." She paused, a salacious grin widening as she added, her voice sinking to the barest breath, "On one occasion, as we were playfully tussling, I spanked his backside with my hairbrush until it turned red. He did quite enjoy that, and when he claimed me completely, it was... very intense for us both."

Victoria's cheeks flushed, and she glanced away, a small smile playing on her lips. "Oh, Mabel," the words escaped on a breath that was half laugh, half gasp. "That is quite scandalous!"

Both ladies fell back against the plush seat backs, their smiles widening as they shared a moment of laughter and camaraderie. The train's rhythmic chug and the warmth of their conversation helped make the forty-minute journey pass quickly. They continued with moments of lighthearted chatter and shared laughter, their voices mingling with the steady hum of the locomotive. The mood was buoyant, a welcome respite from the weight of Victoria's impending visit to her mother.

As the train slowed and came to a halt at Redhill Station, the two women gathered their belongings, their laughter fading into a more subdued but still cheerful demeanor. Stepping onto the platform, they were greeted by the crisp November air and the sight of a waiting carriage. The driver, a jovial man with a ruddy complexion and a slightly battered top hat, tipped his brim and greeted them warmly. "Good morning, ladies!" his voice carrying a note of genuine cheer. "Ready for the ride to the institution?"

He helped them into the small, simple yet impeccably clean carriage, its interior carrying a subtle scent of polished leather and fresh hay. The horses, a pair of sturdy bays, stamped their hooves impatiently, their breath visible in the chilly air. As the driver climbed into his seat and took up the reins, Victoria and Mabel exchanged a glance, their earlier laughter replaced by a quiet understanding of the gravity of the visit ahead. The carriage jolted into motion, its wheels crunching over the gravel drive as they set off toward the imposing gates of The Royal Earlswood Hospital.

They arrived at the ornate iron gates after a quick and quiet fifteen-minute ride. Flanked by two massive stone pylons, the gates stood open, their intricate scrollwork glinting in the pale November daylight. Each pylon transitioned seamlessly into a high stone wall that stretched into the distance, its commanding presence marking the boundary of the hospital grounds. Above the gates, an arched iron sign proclaimed "ROYAL EARLS-WOOD HOSPITAL" in large, bold letters. Sunlight, filtering through the ornate ironwork, threw stark, shadowy letters down upon the gravel. The entrance was awe-inspiring in its scale, but the high walls stretching into the distance spoke less of care and more of keeping something — or someone — contained.

As the carriage came to a halt, Victoria and Mabel stepped out onto the gravel drive, their boots crunching softly against the stones. Before them rose the Royal Earlswood Hospital, its red-brick façade bathed in the pale November sunlight. The building was in the grand Italianate style, reminiscent of a Tuscan villa with its symmetrical design, ornate detailing, and tall, rounded windows, all exuding an air of authority and dignity.

The central block stood three stories tall, its large arched windows reflecting the weak daylight. Above it, a clock tower rose majestically, its face peering down like a watchful guardian. The tower's pinnacle was adorned with a weathervane, which spun lazily in the brisk breeze. To either side of the central block, long wings extended outward, their rows of windows suggesting the orderly lives contained within.

The hospital's ornate stonework tried to lend an air of dignity, and the manicured grounds suggested serenity. But it was all a carefully maintained illusion, shattered by the ivy-choked stone wall that encircled the entire property—a silent, looming barrier.

The main entrance was marked by a broad set of stone steps leading up to imposing, paneled oak doors, flanked by decorative iron lanterns. Above the doors, an arched stone lintel bore the inscription "Royal Earlswood

Hospital" in bold, carved letters. The air was crisp and still, the only sounds the distant chirping of birds and the soft rustling of leaves in the wind.

Victoria adjusted her gloves, her attention captured by the ominous structure before her. The institution's grandeur was undeniable, but something about its scale and symmetry felt slightly foreboding. Mabel, standing beside her, seemed to sense her unease. "It's quite something, isn't it?" she breathed, her words a visible puff in the chilly air.

Victoria nodded, her eyes tracing the lines of the building. "Yes," she responded quietly. "But I can't help feeling it's more like a fortress than a place of healing." Victoria's heart pounded as she approached the hospital, each step bringing her closer to her mother. The imposing scale of the building only heightened her anxiety, its colossal edifice a stark reminder of the barriers—both physical and emotional—that separated them.

The heavy oak doors creaked open, and Dr. Gideon Ashford emerged, his tall, thin frame silhouetted against the dim light of the hospital's interior. He looked much as he had at the charity event: his jet-black hair, streaked with white and gray, was neatly combed, and his short mustache gave him an air of distinguished authority. He descended the broad stone steps with measured strides, his black coat flapping slightly in the brisk November breeze.

The two women ascended the steps to meet him, their skirts brushing against the cold stone. "Good day," Dr. Ashford welcomed them, his voice carrying a note of warmth despite the chill in the air. "Let us get out of the cold." He gestured toward the open doors, ushering the two inside before closing them with a firm thud.

Once inside the grand entrance hall, Dr. Ashford turned to them and extended his hand. "Good day, ladies. I am Dr. Gideon Ashford," he addressed them cordially, his greeting precise, his demeanor one of polished professionalism.

Victoria stepped forward, her gloved hand meeting his in a brief, polite shake. "I am Mrs. Victoria Pembroke," she said, her voice steady. "And this is my traveling companion, Mrs. Mabel Hawthorne."

Mabel offered a nod and a smile, her hands clasped neatly in front of her. Victoria reached into her handbag and produced the telegram, holding it out to Dr. Ashford. "I have the confirmation here—"

Dr. Ashford waved it off with a gentle smile. "No need, Mrs. Pembroke. I am well aware of your visit to see your mother. Please, follow me to my office." He turned and led the way, the sharp tap of his heeled boots echoing against the gleaming marble floor of the hallway.

Upon entering his office, Dr. Ashford motioned toward two chairs positioned in front of his desk. "Please, sit," he directed, his tone polite yet commanding.

Dr. Ashford's office was a portrait of the man himself: ordered, imposing, and steeped in a quiet authority. A large oak desk commanded the center of the room, flanked by a high-backed leather chair and floor-to-ceiling shelves crammed with leatherbound volumes. The titles, though difficult to read from a distance, hinted at a wide range of subjects, from medicine and philosophy to literature and history. The subtle, rich aroma of lemon-oiled wood and aged books filled the air.

The large glass window offered a commanding view of the front grounds, where their carriage stood waiting, the horses shifting and blowing plumes of breath into the crisp air. On the wall opposite the window hung a large oil painting, its frame ornate and gilded. The painting depicted a serene pastoral scene—a sunlit meadow with a gentle stream winding through it, flanked by towering trees and distant hills. At the bottom of the frame, an inscription in elegant script read: "Hope springs eternal in the human breast." A sentiment that felt more like a plea than a promise in this place.

Victoria and Mabel took their seats, their eyes briefly scanning the room before settling on Dr. Ashford as he moved behind his desk.

Dr. Ashford lifted a cut-glass pitcher from his desk, its surface catching the light as he poured water into two matching glasses. He handed one to each of the ladies, his movements precise and deliberate. "I'm sure you are quite parched after your long journey," he offered, his voice maintaining a professional, almost sterile, courtesy.

Settling back into his large leather chair, he recited the stock introduction he had undoubtedly delivered count-less times before. "We here at the Royal Earlswood Hospital primarily care for those with disabilities," he intoned, his voice flat and devoid of inflection, like a clerk reading a ledger. "For nearly a decade now, we have devoted the east wing to the treatment of individuals with various forms of insanity. Our work not only seeks to alleviate their afflictions but also to protect the public from those who may pose a danger to themselves or others."

He opened a leatherbound folder on his desk, its contents neatly organized. Glancing at the papers inside, he continued, "Mrs. Pembroke, your mother has received the best care we can provide for the past four years. However, I must be candid with you. She is not a well woman suffering from melancholia. She is often confused, combative, resists treatments, and can fly into rages without warning. There have been occasions when she has refused to eat, and we have been forced to... shall we say, administer nutrition to ensure her survival."

While Dr. Ashford had been impeccably polite and hospitable, something about his demeanor unsettled Victoria. His words carried an undertone of calculation, as though each sentence had been carefully crafted to elicit a specific response. His penetrating stare lingered a moment too long, and his smiles never quite reached his eyes, leaving her with the distinct impression that his kindness was a veneer masking something far colder.

She couldn't shake the feeling that his warnings about her mother's state were not entirely altruistic. Was he genuinely concerned for her feelings, or was there another reason he seemed so eager to dissuade her from the visit? The thought sent a shiver down her spine, though she quickly dismissed it as paranoia. Still, as she sipped the water he had offered, she couldn't help but notice how the cut-glass pitcher caught the light, its sharp edges glinting like a warning.

He fell silent for a moment, his assessing stare cataloging every nuance of Victoria's reaction. "Given these circumstances, I strongly urge you to reconsider seeing her today. The experience may prove deeply unsettling to your, no doubt, delicate sensibilities."

Slightly taken aback by Dr. Ashford's blunt candor, Victoria straightened her posture and held his stare with unflinching resolve. "Despite your warnings," she declared, her tone leaving no room for debate, "I do need to see my mother."

Dr. Ashford paused; his expression unreadable as he studied her for several long moments. Then, a faint smile touched his lips. "Very well," he acknowledged, the words deliberate and cool. "I will have her brought to our family sitting area. One of my assistants will accompany her and remain with you to ensure everyone's safety." He rose from his chair; his movements deliberate and unhurried. "I have other responsibilities to attend to, so if you will excuse me, I will make the arrangements and meet you again after your visit. Pardon me." With a slight nod, he exited the room, the door swinging shut with a well-oiled click.

Victoria took a deep breath, her hands trembling slightly as she reached for her glass of water. She and Mabel sipped quietly, the silence in the room broken only by the quiet ticking of a clock on the bookshelf. Victoria glanced at Mabel, her eyes searching for reassurance.

Mabel, ever perceptive, offered a warm smile. "Don't worry," she soothed, her voice a low, steady anchor in the room's tense silence. "It will be fine." The gentle assurance seemed to ease the tension in the room, if only for a wistful moment.

10. Behind the Iron Gates

In individuals, insanity is rare; but in groups, parties,
nations, and epochs, it is the rule.
—Friedrich Nietzsche, *Beyond Good and Evil*, 1886

*T*hey sat soundlessly for what felt like an eternity, the slow, rhythmic ticking of the clock etching each passing second. At long last, a short, matronly woman dressed in a starched white uniform and a simple white bonnet entered the room. Her expression was neutral, her hands clasped neatly in front of her. "The doctor has approved your visit," she announced. "Please follow me."

Victoria and Mabel rose from their seats and followed the woman down a short, dimly lit hallway. The walls were lined with dark, varnished paneling, and the sharp, clean scent of antiseptic clung to the air. The gas lamps sputtered, casting long, distorted shadows that seemed to stretch and twist as they walked. At the end of the hallway, the woman stopped at an open door and gestured for them to enter. "Mr. Thomas Cartwright will be present during your visit," she explained. "He will ensure your safety and escort your mother back to her wing afterward. When you are finished, follow the hallway to return to Dr. Ashford's office."

Victoria nodded in understanding, though her pulse quickened as she took a deep breath. With Mabel at her side, she stepped into the room.

The space was plain and sparsely furnished, its walls painted a dull cream and its floor covered with a simple, well-worn rug. Four upholstered easy chairs and a modest couch were arranged in a square, facing each other. Sitting quietly in one of the chairs was a woman who was painfully thin, her black hair long and unstyled but neatly combed. Her face was gaunt, with sharply defined cheekbones, and her eyes sunken and vacant. She seemed to stare into the distance, unaware of her surroundings.

Despite Dr. Ashford's warnings, Victoria gasped softly, her heart sinking as she took in the sight before her. The woman in the chair was a ghost. The once-strong, vibrant, laughing mother of Victoria's memory had been hollowed out, leaving behind a brittle shell; her bony frame seemed almost swallowed by the chair. Her eyes, once so full of light, were now just two dark, vacant pools.

Standing silently nearby was Mr. Thomas Cartwright, his presence as imposing as it was unobtrusive. He was a tall, muscular man, his broad shoulders and sturdy build suggesting a lifetime of physical labor. Dressed in an immaculate white uniform, he stood with his hands clasped behind his back, his expression neutral but watchful. His crisp, white uniform was a stark, almost offensive contrast to the grim decay of the room.

"Mother," Victoria spoke softly, her voice quivering as she approached the frail figure in the chair. "It's Victoria." When there was no response, she knelt on one knee, gently grasping her mother's thin, cold hand. "Mother, do you know who I am?"

Her mother's head turned slightly, her sunken eyes peering toward Victoria with a flicker of recognition. "Victoria?" she breathed, the name a frail whisper on her lips.

A glimmer of hope sparked in Victoria's chest. "Yes, it's me, Victoria," she said, her voice soft but urgent. "And this is my good friend, Mabel."

For a brief moment, her mother's lips curved into a slight smile, but it faded as quickly as it had appeared, replaced by the same blank stare. "My daughter is dead," her mother whispered, her voice hollow. "My husband is dead."

Victoria's heart clenched as she searched her mother's face, desperate for any sign of the woman she once knew. "No, Mother," she insisted, her voice breaking. "I'm not dead. I'm here, right in front of you."

Her frustration simmered beneath the surface, but it was the sight of her mother's eerie quiet that finally broke her composure. "What have you done to her!?" she demanded, her voice rising.

Mr. Cartwright remained impassive, his hands clasped behind his back. "I believe Dr. Ashford explained the serious nature of your mother's illness," he retorted, his tone calm and devoid of emotion.

Tears streamed down Victoria's face, her shoulders trembling as she began to sob. "She was never like this," she choked out, her voice breaking. "Never..." The words hung in the air, heavy with grief and disbelief.

Mabel, her own eyes glistening with unshed tears, knelt beside Victoria. She wrapped her arms around her friend, pulling her into a firm but gentle embrace. "I know," Mabel murmured, her voice soft and soothing. "I know." She held Victoria tightly, offering what little comfort she could in the face of such overwhelming sorrow.

A single, screaming thought eclipsed all others: *What have they done to you?* It was followed by a torrent of others—*Why did I wait so long? What is this place?*—each one a hammer blow of guilt and horror. A storm of rage, grief, and helplessness broke inside her.

Controlling her sobs, her eyes red and swollen from distress, Victoria slowly rose to her feet, her posture squaring as she turned to face the attendant. "Please, Mr. Cartwright," she insisted, "I need to know what she's been through. I can't help her if I don't understand."

For a heartbeat, the hardened expression on Mr. Cartwright's face softened ever so slightly. He let out a slow breath, the sound a quiet concession to her distress. "Ma'am," he began, his tone measured but not unkind, "your mother is receiving the best medical care avail—"

Victoria cut him off, her hands gesturing wildly toward her mother. "Is this the best?" she demanded, her voice rising. "Look at her! How can you call this care?"

Mr. Cartwright continued almost mechanically, his professionalism unwavering. "It's the best medical care available. She receives sedatives and tonics as ordered to help manage her outbursts. She—"

Victoria interrupted him again, her voice sharp with desperation. "I want to see her room."

Mr. Cartwright's patience began to wear thin. "It's not permitted for visitors to venture to the—"

"I wasn't asking," Victoria's voice was a blade of cold steel, a perfect parry to his authoritative stare. "I need to see her room."

The attendant's stance hardened; his lips pressed into a thin line as he fell silent. The tension in the room was palpable.

Mabel, ever the pragmatist, stepped in. She gently took Victoria by the arm and pulled her aside, her voice a low whisper. "My friend—Victoria—these men are not paid well. A few shillings might persuade him to show us more than he should. You know the old saying, honey, not vinegar. Right?"

Without waiting for Victoria's response or consent, Mabel turned and approached Mr. Cartwright. She hesitated for a perilous heartbeat, her fingers tightening around the coin. She knew the risk, but Victoria's desperation left her no choice. "Mr. Cartwright," she began, her voice measured but tinged with urgency, "I know this is highly irregular, but surely you can understand a daughter's concern?" As she spoke, she discreetly slid a gold sovereign into his hand. "All we are asking is a brief tour of the wing where her mother is housed."

Mr. Cartwright hesitated, his eyes flicking to the coin in his palm. "This is against the rules," he responded, his voice low. "If anyone finds out, I could lose my position."

Mabel, sensing his reluctance, leaned in closer, her voice dropping to an almost seductive whisper. "We understand the risk, Mr. Cartwright. And we are deeply grateful for your discretion."

She slipped another coin into his hand, her gaze steady. "This is for your trouble. And there will be more where that came from if you help us."

After a moment of hesitation, Mr. Cartwright nodded, his resolve clearly swayed by the promise of additional compensation. "I will return in a moment," he breathed, the agreement barely audible. Without another word, he briskly left the room, leaving Victoria and Mabel in tense silence. The air felt heavy as they waited, their eyes occasionally darting to Victoria's mother, who sat motionless in a near-catatonic stupor.

Mr. Cartwright returned quickly, accompanied by another man—slightly shorter and less muscular, but dressed in the same immaculate white uniform. "Mr. Stevens will watch your mother while we take a quick look," he explained. "You must follow my instructions exactly. If anyone asks, stay silent—I will handle it. Understood?" Both ladies nodded, their nerves evident. "This will be a short look," he added, his voice dropping to a near whisper. "And you won't mention that this occurred or that I was involved." Again, they nodded, their hearts pounding. "Stay close."

They turned left out of the door and walked down the hall, their footsteps echoing softly on the gleaming, sterile floor. At the end of the corridor stood a large wooden door, its surface worn and marked by years of use. Mr. Cartwright deftly inserted a brass key from the chain on his belt, and the door squeaked open with an old, protesting groan.

Leaving the relatively clean and orderly area behind, they stepped into the restricted wing. The atmosphere shifted immediately. The walls were painted a faded, sickly green, their bare surfaces illuminated by the hazy glow of gas lamps. The air carried the sharp tang of antiseptic mingled with the damp, musty smell of neglect. The oppressive stillness was broken only by the distant cries and disembodied whispers of patients, their voices echoing faintly down the corridor.

As they walked, Victoria and Mabel peered into the day rooms they passed, their shock growing with each step. The scenes before them were harrowing. In one room, patients were confined to crib-like beds, their limbs secured with iron cuffs and hobbles. In another, women sat upright in fixed chairs, their wrists bound by leather straps and their bodies restrained by camisoles. Some were locked in box beds, their arms and legs in a cruel, spread-eagled fashion, while others were secured in racks around the room, their faces blank and lifeless.

Victoria's breath caught in her throat as she took in the sight of women in various states of restraint, their movements restricted by iron chains, handcuffs, and straps. The rooms were devoid of any means of occupation or diversion, leaving the patients noisy and restless, their cries a haunting testament to their suffering.

Mabel gripped Victoria's arm tightly, her own face pale with shock. "This is barbaric," she whispered, her voice shaking. Victoria could only nod, her heart breaking at the thought of her mother enduring such conditions.

They passed several closed doors before halting at one marked by a pallid white "18," the number barely discernible against the aged wooden surface. A small, wired window, clouded with grime, was set into the center, offering only a glimpse of what lay inside. Beyond the door, the stark room lay in eerie stillness—its bare walls enclosing a single disheveled bed, the thin mattress stained and sunken from years of use. Leather straps dangled ominously from the bedframe, their purpose was unmistakable. Beside it stood a rickety washstand, its warped surface marred by water stains, the only other furnishing in the desolate space.

Victoria stared in disbelief, her voice unsteady, barely above a whisper. "This... this is where my mother lives?" Her gaze swept the dimly lit room in frantic, horrified arcs, the flickering gaslight casting grotesque shadows on the peeling, bile-green walls.

Now appreciating the risk he was taking, Mr. Cartwright grew visibly uneasy, his voice trembling slightly as he warned, "We mustn't linger here. It's not safe—for any of us." He shot a glance at the attendants lurking at the end of the hall, their expressions unreadable but their presence ominous.

Tracing their steps back down the same hallway, they passed the day rooms once more. The air seemed heavier now, thick with the stench of unwashed bodies, stale urine, and the acrid tang of carbolic acid used to mask the rot. The muffled cries and vacant stares of the patients cast a pall over the group, their hollow eyes following Victoria as if pleading for rescue or recognition.

The horror was no longer something she imagined; it was in the air she breathed, in the stains on the walls, in the vacant eyes that followed her. The weight of it all pressed down on her chest, making it hard to breathe.

As they continued down the dimly lit corridor, Mr. Cartwright paused abruptly outside a heavy oak door, crisscrossed with formidable iron bands. He hesitated, his hand hovering over the key. For a moment, it seemed he might change his mind and lead them away. Then, with a grim set to his jaw, he turned the key—a metallic *click* reverberated down the hallway.

Finally, he turned to them, his expression grave. "This is the hydrotherapy room," he confided, his voice hushed and grim. "What you're about to see is... perhaps unsettling." His words were deliberate, a warning meant to prepare them for what lay beyond the door.

He pushed it open, revealing a small, tiled chamber that reeked of dampness and antiseptic. The air was thick with steam, and the walls glistened with condensation. On one side of the room stood a large, box-like structure made of solid, lacquered wood and dull, utilitarian metal, its design both clinical and ominous.

The hot water box was a rectangular enclosure, just large enough to confine a person. A small opening at the top allowed the patient's head to protrude, while the rest of their body was submerged in hot water. A metal pipe ran along the top of the box, dripping a steady stream of cold water onto the patient's head. This jarring contrast— heat below and cold above—was believed to "shock" the patient into calmness, a theory rooted in the misguided medical practices of the era.

Inside the box, a woman lay motionless, her face pale and drawn. Her eyes were closed, and her breathing was shallow, as if she had resigned herself to the ordeal. Her hair was plastered to her scalp, and beads of water rolled down her forehead, mingling with the cold droplets from the pipe above. The room was eerily silent, save for the *drip, drip, drip* of water and the slight hiss of steam escaping from the box.

Victoria's hand flew to her mouth, her eyes wide with revulsion. "How can anyone endure this?" she choked out, her voice thick with horror.

Mr. Cartwright's expression darkened, but his tone remained clinical, almost detached. "The treatment is prescribed for agitation or hysteria," he explained, though his voice carried a hint of unease. "The duration varies— sometimes an hour, sometimes twelve. It depends on the patient's... condition."

A crude wooden scaffolding loomed on the other side of the room, its structure towering ominously over the space. A narrow set of stairs led to a platform at the top, where a trapdoor hung precariously, its hinges rusted and moaning lightly in the damp air. Beneath it sat a large, circular wooden pool, filled to the brim with water that glinted coldly under the dim light. The sides of the pool were soft and well-worn, their surfaces grooved and splintered from years of use, as if the very wood bore the scars of the suffering it had witnessed.

The tiled floor surrounding the pool was slick with moisture, and the grout between the tiles was stained dark with mildew. A rusted, ancient drain sat in the corner, its mouth choked with dirt and debris, a thin trickle of murky water snaking from the pool toward it. The air carried the subtle, metallic tang of stagnant water, mingling with the pervasive smell of damp wood and decay. The only sound was the steady *drip, drip, drip* of water leaking from the pool, a rhythmic companion to the relentless drip of water from the other mechanism.

Mr. Cartwright, noticing the women transfixed by the unsettling, alien contraption, stepped forward with an air of practiced nonchalance. "The doctors call this the Bath of Surprise," he began, his voice carrying a tone of detached explanation, as if describing a mundane piece of equipment rather than an instrument of torment. "It's used to help particularly difficult patients—to jolt them out of their hysteria, you see. The sudden immersion in cold water is believed to reset the mind, to—"

Before he could finish, Mabel's grip tightened on Victoria's arm, her fingers digging into the fabric of her sleeve. Her face had gone pallid, her eyes wide with a mixture of disbelief and revulsion. "This is inhumane," she said, the words forced themselves out in a shaken, hushed revulsion. "How can this—how can any of this—be considered treatment?"

Victoria stood frozen; her attention fully locked on the scaffolding. Her mind raced with images of patients—terrified, struggling, helpless—being led up those stairs, perhaps unaware of what awaited them until the trapdoor swung open and they plunged into the cold water below. The thought made her stomach churn. She could almost hear the screams, the splashing, the frantic gasps for air, echoing in the hollow silence of the room.

Mr. Cartwright, seemingly unperturbed by Mabel's outburst, offered a thin, almost apologetic smile. "It's not a pleasant sight, I admit," he declared, his tone softening as if to placate them. "But you must understand, these methods are employed with the best of intentions. The doctors believe it to be necessary for those who cannot be reached by gentler means."

Mabel's grasp on Victoria's arm tightened further, her knuckles whitening. "Intentions?" she hissed, her voice rising now, sharp with anger. "Do you hear yourself? This is torture, not treatment. How can you stand there and defend it?"

Victoria, still silent, felt a surge of nausea rise in her throat. The room seemed to close in around her, the air thick with the weight of what she was witnessing. The Bath of Surprise was not just a tool—it was a symbol of the cruelty and dehumanization that permeated this place. And yet, here was Mr. Cartwright, speaking of it as though it were nothing more than a necessary tool, a routine part of the asylum's operations.

The *drip, drip, drip* of the water seemed to grow louder, each drop a reminder of the suffering that had taken place here. Victoria's heart ached with a mixture of grief and fury, her mind racing with questions she could not yet articulate. *How many patients had endured this? How many had been broken by it? And how could anyone—anyone— believe that this was healing?*

Mr. Cartwright's jaw tightened, but he offered no defense. Instead, he motioned for them to follow him out of the room, clearly eager to move on. As they stepped back into the corridor, Victoria glanced over her shoulder one last time, her heart heavy with the knowledge that her mother might have endured such treatment. The image of the woman in the box would haunt her, a stark reminder of the asylum's clinical cruelty.

They reached the end of the corridor, the large wooden door looming before them like a barrier between two worlds. After passing through, Mr. Cartwright quickly locked the door with a sharp click, the sound ringing ominously in the silence. He ushered Victoria and Mabel back into the sitting room, both women visibly shaken by what they had witnessed. With a curt nod from Mr. Cartwright, the other orderly exited the room, leaving Sarah Jane seated stiffly in her chair, her eyes staring blankly ahead as if she hadn't moved a muscle.

A naked, intense hush filled the room for an eternity of seconds. Slowly recovering from her shock, Victoria felt a surge of anger. She turned to face Mr. Cartwright, her voice unsteady but laced with defiance. "How can you do this to them? How can you call this care?"

Though visibly unsettled and perhaps reconsidering his role in allowing them access to the restricted wing, Mr. Cartwright replied calmly, "We do what we must, ma'am. These treatments are approved by the doctors. Without them, some patients would harm themselves or others." He paused. "I was shocked the first time I saw the restraints too, but they're necessary to keep everyone safe—patients and staff alike."

Victoria's mind flashed to the hydrotherapy contraptions, their clinical brutality etched into her memory. She shuddered, her voice rising in indignation. "And that water box—that monstrous contraption? That water… trapdoor thing? How can you justify that? It's nothing but torture!"

Mr. Cartwright maintained his composure, though a hint of discomfort crossed his face. "The doctors assure us that hydrotherapy is an accepted treatment, ma'am. It's meant to soothe the nerves and restore mental balance. I know it looks… harsh, but it shocks patients into calmness. It—"

Victoria cut him off with a sharp rebuke, her voice cracking with emotion. "This is insane! This place is insane! I'm taking my mother out of here—now."

Mr. Cartwright stepped forward, his tone firm but not unkind. "Ma'am, you can't do that. She's been legally committed and must remain here. She's a danger to herself and—"

Ignoring him, Victoria knelt beside her mother and took her hand, her touch gentle but urgent. "Mabel, help me get mother up." Together, they tried to coax Sarah Jane to her feet, but the moment they touched her, she began to shudder violently, her body stiffening as a piercing scream tore from her throat.

Almost on cue, the door swung open, and Dr. Ashford strode in, his tall frame flanked by two burly orderlies dressed in stark white uniforms. His expression was calm but authoritative, his voice cutting through the chaos like a knife. "Mrs. Pembroke, I must insist you stop this at once. You're distressing your mother… and yourself."

Victoria whirled to face him, her eyes blazing with a mixture of fury and desperation. "You call this care? Look at her! She's terrified—of you, of this place, of everything!"

Dr. Ashford's gaze remained steady. "Your mother is unwell, Mrs. Pembroke. She requires treatment, even if it appears distressing to you. I assure you, everything we do here is in her best interest. I attempted to dissuade you from this visit as it would likely prove deeply unsettling. You ignored my warning, and this is the result."

The orderlies moved closer, their presence looming and unmistakably threatening. Victoria tightened her hold on her mother's hand, her heart pounding as she realized the futility of her defiance. "This isn't over," she hissed, her voice low but fierce. "I won't let you keep her here."

Dr. Ashford's expression softened slightly, though his resolve remained unshaken. "I understand your concern, Mrs. Pembroke. But for now, I must ask you to leave. Your mother needs rest, and this agitation is only harming her."

With a reluctant nod from Mabel, Victoria released her mother's hand, her chest tight with a mixture of grief and rage. Her fingers lingered for a moment, as if reluctant to let go, before she finally withdrew, her heart aching at the sight of her mother's vacant expression. As the orderlies stepped forward to guide Sarah Jane away, Victoria leaned in close, her voice trembling but resolute. "I'll come back for you, mother," she whispered. "I promise. I won't leave you here."

Dr. Ashford motioned to the two men. "Mrs. Pembroke, Mrs. Hawthorne, these gentlemen will escort you to your carriage. I must reiterate—your mother is seriously unwell and requires the care we provide. She has nervous disorders and hysterical fits. I trust you understand the necessity of her remaining here. Good day."

His words left no room for argument. The two orderlies stepped forward, their presence imposing as they gestured toward the door. Victoria shot Dr. Ashford one last defiant glance, her jaw clenched, but she knew there was nothing more she could do.

Victoria's chest tightened as she watched her mother being led away. Anger and guilt warred within her, but beneath the turmoil, a spark of determination ignited. She couldn't undo the past, but she could fight for her mother's future.

The walk to the exit felt interminable, the polished marble floors echoing with the sound of their footsteps. The rhythmic clacking of the orderlies' boots against the stone seemed to amplify the oppressive silence, a resonant reminder of the institution's unyielding control. The orderlies flanked Victoria and Mabel, their presence intimidating and their silence adding to the suffocating atmosphere. As they passed through the grand entrance hall, Victoria couldn't help but notice the grotesque contrast between the asylum's elegant façade and the grim reality within its walls. The high, vaulted ceilings and ornate chandeliers now seemed like a ghoulish joke, a gilded mask hiding a festering truth.

Stepping outside, the institution's front doors closed behind them with a final, resounding *thud*, the sound booming in Victoria's chest. The sharp click of the lock engaging felt like a punctuation mark, sealing her mother's fate. The cold afternoon air hit them like a slap, sharp and bracing after the stifling warmth of the hospital.

Victoria and Mabel stood for a determined instant on the gravel drive, the weight of the asylum's oppressive silence pressing down on them like a suffocating blanket. Above them, the sky had darkened to a solid, oppressive gray.

The carriage stood a few paces away, the only sounds the impatient stamp of hooves and the snort of horses, their breath hanging ghostly in the chill. The driver tipped his hat respectfully but said nothing, his eyes avoiding theirs as if sensing the gravity of their visit. Mabel placed a comforting hand on Victoria's arm, her voice soft but steady. "We'll find a way, Victoria. We'll get her out of there."

The asylum's Gothic architecture loomed like a specter, its pointed arches and barred windows casting long shadows across the grounds. The clock tower stared down like a silent warden, its hands frozen in time, mocking her helplessness.

What have I done? Why didn't I visit earlier? The questions gnawed at her, each a dagger of guilt twisting deeper into her conscience.

She drew a sharp, bracing breath of the cold air, letting it cleanse the lingering scent of antiseptic from her lungs. As she squared her shoulders, the determination that had been a flickering ember within her now erupted into a blaze, fueled by the horrors she had witnessed and a love that no institution could ever cage. "I won't stop until she's free," she vowed, her voice sharp and clear as shattered glass. "No matter what it takes." The words crystallized in the frigid air, a sacred pledge not just to herself, but to the ghost of the woman who had once been her anchor, her protector, her mother.

11. Veils of Despair

Sorrow is a fruit. God does not make it grow on limbs too weak to bear it.
—Victor Hugo, *Les Misérables*, 1862

*T*he carriage ride from the hospital to the train was a somber affair. Victoria sat stiffly, her hands clenched in her lap, her mind racing with the images she had seen—her mother's blank eyes, the leather straps dangling from the bedframe, the woman in the hydrotherapy box, her face pale and lifeless. The air inside the carriage was thick with the scent of damp wool and old wood. The rhythmic clatter of the carriage wheels seemed to echo the relentless ticking of the asylum's clock—*tick, tick, tick*—a constant reminder of time slipping away.

Mabel sat across from her, her expression thoughtful but troubled. She reached across the narrow space and placed a hand on Victoria's knee, breaking the heavy stillness.

"We'll find a way," Mabel reassured her. She hesitated, her attention shifting to the carriage window as if searching for answers in the passing landscape. "But we must be careful. These places… they're not just buildings. They're institutions, protected by laws and men who believe they're doing God's work. If we're to help your mother, we'll need a plan—and allies." Her voice wavered slightly, betraying the fear she tried hard to conceal.

117

Victoria nodded absently, her attention fixed on the shifting scenery. The outskirts of the city were a blur of gray skies and barren trees, their skeletal branches clawing at the heavens as if pleading for mercy. "Allies," she repeated, her voice barely audible over the noise of the carriage. "Who would help us? Who would even care?"

On the train ride back, neither of them spoke much. The weight of the day pressed upon them, rendering words inadequate. They sat side by side as the train car rattled and swayed, the acrid smell of coal smoke seeping through the cracks in the windows. Victoria stared at the soot-streaked glass, her reflection ghostly and fragmented, as the bleak countryside unfurled beyond—a mono-chrome tapestry of gaunt trees and distant smokestacks spewing ribbons of smoke into the ashen sky.

Normally, Mabel's presence was a beacon of light, her spirit irrepressible, her voice always dancing with warmth. But now, her usual vibrancy seemed smothered, beaten down into a strangled hush. The lively hands that so often fluttered with enthusiasm now lay still in her lap. The sparkle in her eyes had dulled, replaced by a shadow of something Victoria recognized all too well—an ache that could not be put into words.

Victoria stole a glance at her friend, wondering how much of today's horrors had seeped into her soul, how much she would carry long after this journey ended. She reached over and gave Mabel's hand a gentle squeeze. After a moment, Mabel returned the gesture, her fingers curling around Victoria's in quiet solidarity. When she finally met Victoria's gaze, she mustered a small, tired smile—not the bright, carefree grin Victoria knew so well, but something softer, something fragile. A promise that, despite everything, they would carry on.

The train rumbled forward, carrying them further away from the towering asylum walls and the ghosts they left behind. But Victoria knew—deep in her bones—that what she had seen today would never truly leave her.

The carriage ride back to Holland Road was just as silent. Both were lost in their thoughts, trying to make sense of what they had experienced. Victoria exited her carriage at Mabel's gold number 86, where the two briefly hugged, and Victoria slowly walked back home. Alone, her thoughts clung more tightly to the horrors, as if the entire ordeal were a living, breathing nightmare.

Arriving at home, she blankly walked up the stairs toward her bedroom. Thankfully, Simon and Annabelle were nowhere to be seen. Someone called after her, "Ma'am... Ma'am," but Victoria couldn't focus on who, nor did she care. She just continued up the steps and finally into her sleeping quarters, where she mindlessly extracted her journal and sat down at her writing desk. She opened it and stared out the window, alone in the dimly lit solitude of her quarters.

The plush carpet beneath her feet, the soft lamplight, the lace curtains—every detail of her room felt like a lie. Each comfort was an accusation. How could this softness exist in the same world as the iron cuffs and the Bath of Surprise? The images of the asylum clawed at the edges of her consciousness, refusing to be silenced by the genteel peace of her bedroom. She was straddling two irreconcilable realities, and the strain was tearing her apart.

Her journal lay open before her, its pages crisp and pristine, eagerly awaiting the imprint of her thoughts. Yet her gaze remained fixed on the window, where the grey

London sky hung heavy with clouds, a brooding expanse of darkness that seemed to mirror her despair. Occasional gusts of wind rattled the panes, sending a scattering of dry, brittle leaves tumbling past the window, their fragile forms spinning aimlessly in the chill autumn air. Soft droplets of rain streaked the glass—*drip, drip, drip*—their descent rhythmic and almost mournful, as though nature itself wept in sympathy for her.

Victoria's tumultuous mind was a whirlwind, a chaotic blur of images she couldn't piece together. Her mother's dead stare—cold, vacant. "My daughter is dead." Blank. Sickly green walls—the smell. Rot. Disinfectant. Despair. "My husband is dead." The flickering gas lamps, shadows crawling—women in crib beds, iron cuffs, leather straps—unwashed bodies, stale urine. Iron chains clinking. The living tomb of a box bed. A faded white "18" painted onto a peeling door. "This is where my mother lives?"

The monstrous water box. *Drip, drip, drip.* The pale woman. Plastered hair. Her head lying unnaturally. *Drip, drip, drip.* Bath of Surprise. Damp wood, decay. *Drip, drip, drip.* Mr. Cartwright's cold, terse voice: "Hydrotherapy is an accepted treatment." Dr. Ashford's voice—blunt. Emotionless. "Your mother is unwell. She requires treatment."

The oak door. Thudding shut. A finality. Closing a tomb. The echo—lingering, like a ghost. The clock tower—staring down. *Tick, tick, tick. Drip, drip, drip.* Unwell. What are they doing to her? The question—sharp. *Why hadn't I visited sooner?* Anger. Frustration. Sadness. Guilt. Twisting —wrapping around her chest. *Drip, drip, drip.* Madness. There was a slight taste of salt and copper on her lips. Had she bitten her tongue?

Teardrops streamed down her face, unchecked and unrelenting, until the raw flood of emotions overwhelmed her. With a choked whimper, she buried her tear-stained face onto the pages of her journal, her sobs racking her body with a violence she hadn't known since the death of her father—no, this was worse, far worse. The sound of her grief filled the room, raw and unfiltered, a testament to the depth of her despair.

After several minutes, her sobs subsided into shallow, shuddering breaths. She lifted her head, her face was streaked with tears and the faded smudges of ink transferred from the journal. She stared at the pages before her, now a chaotic mosaic of blurred words and splotches, the ink running in rivulets where her drops of sorrow had fallen. *Did I try to write?* It was a portrait of her anguish, a tangible record of the pain she could not articulate.

Somewhere in the house, a clock ticked quietly, its rhythm drowned out by the echo of dripping water in her storm of thought—*drip, drip, drip*. A distant *knock, knock* echoed in her distraught inner world. Victoria continued to stare down at her desolate creation, the bleak streaks of black ink mirroring the shadows in her heart. Another rap at the door—*knock, knock*—pulled her from her thoughts. Victoria realized someone was at the door and took a shaky breath, her voice barely audible as she managed a weak, "Come in."

The door opened slowly, and Clara cautiously entered the room, her footsteps soft against the wooden floor. "Ma'am... I brought you some tea," she offered gently, holding a tray with a delicate porcelain teapot and cup, the steam curling upward in fragile tendrils.

Seeing the smear of ink and tears on Victoria's distraught face, Clara quietly put the tray on the floor beside the writing desk and made her way to the ornate porcelain washbasin and matching pitcher on the dresser. She poured some clean water into the basin, the soft splash echoing in the stillness of the space, and then soaked a clean cloth, wringing out the excess. Without a word, she carefully cleaned Victoria's face, tenderly wiping away the tear-ink smears. Looking into Victoria's wound-ed eyes, she soothed, her voice a soft balm, "There, there, Ma'am. It will be alright."

A single tear traced a path down her cheek as she fought against the sob constricting her throat. Victoria breathed, gratitude piercing the heavy shroud of her sorrow, "Thank you... thank you so much. Why are you being so kind to me?"

Clara smiled slightly, her expression softening with a warmth that transcended her station. "You've always treated me—us—kindly, Ma'am."

Without thinking, Victoria hugged Clara, her arms trembling as she clung to the maid, and softly cried, "Thank you, Clara."

Clara hesitated momentarily, her hands hovering uncertainly before she tenderly returned the embrace and whispered gently, "Of course, Ma'am."

As the sobbing subsided, Victoria pulled back slightly, "No... please. Call me Victoria."

Clara hesitated, her eyes widening at the breach of propriety, but after a moment, she nodded and complied, "Of course... Victoria."

That made Victoria's tears well up again, but this time, they fell softly, lightly—a quiet release born from the profound realization that she was surrounded by caring and kind people. In Clara's embrace, she felt a glimmer of hope—a reminder that even in her darkest moments, she was not truly alone.

After disposing of the ink-stained cloth, Clara took another and dipped it into the basin. While holding Victoria's face with one hand, she wiped away the few remnants of ink with the gentle care of a mother tending to a child. Hesitating for a moment, Clara queried, "If I may be so bold, Ma'am... what happened with your mother?"

Biting her lower lip, Victoria responded, "It was horrifying, Clara—truly horrifying, what they've done to her. What goes on out of sight... It's unspeakable. I can't even—" She broke off, unable to finish, her voice trembling as she looked away.

"I'm so sorry, Ma'am... Victoria," Clara said softly, her hands still cradling Victoria's face. "Tragedy seems to follow us all, doesn't it?" She took in a slow breath, her eyes losing focus as she stared into a private memory. "My mother died when I was in my teens. She was kind—so kind. She did everything she could to provide for my sister and me." Clara's voice faltered, her quivering grip betraying her unease as she wrung the cloth. "But the world is cruel to women like her—women with no means, no protection. She... she took in sewing, cleaned houses, did whatever she could to keep us fed. But it was never enough. And when the work dried up..." Clara's eyes dropped, her voice barely audible. "She had no choice but to turn to... other means. Men took advantage of her, and when she could no longer... comply, they cast her aside like rubbish." A shadow flickered across her face, her voice dropping to a near whisper. "They called it consumption, but I think it was the weight of the world—the shame, the cruelty, the way men used her and discarded her—that finally broke her."

Victoria's heart ached as she understood the silent truth. The unspoken reality of Clara's mother's fate hung heavy in the air—a woman forced into prostitution by desperation, only to be abandoned when she was no longer of use. It was a story all too common for impoverished women of the era, their lives dictated by the whims of men and the rigid structures of a society that offered them no escape. With a softness in her voice, Victoria looked at Clara with newfound empathy. "I am so sorry, Clara... Truly."

Drawing in a breath, Clara nodded, her composure returning as she straightened. "It was many years ago, Ma'am... Victoria." She paused in a moment of calm, her eyes fixed on the window where the gray light of the overcast day filtered through. "As they say, time heals all wounds."

Clara's story landed with the force of a physical blow. Her mother's tragedy was different in detail but the same in its essence—a woman broken by a world that had no use for her. The horror wasn't just inside the asylum's walls; it was everywhere, hidden in plain sight, in the struggles of women like Clara's mother. But Clara's kindness and Mabel's fierce loyalty today illuminated a different truth. There was cruelty in the world, yes, but there was also this—this unwavering, sacrificial love.

As Clara left the room, Victoria's gaze settled once more on the journal. The pages were a storm of ink and anguish, but amidst the chaos, a single word stood out, written in bold, deliberate strokes, blurred but legible: "Fight." She drew a sharp breath, her fingertips tracing the letters as if absorbing their strength. And there, in the quiet of the room, something long-dormant uncoiled within her, something stronger than despair stirred—a quiet, unshakable resolve.

12. The Wheels of Justice

Bad men need nothing more to compass their ends, than that good men should look on and do nothing.
—John Stuart Mill, *Inaugural Address Delivered to the University of Saint Andrews*, 1867

*T*he final days of November bled away in a bleak, unrelenting blur, the once-gentle autumn winds now sharp and biting, as if winter were clawing its way into the city. Daylight withered, the sun a feeble, pale coin struggling to pierce the perpetual shroud over London. Plumes of soot and ash billowed from countless hearths and factory stacks, their dark tendrils weaving a suffocating canopy that blotted out the sky. The air itself grew dense, laden with the acrid tang of coal and the metallic sting of industry.

The metropolis seemed to smolder like a vast crater, its streets choked with the grime of progress—a truth so palpable it had earned the grim nickname: *The Big Smoke*. Its inhabitants moved through the gloom like shadows, faces obscured, steps hurried and hunched. It was as if the very earth simmered with discontent, exhaling its frustrations in great, smoky sighs. And at the bottom of this man-made pit, people lived as best they could, a testament to resilience in the face of an unyielding world.

Two such citizens trudged through the pea-soup fog that swallowed the streets, their forms indistinct in the murky haze. Victoria and Mabel forged ahead, handkerchiefs pressed to their faces as if the thin linen could filter the oppression. Each step brought them closer to their destination—a mere few blocks from Number 86—yet the journey felt endless, the soot-choked labyrinth stretching on as if it were the other side of the kingdom.

An eerie quiet hung in the air, the city's usual din muffled by the thick blanket of pollution. The silence was broken only by the hacking cough of a passerby or the rhythmic clomp of hooves on cobblestones as wagons lumbered past. The whir of machinery and groan of carriages provided a jarring beat, a reminder of the city's relentless heart, even in its own suffocation. And through it all, an army of crossing sweepers darted in the yellowed mist, performing their humble, essential duty.

Across the cobblestone street, the lifeless body of a horse lay abandoned, its once-powerful frame now a grim reminder of the city's relentless pace. A common sight, the unfortunate creature, likely overworked and underfed, had succumbed to exhaustion or injury, left to rot in the open air, its ribs showing starkly through its hide. Flies buzzed around its decaying flesh, and the stench of death mingled with the fog, a pungent assault on the senses.

Eventually, men from the knacker's yard—the grim business where dead or useless animals were disposed of—would arrive with their tools to dismember the carcass, carting away the sections for rendering or disposal—a grim but necessary task in a city where the living and the dead coexisted in uneasy proximity.

A few days earlier, Mabel had obtained from an acquaintance the name of a solicitor—Mr. Samuel Whitaker—a man known for his outspoken critiques of asylum conditions and his efforts to rally support for reform. Victoria couldn't help but feel a surge of gratitude for Mabel's ingenuity and unwavering loyalty.

How blessed I am to have such a friend. What would I have done without her? The warm thoughts surfaced, followed immediately by a cold one: *But what has this quest already cost her?*

Since their harrowing visit to see Sarah Jane, Victoria had noticed an unmistakable shift in Mabel. Her usual vivaciousness had dimmed, replaced by a quiet, almost subdued demeanor. The vibrant woman who could light up a room with a joke was gone, replaced by this quiet, haunted figure. Victoria recognized the change; it was the same hollowing she felt in herself after visiting her mother. Some sights, once seen, could not be unseen, and their shadow clung to a person.

Was the change from the weight of what they had witnessed temporary? Or had the experience etched itself too deeply into her soul? Victoria feared the latter. Perhaps this was the inevitable toll of confronting life's tragedies— a piece of one's spirit forever altered. Only time would tell.

Now, standing before the law offices of Whitaker, Smith, and Jacobsen, Victoria felt a mix of apprehension and hope. The building was an imposing structure of red brick and towering Roman columns, its grandeur underscored by a set of gleaming marble stairs that led to a pair of dark oak double doors. The doors were adorned with brass lion door knockers, their fierce visages seeming to guard the entrance with a silent warning: *Enter with purpose, or not at all.*

After a moment's hesitation, Victoria stepped forward and delivered a few brisk raps with the knocker, the sound echoing sharply in the morning air. Moments later, the door creaked open to reveal a young, imposingly tall man, his slender frame draped in a black wool suit with a dark green vest and brass buttons that shone softly in the dim light. His face was striking—a prominent hooked nose, bushy black eyebrows, and calm, deep-set eyes that regarded them with an air of authority. He gestured them inside, then firmly shut the door, blocking out the unpleasant atmosphere.

"Good day, ladies," he boomed, his voice so resonant and measured that it seemed to reverberate in the stillness of the foyer. "May I ask your business here today?"

Victoria hesitated, momentarily taken aback by the man's towering presence. *He must be nearly two feet taller than I am*, she thought, craning her neck to look up at him. "Yes, we're here to see Mr. Whitaker, please," she managed, her voice steady despite her nerves.

"Of course," he stated, stepping aside to usher them in. "Please be seated." He gestured toward a row of rich, dark green leather chairs that lined the entrance hall, their polished surfaces gleaming faintly in the light filtering through the tall windows. "I will inform Mr. Whitaker of your arrival." He paused, his calm eyes lingering expectantly.

"Oh, yes," Victoria added quickly. "Mrs. Victoria Pembroke and Mrs. Mabel Hawthorne."

"Very good," he responded, before turning and striding away with slow, measured steps, his figure disappearing into the shadowed depths of the building.

Mabel and Victoria sat down, exchanging a glance and a slight smile at the oddity of their greeter. For a fleeting second, the old lively Mabel resurfaced, her infectious smile breaking through the weight of the day. Leaning toward Victoria, Mabel whispered with a grin, "Terrance is quite a bit taller than I am, but..." She trailed off, her expression sparkling with amusement, as if the absurdity of the situation had momentarily lifted her spirits.

He returned in the same deliberate manner, his deep tone resonating through the marble hallway. "Please follow me, ladies," he said, gesturing with a long, slow arc of his arm. They rose and followed him, their footsteps echoing softly against the time-worn floor, until they reached an open door. With another graceful gesture, he ushered them inside.

Standing in the doorway was a man noticeably shorter than both of them, dressed in a professional black wool suit that contrasted sharply with his bright, full-of-life demeanor. His round, pudgy face was adorned with a white mustache and long beard, giving him the distinct appearance of a real-life Santa Claus. His features gleamed with warmth, and his smile was so genuine it seemed to light up the room. "Good day, ladies! Come in! Come in! Please, sit," he exclaimed, his tone brimming with enthusiasm. He paused, studying their faces with a twinkle in his eye. "I see you're amused by me and my assistant's height differential!" He chuckled, a rich, hearty sound that filled the office. "No need to be embarrassed. I still find it hilarious myself. Mother always said what I lacked in height, I made up for with mirth."

Victoria and Mabel settled into another pair of rich green leather armchairs, their initial surprise melting into warm smiles as the solicitor's infectious cheerfulness filled the room. His jovial reception was a welcome respite from the serious purpose of their visit, and for a moment, the weight of their mission seemed to lighten.

The solicitor moved with a brisk yet graceful energy, rounding his desk to take his seat. The desk itself was a massive piece of mahogany, its surface polished to a deep, gleaming sheen, scattered with neatly stacked papers, an inkwell, and a few venerable legal tomes. Behind him stretched a floor-to-ceiling bookcase, its shelves crammed with volumes of legal texts, historical treatises, and leatherbound classics, their spines worn from years of use. The room smelled subtly of old paper, lustrous wood, and a hint of pipe tobacco, creating an atmosphere that was both scholarly and inviting.

"Ladies, may I offer you... Oh yes, tea? Tea?" Without waiting for a response, he reached for a handbell with a long black handle and gave it a few brisk shakes. Almost immediately, a figure appeared in the hallway behind them. "Yes, Darjeeling for three! Honey, lemon, etcetera, etcetera!" he shouted, his tone cheerful and commanding. Turning back to Victoria and Mabel, he clasped his hands together and leaned forward slightly, his expression both kind and inquisitive. "Now," he began, his inflection still cheerful but with a note of seriousness creeping in, "what can I do for you lovely ladies today?"

Victoria, relieved to find someone so welcoming and seemingly sympathetic, began, "We have come to understand, Mr. Whitaker, that you are involved in cases concerning asylums."

He leaned forward, his jovial demeanor shifting to one of focused seriousness. "Quite right," he pronounced, his voice now carrying a weight that matched the gravity of the topic.

"Oh, thank goodness," Victoria exclaimed, her words tumbling out in a rush. "You see, my mother is—or rather, has been—a patient at the Royal Earlswood Hospital for several years, where—"

"Yes, I know the place well," Mr. Whitaker interrupted, his brow furrowing. "Dr. Ashford is the director."

"Yes," Victoria confirmed, her words trembling slightly. "And I—we," she added, gesturing to Mabel, "my dear friend Mabel, feel she is being very poorly treated—"

"Yes, to say the least!" Mr. Whitaker interjected, his words cutting through the air like a blade, sharp with indignation. "Can you believe they are still employing those outdated, so-called treatment methods thoroughly discredited by Dr. Conolly over two decades ago?" As he spoke, he reached for a leatherbound book among several on his desk, its edges frayed and cover softened by years of use. The title, embossed in faded gold lettering, read *The Treatment of the Insane without Mechanical Restraints* by John Conolly, MD.

He held the book aloft, shaking it slightly for emphasis as if the weight of its pages could drive his point home. "Written in 1856, mind you! 1856!" he exclaimed, his pitch rising with frustration. "It's an absolute travesty that in our modern times, some institutions still cling to these barbaric practices. Chains, straitjackets, isolation—utterly inhumane! Dr. Conolly proved there was a better way, yet here we are, decades later, still fighting the same battle. Terrible, just terrible!"

Tears welled beneath her lashes as she nodded. "Oh, my God. Yes, we saw it firsthand—in the patient wing. It broke my heart to see what is being done to my mother and the others there."

Mr. Whitaker's features shifted, a mix of horror and empathy in his face. "You saw it firsthand?" he inquired, his voice fraying to a dismayed whisper. "Terrible, just terrible."

"What can we do?" Victoria asked, her inflection tinged with hope, though her eyes betrayed the depth of her distress.

Mr. Whitaker leaned forward, his expression both kind and probing. "First, I need to understand the circumstances. What was she committed for? Who committed her? And how long has she been there?"

Victoria took a shaky breath, her hands clasped tightly in her lap. "She committed herself after my father's —her husband's—death while he was serving in India. She was diagnosed with melancholy and has been there for almost four years." Her voice broke, tears pooling at the corners of her eyes. "I had no idea how badly she was being treated. I didn't... I didn't realize..." She trailed off, her words dissolving into a choked whisper. "She's so lost, so... broken."

Mr. Whitaker's face softened with sympathy and understanding. "Oh, my dear," he spoke softly. "Sadly, I've heard many stories like this." He paused, choosing his next words carefully. "I must be honest with you—since she self-committed and given the length of time she's been there, it will be challenging to secure her release. The law is not on our side in such cases, as they often side with the medical professionals."

Victoria's heart sank, but Mr. Whitaker continued, his tone firm yet sympathetic. "However, there is hope. Our best course of action is to seek her transfer to another institution—one that adheres to Dr. Conolly's principles of kindness, careful supervision, and structured environments. These methods have proven far more effective in managing patients than the cruel and counterproductive use of physical restraints. While it may not be the outcome you hoped for, it would at least ensure she is treated with the dignity and care she deserves."

Victoria's emotions, already threadbare from the rollercoaster of hope and despair, shifted once more—this time toward a fragile, tentative hope. She clung to Mr. Whitaker's words like a lifeline, though his next statement tempered her optimism.

"This is often a long process," he cautioned. "It can be expensive as well. And I must be clear—there is no guarantee of success."

"How long?" The words were a tattered breath, her hands trembling in her lap.

Mr. Whitaker sighed, his expression sympathetic. "Months, at least. I'm sorry to say it, but as they say, the wheels of justice turn slowly."

Victoria nodded, her heart heavy with a deep, resigned understanding. She brought her hands to her face, her fingers pressing against her temples as if to steady herself against the weight of it all. The room seemed to grow quieter, the ticking of the clock on the wall echoing like a solemn reminder of the time ebbing away— time her mother might not have.

13. Forging Friendship

A silent look of affection and regard when all other eyes are turned coldly away... is a hold, a stay, a comfort, in the deepest affliction, which no wealth could purchase, or power bestow.
—Charles Dickens, *The Pickwick Papers*, 1837

Returning from Mr. Whitaker's office, Mabel sank onto the floral-printed chintz sofa in her parlor, Victoria beside her. Their walk through the foggy, soot-laden streets had passed in a heavy silence. The room was warm, an inviting refuge from the chill and gloom outside.

A dainty blue-flowered white porcelain teapot, a cherished piece from Mabel's collection, sat on the low table in front of them, emitting faint wisps of steam from the hot oolong tea inside. The delicate porcelain cups, freshly filled, each held a slice of lemon that bobbed gently on the surface, releasing a muted citrus aroma. A tray of lemon cookies—still untouched—rested nearby, their sweet scent mingling with the earthy fragrance of the tea. The two women sat in silence, their minds heavy with the weight of the day's events.

Mabel took a deep breath, her shoulders rising and falling as she exhaled. She picked up her teacup, the fine china clinking softly against its saucer, and took a sip. Breaking the silence, she sighed, "Well... I'm sure that's not what you wanted to hear." Her voice was gentle, but there was a flicker of her former brightness in her smile as she added, "But I'm sure there are other options. We'll find a way, Victoria. We always do."

Victoria followed suit—a steady breath, a slow exhale, and a sip of tea. She curved her lips into a bittersweet smile, but her eyes welled up with sadness. "No, it wasn't what I wanted to hear," she admitted. "But I need to say this, Mabel. You are an extraordinary friend. I don't know what I would have done these past weeks without you."

She paused, taking another sip of tea. "And I've been thinking about this on the way back... You've done so much for me already. I don't want to burden our friendship with my problems any further. This situation has taken its toll on both of us, and I'll be damned if I let it damage you or what we have."

Mabel's face lit with a deep, soulful smile, and she reached over to hug her dear friend, her arms wrapping around Victoria with a warmth that spoke of unwavering support. "That's what good friends—true friends—are for," she uttered quietly, the simple words carrying the weight of a lifetime of friendship.

Victoria smiled back, her own expression mirroring the depth of Mabel's. "We are truly sisters, are we not?" she spoke with calm assurance filled with affection. Sitting back, her hands resting gently in her lap, she continued, "Now, as a true sister," her smile deepening, "please tell me how things have been with you since the hospital visit. I've been so wrapped up in my own troubles that I haven't asked how you're holding up."

Mabel hesitated for a moment, sensing Victoria's total acceptance and genuine concern. "It... I have to say, it was deeply disturbing," she admitted, her voice quieter now. "I hardly slept for a few days afterward. The images—the sounds—they kept coming back to me."

She looked off into the distance, her gaze fixed on some invisible scene as if reliving the experience. "I've been so fortunate in my life, Victoria. My parents were always there to care for me, and they're still alive and well, as you know, not more than a half mile from here. I met the man of my dreams, and he's so kind and caring. How could things be better?" She paused, her eyes returning to Victoria's, a flicker of her old vivacity shining through. "Oh, and a true sister," she added with a wink and a smile, "I don't know what will come next, but rest assured, I'll be there for you."

Victoria reached out and took Mabel's hand, her grip firm and reassuring. "And I for you," she said, her voice steady and resolute.

"So, have you mentioned any of this to Terrance?" Victoria inquired, leaning forward slightly.

"Heavens, no," Mabel replied, shaking her head emphatically. "Certainly not in a telegram. It's not the kind of news one shares in such a cold, impersonal way." She paused, her expression softening. "I'll tell him everything when he returns after he's had a chance to settle in. He deserves to hear it properly, face to face."

Victoria nodded in understanding, her hands resting lightly on her teacup.

"And you?" Mabel ventured. "Simon? Have you spoken to him?"

Victoria's face clouded with a slight frown, and she exhaled softly as if releasing a burden she'd been carrying. "I tried," she began, her voice tinged with frustration. "I started to tell him about my mother, about how she was before... all of this. But he just nodded and repeated almost the same words as Dr. Ashford—'Your mother is unwell, Victoria. She requires the care they provide.'" She paused, her frown deepening. "I tried to explain, to make him understand, but he just looked at me as if I had two heads. 'Victoria,' he matter-of-factly declared, 'they are doctors. They know what they're doing. You are not an educated doctor, are you?'"

Mabel's expression shifted, her head tilting slightly as she listened. The left corner of her mouth turned up in a half-smile, a mixture of sympathy and mild exasperation. "That is such a shame," she offered quietly, her voice carrying a note of regret.

"I tried to get him to listen," Victoria continued, her hands tightening around her teacup. "And he did, in a way. But he didn't really hear me, if that makes sense."

Mabel nodded; her expression softened with understanding. "It makes perfect sense," she spoke with quiet conviction. "Often people listen, but they don't truly hear."

Victoria sighed, her shoulders slumping slightly. "It's just... he believes what he believes. And nothing I say seems to change that."

Mabel exhaled deeply, her shoulders rising and falling with the weight of her thoughts. "Well, that makes things more complicated... to say the least," she remarked, her voice marked with both concern and determination.

"Truly," Victoria agreed.

Mabel reached out and grasped Victoria's hands tightly, her fingers firm and reassuring. She looked deeply into Victoria's eyes, her gaze steady and unwavering. "Promise me we'll be there for each other, no matter what," she vowed, her voice filled with conviction.

Victoria's smile broadened, though her expression softened with unshed tears. "I promise," she said, her voice quivering slightly. "And you promise the same."

Mabel's own eyes shimmered with moisture, her smile matching Victoria's in its brightness. "Of course... I promise," she replied, her voice trembling with feeling.

Then, as if the old Mabel had returned entirely, she leaned back and gestured toward the tray of lemon cookies with a playful flourish. "Then we should enjoy these lovely cookies... shan't we?" she teased, her tone shifting into the mocking cadence of Annabelle's voice, a familiar tease between them.

Victoria laughed, the sound light and genuine, as she reached for a cookie. "Shan't we," she echoed, popping a lemon cookie into her mouth, her smile wide and unreserved.

With a newly deepened bond now forged, Victoria thought about just how fortunate she had been despite the horrors that had been uncovered. Mabel was a friend beyond compare. The growing closeness with Clara and other household staff—a term that no longer fit, if it ever really did—had also arisen in the crucible of despair. An even closer tie with Annabelle was a tremendous surprise to Victoria. Yet there was one person in her life, much to her chagrin, who seemed to be going in the opposite direction—Simon.

As she swallowed the sweet, lemony crumbs, Victoria held onto the sound of Mabel's laughter. It was a small, bright shield against the looming shadow of Simon's dismissive logic and the immense battle that lay ahead. The path was daunting, but she knew she would not have to walk it alone.

14. Phoenix Rising

Beware, for I am fearless, and therefore powerful.
—Mary Shelley, *Frankenstein*, 1818

*T*he short walk back through the pea-soup thickness of the London haze from Mabel's was also a journey into her own churning emotions—a tangle of grief, anger, guilt, and exasperation. Yet, unexpectedly, she also experienced flickers of gratitude, optimism, hope, and empowerment.

She was moving forward, stepping out of the shadow of the utter helplessness, depression, and panic that had consumed her not long ago. The mist, dense and ghostly, seemed to mirror her inner turmoil, yet it also cloaked her in a strange sense of privacy, as if the world had paused to let her gather her thoughts.

Despite the emotional tempest and the oppressive fog, she managed a slight smile behind her handkerchief as she approached the doorway to her home, its familiar silhouette a small but reassuring beacon. Yet, as her hand rested on the cold brass knob, she hesitated. The doorway, though familiar, now felt like the edge of a stage. Beyond the door awaited a scene she had never rehearsed for.

She took a deep breath, steeling herself for what was to come, and stepped inside, the fog clinging to her coat like a reluctant farewell.

As if to confirm her suspicion of impending turmoil, Clara met her the moment she crossed the threshold, her face etched with a look of concern bordering on panic—an expression Victoria had never before seen on her steadfast maid. Clara quickly helped her remove her coat and, in a hushed tone barely above a trembling whisper, warned, "Ma'am... Mr. Pembroke is in a state. He started shouting vulgarities after receiving that telegram... He's waiting for you in the parlor." Glancing over her shoulder as if fearing his sudden appearance, Clara lowered her voice still further, "And ma'am... he's been drinking... quite heavily, I'm afraid."

Victoria froze, her mind racing as she pieced together the implications of Clara's words. She had no doubt the telegram had something to do with her mother. Simon— enraged and intoxicated? It was unthinkable. In all the years she had known him, he had been the epitome of composure, propriety, and polished decorum. The man who prided himself on his unshakable dignity was now reduced to this?

A familiar, icy sensation began to spread through her veins as she recalled the fragments Simon had shared about his father—a man who had succumbed to the bottle, drinking himself into an early grave long before Victoria had entered Simon's life. The parallels were impossible to ignore, and the thought of Simon following that same path filled her with a deep, gnawing anxiety.

Her first instinct was to turn and flee, to retreat into the foggy streets and delay the confrontation. But she knew that would only postpone the inevitable. Drawing a deep, steadying breath, she squared her shoulders, lifted her chin, and crossed the threshold into the parlor as if wading through deep water. She felt the air grow dense, each breath an effort as she moved into the room.

Simon sat slumped in the large, dark brown leather-backed armchair, an open copy of *The Times* resting in his hands. His dark, curly hair was ruffled, as though he had been running his fingers through it in agitation, and he looked up at Victoria with a deep, unsettling scowl that sent a chill down her spine.

With unsteady breath, she began in a tense, quiet tone, "Sim—"

With a harsh, irritated manner, he cut her off, his words dripping with sarcasm, "Oh, Victoria. So nice of you to be home. Out causing mayhem, I assume?"

Again, she tried, her voice wavering, "Simon, please... I'm sure we can—"

Before she could finish, Simon shot to his feet, his movements abrupt and careless. He mindlessly tossed the newspaper onto the chair he had been sitting on, where it crumpled into a jumbled mess, then picked up a half-full glass next to a nearly depleted bottle of port, and took a deep drink. The sight of him so uncharacteristically unhinged caused Victoria to falter, her words dying in her throat. He snarled, his words sharp and mocking, "We can... We can what? What can we do, Victoria!?"

Instinctively, Victoria took a few steps backward, her heart pounding in her chest. Simon was an imposing figure, fit, muscular, and over six inches taller than she was—a man skilled in fisticuffs and not one to be trifled with. For the first time since she had known Simon, she felt genuine fear—a primal fear that turned her limbs to jelly and curdled the taste in her mouth. "Simon, please..." she pleaded, tears welling in her eyes.

Undeterred, he pointed to the table, where a crumpled telegram lay. His hand shook slightly, whether from fury or the effects of the port, she couldn't tell. "Read it!" he demanded, his snap cracking like a whip.

Shaking, she looked down at the piece of paper as if it were a venomous serpent poised to strike. She froze, her mind racing with the urge to flee until Simon's tone, firm and commanding, cut through her thoughts. "Pick it up and read it."

With a deep exhale, she steadied herself, forcing her quivering fingers to obey. She picked up the telegram, smoothed out the wrinkles, and started reading silently.

"Out loud!" Simon barked.

She steadied herself again, daring a fleeting look at his face. *He's in such a rage. He's drunk. Surely, he's overreacting.* She began reading aloud, her speech shaky but clear, "From the Royal Earlswood Hospital..." She gulped; her worst fears confirmed by the opening words of the message.

"Regarding Mrs. Victoria Pembroke and..." Victoria's breath caught. *Oh God, Mabel is mentioned.* She took another gulp, her throat constricted, and continued, "Mrs. Mabel Hawtorne's visit to Sarah Jane Barr—" Her breath faltered as she broke her attention from the paper, looking at Simon with a beseeching look. "Simon, can we please just talk? You've been drinking, and—"

Before she could finish, Simon's temper erupted. He boiled over with anger, his face flushing crimson as he seized his glass and hurled it furiously into the side of the fireplace. The glass shattered on impact, splinters scattering across the hearth with a sharp, echoing crash reverberating through the room. "Now I'm not drinking. Finish it!" he roared, his tone strained with fury.

"Simon, I really—" Victoria tried again, her voice shaking, her fingers clutching at the edges of the telegram in a futile attempt to steady herself.

Simon scoffed, his expression darkening further. He strode swiftly across the room, his movements sharp and predatory, and snatched the telegram from Victoria's hands. The paper crinkled loudly as he gripped it, his knuckles white with tension.

At that moment, Annabelle swept into the parlor, her presence commanding yet tinged with an undercurrent of concern. "What is going on here?" she demanded, her voice sharp with unquestionable authority. Ever the composed matriarch, Annabelle quickly assessed the scene before her: Simon, visibly inebriated and teetering on the edge of losing control, stood amidst the wreckage of his own making. Shards of glass glinted on the floor, and the jagged remains of a crystal tumbler lay scattered near the fire-place, stark evidence of his unraveling temper.

Victoria, pale and wide-eyed, cowered where she stood. Annabelle's heart clenched as she recognized the look on the young woman's face—it was the same terror she herself had felt years ago when her own husband's rages had turned their home into a battlefield. But even as sympathy stirred within her, a flicker of practicality emerged. *What could Victoria have done to provoke this?*

Simon, still furious, held out the telegram, shaking it violently. "It appears... Victoria has been—"

Annabelle cut him off. "Simon. Stop this. You are obviously—"

"Angry... Of course, I'm angry!" he snapped, the words tearing from him between ragged, furious breaths.

"I was going to say overwrought, dear," Annabelle observed, her voice a delicate blend of maternal concern and unwavering authority. "You know how I feel about excessive drunkenness in my home, especially after what happened to your father."

She paused, her gaze melting briefly with remembered sorrow before steeling itself again. "It's not only self-destructive—it's thoughtless. Thoughtless of the pain this devil's drink has already wrought upon our family."

Then, with a firm and absolute authority that brooked no argument, she gestured to the chair beside her and gently commanded, "Now, please sit down."

Simon, still panting, paused briefly, his mother's words slicing through his rage. He hesitated, his grip on the telegram loosening slightly.

Victoria, in a tense, quiet tone, murmured, "I know this concerns my moth—"

But Simon, infuriated, interrupted her. "You're trying to ruin me with—"

Annabelle interjected once more. "Simon, please give me the telegram... sit down, please."

With the grace of someone accustomed to managing difficult situations, Annabelle strode up to Simon, who stood almost a foot taller than her. She gently but firmly took the telegram from his hand and guided him to the chair. He more collapsed than sat down, the newspaper he had thrown onto the chair earlier rumpling under his weight.

Annabelle took a deep breath, her composure unshaken. "Now. I'm sure we can handle this like civilized people." She glanced at the telegram and began to read aloud, her tone deliberately calm but growing sharper with each word. "From the Royal Earlswood Hospital... et cetera... regarding Mrs. Victoria Pembroke and Mrs. Mabel Hawthorne's visit... et cetera... You were highly disruptive and violated hospital rules by entering..." She paused; her stare locked suddenly on Victoria. "Oh my, Victoria... the restricted and dangerous patient wing? No longer welcome to visit this institution! Legal action pending!" Her tone shifted from calm to incredulous, her eyes riveted on Victoria. "What have you done, Victoria?"

Victoria's heart pounded in her throat as she bit her lower lip, unsure where to begin. "I... I tried to talk to Simon about this when I returned..." she faltered, her voice unsteady. But as she spoke, she began to regain a sense of composure. "However, he refused to listen."

Simon scoffed but remained motionless, his palms resting on his knees as he gazed down at the intricate patterns of the oriental carpet covering the hardwood floor, as if searching for some hidden answer or solace in its woven threads. The room plunged into a silence so deep Victoria could hear the faint hiss of the gas lamps and the ragged edge of Simon's breathing.

Breaking the tense quiet, Annabelle urged Victoria in a firm yet calm tone, "Continue."

Victoria took a shaky breath, her hands clasped tightly before her. "As you know, I went to see my mother at the hospital, expecting her to be in a similar state to when I last saw her a few years ago." She paused, struggling to maintain her composure as tears threatened to spill. "But she was far from that. Her eyes were vacant, her body gaunt... It was as if she were already dead. She..." Victoria's voice cracked, and she swallowed hard. "She thought I was dead. She couldn't even see me, even though I was standing right there. Something was wrong—so very wrong. I could feel it..."

After a quiet pause, Victoria rubbed her hands together nervously, her fingers twisting as if seeking comfort. "So, I insisted... I demanded that the orderly show me where my mother lived. I needed to see... and it was more dreadful than I could have imagined." Her words fell to a whisper. "It was a cold, dark prison. All those women... chained up, locked in horrifying, barred cages like living coffins. And that woman... trapped in that hot water box contraption, with water dripping on her head..." Victoria stopped abruptly, visibly shaking, her hands clutching her arms as if to steady herself. The room was silent for several moments, the weight of her words hanging heavily in the air.

Finally, she continued, scarcely audible, "It was like a dungeon, not a hospital. Mr. Whitaker understands... these so-called treatments are barbaric."

Still motionless, Simon scoffed again, sarcasm curling every syllable. "Who is this Whitaker?"

"He's a solicitor who knows about these cases of abuse at the—" Victoria was mid-sentence when Simon cut her off, his tone laced with a modicum of disgust yet eerily calm.

"So, you think you're far smarter than the doctors who care for these lunatics, but of course, this solicitor— you believe whatever he says." He leaned forward slightly, his eyes narrowing. "Victoria, you're unbelievable... I think you've inherited your mother's insanity."

Simon's biting comment struck Victoria like a blade to the heart. The fear of losing her mind, of becoming like her mother, had haunted her for years, and his words sent an icy chill through her very being. For a wavering moment, she felt frozen, as if the world had stopped. But then, something deep within her stirred—a fierce, unyielding resolve. "No," she exclaimed firmly, her words were level and controlled despite the storm raging inside her. She knew what she had seen, and no one—not even Simon—would make her doubt herself.

Suddenly, a calmness washed over her, born not from indifference but from certainty. "No, Simon. I am not insane. What is insane is that my husband—the man I love, the man I married—would so easily dismiss what I am saying without a moment's consideration." She took a step forward, her look resolute. "I know what I saw and experienced. Were you there? No! You weren't. So how dare you make such a judgment about what I saw and who I am?"

Simon sat back in his chair, his face a mask of stunned disbelief. Victoria's sudden self-confidence had left him momentarily speechless, his usual composure shattered by her unflinching resolve.

Annabelle, who had remained quiet with her fingers clasped in front of her, finally spoke. "Well, this is all unexpected. But if we are to get to the bottom of this, I will visit your mother myself and assess the situation."

Simon's voice wavered, soft and uncertain, as he started, "Mama—"

But Annabelle cut him off with a tone that brooked no argument. "It's settled. I will arrange a visit and see for myself."

15. The Bitter Cry

It may be that, in the sight of Heaven, you are more worthless and less fit to live than millions like this poor man's child.
—Charles Dickens, *A Christmas Carol*, 1843

*T*he cold, blustery days of early December passed quickly as Christmas Day drew near. The Pembroke home, like many others in London, was adorned with the trappings of the season. The traditional fir tree stood proudly in the parlor, its branches heavy with candles, bright red and green ribbons, and silver and gold ornaments depicting cherubs, stars, and an array of holiday motifs. Holly, ivy, and mistletoe draped the mantels and doorways, their vibrant greens and reds starkly contrasting with the frost-kissed windows. Fireplaces crackled with logs ablaze, their warmth a welcome reprieve from the biting winter chill, yet the cozy glow they cast did little to thaw the glacial silence that had settled over the household.

A figurative and literal cold war of silence permeated the house, each room heavy with unspoken tensions. Conversations were limited to necessities, and the only sounds were the sizzle of the flames and the ticking of the grandfather clock. The cheerful decorations seemed almost mocking, their luster emphasizing the emotional distance between the inhabitants.

Victoria moved through the days with quiet determination, her thoughts often drifting to her mother and the unsettling visit to the hospital. Simon, though present, seemed distant, his usual charm replaced by a heavy, sullen quiet. Even Annabelle, typically the anchor of the household, seemed preoccupied, her usual grace tinged with an uncharacteristic unease.

The holiday spirit, so often a time of warmth and togetherness, felt like a distant memory in the Pembroke home. The crackling fireplaces and twinkling candles served as a reminder of what should have been, but the frosty London winter outside seemed to have seeped into the very heart of the house, leaving it cloaked in a cold, unyielding stillness.

Annabelle had sent a letter to the Royal Earlswood Hospital, formally requesting permission to visit Sarah Jane. Thus far, she hadn't received a reply—though it had only been a week since the explosive incident in the parlor with Simon, and since then, the days had dragged on, each one stretching like an eternity.

The status quo held, fragile and tense. Simon's presence was a constant, dark storm cloud on the verge of a deluge. The unanswered question of Annabelle's visit hung in the atmosphere, a shared apprehension no one dared voice.

Despite the many challenges Victoria had faced over the past few months, she now felt a growing sense of confidence and empowerment. Indeed, her reflections often turned to her mother's situation, but she knew she had to bide her time and wait for matters to progress. Throwing herself into managing the household had become an unexpected antidote to the waiting and the worry, making the days feel lighter and more purposeful.

This was especially true since she had come to see the household staff not merely as servants, but as something closer to a family. Working alongside them—not just issuing orders but rolling up her sleeves and joining in the tasks—had become a passion, one that was both remarkably satisfying and, to her surprise, genuinely enjoyable.

Gaston, the French chef with his rich, rolling accent, had taken her under his wing, teaching her how to chop vegetables and meats, how to craft a proper and flavorful soup, and a handful of other culinary skills. He often praised her, calling her a "très bonne élève"—a very good student—and marveling at how quickly she picked up new techniques. Those encouraging words meant the world to her, igniting a spark of motivation she hadn't felt since her days at finishing school.

The kitchen, once a place of strict routines and quiet efficiency, had transformed into a lively hub of activity. Smiles, laughter, and easy conversation now filled the air, creating an atmosphere that felt almost like home. On occasion, Victoria even ventured to assist Clara with the bedrooms, though she was careful to avoid Annabelle's notice, knowing full well how unconventional it would seem for a lady of the house to engage in such tasks. Dusting furniture, properly making beds, and other seemingly mundane chores she had once taken for granted now brought her an unexpected sense of pride and fulfillment.

Through their conversations, Victoria learned more about the lives of those who served in the household. Gaston, for instance, had a family living on the outskirts of Paris in a small farming village—a wife and an eleven-year-old son named Andrée. He missed them dearly, but this position was essential to provide for their needs. His face always lit up when he spoke of them, and he held onto the hope that one day soon, they would be reunited.

While she worked in the kitchen, peeling vegetables and stirring pots under Gaston's watchful eye, Victoria found fleeting moments to reflect on the tumultuous events of the past months. Her thoughts drifted to Mr. Wilby and the way his lecherous advances had once unsettled her so profoundly. Now, in the quiet rhythm of her tasks, the memory of his behavior struck her as almost laughably absurd. *Why did I let that pompous, insufferable man make me so nervous?* she wondered, her hands pausing briefly over the chopping board. *Never again*, she vowed inwardly with a newfound fortitude.

Her bold challenge to Simon and the undeniable impact of her words had awakened something within her —a realization that she possessed a voice, one that could not be ignored or dismissed. *I am much more than 'a fine and sturdy woman,'* she told herself, her jaw tightening with quiet defiance. *I am not a cow, a horse, or a piece of furniture to be appraised and traded. I have thoughts, feelings, and a will of my own.*

This morning, the household was abuzz with activity as they prepared individual gifts for a charity visit to an orphanage, an annual event sponsored by the *Seven Sisters for Sobriety*. The previous year, Victoria had been newly married and preoccupied with settling into her role as a wife, while Mabel had been occupied with her own husband. However, this year, both women decided to participate in the holiday event. Simon, distant and engrossed in his business affairs, was absent, as was Terrance, who remained away on his military campaign.

There was a profound joy in assembling special treats for the less fortunate children of England—delicate lemon cookies, whimsical gingerbread men, and traditional Shrewsbury cakes. Mabel had thoughtfully procured toys to include in each small box—tin soldiers for the boys and charming miniature dolls for the girls. The act of preparing these presents not only brought a sense of purpose, but also reminded Victoria of the warmth and generosity that the holiday season could inspire.

With all the gift boxes securely packed into a few sturdy leather satchels, Victoria and Mabel joined several other members of the Seven Sisters for the walk to the institution. Fortunately, the day dawned bright and clear, with crisp yet mild December air and only the faintest breeze. The pleasant weather made the journey all the more enjoyable as the ladies strolled along, their conversation light and cheerful.

Among the group was a particularly animated woman —a plump, short lady with a wild mane of tangled black hair, known to all as the Seven Sisters' most notorious gossip and chatterbox. She regaled the group with the harrowing tale of an inquest held into the death of an infant who had tragically been eaten by rats at Bellevue Hospital in New York. The mother of the child, a poor Irish immigrant named Mary O'Connor, was said to be utterly devastated and demanding justice for her lost baby. As the story unfolded, the women reacted with a chorus of gasps, "Oh my," "How dreadful," and other expressions of shock and sympathy.

They arrived at the orphanage, a modest, weathered wooden building nestled among various shops and businesses. Its only distinguishing feature was a plain green-painted wooden door, and above it hung a sign with the words "The Haven for Destitute Children" painted in uneven white lettering—a humble but poignant declaration of the building's purpose.

Inside, the group was met with a sprawling, dimly lit space filled with rows of narrow beds crammed along the walls, many occupied by orphans. Some youngsters were playing in the center of the room, their laughter ringing out like small bursts of joy, but others sat quietly, their young features solemn and withdrawn. A handful of women, likely caretakers, moved briskly among the boys and girls, tending to their needs and darting in and out of a doorway at the back of the ward.

Near one of the beds, a man of average height knelt beside a young boy. He had thick, curly black hair and long sideburns that framed his kind face. The man grinned warmly as he gestured to something the boy held in his hands, his voice gentle and encouraging. When he noticed the group had entered, he gave the boy an affectionate pat on the head and rose to his feet, striding over to greet the group.

"Ladies!" he exclaimed, his smile broad and genuine, "Thank you so much for visiting our little sanctuary! The little ones and I are deeply grateful for your kindness," he added with heartfelt gratitude, sweeping his arm in a gesture that encompassed the entire interior and the youngsters being cared for.

He moved swiftly and purposefully, shaking each of the visitors' hands with a warm enthusiasm, accompanied by exuberant greetings of "Welcome," "Thank you," and "So glad you could make it."

With a gracious bow—his right arm crossed over his chest and his left arm tucked behind his back—he introduced himself, "My name is Andrew Mearns, and I work with the *London Congregational Union* to support and uplift the less fortunate in our city."

"If this is your first time visiting a shelter for unwanted children, you might feel a bit uncertain. But there's no need to worry," he continued, a twinkle in his eye. "The children won't bite—well, not usually." His broad smile elicited soft laughter from the group.

Turning slightly to gesture toward the orphans, he encouraged, "Please, take your time and approach these sweet ones gently. Speak a few kind words to them, and if you've brought a box of treasures, feel free to present it. They've been eagerly anticipating your arrival all morning."

With that, the group began to disperse slowly throughout the room, each lady finding a child to greet and offer a small bundle. Mabel and Victoria made their way to a thin, barefoot girl with tangled brown hair, who sat perched on the edge of one of the beds, her eyes wide with curiosity. They knelt before her, gently placing a wrapped parcel into her small, delicate hands. The girl peeled back the lid with trembling fingers, revealing an assortment of treats—a few lemon cookies, a gingerbread man, and a beautifully carved wooden doll with a painted, serene smile, rosy cheeks, and long brown hair.

The little girl's features lit up like the dawn, a beam of pure joy radiating from her as she exclaimed in a tone tinged with wonder, "Thank you, Ma'ams!" Clutching the box to her lap, she picked up the doll, turning it over in her hands as though it were a priceless treasure. Her eyes sparkled as she admired it, her fingers tracing the delicate features of the doll's visage. Then, noticing the cookies, she eagerly grabbed one and popped it into her mouth, chewing with an expression of pure delight as crumbs tumbled down the front of her worn dress.

"What is your name, dear?" Victoria asked, her face alight with joy as she watched the girl's unbridled happiness. To Victoria, the box contained simple, everyday items, but to this child, it was a treasure trove of wonders.

"Mary," the girl answered, her words muffled by the mouthful of lemon cookie, her grin never wavering.

Victoria responded with a warm, mirthful expression, "I am Victoria, and this is my dear friend, Mabel."

Before Victoria could say another word, Mary suddenly reached out and wrapped her small arms around Victoria in a heartfelt hug. The gesture was so genuine and unexpected that it struck her with a force that stole her breath. A wave of tenderness, sharp and sweet, rose in her chest, and for a moment, the grim walls of the orphanage and the cold silence of her own home fell away, leaving only the profound connection of that small, fierce hug. Mabel, not wanting to be excluded from the tender moment, leaned in and gently joined the embrace, creating a heartening group hug that momentarily dissolved the hardships surrounding them.

Mr. Mearns, who had been making his way around the ward and checking on each of the women, came upon the heartfelt scene. Pausing momentarily, he smiled kindly and remarked, "Ladies and Mary, what a beautiful sight to behold. I truly feel God's hand has guided you here today. Thank you for coming."

Mabel spoke, her words soft but sincere, "Thank you for having us. I—" she glanced at Victoria, her eyes conveying a shared understanding, "We hadn't expected to have such a moving experience."

Mr. Mearns' smile broadened, "Yes, that's often the case. Many people feel they must keep their distance from the less fortunate, but the truth is, we are all equal in God's eyes. Everyone deserves a safe place to live, nourishing food, and the comfort of caring companions. As it is written in Proverbs 22:2—'The rich and the poor meet together: the Lord is the maker of them all.'"

The two women nodded thoughtfully in quiet agreement.

Mr. Mearns' grin faded slightly, replaced by a more solemn expression. "Ladies, I cannot dismiss the feeling that Providence has guided you here. There is a particular quality about you—something I can't quite put into words."

"In any case... here in London and other cities across the land, there are tens of thousands of souls living in unimaginable conditions—conditions so dire they evoke the horrors of the middle passage on a slave ship. They dwell in vermin-infested hovels, where fresh air and clean water are scarce luxuries. These dark, damp dens of despair are home to thousands who are crammed together, living in squalor. Yet, they are as much children of God as you or I, part of the race for whom Christ died."

Victoria and Mabel's expressions shifted to one of horror mingled with deep concern.

Lifting his hand in a calming gesture, Mr. Mearns continued, "I know. I know. It's difficult to comprehend, but these suffering souls live right here in our city, often forgotten by society. Yet they are here, and we—alongside our colleagues at the *London Congregational Union*—are working tirelessly to shed light on their plight, to bring attention to the suffering that unfolds in the shadows of our bustling streets. And with awareness comes the potential for change—a change that is already beginning to stir in Parliament. Ladies, I earnestly hope you might join us in raising awareness of the unseen poor."

Victoria, her brow furrowed with a mix of surprise and skepticism, replied, "I don't mean to offend, but this is difficult to believe, as you say."

Mr. Mearns nodded, his demeanor as reassuring as his words. "I understand. It's hard to accept such truths without experiencing them firsthand. That's why, from time to time, I take people to these areas to witness the reality firsthand. Of course, proper precautions must be taken, but I assure you, it is a journey that changes the soul. If you are willing, I would be honored to include you in our next expedition." He let the offer hang in the air momentarily before his voice deepened with solemnity. "It is not an easy thing to witness how the outcasts of London live, but I believe such knowledge will empower you to add your voices to ours to help answer the bitter cry of these forgotten souls."

Victoria and Mabel exchanged a look, in silent communication, before nodding in unison.

Mr. Mearns beamed with gratitude, "Excellent! Thank you, ladies!"

16. Unexpected Developments

Success is the child of audacity.
—Benjamin Disraeli

he December days slipped by, leaving only a week before Christmas Day. Thus far, the winter had been mild, with little snow to speak of, but today, light, fluffy flurries began to fall over London, dusting the city in a delicate white veil. The air carried the crisp, unmistakable scent of winter, and the slight taste of frost lingered on the tongue. By the afternoon, the flurries had accumulated to little more than half an inch, the snowfall's purity marred only where it mingled with the churned mud at the center of the road, trampled by the hooves of horses, the wheels of carriages, and the boots of pedestrians.

Victoria and Mabel plodded through the snowy streets; their woolen cloaks pulled tight against the winter chill as they made their way back to Mr. Samuel Whitaker's office. Their boots left neat, precise prints in the freshly fallen powder, and with each step, the snow emitted a satisfying crunch underfoot that seemed to echo through the quiet, wintry stillness of the afternoon. The lamp-lighters had already lit the gas lamps along the street, their flickering orange glow reflecting off the snow-covered cobblestones.

Victoria's gloved hand clutched the mysterious telegram in her pocket; its sparse message had haunted her since yesterday evening. The curt instruction to come to his office "at your earliest convenience"—with no further explanation—had set her mind racing through endless possibilities. The telegram's ambiguity had become a splinter in her mind, pulling her from sleep each time she drifted off. The night stretched interminably, measured by the slow, solemn chimes of the hallway clock.

They reached the stately law offices of Whitaker, Smith, and Jacobsen, knocked, and Mr. Whitaker's unusually tall assistant opened the door. He greeted them in his deep, baritone voice, delivered with mechanical precision: "Good afternoon, Mrs. Victoria Pembroke and Mrs. Mabel Hawthorne. Kindly take a seat. I shall inform Mr. Whitaker of your arrival." Without awaiting a response, he pivoted on his heel and lumbered down the hallway, his imposing frame moving with the unhurried certainty of a pendulum.

True to his exacting nature, he returned within moments, his gait unchanged. "If you would accompany me, ladies," he intoned, sweeping his arm in the same slow, ceremonious arc as before. Guiding them down the corridor, he ushered them inside with a meticulously practiced gesture.

Mr. Whitaker, anticipating their entry, was already positioned near the doorway, his open palms extended in welcome. He greeted each woman in turn with a vigorous, warm handclasp. "Mrs. Pembroke! Mrs. Hawthorne! What a pleasure to see you both again," he boomed, his whiskered face alight with geniality. "Do make yourselves comfortable." Then, abruptly turning toward the hall, he bellowed, "Tea for three! Oolong, I think—yes, oolong this time! Honey, lemon, etcetera, etcetera!"

160

Unexpected Developments

When they entered the room, it appeared precisely as they had left it—the massive oak desk strewn with neatly stacked papers, an inkwell gleaming dully in the winter light, and a few well-thumbed legal tomes bearing cracked leather spines. The ladies perched nervously on the edge of the dark green leather chairs, their backs rigid with anticipation, while Mr. Whitaker settled behind his desk. He steepled his fingers atop the polished wood, his expression shifting from congenial to serious as he began: "Significant developments have occurred since your last visit."

He paused, clearing his throat with a rumble that seemed to echo in the book-lined room as he visibly ordered his thoughts. "After your departure, I took the liberty of writing to Dr. Ashford regarding our discussion. I confess I expected little to come of it—until recent Parliamentary proceedings altered the situation." He waved a hand dismissively. "I won't bore you with the legal details, but they compelled me to visit Royal Earlswood personally. When—"

The door creaked open, interrupting him as his assistant entered bearing an ornate silver tea service that caught the dim gaslight. With painstaking deliberation, he arranged the tray on Mr. Whitaker's desk, the delicate china cups clinking softly as he poured.

Victoria and Mabel exchanged impatient glances, their teacups untouched, their bodies leaning forward as if willing the solicitor to continue.

"Ah! Capital!" Whitaker exclaimed, plopping a slice of lemon into his cup with unnecessary vigor. He took a noisy slurp, spilling perhaps more than he drank, before setting it down with a clatter. "My thanks, Phineas. Now then—"

161

He blinked, his bushy eyebrows knitting together. "Ah, yes! My talk with Dr. Ashford!"

Victoria's gloved hands clenched in her lap as Whitaker continued: "I presented the Parliamentary developments, etcetera, etcetera, and he listened without remark with that maddening calm of his. Since I was there, I mentioned the possibility of transferring your mother, Mrs. Pembroke, to a London hospital, as I had requested in my letter."

Victoria's breath caught audibly, her lips parting in shock. The solicitor, either oblivious or enjoying the drama, took another deliberate sip before continuing.

"Ah, yes, delicious tea... Then, most unexpectedly, Dr. Ashford calmly informed me he had received my letter and that of your mother-in-law, Mrs. Pembroke senior, requesting a visit and, in lieu of that, a transfer to another hospital due to your being very upset, ease of travel, etcetera, etcetera." He leaned forward conspiratorially. "And there, in that cold little office, he produced your mother's file and announced—in that same detached tone one might use to discuss the weather—that he had just approved a transfer to Hanwell Asylum in West London— an institution that has embraced Dr. Conolly's reforms and has become the most progressive asylum in England!"

The room's air seemed to freeze as a stunned silence followed his declaration. Then, Mr. Whitaker's whiskered face transformed, his bushy sideburns lifting with the force of his triumphant grin as he brought both palms down on his desk with a smack. "Congratulations are in order, madam!" he boomed, his voice ricocheting off the legal tomes lining the walls like a judge's gavel strike.

Victoria's teacup slipped from her fingers, clattering against its saucer, spilling some oolong onto her skirt. Her lips moved soundlessly, the words "Hanwell Asylum" forming but not escaping, while beside her, Mabel gripped the armrests of her chair until the leather groaned in protest.

"This is...this is..." Victoria finally managed, her words barely above a whisper as tears welled in her wide eyes.

"By Jove, this calls for celebration!" Whitaker boomed, his walrus mustache quivering with mirth as he bellowed into the hallway: "Phineas! The Veuve Clicquot, if you please!"

Victoria sat frozen for a heartbeat, her hands trembling against her lips as the magnitude of his words crashed over her. Then—like the first rays of dawn breaking through a storm—joyous tears spilled down her cheeks in glittering tracks. "Oh, merciful heavens!" she gasped, her voice cracking with emotion.

In an instant, both women sprang from their chairs with a most unladylike lack of decorum, embracing so fiercely that Mabel's bonnet went askew. Their delighted shrieks echoed off the mahogany-paneled walls.

Then—in a breach of protocol that would have made their finishing school mistresses faint—they descended upon poor Mr. Whitaker. Flanking the flustered solicitor behind his desk, they smothered him in a most improper double embrace, each planting a resounding kiss on his scarlet-flushed cheeks.

"Good gracious!" Whitaker spluttered, his cravat now hopelessly crumpled, as he fumbled to straighten his attire with sausage-like fingers. The man looked positively apoplectic—equal parts delighted and terrified.

Victoria couldn't contain the happiness bubbling up inside her. "Thank you, dear Mr. Whitaker!" she cried, clutching his hands with uncharacteristic boldness. "A thousand times, thank you!"

17. Christmas Eve Reflections

Reflect upon your present blessings—of which every man has many—not on your past misfortunes, of which all men have some. Fill your glass again, with a merry face and contented heart.
—Charles Dickens, *Sketches by Boz*, 1839

Nearly a week had passed since the astonishing revelation in Mr. Whitaker's office —a Christmas miracle that had left Victoria's heart lighter than the snowflakes drifting down over London. It was a gift beyond any she had ever imagined receiving, a hope she had fiercely guarded but never truly allowed herself to believe in. She and Mabel had showered the poor solicitor with such overwhelming gratitude—embracing him and peppering his crimson cheeks with kisses—that the man had nearly collapsed behind his mountain of legal papers, mopping his brow with an overworked handkerchief. Though Mr. Whitaker had cautioned them as they left his office that bureaucratic wheels turn slowly, "The transfer isn't finalized, ladies—I shall monitor the situation most diligently, etcetera, etcetera," nothing could dampen their elation.

Their journey back to Mabel's residence became a scene of pure, unbridled joy. Arm in arm, they skipped through the snow-dusted streets like schoolgirls, their laughter ringing out crisp and clear in the December air. More than one passerby looked at the two with an astonished gape, while a cluster of housemaids giggled behind their mittens at the spectacle of two well-bred women behaving with such abandon.

Upon reaching Mabel's doorstep, Victoria clasped her dearest friend's hands, the words catching in her throat. "How will I ever thank you? For standing with me through every darkness—" Mabel silenced her with another fierce embrace, the kind that needed no words. Reluctantly pulling away, Victoria adjusted her snow-dampened skirts and prepared to depart. There were others who deserved her gratitude—the loyal staff who were transforming into unlikely friends, and most of all Annabelle, whose stern exterior had concealed a compassion that made this miracle possible. The truth, as stark and clear as the winter air, settled upon her: without Annabelle's intervention, her mother would have had no hope and might have languished in that dungeon forever.

The moment Victoria crossed the threshold of the Pembroke residence, the familiar scent of searing meat and fresh bread wrapped around her like a warm embrace. She made straight for the cooking area, knowing full well the entire household staff would be gathered there at this hour, preparing the evening meal.

Pausing in the doorway, her cheeks flushed from both the winter chill and exhilaration, she announced, "She's coming home! Well—not home precisely, but away from that dreadful place! They're transferring my mother to a proper asylum in West London!"

A ripple of joy passed through the kitchen. Gaston, his chef's knife never breaking rhythm as it danced across the chopping board, boomed: "Félicitations, ma petite lionne!" His use of the affectionate "my little lioness" rather than the formal "ma chère" spoke volumes about how far their relationship had come.

Clara nearly dropped the silverware she was polishing, her face glowing. "Oh, ma'am—Victoria—that's wonderful news!" she corrected herself, still navigating the unfamiliar territory of using her mistress's Christian name.

Alice and Maggie exchanged knowing grins at the hearth as they continued kneading dough and stirring pots, but their expressions glistened with shared happiness. Even the kitchen cat, perched on its usual stool, seemed to blink approvingly before resuming its meticulous grooming.

Victoria leaned against the scrubbed oak table, suddenly overwhelmed by the reality of it all. These people—her unlikely family—were celebrating with her as if Sarah Jane were their own kin. The warmth of the hearth, the clatter of pans, the rich aromas of supper—all of it fused into a moment of perfect contentment she wished she could preserve forever.

Catching her breath against the doorframe, Victoria felt an unexpected warmth blossom in her chest at the thought of Annabelle. How extraordinary—that name which had so recently conjured tension now stirred something akin to gratitude. How swiftly fortunes turn, she marveled, straightening her skirts before addressing Maggie. "Where might I find Mrs. Pembroke?"

The housemaid replied softly, her fingers pausing over the bread dough, "I believe her ladyship is in the study, ma'am."

"Thank you!" Victoria beamed, exiting the kitchen with such haste that she nearly collided with Mary in the narrow passageway. "Oh, Mary!" she gasped, catching the housemaid's shoulders, "They're transferring my mother to Hanwell Asylum—here in London!"

Mary offered one of her characteristically restrained smiles, though her eyes betrayed genuine pleasure. "Most wonderful news indeed, ma'am."

Victoria gathered her petticoats as she hurried toward the library, calling over her shoulder with uncharacteristic impulsivity, "Wish me luck!" The words escaped before she could consider their implication—why should she need luck to speak to her own mother-in-law? She looked down at her own hands, surprised to see them trembling. The ghost of their old dynamic, it seemed, was not so easily banished by good news.

The Pembroke library, while modest compared to the grand literary temples of London's elite, possessed all the warmth and charm befitting a cultured Victorian household. A massive carved oak hearth dominated the room, its roaring flames casting dancing shadows across the leather spines of countless volumes. Every wall from wainscot to cornice stood clad in rosewood bookshelves, their contents a carefully curated universe of knowledge—from gilt-edged poetry collections to well-thumbed historical treatises, each shelf whispering of generations of curious minds.

At the chamber's far end, an imposing portrait of Her Majesty Queen Victoria gazed imperiously over the domain. The monarch, Victoria's royal namesake, sat resplendent in her coronation regalia, the diamond-encrusted Imperial State Crown glittering even in painted form, her stiffly embroidered gown a testament to both royal dignity and the corseted constraints of the age.

Before the hearth, a buttery-soft Chesterfield sofa and two matching wingbacks formed an intimate circle, their horsehair stuffing slightly flattened from years of use. The flickering blaze played across their cognac-colored leather, illuminating faint scars from decades of use—a tea ring here, a cigar burn there—each mark a silent witness to generations of Pembroke contemplation and conversation.

Seated in the wingback chair's embrace, Annabelle perched her pince-nez spectacles on her nose, the firelight glinting off their gold rims as she studied her book. A steaming teacup rested on the piecrust-edged hardwood table beside her. Without glancing up, she remarked in that dry, cultured tone Victoria knew so well, "Victoria, you look positively smug as the cat that got the cream."

Stilling the tremor in her hands, Victoria stepped forward. "I bring wonderful news—and I have you to thank for it." She swallowed. "I'm... more grateful than words can express."

Annabelle peered over her spectacles, brow furrowing. "Good heavens, whatever are you prattling on about, Victoria?"

"Your letter to Dr. Ashford! It's worked! They're transferring Mother from that Godforsaken place to Hanwell Asylum!"

Annabelle snapped her book closed with a soft thud, though her tone remained seriously casual. "Oh? That. I merely wished to understand the situation properly." Her glance flicked up, softening at the edges. "Still, I'm pleased your mother will be nearer. Blood is important."

"You can't possibly understand—it was your suggestion of transfer that swayed them! I'm sure of it." In an uncharacteristic burst of emotion around Annabelle, Victoria sank to her knees beside the chair, capturing

Annabelle's ringed hand between both of hers. "Thank you," she whispered, her voice thick.

Annabelle regarded her for a long moment, a faint upturn of her lips, like sunlight on frost. "I'm gratified to have been of service," she murmured, already reopening her leatherbound companion with a rustle of pages.

Victoria rose, smoothing her skirts, recognizing the finality in that gesture. As she turned toward the door, Annabelle's words halted her mid-step. "Dearest girl..." The endearment hung strangely in the air. "The lion's share of credit belongs to you." Still, Annabelle kept her eyes fastened to her volume, though Victoria noted the slight smile of satisfaction crossing her mother-in-law's face.

Yet when Victoria shared the glad tidings with Simon that evening over supper, her husband merely dabbed his mouth with a napkin before offering his tepid remark. "I suppose you've gotten your way, then."

The silver fork froze midway to Victoria's lips. No questions about Hanwell's reputation. No interest in when the transfer might occur. Just that infuriating nonchalance, like someone discussing the latest price of codfish.

In the days that followed, Victoria made tentative overtures—mentioning future visits, the asylum's modern treatments, even the possibility of hosting her mother for tea once she improved. Each attempt was met with the same maddening indifference: a grunted "As you wish" or the barest inclination of his head as he buried himself in *The Times*. By week's end, Victoria surrendered to the silent stalemate; nevertheless, its injustice prickled like woolen undergarments. If Simon could not—or would not—share in her joy, then she would hoard it like a secret, a private triumph he was determined not to share.

Yet Christmas dawned with resolve. She was determined to transform the holiday into a picture of domestic perfection that might mend this rift. Simon would have his formal dinner—complete with roast goose and claret from the '48 vintage. The dining table gleamed with their prized Wedgwood china—the ivory Queens Ware plates edged in cobalt vines that had been a wedding gift from Simon's aunt. Beside each setting, Georgian sterling silverware—marked with the Pembroke crest—rested atop Belgian linen napkins starched to crisp perfection. The candlelight danced in cut-crystal goblets from Waterford, their facets scattering prismatic sparks across the damask tablecloth like winter stars. The crackers lay like gilded promises at each place setting, their twisted foil ends hiding their extravagances meant to coax a smile from Simon's stony face.

Standing on the dining room's carpet, Victoria adjusted a sprig of holly above the mantelpiece, her fingers lingering on the waxy leaves as if they might divine some answer. *Perhaps this will remind him why he chose me*, she whispered silently in her mind, watching the crimson berries tremble in the candlelight. *Perhaps tomorrow we shall find our way back to one another.*

Yet even as the servants bustled about her—polishing silver, straightening chairbacks—a chill crept up in her that had little to do with the December gales. There was something crouching in the shadows of Simon's silence, something deeper than mere indifference. *What specter haunts my husband?* The question coiled like mist in her mind. It was like the choking London fog that blurred gas lamps and muffled footsteps, obscuring all truth.

18. Shattered Illusions

I gave him my heart, and he took and pinched it to death;
and flung it back to me.
—Emily Brontë, *Wuthering Heights*, 1847

The Christmas dinner had unfolded with flawless precision thus far—a minor miracle of domestic harmony. Platters of roast goose glistened with apple and sage, while the mingled aromas of spiced claret, cinnamon-dusted yams, and beeswax candles wrapped the dining room in festive warmth. To Victoria's quiet amazement, Simon lounged in his chair with an unbuttoned waistcoat, his smiles coming easily as he regaled them with amusing accounts of his business ventures—a tale punctuated by sips of '48 Bordeaux.

Even Annabelle's customary reserve had thawed, her lavender silk skirts rustling softly as she complimented the cook on the chestnut soup. Victoria had spared no effort for this reconciliation feast, donning the same bronze bodice and scarlet cashmere skirt she had worn to the charity ball—though the memory of that evening now seemed to belong to another lifetime.

Simon cut a dashing figure in his bottle-green frock coat and waistcoat, while Annabelle's amethyst brooch caught the light with each graceful gesture. Before dinner, the Westminster Carol Society—twelve boys from Christ Church choir—had stood in the snow-dusted square, their clear voices rising through the frosty air with *"God Rest Ye Merry, Gentlemen."* The last echoes of their harmonies still seemed to linger in the holly-draped hall, blessing this fragile truce of a Christmas.

Mary had just cleared the remains of the third course —a roasted quail in bread sauce that lay nearly untouched on Simon's plate—when suddenly he set down his fork with deliberate, almost theatrical precision. The silver's chime against the bone china rang through the dining room like a judge's gavel.

"Victoria... Mama," Simon began, clearing his throat with a rumble. His eyes darted from one woman to the other before fixing on the warped reflection of himself in his cut-crystal glass rather than meeting their eyes.

"The Westminster Conservative Association has prevailed upon me to contest the approaching by-election. Mr. Southington's recent demise, from cholera presumably, has created a... timely vacancy."

At that moment, a log shifted in the fireplace, sending sparks dancing across the hearth—Providence itself seeming to punctuate Simon's announcement. Across the table, Victoria sat transfixed, her sherry glass suspended midway to her lips, the amber liquid capturing the candlelight.

"A by-election?" Victoria tilted her head in genuine curiosity, her brow furrowing. "I'm afraid you've lost me. What would that entail?"

Simon's visage transformed with the smug radiance of a man seeing his imminent triumph unfold before him as an esteemed member of Parliament. "Why, it means your husband may soon be the Honorable Member for Westminster, my dear. Think of it our name Pembroke finally taking our rightful place in the halls of power!"

His tone turned brisk as he addressed practicalities, that familiar calculating glint returning to his eye as he looked at Victoria. "Naturally, it will require your presence at no fewer than three Tory gatherings weekly—Lady Grantham's drawing-room Thursdays being particularly essential. And Mother..." He inclined his head toward Annabelle, "Your connections with the Ladies' Charity Committee could prove invaluable for securing the parish vote."

His eyes swept over the two startled women, as if taking inventory of his assets, "I trust I can rely on both of you," he stated with a firm smile.

"You may consider my support assured," Annabelle declared dryly, her fingers tracing the rim of her wineglass in a slow, considering circle.

Simon's focus now shifted to Victoria; his gaze insistent on her compliance.

Victoria's sherry glass wobbled precariously as she set it down, leaving a ring on the tablecloth as Simon's announcement hung in the air. She forced her trembling fingers to stay still against her lap.

Victoria blinked and slowly began, "I'm most proud of you, Simon," she managed, her voice betraying none of the rebellion simmering beneath her corset. She let the pause linger just a heartbeat too long before adding, "Might I ask how long this... ambition has occupied your thoughts?"

Simon stared at her as if she'd asked why the sky was blue. "Opportunity knocks when it will. Wilby—"

Victoria's spine stiffened at the name, her lips pressing into a seam.

"—insists my combination of mercantile success and aristocratic bearing makes me ideal."

Again, Simon looked directly at Victoria, still expecting her acceptance of his plans. An unshakable expectation hung between them—her compliance already tallied like a ledger entry in his mind.

Victoria carefully adjusted her posture. "Of course, Simon," she said, her tone measured, "but I've also made commitments to *The Haven for Destitute Children.* Young Mary—"

Simon's brow knotted in a flash of irritation. "Philanthropy lends distinction to any political wife," he conceded, tapping one impatient finger against his water glass, "but this election demands undivided attention. You'll suspend these visits."

The sherry's sweetness curdled to sour milk on Victoria's tongue, "I think that my visits to the orphanage are of great importan—"

"You think?" Simon barked a laugh that rattled the silverware. "Since when do petticoat opinions signify in such things? Capable men will handle these matters. Your position is to support your family."

A hot needle of anger pricked Victoria's throat. "Mary and forty other souls sleep three to a cot in that institution," she shot back, the words tight and breathless. "If gentlemen managed these affairs so capably, why do infants still perish in workhouse gutters?"

Simon snapped, "You may be of some assistance, but men are taking care of these situations."

"Well, if men are taking care of all this, why are there so many orphans and miserable poor?" Victoria quickly retorted. "Mr. Mearns—"

"Who the devil is that?" Simon cut in.

Victoria gripped her napkin so tightly that the monogrammed linen tore. "I've mentioned him before, if you had ever listened to me. Mr. Mearns, a Congregationalist minister, is working to raise awareness about the squalor, overcrowding, and moral decay in the slums, advocating for housing reform and greater social responsibility among—"

Simon now red in the face, "This is all well and good, but you are meddling in things best left to men like Mr. Mearns. Your priority is our family and—"

Victoria quickly snapped back, "I disagree. Mr. Mearns documents what you refuse to see. From the Book of Matthew, Jesus said, Suffer little children—"

Simon let out a derisive snort. "You dare disagree?" He drew himself up to his full height, his starched collar biting into his neck as he pursed his lips like a man tasting vinegar. "Christ and all His angels!" Simon's fist struck the dining surface, making the cutlery jump.

"Do you know why the British Empire has lasted so long, expanding across the world, and why it will no doubt persist for hundreds of years if not longer?" He leaned across the ruined dinner setting, his breath hot against Victoria's face. "Because God entrusted civilization to men of breeding and intellect."

A vein throbbed at his temple, yet he continued, beaming with pride, "We make the world a place of order. Without us, it would be chaos. We alone tame the savage hoards—whether the red-skinned rebels in America, the filthy barbarians of Calcutta, or those barefoot primitives in the dark continent. Without our hand at the tiller—."

His signet ring flashed as he gestured wildly around the gaslit dining room. "—this entire edifice of society would crumble into pagan anarchy! Every china plate, every railway timetabled to the precise minute, every law binding servant to their betters—all made possible by men's reason, not women's whims!"

The clock on the mantel ticked loudly as he seized Victoria's wrist, his grip tight enough to leave imprints, "That is not your position in society. You're here to maintain a well-run home, raise legitimate heirs, and perform your duties in silent compliance! Not to whimsically challenge things that you don't even understand."

Somewhere in the kitchen, a maid dropped a tray with a crash that echoed like cannon fire.

A single tear escaped, tracing a hot path down her cheek. It was born as much from the shocking pain in her wrist as from the horrifying clarity of the man she had married.

"My God, Simon," she whispered, her voice trembling. "Where is the man who knelt in the garden gazebo, calling me his everything the first moment we met? Who stole kisses behind the potted ferns at Lady Ashworth's ball?" Another silver trail followed the first, splashing onto her lace collar like acid on silk. "The man who swore he loved my uncommon fire? Who said he loved me for who I was?"

She twisted in his grasp. "Simon—*please*—" A ragged sob escaped her as she tugged, her wedding ring grinding against bone under his grip. "You're hurting me."

Simon stared at his hand as though it belonged to a possessed dockside ruffian, releasing his grip so abruptly that Victoria fell back in her chair. She cradled her throbbing wrist, the imprint of his signet ring blooming like a bruise on her soul as much as her skin. The man before her now—this cold stranger—bore no resemblance to the eager suitor who had once showered her with compliments and roses.

"See what you provoked?" Simon hissed, adjusting his cuffs with a jerk, his tone dripping with the aloofness of a physician diagnosing hysteria. "We had our courtship, and now we move on with daily life, bettering our position. Grown women concern themselves with managing households and advancing their husbands' prospects."

He paced before the fireplace, his shadow looming monstrously across the room. "This maudlin fixation on romance, this abnormal yearning for love... these orphanage fantasies... I begin to question whether you require medical intervention. Perhaps you need to join your ailing mother in that modern asylum you so cherish," punctuating the word modern with a sneer.

Victoria ran her thumb over the red wounds circling her forearm. She could only stare at the livid marks, a more brutal and honest wedding band than the gold ring that now felt like an iron shackle.

At the table, Annabelle had turned as pale as Wedgwood's finest bone china. Without a word, she rose like a specter from her place, her lavender skirts whispering a lament as she left the room with the slow, heavy steps of someone attending a funeral.

Silence descended, broken only by the crackle of the fire. What remained was a battlefield strewn with invisible casualties—the remnants of Victoria's girlish dreams shattered like the broken crystal tumbler of Simon's earlier fury. The very air seemed thick with gunpowder and tears; the grandeur of the dining room now a hollow stage where their marriage had cracked, revealing the rot beneath. The perfect Christmas scene had fissured, and through the crack, Victoria saw the desolate truth of her future.

The portrait of a youthful Annabelle, positioned regally above the mantel, with her piercing gaze, now seemed to regard the scene below with an air of sorrowful resignation. Her once steadfast eyes, so full of intensity in life, now bore a melancholy weight, their painted depths shimmering as if on the verge of shedding pigmented tears.

19. Picking Up the Pieces

I am no bird; and no net ensnares me: I am a free human
being with an independent will.
—Charlotte Brontë, *Jane Eyre*, 1847

*T*he winter days passed, ushering in the new year without event or fanfare, and the weeks that followed drifted by in quiet succession as the Ides of March crept closer, bringing with them the slow but inevitable turn of the seasons.

The days following Christmas passed in a blur of ashen hours. Victoria moved through them like a ghost; the vital woman she had been seemed to have been snuffed out. Tears came without warning—while brushing her hair or staring out at the frost-laced garden, their saltiness was a rude reminder of all that had broken that Christmas night. She took her meals in her room; the world outside her door too loud, too bright, too full of life. She mourned all she lost—the loss of innocence, the loss of her belief in her marriage, and the fading of a love she had once believed to be true.

On Boxing Day morning, as the gray winter light seeped through the curtains, Simon quietly apologized to Victoria. Yet, it was a hollow act of contrition, in which Simon said he was sorry only for gripping her arm too tightly. What he said—and, more tellingly, what he didn't—was not broached. His tone was measured and calculated, devoid of genuine remorse. It was clear to

Victoria that he was not the man she had once imagined him to be, nor the husband he had pretended to be. This apology was not for her; it was for his own conscience, or more likely, his ambitions. He needed to smooth things over, to ensure his political aspirations did not suffer for his private cruelties. Despite this, Victoria bowed her head and managed a hushed acceptance, her voice empty of feeling. There was too much to process, too much to grieve, and no strength left in her to fight an unwinnable battle.

Slowly, like a plant bending toward a ray of sunlight, Victoria began to reclaim herself. The grief did not vanish, but it settled, becoming a weight she learned to carry. She had endured a gauntlet of hardships and emerged battered but breathing; she would survive this, too. Her spirit, though battered, was not broken.

From that moment on, she resolved to play the role of the compliant wife—keeping up appearances, managing the residence with muted precision, and attending the tedious afternoon teas and charitable committees favored by influential society women to bolster Simon's political ambitions.

She often wondered, as she poured tea and listened to their idle chatter, how many of them were also merely acting out a part. How many were silently shouldering lives they hadn't chosen? Were they all just smiling specters in corseted disguises? She pondered whether all these marriages—held together by social expectation and silence—were little more than elaborate performances on a crumbling stage of facades.

Shared dinners with Simon became a rarity, and when they did occur, they carried the emotional warmth of a drafty parlor in January. Simon would offer a dispassionate summary of his activities—parliamentary gossip, public engagements, the occasional mention of his business with Wilby and company—to which Victoria and Annabelle would reply with little more than nods and muttered platitudes. Annabelle, for her part, had become a quieter version of herself, no longer issuing sharp remarks or reminders of decorum. She seemed content to sit in silence, her hands folded, her eyes far away. It was as if the lifeblood had been drained from her, leaving only a shell that dutifully echoed Simon's words.

Strangely, or perhaps predictably, Simon seemed oblivious to the shift in the household's mood. Or worse, he may have welcomed it—a house hushed and compliant, free of disruption.

Victoria rarely engaged with Annabelle. In truth, they might as well have dwelled in separate parts of London for all they saw of each other. She let the older woman withdraw into her own solitary world while she moved through her days with a new sense of focus, grounded in daily tasks and quiet acts of rebellion.

She threw herself into her kitchen lessons, learning the finer points of sauces, breads, and stews under the tutelage of the ever-patient Gaston. Every day, she sharpened not only her knife skills but her confidence. She was becoming quite the junior chef, welcomed by the kitchen staff with smiles and teasing remarks.

Her visits to the orphanage became more frequent and purposeful. She brought with her baskets of food, hand-stitched garments, and little trinkets, but most of all, time and attention. She spent her afternoons with Mary, who would run to greet her with arms wide and a grin bright enough to light the darkest corners of her heart.

Mary's laughter, untainted by sorrow, felt like balm. Her joy was worth more than all the coins in London.

Mabel, meanwhile, was now often occupied with her husband, who had returned from his overseas campaign in late January, weary but intact. On the rare occasions their paths crossed—mainly at the orphanage—Mabel was her usual radiant self, brimming with energy and affection. She was shocked and outraged by what had unfolded in Victoria's marriage, her loyalty fierce, her friendship unwavering.

"You are the strong, amazing, beautiful woman you always were," she would say, taking Victoria's hands in hers with sincerity that left no room for doubt. "Don't let anyone tell you different." And somehow, hearing it from Mabel made it feel possible.

Mr. Whitaker had been right—the bureaucratic wheels did not turn so much as groan forward with glacial reluctance, especially in matters involving the asylums, it seemed. But at last, toward the waning days of February, a telegram arrived: her mother had been successfully transferred to Hanwell Lunatic Asylum, and a visit would be permitted sometime in March.

She stared at the message in her hand, smiling with a kind of awed disbelief. It had actually happened. Months after that dreadful visit to Redhill, she would soon be able to see her mother. A rush of pride swelled in her chest—a quiet, glowing certainty that she had made this possible, that her persistence had mattered.

For the first time in years—perhaps ever—she felt like the mistress of her own life. Aside from the shadow Simon still cast over her days, she had taken the reins of her future. She moved with more purpose, spoke with more confidence, and held her head a little higher.

And yet...

Something gnawed at the edges of her joy. A vague unease curled in her gut—an ill wind she couldn't name, only feel. *Beware the Ides of March.* The phrase came to her unbidden, from some long-forgotten line of Shakespeare or schoolroom recitation.

What it meant in her present life, she couldn't say. The dread was shapeless, a fog rather than a storm, but it lingered nonetheless. She tried to dismiss it as a trick of the mind, the echo of an overwrought imagination. Still, each time it stirred within her, a chill cascaded down her spine. With no proof and nothing tangible to confront, she buried it beneath reason. But the feeling never quite went away.

After a long day, Victoria entered the library, removed her well-worn shoes, and collapsed onto the edge of one of the wingback chairs, massaging her aching feet. She settled back into the chair, its aged leather creaking as she curled her soles beneath her. The library was a sanctuary of hushed quiet, the scent of aged paper and polished oak surrounding her like a cocoon.

Over the last few weeks, with the unyielding resolve of a warrior, she had committed herself to reading and educating herself as much as she could, despite her increasing daily toil. Many an evening, she would awake in the middle of the night, twisted uncomfortably in the wingback, a book lying askew on the floor. Since she often eschewed her bed after that dreadful Christmas dinner, she would stretch out on the couch or shift her stiff limbs, nestling back into the chair to resume her slumber.

She picked up the volume she had been reading the previous night from the table to her right. She ran her fingers over its embossed cover before opening it, the pages rough beneath her touch—*Advice to Young Men and (Incidentally) to Young Women*—an unassuming title. She turned to the page marked by an azure silk ribbon and began to read.

After some time, she found herself suddenly gripped by William Cobbett's words. Her pulse quickened as his fiery denunciation of vaccination seared across the page. Cobbett's condemnation of the practice was blistering; each sentence laced with scorn. His description of the outbreak in Ringwood sent a chill through her, the weight of his testimony sinking into her chest. *More than a hundred dead—all vaccinated, all told they were safe, only to succumb to the very disease they were promised immunity from.* She reread the passage, her fingers tightening on the page. The excuses—*unskillful operators, staleness of the matter, it not being of genuine quality*—all rang hollow. It was always someone else's fault, never the fault of the practice itself. The authorities had granted Jenner twenty thousand pounds for his work, yet even those he had vaccinated had fallen ill, some perishing as cruelly as the unprotected.

Leaving the ribbon at the damning page, she closed the book with a resounding thump and exhaled slowly, setting it down on her lap. Cobbett had written this half a century ago, his words confirming what Annabelle had told her only weeks before. She felt at her right upper arm, fingertips grazing the faint ridges where the scars of vaccination remained—a mark of an event long past, yet suddenly laden with new meaning. Now she wondered: *was it a blessing or a curse?* How much of the system was simply based on an unwavering faith? She sat pondering whether the many things she had firmly believed were perhaps not so.

Picking Up the Pieces

She woke with a start, jerking upright in the chair, heart thumping against her ribs. The leatherbound companion that had rested on her lap launched into the air and smacked against the floor with a soft, accusing slap. As she righted herself and gathered her scattered senses, she noticed Annabelle seated across from her in the second wingback chair, quietly observing her across the fading glow of the fire.

"Terribly sorry to have awakened you, my dear," Annabelle apologized, her voice as delicate as lace.

Victoria blew a tangled lock of auburn hair from her face, then shook her head briskly—partly to shake her hair into position, mostly to reorient herself to reality. "Oh, that's quite all right. I must have dozed off."

With that, Annabelle rose. "I won't trouble you further."

Victoria stifled a yawn. "No, no... that's quite—please, sit."

Annabelle hesitated, her expression unreadable, then silently lowered herself back into the chair.

Victoria glanced down at the fallen book, which now lay slightly open and oddly tilted with its spine pointing upward. She reached for it, flipping it right-side up, squinting at the cover. "Have you read this...?" she asked, still blinking away the fog of sleep. "Cobbett's book on advice?"

"Yes, of course," Annabelle replied with a slight curve of her lips. "I was quite the voracious reader in my youth."

Victoria flipped to the page where her ribbon had marked her place. "The part about... um... those who were vaccinated by this Jenner and still died of smallpox?" She pursed her lips, her brow furrowing slightly. "Isn't that strange to you?"

Annabelle's mouth curved into a subtle, knowing grin. "Well, perhaps not so strange—not anymore. Even back then, after what I witnessed in my own family, it didn't entirely surprise me." She leaned forward slightly, her voice low and deliberate. "There are many things you'll find that men—particularly men in positions of power—insist are true. But often," she added with a glint in her eye, "they are not."

A hush settled thickly over the room as Victoria pondered. Annabelle began to rise from her chair. "Well, if that is all—"

Victoria offered a small, tentative smile. "No, please, sit a while longer."

Annabelle quietly lowered herself back into the chair, the movement slow, almost reluctant.

Victoria began cautiously, her words catching. "I wanted to... Well, you... You haven't been the same since... Are you alright?"

Annabelle sat still, her usually unreadable face now touched with a trace of sorrow.

"I'll be fine. Thank you for your concern... I've weathered much in my life."

Another, deeper stillness fell between them.

"Simon was a bright, happy boy growing up. So was his sister."

Victoria's eyes widened. "Sister? Simon... you've... you've never mentioned a sister."

Annabelle drew a long breath, her chest rising as though pulling up something long buried. "No. Why would we? It's..."

Victoria's gaze softened, sympathy blooming in her eyes. Sensing this, Annabelle continued.

"His sister was two years older. Her name was Catherine. She took ill with a fever, and my husband insisted on calling a physician. I begged him to let me care for her myself, but he wouldn't hear of it, dismissing my pleas as *'female folly and quackery.'*" She finished with a bitter scowl.

"The doctor repeatedly bled her and gave calomel. Mercury, of all things. But over the days, my..."

Her voice trembled now, emotion cracking through. "...my little girl, Catherine, grew weaker and weaker..."

"We—James, Simon, and I—were quiet, almost ghostlike, on the day of the funeral. But when we returned home, I lost myself. I raged at James and blamed him. I screamed until I was hoarse."

Victoria's eyes glistened, a lump forming in her throat as she fought back tears.

"As I yelled, he struck me," Annabelle whispered. "Grabbed my wrist and backhanded me across the cheek. Then he warned, *'Never raise your voice to me again. This matter is closed.'*"

"He stormed into the library, and that's when I noticed Simon standing nearby, his eyes wide with terror. He ran off before I could speak to him."

Annabelle's own eyes were now glassy with shimmering drops. "James began drinking heavily from that day on. About a year later, I found him slumped in the library... I buried him almost a year to the day I lost my angel, my Catherine."

"I thought Simon would be alright... he was quiet, introspective... but he was coping. Or so I believed."

Her voice faltered. "But something in him has changed... especially after he took up with that damn Wilby."

Then, as if a thunderstorm had unleashed its terrible might on a sandcastle, Annabelle's decades-long composure collapsed into a stream of tears. Her entire body trembled as decades of silence broke open.

"My poor Catherine. My poor angel." She sobbed, her face crumpling. "My God... why didn't I... why didn't I protect her? And Simon..." The sand now washed away in a torrential downpour of grief, spilling forward as Annabelle collapsed back into her chair, her sobs unrestrained and raw.

Victoria slipped from her chair and knelt before her, gently clasping Annabelle's trembling hands in her own. The once impervious Annabelle—a woman who had for years embodied restraint, precision, and social decorum—now crumpled like a house of cards in a sudden gust.

Not long ago, Victoria had imagined what it might be like to see Annabelle's stern façade break—not from grief, but from joy, perhaps from a rare smile or the warmth of shared laughter. She had once longed for a hint of humanity behind the practiced mask. But now, witnessing Annabelle reduced to a vulnerable, grieving mother—expressing a loss so devastating, so long entombed within—Victoria felt her own heart fracture under the weight of it.

In that moment, their quiet antagonism gave way to something else entirely—a painful recognition. Victoria understood, perhaps for the first time, the burden Annabelle had carried alone for decades—a grief bound in silence, pride, and duty.

20. How the Other Half Lives

It is more than usually desirable that we should make some slight provision for the Poor and Destitute, who suffer greatly at the present time. Many thousands are in want of common necessaries; hundreds of thousands are in want of common comforts.
—Charles Dickens, *A Christmas Carol*, 1843

The breeze that swept through West London on that March morning was mild, carrying none of the stench that Victoria and Mabel would soon encounter. They walked along the road toward the orphanage, their conversation an anxious attempt to distract themselves from the expedition Mr. Mearns had planned—a journey into one of the city's most destitute districts, which he had warned would be "not an easy thing to witness."

Blowing warm air into her gloved hands, Mabel asked, "Are you nervous?"

Victoria mimicked the gesture and began to rub her hands briskly together. "Certainly... somewhat... But I'm sure Mr. Mearns will take every measure to keep us safe."

A contemplative silence fell between them as their footsteps echoed over the uneven cobbled street.

Then, with a wry smile, Victoria broke the quiet. "I must tell you about Annabelle. What happened in the library—it was utterly shocking. I was stunned." She paused, gathering her thoughts. "Simon had a sister!"

Mabel's jaw dropped slightly. "What?"

"I know—astonishing, isn't it? One would think, being his wife, I might have heard something of her before..."

Mabel shook her head slowly, giving Victoria a look of incredulous curiosity.

"According to Annabelle," Victoria continued, "her daughter—Simon's sister—fell ill with a fever. The doctor ordered repeated bleedings, and Annabelle was furious, believing the treatment to have done more harm than good. Her husband refused to listen to her, and after the child died, he was never the same. He drank himself to death within a year. And Simon—just a boy at the time—witnessed all of it."

Mabel's expression shifted to one of understanding. She nodded slowly. "Oh. That's why... I see."

"Exactly," Victoria murmured, her voice quieting. "Why Simon never spoke of his father, why his temper and drinking... it all makes sense now. And Annabelle—why she's always been so—"

"—stolid," Mabel supplied.

"Yes!" Victoria replied, her breath catching slightly. "Precisely. And why she urged me so fiercely to attend the *Seven Sisters for Sobriety*. It wasn't just about Simon. She was trying to spare me what she had lived."

Mabel nodded again; her voice soft with thought. "Quite the revelation, indeed."

Another thoughtful silence settled between them, each woman turning inward, digesting the weight of all that had been said.

"And Simon?" Mabel asked gently.

"I haven't seen him in... days," Victoria answered, her voice tinged with resignation. "He comes and goes like a ghost. God knows where he is now."

Mabel gave a slow, understanding nod, her face soft with quiet sympathy.

Victoria shifted slightly, the wind teasing loose strands of hair from beneath her bonnet. "And how are you and Terrance faring, now that he's home again?"

Mabel grinned with her mischievous, cat-that-got-the-cream expression. "The very day Terrance returned, he declared that we must retire to the bedroom without delay. I saluted smartly as he hoisted me over his shoulder like some captured damsel. I gave him a proper thrashing on the back—strictly for show, of course," she added with a wink. "And there, I was thoroughly conquered... again and again." She gave a theatrical sigh. "I could scarcely walk the next morning."

Victoria giggled, "I'm truly glad for you, Mabel. It's good to see you so happy."

"Next week," Mabel continued, "we're heading to the Regent Hotel in Buxton, Derbyshire. The waters there are meant to be quite restorative, and Terrance needs a proper rest," she added, then leaned in conspiratorially, "though I suspect I shall not be spared further... conquest."

Victoria laughed again, shaking her head.

"Oh! And on the way, we'll be stopping in Leicester to call on one of the fellows he served with. Apparently, the poor soul was badly injured and has been convalescing. It seemed only right to pay our respects."

Victoria narrowed her eyes in thought, a flicker of memory stirring at the edges of her mind. "My uncle—my mother's brother—Samuel—he lives in Leicester, I'm quite certain of it. I had nearly forgotten about him, what with everything that's transpired over the past few years... especially with all that happened to my mother."

She paused, eyes distant for a moment before refocusing. "I believe I ought to write to him. Let him know we're alive—and tell him everything that's happened. It feels wrong, somehow, that he's remained in the dark. Would you be a dear and take it with you? It would contain rather personal matters, and I'd prefer not to entrust it to the post."

Mabel arched an amused brow, turned her lip up in a half laugh. She gave a slight shake of her head, "Of course, you goose. You know I will."

Victoria smiled, the corners of her eyes crinkling. "Oh—and I received a telegram. I've been granted permission to visit my mother in just a few days! It'll be the first time I've seen her since that ghastly place in Redhill... that dreadful dungeon."

Mabel returned her smile warmly. "Do you want me to come with you?"

"No, that's quite all right. You've a journey to prepare for—and all that conquesting to attend to," Victoria added with a playful grin. "I shall manage perfectly well on my own. The asylum is only a short carriage ride away."

Mabel grinned, "I'm so very happy for you. I know your mother will be so much better off there."

Victoria nodded as they reached *The Haven for Destitute Children.*

As soon as they entered, several little ones—Mary among them—came scampering forward with delighted cries. Smiles and giggles erupted all around.

"Look what we've brought for you, darlings—some lovely new treats!" Mabel declared, her voice a lilting blend of laughter and affection, as she and Victoria passed out boxes to the eager little hands.

Mr. Mearns, following close behind the children, watched the scene with a warm, approving expression. "Ladies, we must make haste," he said gently. "Please… children, we must leave you for now."

The children, though momentarily disappointed, obediently scampered off to explore their treasures, laughter echoing in their wake.

"This way, if you please," Mr. Mearns added, gesturing toward a door at the rear.

In the back room, a few ladies had already gathered, their expressions a mix of apprehension and resolve.

"Ladies," Mr. Mearns began solemnly, "thank you for coming—to do what is surely God's work. I must again forewarn you: this expedition is not for the faint of heart. We will, of course, see to your safety, but if you have any hesitation—and I say this without judgment—it would be best not to proceed."

He let the words settle, his eyes sweeping across their faces to gauge their mettle.

"Very good," he nodded at last. "Now, to ensure you do not draw unwanted attention, Sister Beatrice and Sister Catherine will assist in outfitting you with the appropriate nun's habit—modest, unassuming, and quite effective at deterring notice and questions."

He stepped aside with a courteous bow. "Please excuse me while you change. When you are ready, we shall depart."

Victoria and Mabel, along with four other women they had never met, changed into full-length grey habits, each consisting of a modest robe, a coif to cover the hair, and a knotted cincture from which rosary beads hung at the waist. Once dressed, they were utterly transformed—

from ladies of comfort and fashion to humble sisters of charity.

Mabel looked down at herself, then at Victoria, with wide, uncertain eyes. "To think we're disguising ourselves as Catholic sisters," she whispered, a nervous tremor in her voice.

"It is a necessary disguise, and a prudent one," Sister Beatrice interjected calmly, overhearing the remark as she adjusted Victoria's coif. "The Irish families in Spitalfields know and trust the sisters. These habits will offer you more protection and welcome than your own fine silks ever could. It is not about our faith, but about speaking to them in a language of charity they understand."

Having completed their transformation, Mr. Mearns reentered the room, accompanied by two broad-shouldered constables in plainclothes, their expressions stoic and alert.

"Ladies," he addressed them with calm authority, "these gentlemen will be accompanying us to ensure your safety. I've made this journey into Spitalfields on many occasions without incident. The residents know us and our mission. Simply stay close, and there should be no cause for concern."

He gave a measured nod as he surveyed the newly disguised group of faux-nuns.

"Each of you will carry a basket filled with foodstuffs and small comforts for the women and children we encounter. Distribute them freely as we walk, but again, do not stray. If at any point you find the circumstances too... unsettling, one of the constables will escort you back to the carriage."

He paused, allowing his words to settle.

"Very good. Let us proceed."

Each woman took a basket filled with fresh rolls, dried fruit, wrapped cheeses, and a few sweetmeats and followed Mr. Mearns out of the orphanage into the brisk afternoon air. Two nondescript black coaches awaited them; their windows shrouded with drawn curtains to obscure the view.

As they climbed inside, the atmosphere was quiet, save for the rustle of robes and the squeak of the carriage doors. The women exchanged nervous glances, the reality of their undertaking settling over them like a thick mist as the journey into London's shadows began.

As they ventured deeper into Spitalfields, the atmosphere grew thick with effluvia—foul-smelling vapors rising from the gutters, cesspits, and heaps of uncollected refuse. The stench, a nauseating brew of human and animal waste, rotting food, and coal smoke, became increasingly difficult to endure. Each turn of the coach wheels seemed to intensify the stench, turning the very act of breathing into a challenge. Somewhere nearby, a woman shrieked—whether in anger or agony, it was impossible to tell. A child's thin, reedy cough followed, echoing from within the dark tenement walls. The air buzzed with the low hum of flies and the distant clang of metal—perhaps a blacksmith, or someone smashing scrap for resale.

Sister Beatrice looked ahead unfazed, her expression composed, while Victoria, Mabel, and the other women pulled their shawls up over their noses, their faces contorted in discomfort. Sister Beatrice, with the slightest hint of amusement, said, "Do not worry, my dears—you'll become accustomed to it soon enough."

They exchanged skeptical glances, their pinched expressions betraying disbelief.

At last, the horse-drawn vehicle came to a halt, and a constable opened the door. To their dismay, an even fouler stench—viler than they could have imagined—invaded the confines of the carriage the moment the door swung open. The constable offered a steadying hand to each nun, and one by one, they stepped down into a landscape that seemed more infernal than earthly, the ground slick with a mire of mud, refuse, and unidentifiable waste. Their boots sank into the slurry with a sickening squelch.

There was scarcely a road to speak of—only a churned mess of filth and debris underfoot. The environment was dense with reeking vapors and acrid coal smoke, and the unseasoned nuns coughed and gagged as their lungs protested this unholy incursion. Nearby, the decaying carcass of a dog lay half-submerged in sludge, teeming with maggots. Rats skittered openly across the path, fearless from overfamiliarity, and cockroaches clung to walls and crates. Black clouds of flies hovered, darting and biting.

Somewhere, a child wept—a long, wailing sound that seemed to rise from the very bones of the place. A man with a bandaged leg dragged himself across the street, muttering nonsense to no one. The air was alive not only with insects but with despair itself.

Mr. Mearns, flanked by the constables, gathered the ladies around him. "Ladies, I know this is an assault on every sense, but I assure you—you will, in time, grow... accustomed. This is daily life for thousands." He gestured broadly, indicating the gaunt, rag-clad figures nearby—children with bare, blistered feet, women clutching infants to their chests, and men slumped in alleyways with vacant eyes. A junk peddler wheeled by with a rickety cart stacked with broken dishes, scraps of cloth, and other fragments of odds and ends.

Several children and women cautiously approached, their limbs stick-thin, their eyes hollow and rimmed in shadow. Sister Beatrice and Sister Catherine began handing out small parcels of food, offering blessings—"Christ be with you"—as they did so. The rest of the ladies followed their lead, reaching into their baskets to distribute what meager offerings they had. One young girl, no more than eight, took and clutched a piece of bread and some cheese with trembling fingers and whispered a "thank you" before vanishing back into the alley like smoke.

Mr. Mearns, his expression etched with both compassion and weariness, addressed the ladies as they continued distributing their parcels. "I see your understandable distress at these conditions. Look around you—these low, blackened tenements are choked with damp and decay; their walls sweat with filth and sorrow. Within, the air is stale and suffocating, the staircases half-collapsed, and the corridors crawling with vermin. To gain entry, one must climb rotted wooden steps and grope through darkness thick with stench and infestation. And to think," he added solemnly, "there are hundreds of thousands of men, women, and children enduring this squalor—living, sleeping, and dying in conditions not fit for beasts."

From an upper window, a pale-faced child peered down through cracked glass, her small hand pressed to the pane, watching the scene below with unreadable eyes. He paused, allowing the weight of his words to settle over them. "I see the distress and nausea on your faces. We shall not remain long. Please return to the carriages. The Sisters and I will see to the remainder of the distribution."

With barely concealed relief, the women climbed back into their respective carriages, their silence thick and unbroken. What they had just seen clung to them like soot, permeating their senses and weighing on their souls. The depth of suffering—the hopelessness, the stench, the desperation—remained lodged in every breath they took. Victoria clutched her stomach, nausea pressing like a fist beneath her ribs. Mabel reached for her hand, and their fingers entwined with quiet misery.

Mabel, her eyes wide and glistening, spoke just above a whisper, "This is beyond horrifying... I could never have imagined such misery existed—so close to our own lives."

Several aching minutes passed before Sister Beatrice returned and shut the carriage door behind her. With a lurch, the vehicle began its return journey—back to the relative comfort and quietude of West London. None among them spoke; each was lost in her own troubled thoughts, sounds, and smells of Spitalfields still clinging to their memory like soot upon a garment.

Victoria sat motionless; her gloved hands clasped tightly in her lap. She stared out the window, though the view was obscured by soot-smeared glass and drawn curtains. Her mind replayed what she had seen—the skeletal limbs of children, the hollow eyes of mothers, the pungent air thick with suffering—the contrast between that world and her own felt obscene.

Mabel reached for her hand and gave it a gentle squeeze. "That was more than I expected, even with Mr. Mearns' warning."

Victoria nodded slowly, her voice soft and brittle. "It changes you. Seeing it. Smelling it. Breathing it in. It's no longer a tale from the papers or a whispered scandal in drawing rooms. It's real."

Mabel stared down at her lap, her expression blank. "And it's not far. Just a few miles away. And yet, it may as well be another country."

Sister Beatrice, seated across from them, studied the pair thoughtfully. "It is good you've come. Bearing witness is the first step. The poor are not invisible—they are simply unseen."

Victoria glanced at her. "How do you bear it, day after day?"

The nun's face softened. "Because they deserve to be seen. And because, in that darkness, there are still glimmers of grace. A child's laugh. A shared crust of bread. A soul comforted in her final hour. We cannot lift them all—but we can lift some. That must be enough."

Mabel's eyes shone with unshed tears. "It's not enough. But it's something."

The carriage rattled on, the cityscape slowly shifting from bleak and broken to polished and presentable. The contrast was jarring—clean, gaslit boulevards, orderly rows of houses, and well-dressed people hurrying along the pavements.

As the orphanage came back into view, the carriage slowed to a gentle stop. Mr. Mearns opened the door and offered each woman a hand as they stepped down, back into the tidy familiarity of their own lives.

"Ladies," he said solemnly, "you've done a great good today. I thank you. I know this trip was short, but extremely difficult to process. Please pray for your own peace and the peace of all who suffer needlessly in our world today."

Victoria turned to him. "It is we who thank you—for opening our eyes."

He inclined his head with a slight smile, then turned to speak with the constables.

Mabel and Victoria stood together a moment, each adjusting her bonnet and cloak. They changed back into their own clothes, but the habits they had worn—and the experience they had lived in them—still clung to them like a second skin.

21. Silencing Sparrows

The best-laid schemes of mice and men, Go often awry.
—Robert Burns, *To a Mouse*, 1785

oday, Victoria would finally see her mother again after being apart for so many months. It was a short carriage ride west, past the manicured lawns of Gunnersbury Park, and to the dusty lanes of Southall. During the half-hour journey, Victoria could not shake the memories of the last few days.

The harrowing experience of the wretched poor in the East London slums had deeply imprinted upon her soul. She had given Mabel her detailed letter to Samuel about life over the many years and what had happened to his sister. Since Mabel had left yesterday, she could not inform him of Sarah Jane's current condition, which would be revealed today. Annabelle was still fairly withdrawn and perhaps embarrassed that her usually impassive façade had collapsed in the library. Still, she seemed a bit more tranquil than before.

Victoria looked out the coach window as they approached the outskirts of Hanwell. The asylum's entrance was imposing and austere, giving Victoria a moment of trepidation. A pair of wrought-iron gates, tall and blackened with age, stood between two weathered stone pillars, each topped with a rusted lantern. The gates groaned open on heavy hinges, revealing a straight, graveled drive lined with clipped hedgerows and skeletal trees that swayed faintly in the crisp March breeze.

They passed down a long drive flanked by greenery that had begun to show some signs of early spring life. Beyond the gates, the main façade of the institution stretched wide, an imposing row of red-brick buildings, their windows high and narrow, each crosshatched with iron bars. A stone archway marked the main entrance, above which was carved the faded inscription: MIDDLE-SEX COUNTY LUNATIC ASYLUM, EST. 1831. The double doors beneath were heavy and dark, fitted with a brass knocker dulled by a thousand anxious hands.

The air was still and muffled, as though the world inside moved to a slower, more solemn rhythm. Even the birds seemed to fall silent as the carriage rolled beneath the arch and slowed to a halt. The door opened, and a willow-thin lady dressed in white emerged and waited at the top of the steps as the coachman helped Victoria descend from the carriage.

A warm smile passed over the lady's face as she extended her open palm to greet Victoria, "Welcome, Mrs. Pembroke. We've been expecting you."

"Yes," Victoria uttered, her voice barely above a whisper.

"Do come in," the woman urged, stepping aside. They entered a lobby with polished white marble floors, where numerous brown leather chairs and couches stood in quiet arrangement, and potted ferns sat in large stone planters scattered about the room. At the far end loomed a large reception desk. "Might I offer you refreshment? Tea, perhaps, or water?"

Victoria shook her head. "No, thank you."

"Of course," the woman said with a gentle smile. "I imagine you're eager to see your mother. If you'd kindly take a seat, I'll inform Dr. Rayner of your arrival."

Victoria perched uneasily at the edge of one of the seats. The receptionist disappeared around the corner, returning moments later with a tall, thin man with spectacles precariously perched on the bridge of a narrow, hooked nose. His brown suit was well-tailored but informal, and his grin was broad and reassuring.

"Mrs. Pembroke," he said politely, motioning for her to remain seated. "A pleasure." He shook her hand briskly before settling into the opposite chair. "I'm Dr. Henry Rayner, superintendent of this facility."

He noted her tension and continued, "You've no need to worry. Your mother is waiting in the arboretum—a far more pleasant setting than these stuffy halls."

"She has made progress," Dr. Rayner explained in an encouraging tone. "She remains withdrawn, as expected, but we are optimistic. Ours is a progressive institution—one of the first in England to abandon mechanical restraints entirely. We believe in the curative power of occupation and fresh air. Our patients tend gardens, labor in workshops, and even assist on our farm. I assure you, straitjackets and chains have no place here—we haven't used them in years, even in the most severe cases."

Victoria nodded, the rigid tension in her shoulders softening.

Dr. Rayner rose, his warm smile broadening. "Shall we?"

He gestured to the portraits lining the walls as they strode down the hallway. "This is Dr. John Conolly, the father of the non-restraint movement, and a superintendent here when we were called Hanwell, before it was renamed Middlesex. His principles guide our work here. I've long argued that environment, not heredity, is the primary cause of mental affliction—and our results speak for themselves."

The arboretum behind the main hospital building stirred with the first whispers of spring. Though most branches remained bare, tight buds had begun to form on the hawthorns and sycamores, and a fine mist clung to the mossy earth beneath. A narrow path of crushed stone curved between plots of young trees—ash, elm, and larch. Sparrows chattered in the hedges, and the air carried the scent of damp bark and thawing soil. Wooden benches were scattered along the paths, their seats worn smooth by years of patients and attendants seeking solace in the quiet embrace of nature.

White-clad attendants moved discreetly among the patients, some of whom sat reading, while others tended to the flowerbeds with careful, deliberate motions. A few looked up curiously as Victoria and Dr. Rayner passed, but most remained absorbed in their tasks.

And then—there she was.

Sarah Jane sat alone on a bench; her face tilted toward the pale midday sun. She was dressed plainly, her hands folded in her lap, her posture both fragile and resolute, as if she were balancing between two worlds.

Victoria's breath caught. She approached slowly, her dress brushing against the damp gravel, before kneeling beside her.

"Mother?"

Sarah Jane turned, her gaze unfocused at first, then sharpening into confusion.

"It's me. Victoria."

Sarah Jane's brow furrowed. "No... my daughter is dead. My husband is dead." She closed her eyes again, retreating into the warmth of the sunlight.

Dr. Rayner leaned close. "Patience, Mrs. Pembroke. Meet her where she is."

Victoria swallowed hard. "No, Mother," she said softly, her fragile smile trembling. "I'm here. I'm your Victoria."

Sarah Jane's eyes flickered open. She studied Victoria's features—the curve of her cheek, the shape of her brow—searching for the child she remembered. "You're too old," she whispered at last. "My little girl was just..." Her voice faded, lost in the fog of memory.

Victoria's eyes glistened, but she held her smile. "I grew up. But I'm still yours."

"They told me you were gone..." she answered, her fingers plucking absently at her sleeve.

"Who told you—" Victoria began, but Dr. Rayner's hand tightened gently on her shoulder, a silent reminder.

"Try a memory," he whispered. "Something only you and she would know."

Victoria took a steadying breath. "Do you remember our picnics? That old red-and-white checkered blanket you used to spread under the oak? And your strawberry and fig jam—you'd pack it in little jars, and we'd eat it with fresh bread..."

A tear slipped down Sarah Jane's cheek. "Victoria?" she breathed—a fragile, hopeful sound. But then she turned her face back to the sky, as if afraid to look too long. "No... You can't be."

Dr. Rayner's voice was barely audible. "This is progress. But it will take time. Sit with her. Let her feel you near."

Nodding, Victoria settled onto the bench and took her mother's hand. The skin was paper-thin, the bones delicate as a bird beneath her fingers. She said nothing more—just held on, as the sparrows sang and the sun climbed higher, pressing its feeble warmth against the cold earth.

Dr. Rayner leaned in slightly, his voice discreet. "Take all the time you need. I must make my rounds, but any attendant can assist you."

Victoria lifted her head, her eyes suspending unshed tears. "Thank you, Doctor... For everything."

With a professional nod that softened at the edges, Dr. Rayner replied, "It's why we are here." He turned on his heel, his boots crunching quietly on the gravel as he retreated toward the facility's looming brick façade.

Time dissolved as Victoria sat with her mother, their shared silence more intimate than conversation. The sun painted a slow arc across the sky until it slipped behind a bank of pewter clouds, leaching warmth from the air.

Sarah Jane flinched as the shadow touched her face, her papery lips forming words like a long-forgotten reflex. "Your father always insisted on picnics, rain or shine. Foolish man." A pause. "Victoria hated cloudy picnics."

Victoria's breath hitched—her mother had spoken her name unprompted. Tears tracked unchecked down her cheeks as she laced their fingers together, feeling the fragile bones beneath parchment skin. "She still does, Mother."

The admission hung between them, delicate as the first frost. The afternoon unspooled in hushed communion, punctuated only by the rustle of awakening leaves and the distant chatter of attendants shepherding patients indoors. Words would have been superfluous; their presence was the bridge across lost years.

As the light gilded toward evening, a starched-aproned attendant approached, her footsteps deliberately audible to avoid startling them. "Beg pardon, ma'am, but supper is at five. The patients do best with routine."

Victoria rose slowly, her skirts whispering against the bench. She bent to press a kiss to her mother's forehead—a gesture she hadn't made since girlhood. Sarah Jane remained still as a portrait, yet the ghost of memory touched her expression: the faintest upturn at the corner of her mouth, like sunlight glimpsed through winter branches.

Stepping out of the asylum's heavy doors, Victoria inhaled the crisp evening air. A profound, quiet joy settled in her chest. Her mother was safe. She was cared for. And for one fleeting, precious moment, she had known her. A smile touched Victoria's lips as she descended the stone steps, the weight of years of fear finally lifting. Everything, at last, was going to be alright.

Her coach waited at the curb, the horses stamping impatiently. Yet as she approached, a prickle of unease crept up her spine. Something felt amiss. *Was the coachman taller? His posture too rigid?* She shook her head, chiding herself for foolish nerves—until the man turned, and she glimpsed a stranger's face beneath the brim of his hat.

Before she could react, the carriage door swung open. Inside sat a thickset man with a jagged scar running from brow to jaw, his eyes cold as flint.

"I—I beg your pardon," Victoria stammered, backpedaling, "this isn't my—"

A vise-like arm hooked around her throat. A sickly-sweet, chemical-smelling cloth clamped over her mouth and nose. Her scream dissolved into a choked gasp as the chemical's syrupy sweetness flooded her lungs. She thrashed, elbows jabbing backward, her gloves tearing against the carriage frame.

"Move, damn you!" snarled a voice behind her as she was shoved bodily into the compartment.

Fire seared her throat. Her muscles locked, then slackened as the world tilted. The sparrows' singing turned muffled, then silent. The ringing in her ears drowned all but fragments— "—*quick, the*—" —before even those words frayed into silence.

The last thing she saw was the scarred man's grin, yellowed teeth bared in triumph as darkness swallowed her whole.

22. Taken

*My dear young lady, crime, like death, is not confined to the
old and withered alone. The youngest and fairest are too
often its chosen victims.*
—Charles Dickens, *Oliver Twist*, 1838

ictoria's vision swam before her with an
uncanny clarity. Her parents' faces loomed
before her, their grins stretched impossibly
wide like carnival masks, their laughter twisting into the
shrill call of distant birds. They sat perched on a mound
covered with a red-and-white checkered blanket, a picnic
basket teetering with each convulsion of their mirth. The
scene rippled like a reflection in a pond. She knew this
memory, yet it slipped away just beyond her grasp.

Then the ground lurched.

With a stomach-dropping realization, she saw the
truth—they weren't on a hill at all, but atop a great gray
elephant, its wrinkled hide shifting like living stone
beneath the blanket.

She tried to scream, but her throat was stuffed with
wool, producing only a rasping cough. James Reginald and
Sarah Jane continued their picnic obliviously, lifting jam-
smeared bread to their smiling mouths as the beast's
trumpet split the air like a war horn.

The world upended.

Victoria was airborne, her parents remained undis-
turbed, with outstretched hands shrinking to doll-size as

she fell. Their voices elongated grotesquely, "Viiicctoorrii-aaaaaa!" into tiny echoes as darkness rushed up to meet her.

Her eyes flew open.

Reality crashed in with the stench of sweat and vomit. Her tongue was shriveled, her mouth a chemical wasteland of chloroform's afterburn. Every cough sent white-hot needles through her temples. She writhed against the scratchy wool blanket, her limbs weighed down as if buried in wet sand.

A sliver of gray light leaked through grimy drapes, revealing a sparse room with a plain wooden table in the center, a commode to the left of the bed she lay on, and a rickety bedside table—no water pitcher, no candle—only the sour proof of her captivity.

Fragments surfaced—the carriage, the scarred man's grin, the sickly-sweet rag pressed to her face. *This isn't my carriage*, she finished in her mind.

Panic ignited her nerves. She wrenched herself onto one elbow, the bedframe squealing in protest, as the questions circled like vultures.

Where am I?

How long have I been here?

God help me—what do they want?

Who are they?

"Easy there, princess." The voice rasped from the corner, so unexpected that Victoria's heart stuttered mid-beat. *How had I missed him?* The shadows there seemed thicker somehow, as if the gloom had congealed into human shape.

The scrape of a chair leg against floorboards. A man stood, his silhouette unfolding to a hulking height. Something glinted in his hand—something shiny catching the feeble light. As he stepped forward, the window's grimy glow slithered across his face, revealing the jagged scar that split his features like a crack in old porcelain.

Victoria jerked backward, her body sliding uselessly against the coarse bedsheets. Every instinct screamed at the sight of him—the carriage, the chloroform, those yellowed teeth now bared in a mockery of kindness.

"Only water, yer highness," he sneered, extending the glass as he bowed. His voice dripped with false courtesy; each word laced with the gravel of London's docks. "Wouldn't want our guest perishin' o' thirst, now, would we?"

Her fingers trembled as she snatched it, half-expecting poison, but desperation overruled caution. The first sip hit her cracked lips like salvation—then she was gulping, water sloshing down her chin as her throat convulsed against what seemed like weeks of dust and chemicals. She coughed and choked, water sputtering from her lips even as she desperately gulped more from the glass.

"Slow, girl." He loomed closer, watching her struggle with vulture-like interest. "Y'ain't no tavern wench chuggin' gin. Dunna drown yerself fore the fun starts." A wet chuckle bubbled from his throat; the sound of a man who'd seen too many women choke on their last breaths.

"W-what... do you... want?" Victoria choked out, each word scraping her raw throat like broken glass. Fear coiled tight in her chest, but beneath it—a spark of defiance.

The man let out a derisive snort, his boots scuffing against the rough floorboards as he ambled back to the shadowed corner. He snatched a tarnished pewter pitcher from the table, its surface dulled by years of neglect, and returned, looming over her like a storm cloud. "Steady them royal hands now," he jeered, tilting the pitcher with exaggerated care. Water sloshed into her glass, a mocking mimicry of fine service.

A drop of spittle escaped his cracked lips as he chuckled, the scent of rotting teeth and cheap gin wafting over her. "No need to piss yer silks, yer majesty. Ain't nobody layin' a finger on ye." The lie slithered off his tongue, slick as oil.

Victoria's mind began sharpening through the lingering fog—*this brute was no mastermind, just a hired thug.* She straightened slightly, channeling every ounce of breeding into her voice. "If it's money you desire, name your price. My family's coffers are deep enough to satisfy even the greediest of men." She thrust her chin up, meeting his gaze. *Let him see that I'm not some whimpering captive.*

She held her chin high, her back firm, a performance of composure she did not truly feel. Behind the mask, the room tilted on its axis, and the sour taste of bile burned at the back of her throat. She willed her trembling hands to be still, pressing them into the rough wool of the blanket to conceal their treachery.

The thug's grin twisted into something predatory as he loomed over her. "Yer thinkin' I'm some slack-jawed idiot what don't know his place and that yer better than me," he hissed, his breath reeking of stale tobacco and rotten meat. A grotesque pink tongue slithered across his chapped lips as his gaze dragged over her like grimy fingers. "A fine-bred pretty bit o' lamb like you'd fetch a pretty penny in Whitechapel... or make a right tasty morsel for them what favors tender meat." He drew closer and growled, "I'd pay a week's wages just to peel that satin bodice off with me teeth—" as his calloused thumb rubbed against her cheek.

Victoria wrenched her face away; her cheek pressed against the mildewed pillow as if distance could cleanse her of his presence. The words and closeness of the man caused nausea to leap higher in her throat.

But pulling back, he held up his grime-crusted pinky finger, mocking aristocratic refinement even as his voice dropped to a conspiratorial growl. "Lucky for you, I value me neck more'n me prick. Ain't stupid enough to cross Mr. Wi—" He caught himself, eyes darting to the door as if expecting a specter. "The guv'nor," he finished, the name Wilby hanging unspoken but undeniable in the damp air as he ambled back to the corner to sit.

Victoria's blood turned to ice. *Wilby!* That depraved wretch—the one who'd pressed too close during the waltz, his clammy palm lingering at her waist as he breathed port-soaked promises in her ear.

You are a remarkable woman.

Have you ever been to India?

I will have to arrange that trip for you.

I do hope we'll have the chance to... converse further.

Now his obsession had curdled into madness. Morphing from terror to rage, her fingers dug into the sour-smelling blanket, the rough wool the only anchor against the dizzying realization.

Fighting to steady her voice despite the bile rising in her throat, Victoria met his stare. "Your... governor," she stressed the word with deliberate disdain, "can't be paying you more than one hundred gold sovereigns for this vile business." She leaned forward slightly, the iron-framed prison creaking beneath her. "I'll double it. Two hundred sovereigns—gold in your hand within the hour—and you'll have my word as a Pembroke that no constable will ever darken your door."

The thug froze, his dirt-encrusted fingernails halting mid-scratch against his stubbled jaw. For a long moment, only the drip of a leaking pipe in the corridor broke the silence.

"An' how'd a fine lady like you be getting' two hundred quid?" he finally rasped, though the greedy gleam in his bloodshot eyes betrayed his interest.

Victoria allowed herself the smallest exhale as she formulated a lie. "My brother-in-law's bank is close to my home. One note from me, and his clerk will open the vault. Or you can explain to the magistrate why you thought kidnapping a Pembroke was sound business."

The man's stool screeched as he rocked back, his shadow stretching grotesquely across the mildewed walls. A bell tolled somewhere beyond the room—five chimes marking the hour. When he spoke again, his voice had lost its mocking lilt: "Two-fifty. An' I wants it in proper gold—yellowboys—none o' them Bank o' England paper." His beady eyes glittered with the madness of sudden greed.

Victoria allowed her shoulders to relax just a fraction, smiling with the surety of a well-seasoned businessman. "Done!" she exclaimed, extending her hand with all the regal grace of a queen granting favor. "We have an agreement... Mister...?"

She let the question hang, watching how his grimy fingers twitched at the implied equality of exchanging names. No, she realized, this gutter-born brute's never been given the courtesy of a surname before.

The door's rusted hinges screamed a second too late as it opened, catching both by surprise.

"Muldoon," came a voice like iced silk, "And... mister Muldoon will be feeding the Thames fish at the bottom this evening."

Victoria's carefully constructed hopes shattered like a champagne flute dropped onto a marble dance floor.

The disfigured brute nearly toppled from his stool in his haste to stand, his grime-blackened nails scraping the floorboards. "S-sir!... Swear on me mum's grave—just play actin'! Never would cross you, guv'nor—"

"How fortunate for you," the silhouette observed, his voice dangerously soft, "that Christian charity stays my hand today."

As the figure stepped forward, pale light from the grimy window excavated his features from the shadows, Victoria's fears were realized—Wilby.

"You are dismissed." He flicked his silver-topped cane toward the door.

As the visibly shaken Muldoon scurried to exit, Wilby suddenly hooked the cane's crook under the thug's jaw, tilting his chin up with lethal delicacy. "But should I ever smell a whiff of such... entrepreneurial spirit again—" He traced the cane along Muldoon's jugular before releasing him with a contemptuous shove. "The fish will dine well that night."

Muldoon ducked his head in a rushed bow and scurried from the room like a rat escaping a sinking schooner.

With a final contemptuous glance at the cowering Muldoon, Wilby turned his full attention to his victim. "Now then, Victoria," he purred.

A tempest of nausea, anxiety, and helplessness—*Why didn't I listen to my intuition?*—carved itself across Victoria's face. "You vile bastard."

Wilby sneered, twirling his cane in a lazy arc that caught the dim light. "I grant these accommodations lack Pembroke House's refinement, but you'll find them... sufficient for our brief association."

"You're not just a lunatic," Victoria spat, her voice trembling with fury, "you're the Devil's footman!"

Wilby adjusted his cravat as if she had commented on the weather. "A servant girl will attend you—food, water, and..." He tapped the commode with his cane, "...those delicate evacuations." A wet snort escaped him, the sound of a man long accustomed to his own wit.

"Do spare attempts to corrupt her," he added, examining his manicured nails. "The unfortunate creature is as deaf as a Westminster bell-ringer. And considerably less talkative."

Victoria wrenched against her lead-heavy limbs, the iron bedframe screeching in protest as she tried to swing her legs over the edge—only to jerk to a halt with a metallic clank. Her right ankle bore a wrought-iron manacle, its chain bolted to the floor with a grim finality. *Oh, merciful God. Wilby wasn't merely a lecher—he was utterly deranged.*

"When my husband—"

A heavy silence settled over the room as a wicked smile slowly curled across Wilby's face.

"What makes you imagine," Wilby interrupted, savoring each syllable, "that dear Simon doesn't know?"

Victoria's heart stuttered mid-beat. An arctic horror flooded her veins. *No. He's lying. He must be.* Yet the restraint around her ankle felt suddenly heavier.

Victoria's rage erupted like a geyser, "You filthy, black-hearted liar!" she howled, her voice ricocheting off the peeling walls.

Wilby tapped his temple with the silver crest of his cane, "What a tragedy—such comely features are marred by hysteria." He paced like a panther circling prey, "Though one can hardly blame you entirely, like mother, like daughter, as they say. First, your theatrical delusions, questioning learned medical men, challenging your position, then even poisoning his own mother's mind against him...Tsk. Tsk." He clucked his tongue in mock sorrow, the sound dripping with venom.

"Naturally," he continued, straightening his waistcoat, "a future Prime Minister can't be shackled to a wife prone to nervous disorders. It required... persuasion... but the boy finally embraced his duty to the family legacy."

Victoria gritted her teeth until her jaw ached, "They'll string you up like a common thief for this."

Wilby erupted in a braying laugh, "Still raving, I see! You won't trouble England's shores much longer."

An ice-cold terror seized Victoria's limbs.

"The official account?" Wilby adjusted his cuffs, "A tragic relapse during your asylum visit. The madwoman wandered into the night... vanished without a trace."

"You undervalue yourself, my dear," Wilby leered, "To certain... collectors... a well-bred English rose is the rarest exotic bloom of all." He tapped her foot with his cane.

India... The word slithered through her mind like a cobra as she pulled her leg back from Wilby with deep revulsion.

He paused at the threshold, running his tongue across cracked lips, "Affairs demand my attention, but fret not— I'll return to... prepare you for the voyage." His gaze crawled over her bodice, "We'll have such... enlightening discussions before your departure."

"The mute girl will bring your supper presently," he added with the indifference of a man reviewing shipping schedules, sweeping out and closing the door with an ominous thud.

As the door clicked shut, the last sliver of light vanished from the room, plunging her into near darkness. The silence he left behind was more terrifying than his voice. A dry, heaving sob escaped her, then another, until she was choking on them, her body convulsing against the iron frame of the bed. She curled into herself; a fist pressed against her mouth to stifle the sounds of her utter desolation. The questions screamed in her mind, but no answers came, only the callous, certain truth of the chain around her ankle and the vast, cold silence.

23. Imprisoned

"Do you find it difficult to endure solitude?" was a question
put by them to one of the prisoners. "Ah, sir," the man
answered, "it is the most horrid punishment that can be
imagined." "Does your health suffer from it?" was the next
inquiry. "No!" he replied, "but my soul is very sick." Of
another it was said, "he cannot speak long without
shedding tears."
—Henry Mayhew and John Binny, *The Criminal Prisons of*
London, 1862

As Wilby had promised, a gaunt, barefoot teenage girl with dirty brown hair dressed in plain beige clothes, silently entered the room carrying a metal tray. A sliver of light from the doorway revealed a portion of roast pheasant, some bread, steamed greens, and a pewter mug with the scent of ale. A coarse linen napkin lay folded beside the dish, conspicuously absent any cutlery.

Victoria thrashed against her chains, waving her arms wildly. "Look at me! For God's sake—can you not see I'm bound?" The young woman blinked placidly, arranged the tray on the table, collected the discarded pitcher and cup, and withdrew like a ghost.

Exasperated, Victoria scooted to the edge of the bed and swung her legs down to the floor. Her legs were returning to normal, though still heavy, and the floor felt oddly strange as her bare feet touched the rough, cold wood. *That disgusting ruffian took my clothes and boots, leaving nothing but my undergarments.* She willed herself to stand, and then, moving slowly, she lurched toward the scarred tabletop, making it to the edge before the metal shackle stopped her from moving any further. She went to move the chair

in front of the table and realized it couldn't be moved —the chair and table had been firmly riveted to the floor. *Damnation.*

As she collapsed onto the unyielding seat, the girl materialized with fresh water. Victoria screamed directly into her face, "I am chained here! Fetch the constable!" The servant cocked her head like a confused spaniel, her vacant half-smile never wavering. Victoria waved frantic hands before those uncomprehending eyes—no spark of recognition, only the dull sheen of a broken mind. *This poor girl is beyond reach*, she thought as the mute figure departed the room.

Alone again, the oppressive hush swallowed Victoria's hope. She devoured the pheasant with her fingers, washed it down with tepid water, but left the ale untouched. The fading light painted bars across the floor as she scoured the cell-like room: the immovable bed, every fixture nailed down with prison-like precision, except for the out-of-reach seat and small table where Muldoon had perched like a ghoul in the gloom. *There must be a weakness somewhere.*

As the last gray light seeped from the room, Victoria's pounding temples and leaden limbs pulled her under, unconsciousness claiming her the moment she reached the bed. She awoke to a darkness so complete it pressed against her eyeballs, her raw throat burning with each swallow. Disoriented, she clutched the scratchy blanket—

then the manacle's bite on her ankle jolted her to grim reality.

Summoning the last of her strength, she repeatedly screamed until her voice frayed: "Help! In God's name, I'm imprisoned!" Her final plea dissolved into a whimper—"Please...help."

Panting like a wounded animal, she was met with a thick silence. *This can't be Spitalfields—no drunken screams, no stench of foul emissions. The country, then? That pheasant was dressed too fine for an asylum...* Her fractured thoughts scattered as another sob wracked her body.

In the void, time lost its meaning. The venom of chloroform still pulsed through her veins, twisting shadows into monsters: Muldoon's scarred face sneering as he reached for her cheek, Wilby's demon-bright eyes flashing as his silver-capped cane jabbed her body, and Simon's skeletal fingers creeping from the dark. They advanced and retreated with her faltering heartbeat, the boundaries between nightmare and waking erased by exhaustion and the sickening poison.

The merciless dawn light stabbed through the grimy window, needling Victoria's closed eyelids until she jolted upright with a gasp. The room stood immutable in its grim austerity, but outside, the cheerful twitter of sparrows and the resonant ringing of a church bell tolling eight times cut through the quiet.

Her pulse quickened. The familiarity—the slightly flat third chime—was unmistakable. *Saint Mary Abbots!* Recognition crashed over her like a wave. I'm in Kensington! As the final bell faded, she strained to measure its proximity. "Dear God in heaven," she whispered, her fingers knotting in the bedsheet. *It can't be more than half a mile to the Pembroke House!* She pressed a trembling hand to the wall as if she might feel the vibration of carriages rolling down Holland Road. *Half a mile, maybe a mile*—a journey she could easily walk in ten or twenty minutes. Yet, the distance might as well have been an ocean.

The cruel irony—to be imprisoned within earshot of her own parish bells, closer to home than she was to her mother at Hanwell—clawed at her throat. Yet this very proximity kindled an ember of defiance in her chest. She eased off the bed and ran her hands along the walls, the iron bedframe, the table, and the chair, searching for anything that might serve as a tool. Nothing yielded hope. Crawling beneath the anchored bed, she disturbed decades of dust and cobwebs, but otherwise found only empty space.

After this futile examination, Victoria collapsed onto the mattress in defeat, absently scratching her tangled hair when—her nails struck cold, thin metal. A single pearl-headed hairpin, lodged stubbornly beneath her fiery tangle of curls, remained in place! She plucked it free with reverent care, its glint catching the dawn light like a beacon of hope.

As the church bells tolled nine, the mute servant girl entered with a fresh tray—eggs, toast, stewed prunes, and a pewter water pitcher. She exchanged it wordlessly for yesterday's tray and vanished like a shadow. The moment the door clicked shut, Victoria hiked up her soiled petticoat and wrenched her shackled ankle onto the bed. Working the hairpin's tip into the lock's mechanism, she twisted with desperate precision. Hours passed, her fingers cramping, but the lock refused to yield.

Blinded by tears of frustration, Victoria lunged upright, seizing the cold iron manacle in both hands. She braced her bare feet against the floorboards, throwing her full weight backward in a series of savage jerks that sent splinters biting into her heels. The wrought-iron bolt held fast. "Release me, you devil's contraption!" she shrieked, her voice raw as butchered meat. She battered the chain against the floor—once, twice—each clang echoing like a prison bell. The final scream, spittle flying from her lips, tore from her throat unbidden. "Come loose, you poxy bastard!"

She collapsed backward onto the thin, straw-stuffed mattress, her breath coming in ragged gulps between sobs. *No, this cannot be happening.* The words were a silent scream in her mind, a denial of the iron reality clamped to her ankle. After what felt like an eternity, Victoria succumbed to exhaustion, sinking into a black, dreamless oblivion.

The faint clatter of the metal tray roused her just enough to peer through heavy-lidded eyes. Feigning sleep, she watched the blank-faced servant girl—moving with the eerie precision of an automaton—complete her tasks and slip away, utterly oblivious to the shackled woman mere feet from her.

Who is this girl?

How can I reach her?

Christ's wounds—not so much as a scrap of paper or charcoal in this damned prison!

Pushing herself upright, Victoria staggered to the table, ignoring the food, and drank deeply from the pitcher like a parched beggar. She scanned the room again as she had already done a hundred times—then froze.

There. A crumbling hole in the corner, no larger than a shilling. She rushed over to the hole as if it were a tunnel to freedom. She fell upon it like a starved hound on a bone, clawing at the rotten plaster until her fingertips wept blood, her nails reduced to ragged, raw edges.

At last—a resistance. She hooked a finger around the edge of something soft and wrenched. Yanking and pulling, the corner of a piece of linen became visible. An old scrap of cloth emerged, its fibers slightly stiff with age. Victoria smoothed it against her thigh with trembling hands, squinting at the faded brown letters:

"HELP ME."

She stared at the words, blinking. A wild, broken, hysterical laugh burst from her lips. *Did I write this?* She pressed the cloth to her face, the musty scent of old ink filling her nose. *Am I going mad?*

"No," she quietly uttered as the laughter morphed into quiet weeping. "I haven't been here that long. No. Dear God... who else has been kept in this hell?" *Someone had been driven to insanity to stuff a note into a hole in the wall.*

As the day edged towards later afternoon, Victoria paced her cell like a caged tigress, her mind circling a terrible truth: *A single day in this hell, and already my thoughts are unravelling. No wonder chained asylum inmates shriek at phantoms.*

A fresh wave of fury burned through her veins as Wilby's face swam before her. "That festering son of a pox-ridden whore," she hissed into the gathering dark, her fingers curling into claws. "I'll see his guts spilled before this is done." *And Simon? My God. How could he?*

The days oozed by like cold molasses, each one a mirror image of wretched monotony—jabbing at the lock, wrenching the manacle, scouring every inch for escape.

After her silent supper, which she forced down like medicine, she would collapse onto the lumpy mattress, drifting into exhaustion-thin sleep until dawn.

By the fourth interminable day, she had begun notching the plaster with her ruined nails—four ragged lines now, like scars on the wall.

At her weakest moments, staring at the sliver of sky beyond the bars, despair whispered: *It's hopeless.* But then she'd see little Mary's gap-toothed grin or hear Mabel's hopeful voice, "You are the strong, amazing, beautiful woman you always were." She remembered her mother's hands holding hers at Hanwell—even Annabelle's haughty glare was punctuated with comments like, "You, my dear, are stronger than you realize." *Wilby might be a troll*, she asserted silently, rubbing the raw skin around her manacle, *but I'll be damned if I let that wretch grind me to dust.*

After the midday tray was delivered on the fourth day, Victoria returned to the crumbling breach in the wall and resumed her clawing. Hours passed with only gritty plaster powder loosening, until, without ceremony, a jagged crack snaked from the hole's upper corner diagonally downward. She wedged her raw fingertips into the fissure, pulling until a palm-sized chunk of wall broke free with a dull snap.

She reached through the breach, her hand trembling as it brushed against decades of filth: matted grime, dry husks of insects, a brittle rib of mouse bone. Her fingers fumbled along the inner edge of the cavity, searching blindly. *A second layer? A passage? Anything... Nothing.* Just the empty breath of a long-dead house, trapped behind paint and paper.

She lay on her side, face pressed to the dirty floor, peering into the small hole. The chain bit at her ankle as she shifted, the sharp tug snapping her back—a grim reminder. She could not follow it far, no matter what she discovered in the dark hole. All that effort for a handful of dust. "This is going nowhere!" she cried out in dejected frustration.

A violent coughing fit seized her as plaster dust invaded her lungs. She staggered upright, gulping water straight from the pewter pitcher to clear her throat. "Hell and damnation! This is—" Her voice failed as she mouthed the word: *Hopeless.*

Then her eyes widened.

The dust! She smoothly unfolded the yellowed linen scrap and began carefully sweeping debris into its center with the edge of her palm. Taking the largest plaster fragment, she methodically scraped it into powder with her hairpin. An hour's meticulous work yielded a chalky mound large enough to coat her palm.

Moving with the care of an apothecary measuring poison, she folded the napkin into a tight packet, trapping the powder inside. Then she sank onto the bed, the linen bundle clutched to her chest, exhausted, yet with the feeling that she had accomplished something—a tenuous plan began to form in her mind.

The sixth morning dawned; its passage marked by six grim scratches on the wall. Victoria sat motionless on the bed, after quickly eating every crumb of her breakfast— poached eggs, toast, and tinned peaches.

In the stillness, she drew slow breaths, rehearsing each step in her mind's eye—the timing, the precise angle, the moment of no return. Then, with the focus of a stage magician perfecting an illusion, she began pantomiming the motions—small, controlled gestures that burned the sequence into her muscles. No room for error. No second chances. She was ready. She had to be.

She knew the timing and sounds of the approaching servant girl—she came thrice daily at mealtimes, ghostly silent. Unlike the servant's near-silent approach, anyone else—especially a man—would announce their presence with the telltale clunks of boots upon the warped, groaning floorboards. It was just a matter of time before Wilby or someone else made their appearance. Now, she needed only to wait—with steady nerves and swift hands.

In the distance, the church bells tolled ten, their mournful chimes drifting faintly through the air. A few minutes later, footsteps approached—the sound she had been waiting for. Victoria took a deep breath, steeling herself. She heard a pause at the door, and then it swung open with a creak, and Wilby stepped across the threshold.

He wore a fine frock coat and cravat, his silver-topped cane tapping against the boards. Arrogance clung to him like perfume. "Victoria, I see you are well."

With tears in her eyes, she pleaded, "Mr. Wil... James, please..." She sobbed as she shifted into a kneeling position on the bed. "I can't stay here any longer. I'll do anything."

Wilby smiled, his lips curling into a grin of victory and lecherous delight. "Well, my girl. We will be leaving today. I daresay we deserve a little time together—just you and I—before the journey begins."

With a seductive allure, she whispered, "James. I know I can make you very happy. If you let me... maybe you'll keep me."

He slipped off his coat and laid it across the table with exaggerated care, then advanced toward her—his eyes gleaming with hunger, his tongue darting across his lips like a beast scenting blood. "We shall see, my dear."

Victoria held his gaze as he drew near. Then, with a quick, practiced motion, she flung a handful of dust into his face. It struck him full in the eyes, nose, and mouth, the fine powder clinging to his lashes, blinding and choking him at once. Wilby recoiled, grabbing at his face with both hands as he sputtered and coughed. "Yo... w... whor—"

As he staggered, blinded, Victoria's right hand shot beneath the blanket, seizing the cold pewter pitcher. With all her might, she swung, the vessel striking the side of his head with a heavy, ringing *crack*. As he reeled, she reversed the arc and delivered a second brutal blow to the opposite side. Wilby's legs buckled, and the bulk of him toppled backward. With a final, crushing impact, his skull struck the edge of the table—a sickening thud silencing him at last.

He crumpled to the ground with a resounding *thump*, lying motionless.

She jumped off the bed near the body, frantically searching through his pockets. *Please, God, let there be keys.* There must be... Her fingers grazed a cold, metallic shape—a ring of keys. Yanking them free, she quickly inserted one into her leg iron—*click*—it snapped open. Tears streamed down her face as her ankle, raw and mottled with bruises, was released.

With only a moment's hesitation, she grabbed Wilby's leg, secured the lock onto his ankle, and fastened it into place with an equally satisfying *click*.

Looking down at Wilby, a triumphant grin curled her lips. "Vile worm," she spat at his still body.

Still clutching the keys, she seized the pitcher in one hand and Wilby's cane in the other, standing with the stance of a warrior armed with makeshift weapons. She didn't know what or whom she might encounter beyond that door—but whatever awaited, she would not go quietly.

She stepped into the hallway and shut the door behind her with a firm, resolute thud.

She dashed down a short hallway—the air musty, her breath ragged—and there, on a chair only feet from her prison, lay her clothes and boots. Setting down her weapons, she dressed as quickly as possible. The feel of the tight bodice against her ribs and the snug fit of her boots brought a strange, grounding comfort—proof that she was herself again.

She hastily descended the straight staircase, each protesting groan a triumphant note in her symphony of escape. At the bottom, she slipped out the back door into a yard behind the main house—a broad, manicured expanse that only made her captivity feel more grotesque.

Quickly orienting herself, she skirted the edge of the estate, keeping low and in shadow, until she reached the front gate. Glancing back once—at the small outbuilding where she'd been held—she resisted the urge to scream.

With no one in sight, she slipped through the gate and out onto the road, teeming with the familiar rhythms of life: the clatter of carriage wheels, the murmur of pedestrians, the bray of a street vendor in the distance. *Oh God, I'm free.* The sounds of the city were a siren song of freedom that lasted only a moment. The danger was still palpable. She was out of the cage, but the hunter was still nearby. She had to disappear.

She ran. Her tangled, fiery hair streamed behind her like a warning flag, her breath coming in gasps. Passersby turned to stare, eyes tracking the wild-eyed woman in wrinkled clothes and unlaced boots holding a pitcher and silver-topped cane.

She turned onto Holland Road, bolting past the Pembroke home, and finally reached Mabel's. She seized the brass knocker and pounded it over and over, frantic.

The door opened, and Samantha blinked in surprise. "Oh, Victor—"

Victoria pushed past her, stumbling into the entryway before collapsing to her knees. Her limbs folded beneath her as she curled into a ball, her weapons and keys falling by her side, the storm of adrenaline breaking at last.

Mabel appeared, Terrance just behind her, and knelt beside her friend, stroking her face. "My God... Victoria, what happened?"

Victoria could only weep—loud, unrestrained sobs that tore from her chest like a wounded animal—a deluge of disbelief and release.

24. Prisoner's Aftermath

London is a modern Babylon.
—Benjamin Disraeli, *Tancred*, 1847

After steadying herself with a sip of brandy, Victoria relayed her ordeal to the horrified trio. As she concluded, Terrance departed for Scotland Yard with all haste, returning with two constables in their distinctive blue uniforms. They escorted Victoria, Mabel, and Terrance back to the Kensington house that had been her prison.

There, they discovered a disheveled Mr. Wilby still shackled to the very room he had constructed into a jail, his once-impeccable waistcoat stained with sweat and fury. "You loathsome bitch!" he spat as the officers restrained him, his humiliation complete, being bested by a woman no less.

The charges read like a ledger of villainy: assault, kidnapping, false imprisonment, attempted white slavery, and conspiracy. Subsequent investigation of his home revealed damning evidence arranged with foolish arrogance on his desk—two first-class passages on the P&O steamship to Bombay, apparently forged medical certificates declaring "Emma Brown" a hysteric requiring confinement, a signed contract with one Mr. Archibald for "transport and maintenance of a delicate patient," and a promissory note from Ranjit Chatterjee for £1,000 in sovereigns, payable upon "safe delivery of the specified commodity." Most astonishing of all—Wilby had made no effort to conceal his scheme.

Upon interrogating the household staff, it became crystal clear that they were wholly ignorant of their employer's crimes. The guest cottage had last been occupied years prior by Wilby's sister, "confined due to violent hysterical episodes"—or so they'd been told. The Spartan furnishings, restraints, and bolted furniture were allegedly installed for her protection. The mute servant girl was her daughter—Wilby's niece—who had known no life beyond caring for her deranged mother. To her, Victoria must have seemed merely another madwoman, or she may even have thought it was her mother. Wilby's sister was said to have died years ago, but the Yard opened a case to investigate, given the scandalous events of the present.

Wilby's private papers revealed a pattern: dozens of coded entries documenting "shipments" of women—all paupers or fallen women—but never a lady of the stature and quality like Victoria. The Yard launched a full inquiry into these suspected white slavery operations, vowing to pursue Chatterjee via diplomatic channels. While Muldoon remained at large, Scotland Yard swiftly confirmed his identity from their rogues' gallery and issued a warrant for his immediate arrest

Notably absent was direct evidence implicating Simon Pembroke. Political correspondence littered Wilby's desk, yet nothing explicitly tied Simon to the plot. Victoria's account of his complicity—delivered under oath at the Magistrates' Court—secured his arrest warrant all the same. The incredibly unusual and scandalous story made front-page news.

THE TIMES

Friday, 4th April 1879

SHOCKING CHARGES OF WHITE SLAVERY
AMONGST THE GENTRY
Lady Victoria Pembroke Alleges Abduction Plot Foiled
by Her Own Hand

LONDON—

A case unprecedented in the annals of English
jurisprudence has rocked society, bridging the divide
between Mayfair parlors and Whitechapel brothels.
Lady Victoria Pembroke (née Barrington) has levied
grave accusations against her husband, the Honorable
Simon Pembroke of South Kensington, and his
associate, Mr. James Wilby, a merchant with extensive
East India Company connections.

According to a sworn deposition before Sir James
Ingham at Bow Street Magistrates' Court, Her
Ladyship was forcibly subdued with chloroform while
visiting her mother at Hanwell Asylum and confined in
a makeshift prison on the Wilby estate. For six days,
her whereabouts were known only to her captors and a
deaf-mute servant girl.

The alleged conspiracy involved her clandestine
removal to Calcutta under fraudulent medical papers
declaring "Emma Brown, a hysteric requiring colonial
convalescence." The grim truth, Her Ladyship asserts,
was indentured servitude to a Ranjit Chatterjee—a
fate narrowly avoided.

In a tale more suited to the Penny Dreadful than the
pages of our respectable publication, Lady Pembroke
described her daring escape: feigning submission, she

234

disabled Wilby by flinging plaster dust into his eyes before striking him senseless with a pewter vessel.

Accompanied by Chief Inspector Frederick Abberline, a magistrate, and this publication's correspondent, Her Ladyship identified the very chamber of her captivity—a converted gardener's cottage where Wilby's allegedly deranged sister once resided. The court observed the iron ankle shackle still bolted to the floor; its rough interior stained with blood.

Mr. Pembroke, when reached at his club, dismissed the allegations as "a hysterical woman unfit to manage her own household, let alone her imagination." He further declared, "My poor Victoria has long suffered from nervous disorders, made worse by recent social enthusiasms and certain radical friendships. It grieves me that her affliction has taken so dramatic a turn."

Wilby, currently held at Newgate, maintains silence. However, documents seized from his residence— including steamer tickets, forged medical certificates, and correspondence referencing "safe delivery of the specified commodity"—have been entered into evidence. The case will proceed to the Old Bailey next month.

Pale and drawn, but resolute, Lady Pembroke addressed the gathered press: "I speak not only for myself," she said quietly as she left the court under police protection, "but for every woman who has been told to hush when she ought to scream."

The nation waits with bated breath.

In the wake of her ordeal, with the specter of Simon's impending arrest, Mabel and Terrance insisted Victoria take refuge in their home. Their guest room—styled in

Victorian elegance and papered in forget-me-nots—became her sanctuary, a stark contrast to the mildewed abyss she had just endured.

After identifying her prison to the constables and witnessing Wilby's snarling arrest, Victoria returned to 86 Holland Road, where Mabel had prepared a bath scented with lavender salts. As the grime of captivity sluiced away, the stains on her psyche remained. Slumped in the tub, she dissolved into shuddering waves of tears—each sob a convulsion that seemed to wrench up fragments of the horror she'd swallowed down those six days. She scrubbed her skin until it was pink and raw, but the feeling of his hands, the odor of the room, the cold bite of the shackles—these had seeped in too deep for any soap to cleanse.

The days slipped by in a foggy daze of disbelief and legal obligations. She gave statements at Bow Street Magistrates' Court, revisited the gardener's cottage to point out the blood-stained shackle, and hid from the ravenous press behind the sanctuary of drawn velvet curtains. Reporters clustered outside like ravens, their shouted questions clawing at her chest until she longed to tear their beaks from out of her heart. In her mind, the word *Nevermore* tolled again and again, an echo she could not silence. She dug her fingernails into her own flesh, as if she could physically scrape the memory from her mind. The horror of it was a film over everything, distorting the world into a haunt of endless threat.

Nights were the longest—the true trial—interminable and thick with dread. Though she now lay in a clean, safe space, sleep remained a battlefield. She kept a battalion of beeswax candles burning through the dark hours, their golden glow warding off the memory of that lightless cell. But when exhaustion finally dragged her under, the terrors surged like a foul tide.

The phantom of Muldoon always came first.

His gin-sour breath slid across her neck as he pinned her shackled body beneath his rancid bulk, his scarred face leering with a lascivious grin. "Funny thing," he rasped, lips peeling back from rotting teeth clinging to inflamed gums, "I actually value me prick more'n me neck." His teeth twisted into fangs as his mouth shredded her bodice, his calloused hands groping the flesh beneath.

Then came Wilby.

He stepped from the blackness, his silver-tipped cane catching firelight in the hellish gleam of his eyes. His tongue flicked over cracked lips as she lay paralyzed, her limbs leaden as coffin lids. His arms slithered over her like vipers, his massive grin a grotesque delight in her utter helplessness.

The scene shifted.

A maharaja lounged on a divan, his oiled chest glistening beneath strands of pearls. A mangy tiger gnawed lazily at the ankle chains of half-naked Indian women who encircled him in silence. "You are my well-bred English rose," he crooned, yanking her chain until she fell to her knees. "I paid for you. I own you."

But perhaps the worst was Westminster.

Simon sat enthroned, draped in Parliamentary ermine, flanked by Wilby and a porcelain-skinned golden-haired duchess clad in Victoria's stolen ball gown—the rich scarlet skirt, the bronze bodice now stretched across another woman's breasts. "Pity you went mad," Simon murmured, sipping claret. "Now you're nothing... no one... worthless." Grime-caked Indian men advanced, rough hands reaching. "Now you're just... merchandise."

In each of these visions, Victoria awoke with a hysterical scream, thrashing violently, as if to fend off the phantoms that haunted her sleep. The bedclothes had twisted around her limbs like manacles, binding her in terror. "Make them stop! No! Stop!" she would cry, over and over, until her throat was raw and aching. More than once, Mabel—roused by the piercing shrieks—would come rushing in, gathering Victoria into her arms and holding her tightly, as if to anchor her to the present. She'd rock her gently, humming half-forgotten lullabies, until the tremors quieted and the bad dreams began to fade.

After several interminable days and harrowing nights, Victoria felt she could not endure another moment. She sat at the window on a mild afternoon in mid-April, staring blankly as birds trilled in the hedgerows and the world beyond the glass burst into a riot of color—greens, blues, reds, and purples in jubilant bloom. The sun warmed her skin, but it couldn't melt the ice that trauma had laid around her heart.

A soft rap at the door preceded Mabel's entrance. Her friend's skirt whispered against the doorframe as she swept in. She pressed a fleeting kiss to Victoria's temple before chirping, "Darling, you're wanted in the parlor."

Victoria twisted a loose thread from her dress around her finger. "I don't think... I... I'm very tired." The words came out leaden, dull as the gray of an overcast sky.

Mabel softly scoffed like a governess scolding a pupil, "Pish-posh! Five minutes won't kill you." She extended a hand.

Reluctantly, Victoria took her friend's hand, letting her lead the way. The grand staircase yawned before them like a precipice, but Mabel's arm anchored her as they descended. At the parlor threshold, Victoria froze.

The room was filled with familiar faces: smiling children from the orphanage, who squealed with delight and ran to encircle her. Little Mary threw her arms around Victoria's waist and beamed up at her with a gappy, radiant grin. "I missed you," she exclaimed happily.

Behind the little ones stood Mr. Mearns, with his ever-kind eyes, and Mr. Whitaker, with his rosy cheeks and Santa-like cheerfulness. The Pembroke family—Clara, Mary, Alice, Maggie, and Gaston—stood together, and at the very back, Annabelle.

Victoria's hands flew to her mouth, her knees buckling under the weight of this unexpected blessing. Mabel's grip tightened, becoming both tether and lifeline.

"Some people who refuse to let you drown," Mabel said, the words husky with shared emotion.

Glistening drops fell freely now, splashing onto Mary's braids as Victoria gathered the girl close. "This..." She swallowed against the lump in her throat, "This is the first day I've believed the world might still hold goodness." Choking back sobs, Victoria whispered, "Oh my God... I... I don't know what to say..." Her face broke into a smile. "Thank you. This means more to me than anything in all of England... in all the world."

The afternoon unfurled like a stolen piece of heaven. Over the next couple of hours, the youngsters embraced her and giggled.

Little Mary thrust her wooden doll forward, now dressed in a satin ball gown, announcing, "Meet Queen Victoria!" Her gap-toothed grin widened when the real Victoria burst into genuine laughter—a sound that startled even herself, so long had it been absent.

There were many warm wishes from the Pembroke family. Gaston told her as he looked her squarely in the eyes, "Tu es forte, ma petite lionne—you are strong." Clara, with a smile and a wink, added, "Don't let any man stop you now, milady." Annabelle approached with a quiet uncertainty, "My dear... well, I don't know what to say. I..." Victoria reached out and held her hand, their eyes meeting, each silently acknowledging what words could not convey.

Mr. Whitaker, his twinkling eyes full of warmth and a genuine grin, offered his sage advice, "Remember that the greatest weapons of battle were made in the hottest forges of adversity." She clasped his hands, eyes brimming with gratitude, "Thank you."

As shadows lengthened across the parquet floor, Mr. Mearns consulted his silver pocket watch and sighed. "The devil whispers lies to survivors," he observed, gathering the orphans with a shepherd's gentle firmness, "but these children? They're living proof you've done God's work. The world needs its angels earthbound a while longer."

At the door, Mary turned back, her doll clutched to her chest. "Will you visit on Tuesday?"

Victoria's smile trembled, "Wild horses couldn't keep me away."

From that day forward, the lifeline Mabel and the others had thrown her transformed into a steadfast anchor upon which her recovery was moored. Over the ensuing weeks, she summoned the strength to visit both the orphanage and her mother.

Her mother had made modest progress, and on occasion, even appeared to recognize her—sometimes offering the faintest of smiles as Victoria sat quietly by her side.

The nightmares still came—the phantom bite of the iron shackle at her ankle, the hissing whispers of demons lurking in the dark—but their claws grew duller with each passing week. As the days grew longer and brighter, by the close of April, she was able to sleep through most nights. Thoughts of Simon still slithered in unbidden, but she pushed them aside. There would be time enough to reckon with her husband's betrayal after Wilby's trial at the Old Bailey.

Standing before her dressing-table mirror, Victoria regarded her reflection with steely resolve, her mind fixed on Wilby. I will see him punished. I will make the world hear how he trades in flesh. And by God, I'll ensure no woman ever fears his shadow again.

Outside, a newsboy's cry rose through the open window—"Read all about it! White slavery scandal shocks London! Respected businessman on trial!"

Her reflection did not waver.

25. Trial and Tribulation

In drawing an inference or conclusion from facts proved,
regard must always be had to the nature of the particular
case, and the facility that appears to be afforded, either of
explanation or contradiction.
—Charles Abbott, *King v. Burdett*, 1820

*O*n a crisp, bright, cloudless morning—the fifth of May, 1879—a large and restless crowd gathered before the soot-streaked facade of the Old Bailey. A current of curiosity and excitement hummed through them, a palpable energy stirred by the sensational trial that had seized the public imagination and dominated every major newspaper.

Victoria sat as rigid as the marble columns that lined the packed courtroom, her white-knuckled hands clenched tightly in her lap. Wedged between Mabel and Terrance amidst a sea of spectators, she remained motionless. The air purred with barely suppressed anticipation, the occasional cough or rustle of petticoats punctuating the low hum.

The twelve jurors—all men, as was the custom of the time—were already seated, their expressions solemn as the Lord Chief Justice, resplendent in his scarlet robes, ascended the bench with grave ceremony. Across the aisle, Wilby allowed a smirk to creep across his face as he exchanged words with the renowned Montagu Williams, Queen's Counsel, who adjusted his powdered horsehair wig with the casual expertise of a man steeped in the grand traditions of the legal profession. Victoria's own barrister, Sir Hardinge Giffard, Queen's Counsel, offered her a reassuring nod. His sharp, intelligent eyes betraying nothing but the steady determination of a seasoned advocate.

The clerk rose, his black-robed figure cutting a somber silhouette against the dark, age-polished oak-paneled walls of the court. He began to read solemnly, his voice echoing beneath the high vaulted ceiling.

"James Reginald Wilby, you stand indicted before this court."

The clerk's voice echoed in the hushed room. He paused, letting the full weight of the name settle, before continuing.

"For that you, on the fifteenth day of March in the year of our Lord eighteen hundred and seventy-nine, did unlawfully, willfully, and with malice aforethought seize, confine, and carry away one Lady Victoria Pembroke, a peeress of this realm, against her will."

Another deliberate pause filled the air.

"And by means of foul artifice—namely, the administration of chloroform and the use of forged medical certificates—with intent to forcibly transport her beyond the seas, namely to the East Indies, there to be sold into a condition of servitude most vile and contrary to the laws of God and man."

A weighted silence fell over the courtroom as the clerk finished, his words hanging in the air like a sentence already pronounced. At the urging of his barrister, Wilby rose, his polished demeanor at odds with the gravity of the charge.

"How plead you, James Reginald Wilby?" the clerk intoned. "Guilty or not guilty?"

Drawing himself up with theatrical defiance, Wilby declared in a voice that rang clear across the gallery, "Not guilty, my lord!" His words seemed to hang in the suddenly electrified air, followed by an instant of stunned silence before the gallery erupted in a storm of whispers and gasps as spectators leaned forward in their seats. The journalists in the press gallery scribbled furiously, their pens scratching against paper.

Sir Giffard rose and approached the jury box with deliberate calm. He moved slowly before the twelve men, meeting each gaze in turn. A stark cross-section of Victorian society sat before him—a butcher, a dock worker, a clerk, a shopkeeper, even a retired colonel— each watching intently as the Queen's Counsel paced before them, his silk robe whispering against the sawdust-strewn floor.

He cleared his throat and began in a low, resonant tone: "My lords and gentlemen of the jury,"—he paused, letting the weight of silence settle—"today, you shall bear witness to a conspiracy so vile, so grotesque in its machinations, that it would shame even the most lurid tales of the penny dreadfuls." He turned sharply to point at Wilby. "Before you sits a man who cloaks himself in the guise of respectability—a merchant of means, a pillar of society—yet beneath that veneer lies a heart blackened by greed and deceit." With a measured sweep of his arm toward Victoria, he declared, "The Crown shall prove, by ironclad evidence, that this man employed the vilest of means—chloroform to still her voice, manacles to bind her limbs, and forged certificates bearing the names of a fictitious physician—all to reduce Lady Victoria Pembroke, a noblewoman of this realm, to mere chattel, destined for foreign bondage."

As the gasps and whispers of the spectators died down, Sir Giffard turned toward the bench. "My Lord, with the court's permission, I call the victim of this outrage—Lady Victoria Pembroke to testify."

The Lord Chief Justice waved a liver-spotted hand. "Let the witness be sworn."

A court usher escorted Victoria to the witness box. Though the shadows beneath her eyes betrayed the toll of her ordeal, her posture remained poised—her back straight as an iron bar, her white-gloved hands resting lightly on the oak railing.

Sir Giffard approached, his tone low and steady. "Lady Pembroke, please take us back to the evening of March fifteenth."

Victoria took a measured breath. "Gentlemen of the jury... what I shall recount may strain belief. But I swear upon my mother's soul and the Holy Gospel—every syllable I speak is truth, branded upon my memory as though by fire."

A reverent hush settled over the courtroom, broken only by the scratch of the court reporter's pen.

"That evening at Hanwell Asylum, as I stepped into the dusk, I carried with me the fragile hope that my mother's fleeting recognition had rekindled." Her voice, initially soft as old parchment, hardened like forged steel. "But the carriage awaiting me was a wolf in sheep's clothing—the wrong coachman, the wrong horses... yet by the time I sensed the trap, the jaws had already snapped shut."

Sir Giffard leaned forward, his wig casting a shadow across his face as he gave her a nod of encouragement.

"Describe the moment of your abduction, Lady Pembroke."

Victoria closed her eyes, her fingers tightening around the railing as if it alone could anchor her to the present. "A stranger's arm—thick as a hangman's rope—locked about my throat. A rag drenched in chloroform was forced against my face... it reeked of overripe pears left to fester in the sun. I fought—God Almighty knows I fought—but the world dissolved into spinning shadows and that scarred demon's grin leering through the haze. For one horrifying instant, I truly believed Lucifer himself had come to claim me!"

A collective shudder ran through the hushed hall. Several spectators clutched at their throats in sympathy; the butcher in the jury box and several others in the gallery made the sign of the cross with trembling fingers.

Sir Giffard lowered his voice to a hush that compelled listening. "And when you awoke?"

Victoria's breath hitched, as though the memory alone could resurrect the poison in her veins. "My skull split asunder with pain, my stomach heaving as if I'd swallowed hot embers. My limbs lay heavy as lead shot, still shackled by the chloroform's venom." Then, like a storm breaking, her voice rose, sharp with revulsion: "And there he stood—Muldoon, I later learned his name—leering down at me like someone appraising a side of mutton at Smithfield Market. I found myself manacled like a rabid dog!"

The room erupted in pandemonium. A woman's shriek pierced the din; a reporter near the front scrambled to blot his spilled ink.

The Lord Chief Justice's gavel struck like a pistol shot. "Order! I will have order in this court!"

Victoria's words cut through the chaos like a blade. "I was wrong. That scarred brute was no devil. Merely the devil's footman. The true architect of this horror—" She whirled, her finger leveling at Wilby like a dueling pistol. "—the Devil himself, soon entered that room, smirking over his silver-topped cane!"

Another explosion of shouts. The judge's face turned purple as he hammered the bench. "One more outburst, and I'll clear the gallery!"

Victoria continued, each word dripping with righteous fury. "He boasted that he had persuaded my own husband—for the sake of his precious political career—to sign away my life. That I would be shipped to India like a crate of merchandise, while people I knew would believe me as another hysteric who'd thrown herself into the Thames." Her voice dropped to a whisper that somehow carried to the farthest corner of the room. "And before the sale—as if I were a horse, or a piece of furniture—was done... he promised to take his pleasures with me—not as a lover, but nothing more than a lecherous trophy."

The gallery's roar was volcanic, a seething, thunderous eruption of outrage that rattled the very rafters of the court.

Wilby's barrister rose with a theatrical sigh. "My Lord, must we entertain these fantastical tales? The witness clearly suffers from the same female hysterics that afflicted her mother. This is the ranting of an overwrought imagination!"

Sir Giffard was on his feet before the final syllable faded. "My learned friend insults not only Lady Pembroke, but this court's intelligence! Does an overwrought imagination also forge iron manacles?" He snatched the shackle and chain from the evidence table and dropped it.

The loud clang against the wooden table silenced the room. "Or perhaps the defense would care to explain why this melodrama matches precisely the testimony of Hanwell's head gardener, who saw the abduction? Or the dockside worker who'll swear under oath he was offered a highborn lady's passage to Calcutta?"

A deadly silence fell. Even the judge seemed to hold his breath.

Sir Giffard solemnly faced Victoria, "Please continue. How did you escape?"

Victoria lifted her chin high, "With a hairpin, plaster dust, and a pewter pitcher, but chiefly, gentlemen, I escaped with the cold determination of a woman who refused to be inventoried alongside tea and opium in some trader's manifest." Pausing to take in a deep breath, she explained, "When I struck the devil down—" she turned to stare directly at Wilby, "—I confess I thought about stopping his last breath, but my values—unlike his—forbade me from doing what he would have done without hesitation. She hoisted her still-red ankle onto the witness box railing, the mark of the manacle visible to all, "I understood how easily one might become the monster they believed I was."

A collective gasp swept through the gallery like a winter's gale, and then erupted. The judge's shouts for order went unheard as Victoria let out a breath of relief as she finished her testimony.

Through the maelstrom, Victoria remained statuesque—her ordeal laid bare. As the bailiffs struggled to restore order, she exhaled a shuddering breath of liberation that carried six days of terror into the ether.

After calm and quiet fell over the court, Montagu Williams rose with the grace of a dueling master retrieving his pistol. His silk robe whispered across the floor as he approached the witness box. "My Lady," he began, his voice dripping with false kindness, "I perceive you are quite overwrought. Would the court's indulgence grant you a moment to collect your scattered nerves?"

Victoria's white gloved hands flexed against the oak railing, the wood creaking slightly. "No. Thank you."

Williams tilted his head, his powdered wig catching the gaslight, "Are you quite certain? These proceedings could adjourn briefly to spare your delicate constitution."

"No. Thank you," Victoria repeated, each syllable sharp as a stiletto.

With a sly smile, Williams pivoted. "How remarkable that a gently-reared lady—supposedly comatose from chloroform—recalls conversations with such... theatrical precision." He circled the witness box like a vulture. "Can you explain this exquisite recall?"

Victoria's eyes flashed emerald fire. "If you had endured—"

"Ah!" Williams slashed the air with his hand, his signet ring glinting. "But by your own sworn testimony, you were shackled by the chloroform's venom." He turned to the twelve men, his robe swirling dramatically. "Those were your precise words, were they not?"

"Yes, but—"

Williams executed a perfect about-face and marched to the defense table. "With the court's permission." He lifted a leatherbound volume, its pages marked with scarlet ribbons. "This is the seminal work *On Chloroform and Other Anaesthetics* by Dr. John Snow—a well-respected medical book."

The courtroom quietly leaned forward as one.

Balancing the book in one hand while waving his other about like a preacher with his Bible, Williams read, "Upon awakening, patients often experienced disorientation, confusion, and difficulty recalling events leading up to and following the anesthetic state. Memories may be confused and fragmented. Patients can have difficulty separating dream from reality." He snapped the book shut with the authority of a judge's gavel. "Given this irrefutable medical certainty, isn't it likely you were confused? That in your confused state, you conjured the specter of the Devil himself and unjustly fixed it upon my client, the respected businessman, Mr. Wilby?"

Victoria's knuckles turned corpse-white against the railing. "No! He and his henchman did—"

"Or perhaps—" Williams mused, catching a juror's gaze, "—isn't it likely that you are suffering from a mental infirmity you inherited from your mother?" He suddenly braced both hands on the witness box, invading Victoria's space. "Isn't it true that much of what you think is true is nothing more than phantasm, hallucination, delusion? Between the chloroform and your inherited hysterics, how can this court trust anything you claim is true?"

Victoria rocked back as if struck, her breath coming in short gasps. "No! You weren't there!"

Williams straightened and smiled, "Precisely, Mrs. Pembroke. I was not. Nor was anyone else. We have only your... colorful narrative." He smoothed his waistcoat, the embroidered silk gleaming. "No further questions for this... imaginative witness."

Victoria lowered herself into her seat, the wood of the chair feeling like an ice block against her burning skin. She kept her eyes fixed on her lap, unwilling to meet the stares of the onlookers.

The silence that followed was cathedral-like in its absoluteness—so profound one might have heard a spider weaving its web in the rafters.

Over the course of the day, Sir Hardinge Giffard called forward several witnesses for the defense, each one methodically cross-examined by Montagu Williams

First to take the stand was Simon le Maire, head gardener at Hanwell Asylum, his work-roughened hands clutching his cap as he spoke. "I were pruning the hedge-rows by the east gate when I seen 'er ladyship come out," he testified in a thick Berkshire accent. "Proper lady, she were—walkin' all graceful-like toward 'er carriage. Then this great hulkin' brute of a man comes up behind 'er and covers 'er face." The gardener's tone dropped to a horrified whisper: "He grabbed 'er round the middle like she were a sack o' turnips and flung 'er inside. The 'orses took off at a gallop fit to wake the dead."

Williams rose to cross-examine, positioning himself to subtly block Victoria from the gardener's view. "How can you be sure this wasn't someone else you saw? Can you describe Lady Victoria in detail?"

The gardener attempted a fumbled response, stammered, and fell silent, to which Williams quickly interjected with a feigned sigh, "Perhaps not so sure? No more questions for the witness."

Next came Mr. Archibald, a shipping clerk from the East India Docks, his spectacles glinting as he produced a leatherbound ledger. "The defendant booked first-class passage on the SS Bengal Tiger departing March twenty-second," he stated primly, adjusting his cravat. "When I inquired about the female companion listed on the manifest—an Emma Brown—described as suffering quote 'severe hysterical fits'—Mr. Wilby assured me the poor creature would be sedated for the voyage." His nose wrinkled in distaste. "Said she ranted all manner of inanities and needed to be ignored and left be."

With practiced ease, Williams rose, smiled, and politely asked, "Isn't it possible that this trip was arranged to provide respite for a lady suffering from severe hysterical fits, traveling under an assumed name to spare Mr. Pembroke public embarrassment?"

Mr. Archibald quietly began to reply, "Yes, of course— "

Williams finished quickly, cutting him off with a gracious nod, "Thank you. No more questions."

Forgery expert Mr. Carlson took the stand next, his cadaverous frame seeming to float within his academic robes. "The document purportedly signed by Dr. Elias Whitcombe of St. Bartholomew's Hospital is expertly fashioned," he declared, holding up the fake medical certificate. "It matches genuine paper stock. However—" He paused with theatrical flair, "—no Emma Brown appears in any asylum registry from Cornwall to Newcastle. Moreover, the doctor listed does not exist—he is a fiction."

With effortless charm, Williams approached the witness box, grinned, and asked, "Could it not be that this journey was arranged to offer a reprieve for a lady afflicted with violent hysterical episodes, requiring travel under an assumed name to protect Mr. Pembroke's reputation?"

Mr. Carlson, "That would be quite irregular and of—"

Williams quietly interrupted, "Of course, Doctor. But again, given the sensitive nature of the situation, a good possibility?"

Mr. Carlson, adjusting his robes, muttered, "I suppose someone might be inclined to do something—unorthodox."

Williams concluded briskly, "Thank you. I have no further questions."

Next, Dr. Charles Garland's medical testimony sent shockwaves through the packed gallery. The distinguished physician—his muttonchop whiskers quivering with indignation—described examining Victoria upon her escape. "The abrasions on her ladyship's ankle exhibit the distinctive pattern of a wrought-iron manacle," he pronounced, displaying a detailed anatomical drawing. "Note the crescent-shaped contusions here and here—precisely where the hinge would pinch. Furthermore," his voice grew somber, "the muscle atrophy, dehydration marks, and light sensitivity all confirm prolonged confinement in darkness. In my professional opinion, these injuries could not possibly be self-inflicted."

Williams arose and asked with an air of confidence, "Good doctor, can you ascertain why she was perhaps restrained? Haven't you seen similar symptoms in hysterical patients?"

Dr. Charles Garland confidently replied, "Yes. I have seen this in other patients with a variety of mental infirmities."

Williams smirked, "I see, you say, 'in other patients,'" slowly accentuating, *other patients* and offering a slight bow. "Thank you, Doctor. I have no further questions."

Finally, Sir Hardinge Giffard stood up, holding aloft a document for all to see. "I hold here a promissory note from a Mr. Ranjit Chatterjee for £1,000 in sovereigns, payable upon safe delivery of Mrs. Pembroke. One thousand gold sovereigns!" he thundered, his voice ringing through the hushed court. "Imagine it! Clearly, this was not for any alleged medical treatment, but for the vile sale of Mrs. Pembroke into white slavery!"

Williams chuckled as he rose, bracing his hands firmly on the defense table. "No such mention is made of Mrs. Pembroke in this document!" he declared, his tone laced with incredulity. "That is the product of the prosecutor's imagination! The paperwork plainly concerns armaments and other goods deemed necessary for the advancement of the British Empire. Nothing more."

Yet, as the damning testimony and physical evidence accumulated through the course of the day, Wilby's smirk withered, fading like a candle guttering in a tomb's chill air.

As the final witness was dismissed, the tension in Victoria's shoulders lessened by a fraction. She allowed herself a single, deep breath, the first she felt she'd taken all day. The mountain of evidence was there for all to see.

Judge Simmons, expression stern, briskly banged his gavel. "This court shall reconvene on the morrow. Until then, we stand adjourned."

26. Wilby Strikes Back

All we see about us, Kings, Lords, and Commons, the whole machinery of the State, all the apparatus of the system, and its varied workings, end in simply bringing twelve good men into a box.
—Henry Brougham, 1828

*T*he second day of the trial crackled with tension more intense than the first; the air was thick with anticipation, both inside the overcrowded courtroom and among the restless crowds gathered in the street beyond. The first day had drained Victoria, leaving her feeling hollowed out, but her steadfastness had only hardened into something cold and sharp. She would see this through. Now, as she waited for the defense to present its case, her conviction hardened. *That vile wretch, Wilby, will answer for the depravities he inflicted upon me.*

Beside her, the formidable Sir Hardinge Giffard, Queen's Counsel, exuded quiet confidence. He had reassured her repeatedly that their case was strong, the proof damning and irrefutable. Yet he also warned her to brace for battle. Leaning in, he cautioned, "I know Montagu Williams quite well. He is a shrewd man, masterful in the art of persuasion, and he will pull no punches in defending his client. You must remain composed, no matter how he provokes you. If he can goad you into reacting, he will paint you as a hysteric before the jury—and that is precisely what he wants and we certainly do not. The case could easily pivot on your equanimity."

Victoria nodded, steeling herself. She would not give Williams, and for that matter, Wilby, the satisfaction. Let him twist his words and spin illusions—she would meet them with the unflinching stillness of ice.

Montagu Williams rose and advanced with a serpent's grace, his black silk gown rustling against the oak bench as he approached the jury box with prowling elegance. He paused before each juror—the butcher, the shopkeeper, the retired colonel—allowing the weight of his gaze to linger on their faces

"Gentlemen of the jury," he began in a quiet, reserved voice, "my client stands before you—guilty." A whisper of shock rippled through the gallery. "Guilty. Guilty. Guilty!" The whispers swelled into gasps, and the twelve men appeared visibly confounded, some narrowing their eyes, others letting their jaws fall slack.

"Guilty!" The defense counsel repeated, slapping the hardwood rail hard enough to make the clerk's inkwell quiver.

"Guilty of being an esteemed businessman and a gentleman! Guilty of expanding Her Majesty's commercial empire across the breadth of the globe! Guilty of aiding a man of unassailable character, his friend and business partner—the Honorable Simon Pembroke—destined not only to be a distinguished member of Parliament but, dare I say, a future Prime Minister of the realm! Guilty!"

Stepping back, he drew a deep breath and continued, now more softly. "And how, pray, did Mr. James Wilby assist Mr. Pembroke? Ah—that is the crux of the case. His wife had become increasingly unstable—hysterical, by any reputable physician's account. So, as any good friend and trusted associate might, he volunteered to assist this fine man in securing his wife—" He wheeled toward Victoria, motioning to her with a flourish both graceful and contemptuous, "—God pity her—so that she might not pose a danger to herself... or to society at large."

Now raising his voice again, gesturing toward the hushed gallery and the twelve men, "To us! All of us! What loyal Englishman among you would not act to protect his friend's deranged wife—especially when her own mother languishes in a lunatic asylum?"

The gallery erupted into murmurs and knowing nods. Victoria pursed her lips, but otherwise remained motionless.

Lowering his voice again, almost conspiratorially, he continued. "Yes, we concede that Mrs. Pembroke was taken to a house the accused had previously used to confine his own unfortunate mad sister, that she might be restrained with care before formal commitment proceedings could be undertaken. It is, indeed, that simple." He scanned the twelve men once more. "Each of you—men of honor, bound by friendship and duty— would have done the same. Would you not?"

With a final pivot, his gown billowed like a ship's sail, and he fixed Victoria with a look of well-rehearsed pity. "Let us speak plainly. Mrs. Victoria Pembroke's tale—and I have no doubt she believes it—is nothing more than the fevered delusion of a woman plagued by maladies of the mind. And we shall demonstrate this as fact. Will you trust the word of such a woman over the unimpeachable reputation of a gentleman? Thank you, my good men, for your discernment—and your impartiality."

With a precise, almost reverent bow, he retreated, leaving silence thick enough to choke on. He waited just long enough for the tension to crystallize before his voice shattered the stillness, "I call forth the esteemed Dr. Gideon Ashford."

Victoria's breath hitched as Dr. Ashford quietly took the stand.

"Good day, Dr. Ashford," the barrister began, his tone butter-smooth. "We are grateful you've taken time from your noble work of healing the afflicted to lend your expertise to these proceedings."

Ashford's reply was practiced and polished, "Of course. It is both my duty and privilege to serve the public in any capacity required."

"Would you kindly enlighten the court as to your qualifications?"

The doctor straightened, his voice expanding to fill the chamber with authority.

"For sixteen years, I have served as director of the Royal Earlswood Hospital, where we provide sanctuary and treatment for those burdened by defects of both body and mind. Our institution stands as a bulwark—offering compassion to the afflicted while ensuring the safety of the public. Additionally, I am regularly consulted by the Royal Surrey County Hospital, an establishment renowned for its cutting-edge medical innovations."

Williams leaned forward, his gown pooling like spilled ink across the floor. "Doctor Ashford," he began, infusing his voice with honeyed reverence, "Your qualifycations and dedication to those who suffer maladies of the mind are unparalleled."

Doctor Ashford nodded curtly, "We at the hospital all work together to the best of our ability."

"Modesty!" Williams chuckled, turning to the jury with a conspiratorial smile. "I believe we all here would agree that you are much too modest." He allowed the compliment to linger, basking in the ripple of approving nods from the gallery.

"You encountered the alleged victim on November 19th of the previous year, did you not?" He flipped a dismissive hand toward Victoria.

Ashford adjusted his spectacles. "Yes. Mrs. Pembroke and Mrs. Hawthorne visited regarding her mother, Sarah Jane Barrington, who suffers from a grave form of melancholia punctuated by violent episodes."

Williams arched a brow. "And you advised against the visit?"

"Emphatically. Given the serious nature of the patient's condition and the daughter's—" His eyes flicked to Victoria, "—evident familial predisposition."

Montagu feigned astonishment. "Doctor! Are you suggesting this woman—" he jabbed a dramatic finger toward Victoria "—has inherited her mother's madness?"

"I made no formal diagnosis. However, given the severity of her mother's affliction, and that daughters often exhibit similar disturbances, coupled with my many years of clinical experience, I could surmise that this was a strong possibility."

Williams scowled and shook his head, "Well, it does seem you were entirely correct—"

Sir Hardinge sprang up, his robes flaring like a banner caught in a sudden gale. "My Lord! This is rank conjecture! The good doctor admits he never examined Lady Pembroke, yet presumes to—"

Judge Simmons raised a skeletal hand. "The jury will disregard the last remark as speculative."

Montagu nodded dismissively and continued, "In any event, please describe the rest of your encounter with Mrs. Pembroke."

Continuing in his characteristically dispassionate tone, Dr. Ashford resumed, "Despite my explicit warnings regarding the patient's volatility, I reluctantly permitted a supervised visit—"

Victoria braced herself as she knew what Ashford would undoubtedly say next.

"—But unfortunately, Mrs. Pembroke almost immediately became highly agitated. She then—" he said with a theatrical pause as he turned toward the jury, "—bribed the orderly to grant them access to the restricted wing."

A collective gasp rippled through the room, the din rising as the jurors shook their heads in disapproval.

"This caused a great deal of disruption and, in the end, inflicted considerable distress upon both the patient and herself. I was compelled to have the ladies removed from the premises. It took several hours to restore order to the institute."

A hiss slithered through the crowd, followed by a scattering of boos and derisive mutters.

Victoria's hands tightened together on her lap as she focused on controlling her breathing. Beneath her skirts, her ankles crossed tightly, as if physically restraining the scream building in her chest.

Williams sighed, as if mourning human frailty. "How tragically predictable." He waved a languid hand. "No further questions."

Sir Hardinge Giffard slowly rose and approached the witness box with a smiling confidence that seemed almost leisurely, his robes swishing along the floorboards. "Doctor, are you aware that since Mrs. Barrington's transfer to Hanwell Asylum, her physical and mental condition has markedly improved?"

"She is no longer our patient," Ashford responded curtly.

"According to the attending physicians at Hanwell, she has, in fact, improved considerably." Sir Giffard rested his fingertips lightly upon the edge of the witness box, his voice mild but firm. "Is it not possible, Doctor, that Mrs. Pembroke's actions—however ill-advised in your estimation—were motivated purely by concern for her mother's wellbeing, and that the resulting change in circumstance has led to a positive outcome?"

"We at the Royal Earlswood provide the b—" Ashford began stiffly.

"Of course, Doctor," Sir Giffard interjected smoothly, his interruption wrapped in the silk of courtesy. "But I ask again—is it not possible that Mrs. Pembroke's behavior was the natural consequence of familial devotion, and that it has, in some measure, contributed to her mother's recovery under different care?"

"Well, of course, anything is possible, but—"

Sir Giffard straightened, offering the slightest of bows. "Thank you, Doctor. No further questions."

As the echoes of the courtroom slowly dissipated, Williams sauntered toward the twelve men of the jury, his tone smooth as satin. "Gentlemen," he intoned, then turned toward the judge and finally swept his gaze over the hushed hall. Now we will hear from Mrs. Victoria Pembroke herself regarding her own mental state."

Facing Victoria, he paused, his expression calculating as he gauged her reaction. "In her very own words," he continued, fixing her with an unblinking, predatory stare, as if daring her to flinch.

Confused, Victoria looked to her barrister, who, sensing her distress, stood and said crisply, "Your Honor, I am unsure what Mr. Williams is proposing. Mrs. Pembroke has already given her sworn statement."

Montagu allowed himself a tight, knowing smile as he sauntered back to the defense table. "Well, we shall indeed hear from Mrs. Pembroke, but not from her lips—" he declared, producing a worn, brown, leatherbound diary from underneath a sheaf of papers and holding it aloft like a trophy, "—but from her personal journal!"

Victoria's heart skipped, her eyes grew to the size of teacup saucers, and her entire being froze in a suffocating wave of anxiety. *My God in Heaven! How did he get that?*

Smiling triumphantly, Williams opened the leatherbound book to a page marked by a thin red silk ribbon. "I have no desire to embarrass Mrs. Pembroke," he declared with mock sincerity, "however, one entry in particular is vital to this case."

The entire courtroom froze, breathless, every eye riveted to Victoria, as if moving in unison with her mounting horror.

Clearing his throat and scanning the twelve jurors with a slow, deliberate gaze, he read aloud. "Mother suffered from melancholy after Father's death, and she never recovered. She remains confined at the Royal Earlswood Hospital, a shadow of the woman she once was. Am I doomed to the same fate? Is this the beginning of some inherited madness, or perhaps hysteria? The very idea fills me with dread."

With devastating finality, Williams snapped the diary shut, the sharp crack echoing through the chamber like a cannon.

Montagu repeated slowly, "Mrs. Pembroke's own words—Is this the beginning of some inherited madness, or perhaps hysteria?" He paused dramatically, then slammed the leatherbound book hard against the table with a resounding thump that echoed through the court, "I think we all know now that even the so-called victim knew she had slipped into insanity," he sneered, finishing with a disjointed, mocking flare, "Just—like—her—mother!"

The room was as silent as the grave. Even the scratching of pens had ceased.

The stunned Hardinge leaned over and whispered urgently to Victoria, "Is this your journal?"

Victoria could only nod, her face pale, her eyes staring forward in mute shock.

"Your Honor," Sir Giffard called out, regaining his composure, "we respectfully request a recess to examine the authenticity of this so-called personal journal."

Judge Simmons banged his gavel twice, the sound breaking the eerie stillness. "The court is in recess for ten minutes."

Williams deftly handed the book to Hardinge, who immediately opened it to the marked entry. His eyes narrowed slightly as he read, his free hand absently stroking his jawline in thought.

Ascertaining the contents, he leaned over and whispered urgently to Victoria, "Mrs. Pembroke, you must compose yourself and fully grasp the gravity of this development."

Victoria drew in a deep, steadying breath, struggling to master the pounding of her heart.

With a look of measured compassion, Giffard continued, "You must take the stand and explain what you wrote.

You must do so with confidence—with clarity—and above all, without emotion."

Gripping her shoulders gently but with crystal-clear urgency, he added, "Do you understand? The entire case may hinge upon your conduct in these next few moments."

A cold, sharp fear cut through her. She bit down on her lip, the metallic taste of blood a tiny, grounding pain against the depth of this unexpected betrayal.

Mabel, who had sat quietly through most of the proceedings, reached over and grasped her trembling hand. "Victoria," she said gently, her voice a lifeline, "you can do this."

Facing Mabel, Victoria clutched her friend's hands. Mabel's eyes were an anchor, and Victoria felt a resurgence of bravery steady her. "I will," she whispered fiercely. "I can do this."

Judge Simmons banged his gavel twice, his expression grave. "Court is now back in session," he declared briskly. "How do you wish to proceed, Sir Giffard?"

"Your Honor, I call Mrs. Pembroke to the stand to elucidate what she had written in her journal."

Sir Giffard nodded curtly and passed the book to Victoria, who rose and slowly approached the stand.

She sat and opened the leatherbound book, her limbs quivering beneath the taut fabric of her sleeves.

Reading the words quietly to herself, a fierce determination began to kindle deep within her chest. *This is all because of that horror, Wilby. I must not falter. I shall not falter.*

Sitting tall, her back as straight as a ship's mast, she declared, "Gentlemen of the jury, I can verify that this is indeed my private journal."

A ripple of shocked reaction stirred through the courtroom.

"These are—or rather, were—my private thoughts. Thoughts I wrote down in an attempt to make sense of a world that had grown increasingly perilous to me."

She moistened her lips and continued, "I believe this is something many people discreetly do as they attempt to understand their own experiences and determine the course of action they must take."

Gathering her resolve, she pressed on, "I found solace in committing my reflections to paper, and in this particular entry, I was grappling with the lewd advances of Mr. Wilby at a charity ball I attended this past autumn."

Feeling ever more confident, her voice stiffened with controlled indignation as she read directly from what had once been private musings.

'The occurrences and revelations of last night were, to say the least, profoundly disturbing. Mr. Wilby's penetrating and lurid stare was unlike anything I have ever experienced before. It felt as though his gaze reached into the very depths of my soul, leaving me exposed and vulnerable. What could it all mean? He has always struck me as pompous, yes, but even at the business dinner, his eyes never held such lewdness—no, such imposing domination. That was the feeling, unmistakable and chilling.'

Looking up from her journal, she said, "For a fleeting moment, I doubted myself—as anyone might wonder if what they felt was but the product of imagination. Yet it was certainly not! And as I wrote in my journal following my self-examination for madness—'No! I know what I felt. It was real.'"

Victoria got to her feet, her bearing regal and unwavering, and turned to face Wilby directly, repeating in a clarion voice, "No, I am not mad!"

She continued, her voice now hard as tempered steel, "From the very beginning, this man fixed upon me with the mind of a predator. Ultimately, he kidnapped me, imprisoned me, and treated me as no more than a commodity to be traded and sold—to him, I was no more than a sack of wheat or a box of rivets."

As Victoria released this righteous tirade, Wilby seemed to shrink visibly into his chair, a crimson flush creeping up his neck as he realized he was once again being bested by a woman.

She struck the witness stand railing with her fist, the impact exploding with a resounding crack,

"No! I am not insane! Absolutely not!"

"But this man," she said, pointing an accusing finger at Wilby, "is nothing more than a lewd, arrogant, heartless criminal, utterly bereft of morals, who violated me in the most vile and inhumane manner imaginable!"

"And, gentlemen of the jury," she implored, her voice ringing with passion, "I beseech you to deliver justice in this case!"

Having finished her address, Victoria stood tall and proud, her chin lifted in defiance, as a spontaneous ovation rose from the gallery.

The judge rapped his gavel sharply for order, but the applause continued unabated as a small, triumphant smile touched the corners of Victoria's mouth.

As the commotion in the courtroom finally died down, each of the barristers presented their most impassioned closing arguments. However, after Victoria had turned what Wilby and his counsel had envisioned as their coup de grâce into her stunning deliverance, the verdict seemed all but inevitable. Wilby sat quietly and sullen, his hopes having evaporated like a shallow puddle beneath the relentless sun of the Sahara.

The jury returned in just under an hour—a remarkably short time that spoke volumes. Although Wilby was found not guilty of the charges of attempted white slavery and conspiracy, he was found guilty of the other charges of assault, kidnapping, and false imprisonment. Victoria did not move, absorbing every word of the sentence as a salve on her battered soul. Across the aisle, Wilby seemed to collapse in on himself, his shoulders slumping as the weight of his future came crashing down around him.

"James Reginald Wilby, for your loathsome crimes— the vile assault, the calculated abduction, and the depraved imprisonment of a helpless woman—you are hereby sentenced to twenty years' hard labor and fined one thousand sovereigns, a pitiful sum against the enormity of your disgrace—and may the righteous contempt of all decent men and women dog your steps until the end of your miserable days. Court is adjourned!"

27. An Unforeseen Meeting

It is said that every life has its roses and thorns.
—Charles Dickens, *Hard Times*, 1854

*J*n the days following Wilby's conviction, a quiet sense of justice settled over Victoria. The image of him being led away to twenty years of hard labor was a balm on the raw memory of her captivity. The world was rid of one monster at least. She was deeply gratified to know that others would be spared a similar fate at the hands of someone who had so cunningly masked his monstrous nature behind the curtain of respectability.

Patrick Muldoon had yet to resurface and remained a fugitive, still wanted by Scotland Yard. Whispers on the street suggested he had either fled London or was merely keeping to the shadows.

Victoria knew without question that Mabel was a priceless friend. She had stood by her through every shadowed hour, unwavering and true, and Victoria felt with crystalline certainty that nothing could ever come between them.

Over the next week, Victoria remained in the Forget-Me-Not room, splitting her time between the orphanage and visits to her mother. To Victoria's joy, her mother had begun smiling more frequently—and once, in a moment of unexpected tenderness, she had reached for Victoria's hand as they admired the blooming garden flowers.

Still, one question lingered—what was to be done about Simon?

An officer from Scotland Yard had informed her that the case against her husband had been dropped due to a lack of evidence. There was nothing but the accusation of a convicted scoundrel to suggest his complicity. *Had he known what Wilby was plotting?* Victoria confessed to herself that she truly did not know.

They had not spoken since before the kidnapping—and, in truth, had exchanged barely a word since the disastrous Christmas dinner, now over three months past. Her feelings for Simon had withered. He was no longer the man she had once believed him to be, and she could not imagine how their bond could ever be restored. And yet—despite the hurt, despite the betrayal—she could not fully believe he was a heartless criminal. *Kidnapping? Bartered into sinful servitude?*

To add another intriguing dimension to Victoria's already unsettled days, a curious note had arrived just two mornings prior. The letter was discreetly slipped through the front door's brass mail slot, enclosed in an unremarkable white envelope bearing only a neatly penned, elegant inscription: "To Mrs. Victoria Pembroke." The contents proved no less enigmatic.

Dear Mrs. Pembroke,

I write with the hope that you will grant me a brief audience. Recent events compel me to speak with you in person, as I believe we may find some measure of clarity or resolution through conversation.

Should you be willing, I shall be seated at the corner table of Twinings Tea Shop on the Strand at two o'clock in the afternoon, Wednesday the fourteenth of May. To make myself known without undue attention, I will place a single white rose upon the table before me.

With the utmost respect,

M. Hutchinson

The handwriting was finely sloped and practiced, the ink steady and deliberate—clearly the work of someone educated and refined—certainly not the scrawl of some brutish Muldoon associate. Victoria had turned the letter over in her mind ever since it had arrived. *Who is this Mr. Hutchinson? Some crony of Wilby's? The name stirs no memory.*

She shivered at the thought. Yet nothing in the correspondence carried a tone of menace; rather, it read as a courteous, if cryptic, invitation, and a meeting in a frequented, reputable establishment at that. A public venue on the Strand would hardly be the setting for anything nefarious. No, she resolved, the only way to uncover the truth is to go and meet this Mr. Hutchinson face-to-face.

When Victoria reached *Twinings* on the Strand, the ornately carved wooden doors stood open, framed by elegant white-painted columns on either side. Above the entrance, a polished bronze plaque proudly proclaimed in bold letters: "TWININGS, EST. 1706." Several feet above that, a regal bronze lion—its bronze windswept mane lay in dignified repose, its gaze cast into the distance as if safeguarding the establishment's decades of tradition.

Victoria paused at the threshold and glanced up and down the bustling thoroughfare, scanning for any recognizable faces or lingering eyes. There were none—only the usual hum of midday London.

A few minutes later, the St. Mary's bells tolled twice, the sound echoing above the rooftops, their loud clangs scattering pigeons across the soot-stained sky. Drawing in a steadying breath, Victoria gathered her skirts and stepped purposefully across the threshold of the venerable teahouse.

She stopped just inside the entrance, taking in the whispers and clinking porcelain of the bustling tea room. Most of the tables were graced by pairs or small groups, engaged in low conversation as they savored steaming cups of tea and an assortment of golden scones, tarts, and other confections.

At a front window table, a stout gentleman wearing a brown bowler hat sat alone, a well-folded copy of *The Times* held before his face. He appeared to be deeply absorbed in the editorial page, showing no sign of anticipation or recognition—clearly not awaiting company.

Victoria's gaze drifted along the periphery of the shop, methodically searching the corners, each occupied by animated couples or chattering ladies in groups—save one. In the far back, a solitary woman of unmistakable refinement sat elegantly in a teal silk walking dress accented with a high lace collar. She raised her teacup with practiced grace. Their eyes met, and the woman's teacup froze mid-arc, her eyes fixed upon Victoria with a measured, almost contemplative expression.

On the table before her, a single white rose lay against the polished wood—its stem precisely parallel to the edge of the table. *It hadn't been a man who sent the letter—but this woman.*

As Victoria approached, the woman rose from her seat, offered a polite nod, and gestured to the chair opposite her with a subtle, almost hesitant motion. She was slightly taller than Victoria, with medium-length, straight, chestnut-brown hair. On top of her head, she wore a smart-looking, matching teal bonnet adorned with a small flower and a bow. Her face was well-proportioned, with a thin, straight nose, full lips, and sea-green eyes that perfectly accented her outfit—by all measures, a strikingly beautiful woman.

As they both sat down, it became clear the woman was visibly uneasy. A flush had crept across her cheeks, and her hands trembled faintly as they returned to her lap, clasped tightly together in a vain attempt at composure.

"Mrs. Pembroke," the woman began, her words tumbling out a little too rapidly, betraying her nerves.

"Mrs. Hutchinson, I presume," Victoria replied calmly, her tone contrasting with composed curiosity.

"Miss Hutchinson—Miss Margaret Hutchinson," she corrected herself.

Victoria regarded her with a mildly puzzled look that beckoned the woman to continue.

"Yes, of course... I..." Miss Hutchinson faltered, her hands tightening slightly in her lap. "I had it all arranged in my mind—what I wanted to say—but now..."

Victoria offered a gentle smile and nodded with quiet reassurance. "It's quite all right. Just begin where you feel able."

"I was present at the court—during your testimony... I mean, during the prosecution of that monster Wilby." She paused, gathering herself. "You spoke with such... such contained fire. Not at all the raving hysteric they painted you."

Victoria, her brow slightly furrowed in confusion, inquired evenly, "I am unclear as to the purpose of this clandestine meeting, Miss Hutchinson."

Margaret shifted uneasily in her seat, her gloved fingers twisting in her lap. "Well... it commenced last year... we met... and I am utterly mortified to admit this."

Victoria remained silent, her expression composed but expectant, waiting for her to continue.

"Last August, at a Royal Botanical Gardens soirée," Margaret began again, her voice low and unsteady. "I was introduced to your husband... He never mentioned he was wedded."

Victoria felt as if the air had thickened. For a moment, she remained silent. A flicker of something colder than shock—perhaps confirmation of something she had deeply suspected—passed behind her eyes. Her spine straightened ever so slightly.

"I see," she said, her tone measured.

Margaret rushed on, as though desperate to stem the silence. "Please believe me, I didn't know... Not then... He told me his name was Simon, but never mentioned you— never spoke of a wife at all."

After a moment, Victoria inquired gently, "And when did you find out?"

"October. I was at the Children's Hospital Ball... Simon stopped to talk to me... A woman asked about his dear Mrs. Pembroke. The look he gave her... I fled to the terrace, and he followed. We exchanged heated words out in the night

273

air, just beyond the lanterns, our breath fogging in the cold... He looked flustered and said it shouldn't have happened, and then he turned and went back inside." She paused, taking a sip of tea, "Perhaps he thought I would follow, but instead I left."

Victoria closed her eyes, seeing with terrible clarity Simon's abrupt disappearance that night—the night Wilby had first leered at her during that dance. Later, he reappeared, asked her to dance, and seemed distracted, as if he were looking for someone. As the cold revelation settled into her, it all made perfect sense.

"What shouldn't have happened?"

"The August flirtation... the passionate words that passed between us... the embrace."

Victoria scowled as Margaret spoke, but otherwise remained stationary.

"And that was meant to be the end of it. But then, in January, we crossed paths again—happenstance. He claimed you were... deteriorating like your mother. He spoke of asylums."

Victoria exhaled sharply, lifting her hands to her face and pressing them over her eyes. "Lord in heaven."

"Mrs. Pembroke, I swear it—on my mother's grave—" Margaret's gloved fingers closed around the stem of the white rose, thorns piercing through the fine leather, unnoticed. "Our meetings were chaste. Nothing untoward ever passed between us. He spoke of you frequently— dwelling on what he called your fragile state of mind." Her voice faltered, cracking under the weight of the moment. "I believe... I know he said Mr. Wilby advised that having you committed would serve to protect his political ambitions."

Victoria slowly lowered her hands from her face, her expression turning to stone.

Margaret's voice softened to a tremble. "He is a man of decorum, to be sure—a creature of duty and appearances—but also deeply conflicted."

Victoria's lips pressed into a thin, controlled line. "Did he ever say outright that he planned to have me abducted?"

Margaret's eyes widened. "Heavens, no! At least... not that I ever heard. I can't imagine he would go that far—but then, so much has transpired, so many disconcerting events—what I've read in the papers, what I heard at the trial..." She hesitated, visibly anguished. "I truthfully don't know anymore."

A heavy silence fell between them, filled by the low drone of the teashop conversation and the sharp, occasional clink of a porcelain cup.

Margaret looked admiringly at Victoria. "I had the misfortune of encountering Mr. Wilby on several occasions, and I daresay he was precisely as you described —the Devil himself. He had a way of looking straight through you, as though divining your deepest secrets... I am truly grateful for your valor. Thank you for exposing him."

Victoria studied Margaret anew, no longer as a rival, but as another victim ensnared in Wilby's treacherous designs. The girl's flushed cheeks and trembling voice revealed no artifice—this was not a woman bent on confrontation. This was a soul burdened by regret and quietly offering gratitude.

She placed her gloved hand gently over Margaret's. "I appreciate your coming forward to meet with me. It took no small measure of bravery. I can see now that you're a decent, honorable woman, and I hold no animosity toward you."

Margaret visibly relaxed, a slight smile softening her face.

Victoria stood from her chair. "Thank you. You've given me much to reflect upon. It seems we have both been taught hard lessons these past months."

Margaret rose as well and offered a respectful nod. "Indeed."

28. Simon Says

*I have not broken your heart—you have broken it; and in
breaking it, you have broken mine.*
—Emily Brontë, *Wuthering Heights*, 1847

After the meeting with Miss Hutchinson, Victoria now resolutely knew that she must meet with Simon and resolve how she would proceed with her life. She had sent Simon a brief letter indicating her desire to meet and discuss matters. After several dispatches, they had agreed to meet at Saint Mary Abbots on Friday, the twenty-third of May, at midday. That formal and virtuous setting felt suitable for the seriousness of the conversation.

A few days before their proposed meeting, the Muldoon situation had been settled in a gruesome manner. According to *The Times*, Scotland Yard officially closed the investigation into the death of Patrick Muldoon. His body had been discovered by dockworkers along the edge of the Thames, bobbing along with driftwood, excrement, and other refuse—savagely stabbed, bloated from days in the water, and with his face partially devoured by rats. He was identified by the black silk suit he wore, the inside lapel bearing a monogrammed name: *Patrick Muldoon*.

As reported, investigators surmised that Muldoon, having received a sizable sum for his role in the abduction of Mrs. Pembroke, squandered it on ostentatious clothing—thereby attracting the notice of less fortunate cutthroats. He was, the article stated, "likely set upon by fellow criminals, robbed, murdered, and cast into the river." Victoria let a curt smile cross her face as she read the news—*a fitting end to such a vile brute.*

Victoria stepped out into the oppressive London air, her tightly furled umbrella clutched in her hand as dark storm clouds churned above the rooftops. The stench of horse manure and coal smoke clung to the damp cobble-stones, forcing her to lift her skirts higher than propriety allowed to avoid the most odious piles of refuse along the street.

Near the Pembroke home, a flash of emerald green caught her eye—a splash of color amid the mud and soot. She bent to inspect it, her corset stays protesting the movement, and retrieved a weather-beaten boy's cap, its once-proud pigeon feather now snapped in two. *Where was that scrawny crossing sweeper who usually lingered on these streets?* She scanned the street, but no familiar grime-streaked face appeared.

A cold droplet struck her cheek—the storm's first warning.

She brushed the worst of the gutter filth from the cap and tucked it into her bag. As she dashed toward the cathedral's looming spire, the heavens opened with sudden fury, turning the streets into a quagmire of swirling refuse, ash, and rainwater. Her umbrella snapped open just in time, its black silk canopy blooming against the downpour.

She hurried, skirts swishing and boots splashing, down the slick footpath toward the entrance of the gothic stone church, its soaring spires and elongated stained-glass windows nearly swallowed by the thick fog and pounding rain. She paused briefly beneath the carved

278

stone archway, droplets streaming from the edge of her bonnet, then pulled open one of the towering mahogany doors, collapsing her umbrella with a practiced snap as she stepped into the sanctuary.

As the heavy door closed behind her with a muffled thud, the clatter of the storm gave way to a hush of sacred stillness. A soft golden glow bathed the aisles, cast by scores of flickering candles held aloft in wrought-iron candelabras suspended from the soaring, vaulted ceiling, supported by massive stone columns and ribbed arches. The air was thick with the pungent scent of incense, curling through the four orderly columns of dark oak pews.

A few rows ahead, on the right, Simon sat alone in quiet contemplation, his back straight, hands folded, eyes fixed in somber reflection upon the stained-glass windows that rose in majesty behind the gilded altar, their vibrant colors dimmed by the storm's gloom outside.

As she slipped into the bench next to him, he quietly spoke, looking up at the vaulted ceiling far above. "Do you remember our wedding day?" he asked, his voice barely more than a whisper.

Staring straight ahead, she answered wistfully, "Yes. It was beautiful."

A long silence stretched between them before he spoke again. "How did things go so wrong?"

Victoria frowned slightly and turned her head to face him. "Did you plot with Wilby to abduct me?"

Simon scowled slightly, "No. I did not."

Victoria still frowning, "Then why—."

Simon interrupted, "I made a mistake." Shaking his head, but still facing forward, "A terrible error in judgment. I thought Wilby was a shrewd businessman and trustworthy confidant. I thought... ambitious and perhaps ruthless... but what has recently come out..." His expression darkened, "I had no idea."

Victoria's eyes moistened. "Why should I trust you?"

Simon took a deep breath. "Well, I can't answer that. I'm not sure if I even trust myself."

A silence fell, broken only by the rustle of prayer books and the muted whispers of worshippers.

"How did Wilby get my personal journal?" Victoria asked, not letting the silence linger.

Simon hesitated. "Ahh... when you vanished, I contacted Scotland Yard to investigate, although Wilby advised I would probably find that you had lost your mind and had thrown yourself into the Thames."

Victoria grimaced slightly, her back stiffening.

"The constables suggested searching the home for clues. I assured them they would find nothing, but I was proved wrong as one of them returned with your journal. How it made it from Scotland Yard to Wilby's lawyer's hands... I don't know."

He twisted his mouth askew, "It was... disturbing. That phrase—mausoleum of expectations—is that how you thought of our lives together?"

Victoria sat quietly.

"And your note of how Wilby made you feel at the charity ball last year—that I was a stranger to you..."

Victoria turned; her lips pressed into a thin line. "I know about Margaret."

Simon's head snapped in her direction as he frowned, and then he let out a breath. "That... was a mistake. A rash, impulsive moment. I—"

Her voice rose, trembling with emotion. "My God, Simon. I felt so utterly alone... What were you thinking?"

He matched her tone, his own voice cracking under the weight of suppressed frustration.

"I wanted to build something magnificent—for me, for us. But more than that, I knew I needed to leave my mark on the world. I know men of worth make important contributions. Everyone else is forgotten. Nothing."

"Didn't I matter?"

"No man of vision has ever squandered his life chasing happiness. It is toil, sacrifice, duty that gives life meaning—not joy."

"And Margaret? Was she part of your life of worth?" she snapped.

His face furrowed. "We are born alone and we die alone, Victoria. People forget that. We live as if tomorrow is promised. But it is not. There is only the legacy we leave behind. Margaret was... a moment of fleeting desire. And one I regret."

A tear slowly made its way down Victoria's flushed face. "And how did I fit into your legacy?"

"We have a duty to England—to bring order. To uphold principles. To establish rules that—"

Victoria interrupted thick with emotion, "Like your father? Your father, who followed the rules?"

Visibly angry, "My father was an honorable man. He —"

She finished bitterly, "—let your sister die because he wouldn't listen to his wife. Because he obeyed the rules."

"Damn you!" he barked, slamming his hands against the bench before them. "That's enough—"

The commotion drew a swift response. A sister of charity approached, her habit whispering across the stone floor. "Quiet," she commanded sternly. "This is a house of worship. We do not tolerate blasphemy here."

Simon lowered his eyes, lips drawn tight. "We beg your forgiveness, Sister."

She nodded curtly. "If you must profane, do it elsewhere." She crossed herself and departed as silently as she had arrived.

The stillness that followed was rigid with words unspoken. After a long moment, Simon murmured,

"My father was a great man. If I could be half the man he was, I would consider myself fortunate." He squared his shoulders. "This matter is closed."

She frowned slightly, her voice barely carrying. "That is your father speaking. You don't—"

He turned sharply, his gaze hard with anger. A look that spoke volumes.

Another tear followed the furrow of the first, leaving a second glistening streak. "You thought I was insane," she whispered. "My Heavens, Simon... you... you didn't have any faith in me."

Simon pressed his lips into a flat line. "The doctors say madness in women is hereditary. That's what the literature says. What else was I to believe? That they were all wrong?" He looked upward, then gestured to the vast space of the house of worship. "That everything we've built is based on lies?"

More tears flowed freely. She gave a choked laugh. "There is faith, Simon. And love. But you—you had neither."

He looked at her, utterly perplexed as if she had completely lost her mind.

Victoria lowered her head, wiped her eyes, and rose to her feet. Her voice, though soft, carried, "Goodbye, Simon."

She stood, walked to the aisle, turned, and moved towards the cathedral doors. The only light in the heart of the church came from the storm-dimmed stained glass and the guttering candles, casting their final moment in a wash of sorrowful color and shadow.

Simon half-rose, then stopped, frozen in place as he watched her go. The great doors opened and closed behind her with a hollow thud—a sound like the lid sealing a tomb.

He sank back into the pew, shoulders slumped, eyes vacant. Utterly alone.

29. The Nineteenth of June

*That was a memorable day to me, for it made great
changes in me. But it is the same with any life. Imagine one
selected day struck out of it, and think how different its
course would have been.*
—Charles Dickens, *Great Expectations*, 1861

ictoria sat quietly at the writing desk in the Forget-Me-Not room, holding the emerald green cap with its cracked feather in her hands as if it were a sacred relic. She had searched sporadically for the mysterious boy, but he never reappeared. What haunted her most was that she had never asked his name. He had seemed no more than seven years old, with eyes that sparkled every time he bowed and greeted 'Good day, Miss.'

What had become of him? Had he darted into the road and been struck by a passing carriage? Or had he been sent to a factory, or the coal pits in the north, like so many others? She had to accept the bitter truth: she would never know. Life, she had come to realize, was a series of twists and turns, its joys and sorrows interwoven like threads in a fraying tapestry—ever so fragile, and ever so fleeting. That was a lesson Victoria had learned all too well over the past year.

She gently placed the cap into the large steamer trunk at the foot of her bed, which was already neatly packed with her few valued possessions and practical necessities.

Over the past month, she had fostered a correspond-ence with her Uncle Samuel, an exchange sparked by the lengthy, heartfelt letter Mabel had delivered in March. When he and his wife, Aunt Olivia, suggested Victoria come to live on their family farm just south of Leicester, she had initially dismissed the idea. But as the days wore on—and with the summer air in the city more stifling than ever—she realized that this might be the very path she needed to walk. A change from the trap of London propriety to the rural pace of country life might offer the peace she had long imagined: babbling brooks, boundless fields, and the rarest of treasures—freedom.

She had consulted Mr. Whitaker regarding the legal documents she needed to complete before traveling north. A portion of the compensation from the Wilby trial had been disbursed, and though modest, it would suffice to finance her journey and help her settle at the farm.

To her astonishment, Simon received and signed the annulment with unexpected grace. He gave a curt nod and wished Victoria well, his composure held, save for a single muscle twitching in his jaw and a sheen in his eyes that he blinked away, refusing to let it fall. With a final deep breath and a faint, wistful smile, he turned and exited Mr. Whitaker's law office without another word.

She had also had tea with Annabelle at *Twinings*, where they shared a pot of oolong and a plate of scones. Annabelle was more relaxed than Victoria had ever seen her. Despite the dissolution of the marriage, she admitted —with rare candor—that without the oppressive pres-ence of that "pompous blowhard" Wilby, Simon might yet return to himself. She spoke kindly, even fondly, saying, "I told you that you were stronger than you realized." And when they parted at the teashop's door, Annabelle did something truly unexpected: she hugged Victoria, offered her a grin, and added with a laugh, "Perhaps I'm not quite the old shrew you once believed me to be."

She also received a visit from the Pembroke household staff—Gaston, Clara, Mary, Alice, and Maggie—for one final farewell. She hugged each of them warmly, one by one, and asked them to reach out should they ever find themselves in need. From the modest compensation awarded after the Wilby case, she presented each of them with two gleaming gold sovereigns, a gesture of heartfelt gratitude for their unexpected and dearly treasured friendship.

As their eyes glistened with emotion, and even Gaston blinked rapidly to hold back tears, Victoria smiled and offered softly, yet with warmth and conviction, "A small token, for each of you—to bring a little brightness to your days, and to help make your lives all the better."

She and Mabel made their final visit to the orphanage together, arriving with two extra-large crates brimming with treats, books, and garments for the wide-eyed, delighted youngsters. Victoria took time to kneel beside each little one, sharing a kind word or a gentle touch. Before leaving, she took Mr. Mearns aside and promised him solemnly that she would continue to support the orphaned and destitute children of London, no matter where life took her.

As a pledge of that promise, she pressed ten gleaming gold coins into his hand—a generous sum intended for the benefit of the children's home, to be spent as he deemed best. His face lit up with such joy that it seemed to illuminate the entire hall. "God bless you, Miss Barrington," he uttered, voice thick with emotion. "You are truly one of the Almighty's blessings upon us. Thank you—from the bottom of our hearts."

Last week, Victoria visited her mother one final time before her departure for Leicester. She promised she would return often once she was settled and vowed to give her uncle a big kiss from her. To Victoria's surprise, her mother reached across the table and gently embraced her, whispering, "You look just like your grandmother—beautiful, inside and out." The words moved Victoria deeply, tears brimming as she realized that all she had done for her mother was, in that moment, worth more than all the gold in England.

Two weeks ago, Mabel had confided—half blushing, half beaming—that she was with child. "I've been conquered often enough, it seems," she said with a grin. When she shared the news, Victoria threw her arms around her dear friend, peppering her cheeks with kisses as they twirled like wild girls in the parlor. Though the baby would not arrive until the new year, the news brought joy to Victoria's heart and, with it, the final push to surrender her room—soon to be transformed into a nursery—to begin the next chapter of Mabel's life.

It was Thursday, the nineteenth of June, 1879, and Samantha informed Victoria that the carriage had arrived. Victoria cast one last fond glance around the sunlit room, then gathered her skirts and descended the grand staircase with deliberate grace, savoring each step as if committing the house to memory.

At the bottom stood her dearest friend, Mabel—radiant, effervescent, and now unmistakably with child. "Well, it's time for you both to go," Mabel declared, her smile as luminous as ever. Then, placing her hands firmly on her hips and flashing a mischievous grin, she added,

"You'd best visit often, or you'll have me to contend with, Miss!"

Victoria smiled through the sting of tears and embraced her tightly.

"Careful!" Mabel laughed. "There's a child in there!"

Victoria laughed too—a bright, unrestrained burst of joy that bubbled up from deep within her. "I love you, Mabel."

"I love you too," Mabel replied, and then, with a teasing curtsey and a glint in her eye, added, "Queen Victoria."

"You goose!" Victoria chuckled.

Then, glancing about the foyer, she asked, "Speaking of queens—where is that child?"

Mabel called toward the parlor, "Mary! Time to go!"

Mary came bounding in, clutching her treasured doll, her brown hair tied back in a neat ponytail that bounced with every step. She wrapped her arms around Victoria's waist and beamed up at her. She held up her doll and proclaimed, "Mama! We're ready!"

With that, the two of them stepped out the door of Number Eighty-Six, the sunlight bathing them in gold, as they set off to begin their new chapter—together.

30. New Beginnings

Wear a smile and have friends; wear a scowl and have wrinkles. What do we live for if not to make the world less difficult for each other?
—George Eliot, *Middlemarch*, 1871

*T*he journey from Kensington to the railway station by horse-drawn carriage, followed by the Midland Railway's express train to Leicester, consumed the better part of the morning. Yet to young Mary, the entire expedition was a marvel of steam and speed, a torrent of unfamiliar sights, sounds, and smells.

Being an orphan, no one knew Mary's exact age, but Mr. Mearns had estimated she was scarcely five years old when she was brought to the orphanage—a scrappy girl with tangled hair and threadbare clothing. That was nearly two years ago, making Mary now a girl of seven, all energy and impulse, her curiosity as boundless as the countryside rushing past the window.

She pressed her palms against the glass, her breath fogging the pane as she gasped at the rushing panorama of the world—the soot-stained brick of London's outskirts yielding to green pastures, flocks of sheep scattering like tiny clouds, and the occasional red-cheeked boy watching the locomotive thunder by with wonder. She clapped her hands in delight each time the steam engine let loose its piercing whistle, a sound that made her heart leap into her throat with a mixture of terror and delight.

As Victoria watched Mary's raw, undiluted delight, she knew she had made the right choice in adopting the girl who had stolen her heart with a single lemon cookie crumb-smeared smile months earlier—Mr. Whitaker had certified that all the legal papers were properly filed to make Mary her legitimate daughter. That day in the orphanage—the way Mary's grubby fingers had clutched the wooden doll, now christened "Queen Victoria," and how she'd hugged Victoria with a strength that belied her petite frame—had etched itself into Victoria's heart and soul.

Leaning forward, Victoria adjusted the ribbon in Mary's hair and adopted a mock-serious tone. "Now, Mary, we have a matter of great importance to attend to."

With her characteristic boldness, Mary crinkled her nose, the scattered freckles on her cheeks shifting upward, while she bounced on the plush train seat, her boots kicking the air. "What, Mama?"

Victoria's feigned sternness melted into a genuine laugh. "We must declare a proper date for your birthday. Since we don't know the true one, how about today? The nineteenth of June, in the year of our Lord 1872? That makes you seven today!"

"Oh yes, Momma!" Mary agreed, as if bestowing birthdays were an everyday affair.

"And what's a birthday without a gift?" Victoria asked, her eyes sparkling, drawing a small velvet box from her handbag.

Mary's eyes grew wide and unblinking. "Yes! Please!" she squealed, her hands smacking together in a frantic, silent clap.

Snapping open the box, Victoria lifted a delicate silver locket and held it up, letting it dangle before her. "Look closely—it's engraved with your name." The pendant caught the sunlight, throwing a single, brilliant shard of light that wobbled and skittered across the dark wood of the seat-back like a captured star before she placed it around Mary's neck.

The world seemed to halt as Mary stared down at the hanging locket, her lips parted in awe. Then, with a shriek of joy, she launched herself at Victoria, wrapping her arms around her neck with enough force to topple them both backward if the train seat had not stopped them. "My very own treasure!" she whispered, the words flooding out in a stream of pure delight.

Victoria hugged her back, breathing in the scent of rosewater soap and the faint, stubborn tang of coal smoke clinging to Mary's hair. In that moment, the rattle of the locomotive, the soot-streaked windows, even the weight of her past—all of it fell away. There was only this: her daughter's heartbeat against hers. In finding Mary, she had reclaimed a piece of herself she never knew was lost.

After arriving at Leicester Midland Railway Station, a porter hoisted their steamer trunk onto a cart as they stepped onto the broad stone platform. Victoria quickly spotted her uncle Samuel standing alongside a broad, flat milk cart with its four large, spoked wooden wheels caked with the dirt of morning deliveries. The parked cart was hitched to two immense, placid draft horses, their white coats dulled with dust. In the rear, about two dozen gleaming tin milk churns bore brass tags etched with the name "Barrington Farms."

Samuel was a man of average height, clean-shaven, dressed in a modest brown suit and a crisp white shirt, topped with a broad-brimmed white straw hat that shaded his eyes, which crinkled at the corners.

As he stepped forward, he waved. "Victoria!" he called with a grin, pulling her into an enveloping hug that smelled of fresh hay and sunshine. "Gracious, girl, I haven't seen you in... what, six years? Look at you—a grown woman!"

Without pause, he bent down with his face alight with good humor. "And this must be Mary!" he exclaimed, beaming as he gently embraced her. "Are you ready to take a ride out to the farm?"

Mary, wide-eyed and speechless, gave a furious nod, a grin that seemed to split her face in two.

"Uncle Samuel," Victoria spoke, her voice quivering with gratitude, "we're so grateful—for coming to get us... and for taking us in."

"Don't be silly—this is what families are for," he replied warmly.

The porter finished loading their luggage, tucking it securely beside the milk churns. Her uncle extended a hand to help Victoria onto the wooden bench at the front of the cart, then lifted Mary to sit snugly between them. With a familiar, gentle shake of the reins and a few sharp clicks of his tongue, the horses started forward, hooves clunking in rhythm as they set off toward the open rolling hills.

"I hope you're both hungry—your aunt and the ladies have prepared quite a feast," Samuel grinned with a wink.

A genuine smile broke through her tiredness. "I'm truly famished," she remarked, while Mary nodded with gusto. "Me too!"

"As I wrote," he continued, "the farm's grown a good bit since you were last here as a young lady. There's the main house—where you'll both be staying—the barn, the dairy barn, the chicken coops, the hands' quarters... Well, you'll see it all soon enough." He spoke with a palpable, understated pride, his eyes on the road ahead. "It'll be quite a change from London life, I imagine."

Victoria inhaled deeply, the crisp countryside air tinged with the scent of wildflowers and earth. "Goodness—the air! I'd forgotten how clean it smells. You get so used to the coal smoke, soot, and filth in London, you hardly notice it anymore... until you escape it."

Samuel shook his head slightly. "Never understood why Sarah Jane insisted on staying in that city." His tone softened. "Anyway, we've got quite the household out here, and I treat everyone like kin. There's me, your aunt Olivia, and the farmhands—Patrick and his wife, Charlotte; Andrew, Nathan, Russell, Emmett, Benjamin, and Tillie. Don't let them overwhelm you—they'll likely pepper you with questions the moment you step down from the cart!"

As they approached, the farm revealed itself—rolling green hills dotted with cows, goats, and sheep grazing lazily in the afternoon sun. They passed a scattering of outbuildings and cultivated plots: weathered barns, a spacious chicken coop, neat vegetable plots, and orderly rows of apple trees mingled with pear and plum. The main house soon came into view—a stately two-story white structure with a thin, grey curl of smoke rising from its red brick chimney, nestled among tall, slender elms and a few ancient oaks that cast long shadows across the yard.

As the wagon rolled to a gentle stop, a pair of large farm dogs came bounding across the yard, tails wagging furiously, their deep, joyous barks echoing through the crisp country air. They jumped up against the side of the wagon, eager for the generous pats they knew were coming.

Two young men, clad in well-worn trousers and work shirts, followed just behind the energetic hounds. Samuel climbed down and extended his hand to assist Victoria and Mary. "Andrew and Emmett will see to your luggage and carry it up to your rooms."

The two men smiled politely, nodding in silent welcome as they passed. Emmett's eyes met Victoria's for a half-second too long, a silent, curious appraisal before his cheeks colored slightly and he turned his attention back to unloading the wagon.

Inside the house, the door opened to a rich, complex wave of smells—freshly baked bread, roasted meat, and herbs—mingled with the warm din of conversation and clinking dishes. The air itself seemed to hum with life—a cacophony of laughter, the clatter of pottery, and the rich, savory smells of a meal prepared for a crowd.

A petite woman with wiry auburn hair pinned into a neat bun emerged from the back of the house. She wore a faded floral house dress beneath a rose-pink apron, lightly marked with the day's cooking. At the entrance, she greeted them with open arms and a look of immense warmth. Rising on her toes, she kissed Samuel on the cheek. "Welcome home, my dearest," she whispered, her voice brimming with quiet joy.

With a broad smile, she pulled Victoria into a tight, lingering hug. "Welcome, my dear."

Then, bending at the waist with twinkling eyes, she grinned down at Mary. "And hello, my little darling."

Turning with a rustle of her skirt, she gestured toward the inviting glow of the dining room. "Come along now. You're just in time—supper's being laid out, and everyone's half-starved already."

A comfortable chaos swirled around the long wooden table—dishes passed from hand to hand, steaming platters set down, chairs scraped across the floor as everyone found their places and settled in. Samuel gestured warmly to two empty chairs, and Victoria gently guided Mary to sit beside her.

Without a word, hands reached around the table—clasping together in quiet reverence.

Samuel bowed his head slightly and spoke in a low, steady voice. "Lord, we give thanks for this abundance, for the hands that prepared it, and for the blessing of family—now made fuller with the arrival of two beloved souls." He opened his eyes and his gaze settled warmly on Victoria and Mary.

Lifting his head, his voice brightened. "Life here on the farm will be a far cry from the bustle of London. We labor hard—not for riches, but for a good life. Here, health and happiness are our true wealth. Because we stay strong and well, we've little need for the remedies and tonics being peddled in town."

He looked around the table, then back at Victoria and Mary. "If ever you're unwell, speak to one of us—Olivia and Tillie have a gift for healing, passed down from mother to daughter for longer than anyone can remember. God has provided every cure we need in the plants and earth around us."

Samuel chuckled, breaking the solemnity, "Ah, well, now you've all heard me carry on... let's eat before the food grows cold!"

The country fare was delicious, not grand or ostentatious, but hearty and soul-satisfying, a stark contrast to the elaborate spectacles Victoria had been accustomed to. The humble ingredients blended into a perfect harmony of flavors: roasted vegetables, savory stews, crusty bread still warm from the oven, and farm-fresh butter. But what truly made the meal remarkable was the company. There was no pretense, rigid etiquette, or forced conversation, only genuine laughter and stories traded like currency shared around the long oak table.

Instead of polite small talk and hushed tones, there were animated tales of livestock mischief, weather mishaps, and Emmett's near collision with a runaway hay cart. Laughter was a constant undertone, and the meal didn't feel like something to be endured, but a gathering one hoped would never end.

After the main course had been cleared and hands wiped on well-used homespun linen napkins, they lingered at the table, sipping black tea and enjoying the easy, post-meal chatter. Then, with a triumphant flourish, Olivia appeared with two golden-brown pies—one apple, the other brimming with plump, deep purple blueberries—their warm scent alone caused mouths to water. They were perhaps the finest Victoria had ever tasted, featuring a luxuriously buttery, flaky crust and a filling with just the right touch of sugar.

Mary, completely taken with the blueberry, devoured her slice with such enthusiasm that her fingers, cheeks, chin, and even the tip of her nose turned a vivid shade of indigo—transforming her into something resembling a berry-stained woodland nymph more than a little girl.

After the meal, the company moved outdoors to a well-used fire pit encircled by rough-hewn benches and chairs. The fire crackled, sparked, and hissed, sending flames shooting up into the crisp, star-filled sky. Someone produced a jug of apple cider, and the singing began—a medley of hymns, old folk ballads, and the occasional silly tune that had everyone laughing.

Samuel brought out a well-loved fiddle, its varnish dulled by years of use, and played with the ease of long practice. He tapped his boot in time and coaxed lively notes from the strings, the melodies echoing into the night.

Emmett, somewhat sheepish, held up a guitar. "I'm not very good," he said with a smirk, "but I'm learning." He strummed a carefree rhythm and launched into a comical song—one he claimed to have written himself—about a pompous London banker and an ill-fated encounter with a belligerent goat. The verses grew more absurd with each stanza, leaving the group roaring with laughter.

> Oh, Mister Goldmiser, banker stout,
> With a pocket watch and a paunch about,
> Did tip his hat with a haughty air,
> Till met a goat with a furious stare.

> In Blueberry Lane, it took its stand,
> A beast of most unruly brand,
> It bowed its horned head, then gave a leap,
> And sent the banker tumbling in an embarrassing heap.

As the evening wound down, everyone exchanged fond goodnights and disappeared into the various corners of the farm. Victoria and Mary were shown to a small but tidy room with plain, sturdy furniture, and a scent of cool night air and dry hay wafting through the half-open window, the silence interrupted by the chirping of crickets.

As Victoria changed into her nightgown, she noticed Mary had already curled up on her bed, sound asleep in her clothes, her arms wrapped around her wooden doll. Smiling, Victoria gently removed her shoes and tucked the blanket around her before lying down beside her.

Her body ached pleasantly from the day's travel and newness, but her mind was calm. With the scent of wood-smoke and pie still lingering in the air, she thought. Every smell and sound of the day settled into a profound and quiet certainty. *This is home.* And with that, she drifted into the deepest, most restful sleep she had ever known.

31. The Good Life

The kindness of people is enough to break one's heart.
—Charles Dickens, *Martin Chuzzlewit*, 1844

*T*he summer days quickly slipped by like a red fox darting through the forest, pursued by baying hounds and thundering hooves. Since their joyous arrival celebration—now five weeks past—the rhythm of farm life had settled into its unrelenting yet comforting routine. The skills Victoria had learned from Gaston proved helpful as she took her place in the kitchen, though she quickly realized how much more there was to learn.

Plucking and dressing a chicken had been foreign to her—the sharp knife slicing through sinew and bone, the warmth of feathers giving way to slick flesh, the metallic tang of blood clinging to her hands. At first, the process seemed brutal, almost barbaric, but after a few repetitions, her hands grew steadier. Though she never grew fond of the task, she understood its necessity.

The real test came when Patrick demonstrated how to dispatch a bird. He used the "stump and hatchet" method —pinning the chicken's wings with one hand, positioning its neck over a weathered stump, and bringing the blade down in one swift motion. The head tumbled into the dirt, and for a few ghastly moments, the body convulsed, wings flapping wildly as crimson arcs painted the ground. Victoria recoiled, her stomach turning.

Patrick, wiping his hands on his apron, shook his head and chuckled, "Aye, city women."

She resolved to leave the grisly affair of the hatchet to him.

There was no shortage of other chores: tending the ever-hungry hearth, kneading dough for the day's bread, stirring iron pots of simmering stew, scrubbing floors until her knees ached, and beating dust from linens under the open sky. Even the chickens demanded more attention than she'd imagined—collecting warm eggs from straw-lined nests, scattering grain while the flock clucked and pecked at her skirts, hauling buckets of fresh water from the well. Mary, ever her shadow, adored rising at dawn to chase the fluttering birds, her laughter ringing across the yard.

Farm life was an education in humility. Emmett, grinning like a schoolboy, once tried to teach her to split wood. She swung the axe with all her might—only to overbalance, the blade burying itself harmlessly in the dirt as she landed hard on her backside. Emmett roared with laughter before hauling her upright, his calloused hands rough against hers. "Maybe you should leave this to us lumbering oafs," he teased. She didn't argue, at least for the time being.

Dawn to dusk, her muscles burned, her hands grew rough, and each night she fell into bed as if sinking into a feather-filled cloud. Yet for the first time in years, her sleep was dreamless, her exhaustion sweet with purpose. Her new family never scolded her for her lack of knowledge or clumsiness; they only offered patient corrections and warm encouragement. The rigid decorum of her past life—the stifling silences, the measured smiles—felt like a distant, disturbed dream.

Was happiness truly this simple? No ball gowns, no rigid top hats, no stilted conversations over elaborately decorated table settings. No posturing for society's approval, no hollow accumulation of trinkets, no crushing corsets cinched to the point of breathlessness. Instead: the crisp snap of a carrot pulled fresh from the earth, the scent of rosemary crushed between her fingers, the aroma of recently baked bread just removed from the oven. Relaxed conversations and laughter around an old, long oak table, Emmett's off-key singing as he repaired a fence, Mary's hand sticky with berry remnants sliding into hers without reluctance.

How had she not seen it before?

Had life always been this easy?

In the quiet pauses between farm duties or as the evening fire cast dancing shadows on the walls, Victoria and the others took turns teaching Mary. Lessons were woven into the fabric of daily life: sounding out letters and words from a cookbook, counting beans into a tin cup for sums, or striking flint against steel until a spark leapt to the waiting tinder. The whole family delighted in guiding her, and Mary absorbed their lessons with the boundless curiosity of a child who had never been told that learning was an obligation rather than a delight.

This was no childhood of grime-choked London alleys, no dawn-to-dusk terror beneath the factory whistle's scream, no small lungs and hands blackened by coal dust in the mines, no desperate darting between carriage wheels to scoop horse dung for a penny. Here, knowledge was not hoarded or harshly delivered—it was passed like a shared loaf of bread: warm, nourishing, and meant for all. There was no hurry, no scolding, only the unspoken understanding that every scrap of learning was a gift.

And in those moments—with Mary's brow furrowed in concentration as she blew gently on her first fledgling flame, or her triumphant giggle when she spelled "chicken" without help—Victoria felt something more pro-found than pride. She felt certainty. *This* was how a child ought to grow. Not just safe, but cherished. Not just fed, but nourished in body, mind, and spirit—in every way that mattered.

Between fixing split-rail fences, managing livestock, fumbling through guitar chords by firelight, and countless other activities, Emmett still managed to whittle wonders from scraps of wood. Perhaps his most breathtaking creation was an owl, regally perched on a crooked branch. It peered down at the oak table with such uncanny presence that the first time Victoria saw it, she thought there was a genuine owl in the room ready to pounce.

With his talent, he took to shaping a menagerie for "Her Majesty's royal court"—a border collie curled as if sleeping by a hearth, a stallion mid-gallop with mane frozen in eternal wind. Mary—"Mare" or "Nightmare," silly nicknames Emmett insisted on calling her—would clutch each new creature to her chest, her laughter bubbling up like a spring creek.

No one had ever carved joy before—not for Victoria, not for Mary. It astonished her how kindness flowed so freely through this farm, as if generosity were just another crop, sown and harvested with the seasons.

Victoria couldn't help but notice that Emmett had taken a special interest in Mary—and in her. But there was no awkwardness, no pressure—only a quiet attentiveness that felt as natural as sunlight. She found herself smiling wider when he was near, her heart lifting with warmth.

The air hung thick on that final July evening, the three of them leaning back against the old log of a fallen oak, just beyond the ring of fading firelight. The fire had disintegrated into a pile of embers that pulsed with a deep orange glow, their light too weak to compete with the vast, brilliant arc of stars overhead. The others had retired, and Mary lay curled against Victoria's lap, eyes closed, breath slow and steady.

Victoria studied Emmett's profile as he gazed up at the twinkling celestial display overhead. His wavy, sandy-brown hair brushed his shoulders. The soft Roman curve of his nose and the dimple in his chin suited his face well. He had a small scar over his brow, a souvenir from a cantankerous goat's kick—an incident forever immortalized in one of Emmett's songs. His full lips were often fixed into a smile. By all measures, a handsome man, but what truly made him distinct was his quiet strength and gentle soul. It wasn't a façade—it was simply who he was.

"I never tire of looking at the heavens," he peacefully observed. "I wonder who might be looking back from one of those flickers of light." His voice was low and thoughtful.

Victoria inhaled the perfume of warm earth and woodsmoke, following his gaze to the sprawling splash of the Milky Way, a spray of countless stars dusted across the dark. "How long have you called this place home?"

"Three summers now," he mused as he ran his fingers through his hair.

With a smile, she observed, "Everyone seems content… happy… most of the time anyway. It's so unlike life in the city."

"I have to say, Samuel is a great man. Not because he has a title, celebrity, and wealth. He built something rare—

a patch of earth where we are all equal. We share in the labor and reap the harvest together."

With a laugh, barely audible, she uttered, "I can't imagine ever returning to life in that... in London."

"I understand. My da died in the pits when I was knee-high. My ma had no way to support us, so we all ended up in the cotton mills up north—my sister's fingers bloodied by the looms, my baby brother coughing lint from his lungs. Twelve hours a day, six—sometimes seven—days a week. The day shift swapped beds with the night shift— we used to say our beds never had time to go cold."

His face hardened with recollection, "The masters there were cruel and..." His voice broke, "I escaped the brutality, but lost my brother and sister.... to fever, to exhaustion, to neglect. Years later, I made my way here, and I doubt I'd ever leave."

Victoria gently placed her hands on top of his—the hushed moment speaking volumes.

He smiled, then thoughtfully commented, "Men can be so cruel sometimes, chasing gold like it's the only thing that matters. They build big wooden ships to far-off places to get more, then erect gilded palaces to prove their worth—and still, it's never enough." He waved his hand across the front of himself. "They forget what real wealth is."

She followed the movement of his hand, then looked past it—to the stars. "Maybe real wealth is this," she whispered. "This sky, this stillness, a warm fire, a child safe in your arms."

He glanced at Mary, still curled against Victoria, her tiny hand resting on her chest like a leaf fallen gently from a tree. "I reckon you're right," he added quietly. "Peace like this doesn't come easy. Some folks never find it at all."

A night owl hooted from the trees, low and mournful. Emmett shifted but didn't speak. Victoria leaned back against the oak, closing her eyes, letting the night air and silence wrap around them like a quilt stitched from starlight and serenity.

32. Market Square

Disobedience is the true foundation of liberty. The obedient must be slaves.
—Henry David Thoreau, *Resistance to Civil Government,* 1849

*T*he first hints of fall whispered through the homestead, transforming the sultry summer heat into cool breezes laced with the scent of apples, pumpkins, and woodsmoke. The maple leaves blushed crimson at their edges, while the oaks dressed themselves in amber—the landscape changed into a riot of fire and gold. For Victoria, autumn had always stirred nostalgia—memories of youthful walks through the countryside, her small hands tucked in her parents', kicking up drifts of red and yellow leaves. But this year, with her roots sinking deeper into the fertile soil of Barrington Farms, the joy ran deeper and sweeter.

Life on the homestead demanded callouses and sweat. Yet, each sunset brought a satisfaction London's ballrooms never offered—the weight of a basket brimming with potatoes she'd dug herself, the creak of the barn door closing behind her after tending to the cows, the chorus of crickets finishing off another day's honest labor. A deep sense of accomplishment settled in her bones, a feeling of belonging that was as tangible as the rough wood of the barn door, a contentment she had earned with every ache and callus.

Mary thrived like a wildflower in sunshine, her curiosity and imagination blooming daily. She wondered aloud,

"Why do spiders spin circles?"

"Why do bees make honey?"

"Why do clouds change shape?"

"Can I name the new calf Cinnamon?"

Their bond with Emmett had deepened as naturally as a growing thicket. When they weren't busy with the daily work on their patch of earth, they gathered around his guitar as he plucked newly fashioned songs, or lay shoulder-to-shoulder beneath the sky against that old log, pointing at clouds—a waterfall made of sheep, a pirate ship sailing into the mist, a grumpy chicken flapping into the ether.

At her walnut writing desk—its surface scarred from generations of use—Victoria penned letters by lamplight. Mabel's latest came scrawled with her usual humor, claiming she was now "as big as a fat ox." Hanwell wrote that her mother improved as she took a more active role in tending the gardens. Victoria foresaw a day when perhaps her mother would join them at her brother's farm—a proposition that Samuel was delighted about. Mr. Mearns was elated to let Victoria know they were working on constructing a new orphanage to help more of the city's poor and disadvantaged innocents—a four-story building of clean brick and bright windows, where ragged children would learn tailoring and arithmetic instead of picking pockets.

Only Annabelle's letter struck a dispassionate note, stating that the household was "operating at satisfactory efficiency," although she did confess that Simon was still "despondent over events." Victoria imagined her former husband sitting in the library, gazing into his crystal tumbler filled with port, his reflection broken into splinters. How strange it felt—that the image now stirred pity rather than pain.

Mary had recently begun attending informal, rotating lessons held at nearby farms—a kind of patchwork country schoolhouse. There, she mingled with children ranging in age from five to fourteen, each gathering hosted by a different family, with a new slate of teachers every day. Her education spanned from the practical—starting and tending a fire, picking and shucking corn—to the academic, including natural science, history, and classical literature.

"Mama," she exclaimed one evening, eyes wide with discovery, "did you know Queen Victoria became queen when she was just eighteen?" She delivered the fact with the seriousness of someone unearthing a royal secret from centuries past. Then, after a moment of intense contemplation—lips pursed, brow furrowed, and a decisive nod—she declared, "I want to be queen when I'm eighteen, too!" To that, Victoria smiled with exaggerated reverence, dipped into a graceful curtsy, and declared, "But of course, Your Majesty."

Today, Victoria had agreed to accompany Emmett to Leicester to deliver milk while Mary was at one of her lessons. She hadn't ventured into the city since arriving in Leicester, preferring the quiet rhythm of homestead life, but today she felt it was time to see more of the world beyond Barrington Farms—a world she'd glimpsed only fleetingly when first stepping off the train weeks ago.

Leicester revealed itself through a haze of coal smoke and the relentless hum of industry. The tall, soot-streaked spire of St. Martin's Church pierced the skyline, its Gothic arches casting long shadows across the city's heart.

Market Place bustled with stalls brimming with cheese, coarse-woven linens, and hand-forged tools, their vendors shouting to be heard over the din of haggling housewives, barking dogs, and rolling cart wheels. Horse-drawn carriages clattered past gas-lit shopfronts, while soot-smeared laborers hauled crates or hammered iron, their voices mixing with the distant shriek of a locomotive at the Midland Railway Station. The recently cobbled streets near the ornate new Town Hall teemed with clerks in stiff collars, men in top hats, and women balancing shopping baskets on their hips.

Everywhere, the city throbbed with the symphony of progress—the churn of factory looms, the clatter of iron wheels, and the sharp sound of church bells ringing on the hour. Small by London standards, Leicester still impressed her with its energy and industry—half-medieval, half-modern. Victoria, accustomed now to the open skies and fragrant breezes of the countryside, wrinkled her nose at the acrid staleness of coal smoke that seemed to cling to everything.

After they unloaded their milk churns and exchanged them for empty ones at a bustling cheese shop, Emmett turned to her and asked with a grin, "Care to see what the market's got on offer?"

The Market Square pulsed with the rhythm of daily life—a cacophony of trade, chatter, and competing convictions. Soapbox orators balanced on overturned crates, shouting themselves hoarse to passersby. One man, dressed in a threadbare coat, handed out pamphlets while proclaiming, "Children belong in schools—not sweatshops or mills!" Another announced, "Eight hours for work, eight for sleep, eight for what we will!" Near the pump where horses drank, a red-faced preacher waved a tattered Bible and roared about the evils of drink to a jeering crowd of factory workers on break.

Farmers in mud-caked boots and patched overalls bellowed prices over the clamor, their stalls heaped with the week's bounty. "Sweet butter, churned just this morn —none finer in all the county!" called a ruddy-faced dairyman, slapping a wooden paddle onto a mound of yellow cream. A wiry old woman arranged brown-speckled eggs in perfect pyramids, pausing to polish each shell with a scrap of linen. The earthy scent of new-dug potatoes mingled with the sharp tang of well-aged cheeses, their muslin-wrapped rinds protecting them from numerous buzzing flies.

But not every trade was so honest. A flashily dressed vendor in a grease-spattered waistcoat hawked "Genuine French Hair Dressing Pomade" from chipped porcelain jars—though the odor suggested lard mixed with cheap lavender oil. A one-legged veteran nearby hunched over a splintered crate, selling hand-whittled whistles and dolls, his tattered military ribbons barely clinging to a threadbare coat—a faded reminder of glory traded for hunger and street dust. At the square's edge, a fortune-teller swathed in faded silks drew clusters of giggling girls with promises of dark-eyed strangers and unexpected riches, her copper bangles clinking with each exaggerated wave.

The air was thick with overlapping smells—sizzling meat pies, bruised fruit, sawdust, horse dung, and the damp musk of wool and horse sweat—a pungent fragrance of commerce and humanity.

Beneath the graceful arches of the Corn Exchange, finer goods beckoned: Turkish tobacco wrapped in brown paper, Brazilian coffee in burlap sacks, and Dutch cocoa offered by the ounce. In one shadowy corner shop, Victoria spied a table stacked with second-hand Dickens novels. She smiled and remarked fondly, "I read every one of his books when I lived in London."

After browsing the stalls for some time, the pair drifted toward the bustling heart of Market Square. The square stretched wide and uneven, its weatherworn cobblestones slick with the debris of decades—spilled ale, trodden horse dung, coal dust ground deep into every groove by thousands of boots and iron-shod cart wheels.

At its center stood a raised platform—a semi-permanent speaker's stage, its planks warped and splintered by years of wind, rain, and frost. A faded Union Jack hung limply from one corner, its once-bright reds and blues now bleached to rust and ash by sun and soot. The platform's steps had been worn smooth by use, their edges chipped and battered from the stomping of workmen's boots during tumultuous rallies and union protests. A few tattered handbills clung to the lower boards—crumbling notices for political gatherings, temperance lectures, and dramatic readings. Knife-carved initials and crude sketches scarred the wood, mingling with blackened scorch marks from past torchlit vigils.

A cloth banner hung across the front of the stage, fluttering in the wind: *A Great Crime of Our Time*. Nearby, a pamphleteer paced back and forth, thrusting leaflets into open hands and crying, "Listen to a public vaccinator—today at noon! Hear the truth they don't want you to hear!" Victoria and Emmett joined the swelling, murmuring onlookers as St. Martin's bell began to toll. With each clang, heads turned toward the stage.

At the twelfth chime, a man ascended the sun-bleached steps, his boots landing heavily on the warped planks. He was tall and lean, dressed in a frayed black frock coat, his features gaunt but animated, eyes sharp with passion. The sea of faces—a rough assembly of factory hands in flat caps, mothers clutching infants, and curious tradesmen—pressed closer as he unfolded a sheaf of handwritten notes.

"Friends! My name is Dr. Thomas Brett," he bellowed, his voice slicing cleanly through the rising buzz. "I am a doctor with fifty years of experience!" He paused, his gaze sweeping over the upturned faces. "Yes—fifty years!"

He lifted his notes slightly and continued, his voice steady but impassioned. "In those decades, I tended to many a man, woman, and child. And when called to vaccinate, I did so. Why? Because we were told that, nearly eighty years ago, a great physician—Edward Jenner—had gifted us with a miracle. That his discovery would shield us from the scourge of smallpox. That it was safe. That it would eradicate disease."

He paused again, letting the memory of that trust settle into the throng. Then, slowly, emphatically, "But after fifty years, I have come to a grave conclusion. Vaccination is not merely ineffective; it is dangerous."

A murmur ran through the gathering—some gasps, a few nods, and a raspy "Hear him!" from a man whose pockmarked cheeks lent weight to the claim.

The speaker straightened. "I refuse the risk of vaccination!" he shouted, slapping his papers against his palm. "And I would not inflict it upon my bitterest enemy!"

A cheer burst from the onlookers' front ranks. Near the edge of the stage, a woman in a threadbare shawl tightened her hold on a sleepy toddler, her eyes round and wet.

He pressed on. "It is the convenient habit of vaccinators to claim their product is uniform—that this vaccine is as reliable and measurable as a grain of salt or a drop of water. But nothing could be further from the truth! The contents of their lancets are undefined, their effects unpredictable."

He stepped forward, gripping the splintered rail. "This so-called pure glycerinated calf lymph—used across the Empire—descends from a foul lineage: cowpox, horse grease, swine-pox, donkey-pox, goat-pox, buffalo-pox, humanized lymph, and other beastly poisons. You all know full well how the vaccinators wield their infernal lancet—cutting into your very flesh to force in their vile brew!"

Gasps and shudders rippled through the square. "Here! Here!" Many in the group exclaimed. A mother's voice from the crowd yelled, "That cursed poison injured my Andrew. He's still not well."

Emboldened by this testament, the speaker leaned further over the rail.

"This dangerous concoction is drawn into tubes and forced into the arms of three-month-old babes—and adults, too, who seek to enter the army, the navy, the railway service, or the civil bureaucracy. And the very calves used in its production are then sold at a discount to butchers, and the public unknowingly consumes them!"

A shocked silence fell, broken only by a shriek from a startled child.

The speaker's voice dropped to a bitter rasp. "The law calls us criminals for refusing this filth—but I say they are the criminals!" His voice cracked with fury. A murmur of agreement spread, though a well-dressed clerk on the outskirts scowled and muttered "quackery" before stalking off.

The platform moaned under his shifting weight as he turned, flinging an arm toward the looming silhouette of the Town Hall.

"They fine us, they jail us—for what? For safeguarding our children's blood? For demanding the right to say no?"

A cry of "Shame!" rose up. A few fists punched the air.

He smashed his hands on the platform's rail, exclaiming loudly, "Are we not a nation of free people? We demand freedom!"

At the square's edge, a uniformed constable shifted uneasily, his fingers grazing the handle of his truncheon—but he made no move.

The doctor's final words were lost in the din, but the mood had already turned. The crowd surged forward with renewed fire, chanting:

"No more vaccines!"

"No more fines!"

"Freedom!"

Handbills swirled like leaves, caught in an autumn breeze. Men shouted, women wept, and the afternoon light cast long, wavering shadows across the battered planks—a testament to a city and a people on the edge of rebellion.

Victoria recalled how Simon had once proclaimed that men—men of breeding, of intellect—had forged a world of order. That men of reason had laid railways across continents, launched great ships across oceans, and invented marvelous machines from which all humanity now benefited. But what he failed to mention, she thought bitterly, was that these same men also built the factories and mines where the poor men, women, and even children labored until their bodies broke and their lives flickered out. That they filled asylums with women deemed inconvenient, branding them mad and subjecting them to so-called treatments that amounted to torture. That they devised implements of war capable of tearing men to pieces half a world away. And perhaps most insidious of all, that they created the vile concoction of blood-poisoning—now forced upon free men, women, and babes scarcely three months old.

Yes, the world was more civilized, more ordered, and forever reaching toward new wonders... but at what cost?

33. Harvest of the Heart

How do I love thee? Let me count the ways.
I love thee to the depth and breadth and height
My soul can reach...
—Elizabeth Barrett Browning, *Sonnets from the*
Portuguese, 1850

ictoria's heavy eyelids fluttered open, her deep, velvet-brown eyes adjusting to the pearl-grey wash of winter light filtering through the frosted window. Delicate feathers of snow traced crystalline arcs along the edges of the glass panes, while beyond, flurries spiraled and danced toward the lace-draped ground below. The sun, veiled by a low ceiling of pewter-hued clouds, cast a dim, silvery glow. She elongated her spine, giving a gratifying pop as she raised her arms skyward, stretching her body into a long line against the cold morning air beneath the heavy, hand-stitched patchwork quilt—its frayed seams a testament to countless winters past.

With a cunning grin, she peeked to her right and peeled back a corner of the quilt, revealing two tiny, dirt-smudged feet. *That girl ends up in the oddest positions*, she smirked. Dancing her fingers over the soles like a pianist playing a scale, she was rewarded with a reflexive curl of toes and the sudden vanishing of feet beneath the layers. A giggling shriek erupted from the depths of the bedding, bright and effervescent as cider bubbles.

"Rise and shine, my little piglet," Victoria crooned.

Mary's sunbeam-bright face burst into view at a wildly improbable angle, sticking out of the left side of the bed, her cheeks flushed apple-red from sleep, eyes alight with the reflection of the snowy window, and a grin wide enough it might split a pumpkin. Even her dusting of freckles seemed to dance across her cheeks and nose. "Mornin', Mama!" she chirped, her voice still syrup-thick with sleep, adding "I'm not a piglet!"

Victoria, with a chuckle and a twisted smile, tweaked Mary's toe. "Sweetheart, you sleep like a pretzel dunked in a cup of chaos. I'll never understand how you twist yourself into such odd positions while you sleep. Were you raised in a circus?"

Mary's face vanished back under the covers with a rustling like a hedgehog burrowing into leaves. There was a flurry of wriggles, then suddenly—*pop!*—her head reappeared, hovering just inches from Victoria's face, her braids dangling like bell ropes. "I dunno, Mama. Maybe I'm a corn... tor... fish... nest?" she declared proudly.

Victoria's glee bubbled up, "Contortionist, you ridiculous goose!"

"That's what I said!" Mary insisted, her tongue tripping gloriously. "Cork-tor-fin-ist!"

Their mingling laughter echoed through the room as Victoria dug her fingers into Mary's ribs, sending the girl squealing like a panic-stricken piglet. With a dramatic gasp, Victoria swung her legs over the bed's edge, her bare feet meeting the plank floor with a shock of cold that shot straight up her legs.

"Mercy me!" she exclaimed. "I must remember to get a bedside rug before we both freeze our toes off!"

After dressing in woolen stockings, heavy petticoats, thick skirts, and shawls, they descended the narrow, creaking staircase of the old farmhouse, enticed by the warmth and mouthwatering aromas rising from the kitchen below. Olivia, her sleeves pushed high above her elbows, stood over the cast-iron stove, turning plump sausages with a worn, browned wooden spoon. Meanwhile, Tillie kneaded the bread dough with practiced hands, her hand-stitched apron whitened with flour like the first dusting of a winter flurry. The savory scent of spitting pork fat and cinnamon apples drifted through the room, as a chorus of "Good mornings" rippled through the air.

They both laced their boots and buttoned up their coats before braving the bitter sting of the winter morning. The moment the door cracked open, Biscuit and Marmalade—a blur of dusty pearl and orange fur—barreled past like runaway stagecoaches, their tails wagging as they snuffled their snouts into the new snow, barking joyfully into the crisp air.

Victoria hitched her skirts against the snow as they trudged the well-worn path to the outhouse. The icy seat provoked a most unladylike yelp from Mary, whose giggles turned to shrieks when the wind ominously rattled the door. Victoria thought, rubbing her frozen hands together, *This is the one part of farm life I'd gladly trade for a London water closet.*

Back in the kitchen's warm embrace, Victoria tied on an apron and joined the morning activities—peeling potatoes, while Olivia shared the latest gossip from the previous market day. At the long oak table, its surface scarred by generations of homestead life, Mary sat perched on a thick dictionary to reach the table, her finger tracing each line of *Aesop's Fables* with the serious face of a Cambridge scholar.

As the last breakfast dishes were cleared, the farmhouse erupted into a cheerful frenzy of Christmas preparations. Garlands of evergreen—their piney fragrance mingling with woodsmoke—were draped along the mantelpiece, brightened with clusters of holly berries. A branch of mistletoe, tied with scarlet ribbons, was hung from the ceiling beam.

In the kitchen, the air grew thick with the lip-smacking aroma of holiday dinner—the earthy sweetness of apples and onions stuffed into the goose, farm-fresh butter mixed with sage and rosemary from the garden rubbed onto the turkey's golden skin. Wild mushrooms, foraged and dried last autumn, soaked in cream for the gravy, while potatoes waited in their salty bath, ready to be mashed with generous lumps of yellow butter. Ears of corn, their kernels still plump from the late harvest, toasted in a black iron skillet as Tillie hummed *"God Rest Ye Merry, Gentlemen"* while basting the birds with their own glistening drippings.

Unlike the frantic London Christmases Victoria remembered—where servants scrambled to fulfill a hundred exacting traditions—this day unfolded like a well-worn quilt: warm, familiar, and stitched with love. Olivia, Charlotte, and Tillie gathered by the parlor window, their needles darting deftly as they added stitches to the communal quilt, its square patches made of three generations' worth of flour sacks and worn Sunday dresses. Nearby, Samuel and Patrick lounged in ladder-back chairs, reading leather-spined volumes from the small farmhouse library.

At the table's far end, Andrew and Russell hunched over a chessboard carved from maple and walnut, their knuckles hovering over the pieces before each decisive move, while Nathan and Benjamin looked on, puzzling over and commenting on every decision.

Mary, curled against Victoria's side like a contented kitten, sounded out words from "The Night Before Christmas," her finger tracing each ornate letter in the newly-illustrated edition. Only Emmett was absent—vanishing after breakfast with a cryptic mumble about "finishing touches."

As she turned a page, Victoria's attention drifted to the frost-laced window. What a contrast from last Christmas—that terrible day when Simon seized her wrist like a lunatic and shattered the remaining fragile remnants of their marriage with his cruel tirade. Now, the only sparks came from the hearth's merry crackle, and the only flames were the amber tongues of candlelight illuminating Mary's delighted face.

She thought, with a quiet smile, What a difference a year has made. *What grace to wake in such peace—and be surrounded by love.*

As the last golden light of Christmas afternoon slipped beyond the frosted windows, the family gathered around the long table—its surface a tapestry of steaming dishes that sent fragrant curls of steam into the candlelit air. Hands joined in a circle; heads bowed in quiet, reverent silence.

Samuel's voice broke the hush. "Heavenly Father, we thank Thee for this bounty, and for the hands that prepared it." His work-roughened fingers tightened briefly around Victoria's before he continued: "We're especially grateful this night for new souls who've found their way home. Victoria, would you like to say a word or two?"

All eyes turned to her—the flickering illumination catching the moisture gathering in her lashes as she swallowed against the sudden lump in her throat. "I..." Her voice caught, then steadied as Mary's small hand slipped into hers. "A year ago, I thought I'd forgotten what family felt like. You've shown me—shown us—" She squeezed Mary's little fingers, "that home isn't a place, but the people who live within it. Thank you all from the bottom of my heart."

A sniffle came from Olivia's direction as Samuel turned to Mary with theatrical gravity, "And what says our littlest angel?"

Mary's nose scrunched in fierce concentration, her eyes tracking across the smoke-darkened ceiling beams as if reading divine script. "Thank you..." she began with ceremonial solemnity, then launched into a rapid-fire litany. "Uncle Patrick for letting me taste the pudding, Uncle Andrew for the funny faces he makes, Uncle Nathan for not telling Mama about the jam jar, Uncle Russell for the piggyback rides, Uncle Benjamin for the secret peppermints—"

Emmett coughed into his napkin to hide a laugh as she continued, undaunted. "Uncle Emmett for hum-er-us songs, Aunt Olivia for the warm mittens, Aunt Tillie for extra raisins in my porridge, Aunt Charlotte for not being cross when I spilled the milk—"

The adults exchanged amused glances as Mary drew a dramatic breath for round three. "And Biscuit for licking my face! And Marmy-lade... for licking my face! And—"

Victoria's hand descended in a playful head-ruffle, sending Mary's chestnut curls bouncing. "Enough, you magpie!" she laughed, her tone soft and teasing. "At this rate, the gravy will grow cold before you finish thanking every chicken in the coop!"

"And Cinnamon! Paprika the Chicken—" Her list was interrupted by her own shrieks of laughter as Victoria tickled her sides.

As laughter rippled around the table, the spell of solemnity broke into joyful chaos—platters being passed, glasses clinking, and a dozen conversations blooming at once. Only the Christmas candles bore witness to the tear Victoria quickly blinked away as she watched Mary steal a roast potato from Emmett's plate, the man pretending not to notice.

As everyone finished, Emmett rose from his chair and reached for his guitar propped near the hearth, strumming it a few times as he looked at Mary. "I've composed a little tune for someone very special," he declared with a grin and a twinkle in his eye. He improvised a relaxed rhythm, his fingers picking out a gentle melody, and began to sing. Mary let out a squeal of delight, covering her face with both hands as Emmett played his tune.

Oh Mary. Oh Mary. Oh Mary.

There once was a girl named Mary,
Was she a girl or just a fairy?
She danced in meadows, sang in the rain,
With sparkling eyes, a heart, and even a brain.

With a crown of flowers and feet so bare,
She ruled with laughter and love to spare.
She grew up and turned eighteen,
All the towns bowed, and she became Queen!

Oh Mary. Queen Mary! Queen Mary!

As the last chord of the guitar and laughter faded, Emmett produced a mysterious lump shrouded in burlap, setting it before Mary with the solemn ceremony of a royal ambassador. "And what," he uttered, his hands poised dramatically on the rough fabric, "is a queen without a—" With a magician's flare, he yanked away the sack, revealing his masterpiece: "—a castle fit for Her Majesty!"

He revealed a small wooden castle, like a storybook dream. Slender towers reached skyward, their four turrets crowned with steeply pitched roofs of small cedar shingles—a delicate balcony with posts curved beneath the clock tower, where painted hands forever pointed to midnight. Tiny leaded windows of real glass winked in the candlelight, and a functional drawbridge dangled on hemp rope chains.

Mary's shriek of delight almost startled his carved owl from the rafters. She launched herself at Emmett with the force of a small locomotive, her arms locking around his neck so fiercely his ears turned scarlet. "It's perfect! Look at the little flags! And—and the staircase!" Her joyous babbling dissolved into a dozen incoherent thank-yous.

Victoria pressed both hands to her mouth, her eyes shining brighter than the Christmas candles. "You carved this? All of it?" Her fingers traced a tower, imagining the hours he must have spent hunched over his workbench while she thought he was mending fences. "It's... I've never seen anything so wonderful."

Emmett leaned back, satisfaction warming his chest as Mary danced around her new miniature kingdom—her laughter brighter than the firelight, Victoria's grateful smile worth every splintered hour spent carving.

Later, as the hearth burned low, Nathan and Benjamin made their grand bow before the assembled family, their shadows leaping up the walls like Marley's ghost himself.

Nathan—his voice suddenly twenty years older—hunched into Scrooge's miserly snarl. "I do. I must. But why do spirits walk the earth, and why do they come to me?"

Benjamin, draped in a moth-eaten sheet, wailed like a banshee while flapping his arms with such excitement he knocked over a candlestick. "It is required of every man that the spirit within him should walk abroad among his fellow-men..."

Nathan recoiled with terror, toppling backward into an armchair as Benjamin advanced, rattling a length of actual metal chain. "Forged link by link!" he howled, nearly hitting Russell with a wild swing.

When Nathan, as Scrooge, attempted his feeble defense. "You may be an undigested bit of beef!"

Benjamin let loose a moan so ghastly that Biscuit fled howling into the kitchen.

The ensuing chaos—Benjamin chasing Nathan around the table, Tillie crying with laughter, Mary cheering for "more ghosts!"—continued until everyone collapsed from exertion and laughter.

As everyone settled down for the evening, Emmett waved for Victoria to follow him.

Victoria looked at him with enormous adoration, "You're amazing. You made Mary... and me very happy."

Emmett gently smiled, "I want to give you something, Vic."

Victoria, wide-eyed and blushing, stammered, "Oh no, Emmett. I didn't get you anything."

"Oh, I don't care about that."

He presented Victoria with a closed, upturned hand that he slowly opened, "I have a friend who is a master metal crafter. I hope you like it."

The ring glowed in the firelight—three metals woven like wild vines into a lover's knot. Copper tendrils curled with the untamed grace of blackberry brambles, their textured leaves sprouting from the band and trembling at her touch, while the silver core gleamed between dark bronze bands.

With moist eyes, she picked up the delicate creation, holding it close to her eyes, "Oh my God. It's beautiful."

"I was hoping you would wear it." And then pausing a moment with a twinkle in his eyes, "I was hoping you would marry me."

Victoria stood frozen; her eyes wide, completely thunderstruck.

Emmett chuckled, "It's not like you to be speechless."

Slowly, Victoria gained her voice, her eyes wide and damp. "Oh—My—God," she slowly whispered.

His brow furrowed now, boot scuffing the floorboards, "I know this is maybe too quick, with all that—"

She kissed him.

Not the polite peck of London ballrooms, but a full-bodied collision of joy—her fingers spearing through his hair, her tear-damp cheek scraping his beard, the ring clutched between their pounding hearts. "Yes!" she laughed against his mouth. "Yes, you impossible, wonderful man!"

She wrapped her arms around him with a love she had never felt before—the mistletoe swaying just above their heads.

34. A Friend in Need

Fog everywhere. Fog up the river, where it flows among green aits and meadows; fog down the river, where it rolls defiled among the tiers of shipping and the waterside pollutions of a great (and dirty) city. Fog on the Essex marshes, fog on the Kentish heights. Fog creeping into the cabooses of collier-brigs; fog lying out on the yards and hovering in the rigging of great ships; fog drooping on the gunwales of barges and small boats.
—Charles Dickens, *Bleak House*, 1853

ictoria couldn't believe she was back in St. Mary's, the familiar honeyed glow of hundreds of beeswax candles flickering in the wrought-iron chandeliers above—while sunlight spilled through the tall stained-glass windows in a kaleidoscope of jeweled hues. The cathedral ceiling was braced by massive stone columns and arches, conjuring the wonder of reaching toward heaven itself. The scent of frankincense clung to the air, so thick she could taste it—a far cry from the crisp pine-and-snow fragrance of winter at the farmhouse. Unlike her last visit here with Simon, the dark oak pews were packed with people all dressed in their finest attire.

Victoria was deep in thought about all that had transpired over the last couple of weeks, only vaguely aware of the minister's voice, catching fragments like, "...an honorable... ...served the Crown..."

A Friend in Need

She had been enjoying the biting yet enchanting cold of January when the telegram arrived. It was short—frighteningly so—but its urgency was unmistakable:

I NEED YOU. PLEASE COME

Despite its brevity, Victoria felt the gravity of Mabel's desperation. Her dearest friend, who had stood by her through every trial, now needed her in return—and Victoria knew deep in her soul she must go.

She explained everything to Mary and the rest of the family. With unwavering support, they insisted she leave at once. They would tend to Mary, and there would be no need to worry while she was gone.

Emmett gave her a ride to the station the next morning, his strong arms wrapped around her as he pressed a farewell kiss to her lips. "Vic," he promised gently, "don't worry about Mary or anything. Everything will be taken care of." Emmett's farewell still burned on her lips—as well as the memory of how he'd cupped her face in his work-roughened hands, his whispered "Come back to me" partially swallowed by the locomotive's shriek.

The rattling train ride and jolting carriage journey gave Victoria ample time to worry. *Dear God, let it not be the baby*, she prayed. Beyond that, she could only guess at what crisis had compelled Mabel to send such a desperate plea.

Upon reaching number eighty-six, Victoria hammered the lion-head knocker until Samantha, hollow-eyed and trembling, wrenched open the door. "Oh, Miss Victoria!" The maid's chapped fingers clutched at her traveling cloak. "She's… she's in the parlor, ma'am."

"Thank you very much, Samantha," she said hurriedly, giving the maid a quick hug before she dashed off to the parlor.

The sight stopped Victoria in the doorway, the air knocked from her lungs. Mabel—vibrant, effervescent Mabel—sat hunched like a crumpled paper doll, her swollen belly at odds with her skeletal pallor. Tear tracks glistened on cheeks gone gaunt, her unbound hair strewn about her shoulders like storm wreckage. By the fireplace, Mr. Anderton stood with his back militarily straight, his eyes hollow. Mrs. Anderton sat beside Mabel, pressing a handkerchief into her hand.

Mabel launched upward with a wounded cry, her distended belly brushing Victoria's ribs as she collapsed into her arms. "My God, Victoria—" The words dissolved into great, heaving sobs that shook them both.

Over Mabel's shuddering shoulder, Victoria locked eyes with Mr. Anderton. The old soldier's voice cracked like thin ice. "Terrance is missing. We fear... the worst."

Mabel wrenched free, her face blotched with fury and despair. "You don't know that! You don't—"

Victoria guided her friend back to the sofa and sat with her, holding her tight. Mabel's sobs stopped as she slipped into a moment of withdrawn quiet.

Mr. Anderton continued, his voice, usually so commanding, splintered and hitched. "It was Monday, the twenty-sixth of January. Without warning, a dense fog rolled over the city—worse than anything I've ever seen. It was as if hell itself had expelled its infernal gases onto the world."

Mrs. Anderton added, her voice struggling with gloom, "They say over two thousand souls died during those four terrible days."

Mr. Anderton nodded grimly. "It was one of the worst pea-souper fogs on record. The temperature dropped to freezing, and the smog grew so thick that by midday the sun was completely blotted out. You couldn't see the tops of the houses, let alone the street beneath your feet."

He coughed, clearing his throat of lingering congestion. "The fog thickened into a choking yellow-black mass. It burned the throat, stung the eyes. It reeked of sulphur and soot. Trains were halted. Ships collided in the Thames. Pedestrians lit lanterns at noon."

Fearing the worst, Victoria looked up at Mabel's father, eyes shimmering with unshed tears. "And Terrance?" The question was barely audible, dread tightening her chest.

"In the chaos, there were reports of carriages overturned, cries in the dark... gunshots. Children vanished into the haze..." He faltered, then continued. "A maid pounded on his door, begging for assistance. Terrance grabbed his saber and revolver, wrapped a damp scarf over his face, and stepped into that cursed fog to help."

Mabel quietly added in an almost catatonic state, "He kissed me on the forehead and said, '*Don't worry, I'll be back before you know it...*'"

Mabel stared into the fire; her voice no more than a breath. "He stepped out and..." Her words dissolved into silence.

Mrs. Anderton finished quietly, "He hasn't been seen since."

Mabel's fingers clutched Victoria's sleeves with desperate, trembling strength. Her voice rasped from a raw throat. "He promised..."

A fragment of the minister's speech penetrated Victoria's thoughts. "...he saved women and children..."

A Friend in Need

For two endless days, Victoria kept vigil at Mabel's side, their hands clenched together as they waited. The grandfather clock in the hall ticked louder with each passing hour, its relentless pendulum swinging like a blade above their hopes. When the news finally came, it landed with the weight of a tombstone. Mabel's husband's body had been pulled from the ice-rimmed Thames near Battersea Bridge, his uniform buttons still gleaming dully through the filth.

The police surgeon's report lay between them on the sofa, its clinical words burning like acid. "Subject suffered probable concussion from vehicular impact prior to immersion. Hypothermia and death hastened by preexisting inhalation of toxic vapors..." Mabel's fingernails tore at the fabric as she read how he'd shepherded women and soot-blind children to safety before—dazed, bleeding from the temple—he'd stumbled toward what he thought was a street light's glow... and found only the river's hungry embrace.

Mabel cradled Terrance's silver pocket watch, its polished surface dulled by soot and time, which had been returned to her by the police. It had been a wedding gift—engraved with their initials entwined in ivy—and now she clutched it like a sacred talisman, her thumb tracing the crack across its glass face where it had struck the ground. Though its gears still sputtered a faint, irregular ticking, the hands were frozen in perpetuity at 2:07—the precise moment the coroner declared life extinct.

Later, when The Times arrived with its black-bordered tribute, Victoria had to read it aloud because Mabel's hands shook too violently to hold the paper:

A SOLDIER'S LAST PATROL

Captain T. Hawthorne, 33rd Regiment, perished in
Monday's catastrophic fog after delivering no fewer
than fourteen souls to safety at...

The ink blurred as Mabel's tears fell, creating tiny
inky pools in the newsprint.

Now, in the cavernous belly of St. Mary Abbots,
Victoria felt the clergyman's eulogy wash over her like
distant thunder: "...a life of service to Queen and Country..."
The words meant nothing against the reality of Mabel
beside her—a wraith in a jet-black cape, her swollen belly
a cruel mockery of life amidst death. When the minister
gestured to the lectern, Victoria half-carried her friend
forward, their mourning skirts whispering like phantoms
against the marble steps.

Mabel gripped the pulpit as if it were the last solid
thing on earth, her voice breaking.

"My husband..." A wet, rattling cough interrupted her.
The handkerchief came away streaked with black
smudges, the telltale mark of London's killer shroud still
lingering in her lungs.

"Terrance was... he was..." Her fingers convulsed,
crushing the eulogy into a paper ball. Suddenly, she
slammed her palms on the lectern, the impact echoing
through the silent church. "Terrance was loving and kind.
The years I knew him, he was always... always... he never
raised his voice or... he was everything to me and—" Her
wail bounced off the stained-glass saints, "—taken by that
devil's breath!"

The congregation collectively recoiled, as if they had
been scalded by boiling water. Mabel swayed, her knees
buckling beneath her like broken reeds as another violent

fit of coughing overtook her—this time ending in a splash of crimson staining the white linen of her handkerchief. Victoria lunged forward and caught her just as the world seemed to dim, Mabel collapsing like a discarded ragdoll into her arms, her full weight suddenly and terrifyingly limp in Victoria's arms. She cradled her friend's fragile, slack form against her trembling chest, heart pounding with helpless dread.

Somewhere in the background, a woman shrieked, "Smelling salts—quickly!", her voice sharp as broken glass. But Victoria heard none of it. Her entire world narrowed to the ragged breath on her shoulder and the faint, fading whisper that escaped Mabel's cracked lips—

"Please. Please... make it stop."

A heavy silence fell over the church, pressing down like the hush before a storm. Then, from beyond the open door, a distant foghorn moaned—its low, mournful call cutting through the stunned stillness, as if the city itself had taken notice.

35. A Breath of Brimstone

If mothers or doctors deal out calomel to children or others, we can only commend them to the mercy of heaven.
—Wooster Beach, MD, *The American Practice Condensed: Or, The Family Physician*, 1850

Mabel and Terrance strolled through Hyde Park beneath a brilliant spring morning sky. The sparrows sang cheerfully in the hedges, and golden sunlight danced across the budding trees. Mabel glanced at Terrance, a soft smile playing on her lips. Everything about the day felt perfect—idyllic, almost dreamlike.

But something was wrong.

A subtle, unshakable dread.

Her look of contentment faded as a shadow of unease crept in. She couldn't name it, couldn't place it—only that something about the world felt ever so slightly askew. Mabel frowned, her brow furrowing as she tried to puzzle out the source of the disquiet.

Suddenly, there was an ominous crack of thunder. The atmosphere grew brutally cold as tendrils of an unnatural mist slithered along the ground from the west. The bright, clear sky quickly darkened and thickened while spirals of soot and ash billowed endlessly from the numerous coal-fired hearths and factory chimneys that seemed to have materialized from nowhere. Their dark tendrils inter-twined into a suffocating canopy that blocked out the sky. The birdsong ceased as if it had never existed, replaced by distant shrieks, pistol shots, and the clattering thunder of insistent hooves against the cobblestones.

Out of the western fumes, a pair of hellish, red-glowing eyes materialized, followed by another pair. The piercing neighs of two jet-black stallions cut through the haze, their sweat-slicked muscles bulging as they galloped at a frightful pace, jets of fire and brimstone belching from their nostrils with great smoky groans. The dark horses pulled an even darker carriage, steered by a hooded driver, his face obscured by shadows, as he whipped the beasts, a gleaming scythe by his side. The ghastly whirring of the wheels and the groaning of the carriage mixed with the clomping hooves as it barreled down at Mabel, who stood frozen with dread.

The hellish carriage passed her, leaving her surrounded by an endless, smoldering panorama. She noticed, with sudden fright, that Terrance was gone. Through the unrelenting, suffocating haze, she saw a man stumbling away from her. In the eerie silence, she chased him. He disappeared, then reappeared over and over. She finally caught him and put her hand on his clammy shoulder, causing him to turn slowly. Terrance was pale as death, his eyes black and lifeless. Black ichor leaked from his mouth as he choked, "I told you I would be back."

Mabel's heart stuttered. She stepped back and opened her mouth to let out a cry, but only a hoarse, muffled groan came out. She tried to scream a second time. A third. She snapped awake in fright the moment she finally found her voice, shrieking and crying in raw terror and grief. Arms held her tight as she continued to thrash and scream, her body wracked with sobs as torrents of salty tears fell from her lashes. Victoria whispered as she stroked her friend's damp face, "It's all right. Hush now. It's only a dream… It's me, Victoria."

Holding her friend tighter, she continued quietly, "Shh… we'll get through this… it will be alright," knowing very well things were far from alright.

The funeral had been mercifully short but unbearably grim, the scent of lilies mingling with frankincense, clinging to their clothes like sorrow itself. Afterward, they returned to Mabel's residence in a deafening silence. Mabel coughed now and then, a sound that still made Victoria's stomach ache, though happily, it was no longer streaked with blood.

Victoria instructed the kitchen staff to acquire the same broths and herbal infusions that she and Annabelle had relied on. Shortly thereafter, to Victoria's quiet surprise, Annabelle and Gaston arrived unannounced. They came not out of duty, but with a gravity that spoke of genuine concern.

Without hesitation and with a sorrowful, yet grateful smile, Victoria embraced them both warmly. "You didn't have to come."

With muted warmth in her eyes, Annabelle replied, "Nonsense. That is what family is for."

The words, so uncharacteristically tender, drew a brighter smile from Victoria and softened her features with sudden, grateful tears.

With a deep, solemn sigh, she gathered herself. "Thank you. Truly… Mabel's husband—he lost his life in that dreadful fog. She is heartbroken, and the child is expected to arrive any day. If you could prepare something strengthening—"

Annabelle nodded. "—Yes, of course. We'll see to it at once."

Gaston added, "Bien sûr, ma petite lionne... We're here for you."

With that, they both quickly disappeared toward the kitchen.

Still bone-weary from grief and illness, Mabel leaned on Victoria's arm as they climbed the stairs, the air below rich with the fresh scent of simmering broth and steeping herbs.

Meanwhile, Mabel's parents had sent for the family physician to examine their daughter. Dr. Harrington arrived a few minutes after Victoria had put Mabel into bed to rest. Escorted by Mr. Anderton, a grim-faced physician entered the room, his small black leather bag swinging at his side with the gravity of bad news. He approached Mabel's bedside with methodical precision. He placed the cold stethoscope onto various points along Mabel's chest, instructing her to breathe deeply, then to cough.

After a cursory examination, the physician straightened, removing his spectacles to polish them against his sleeve before addressing the room. "Mrs. Hawthorne is in the early stages of consumption—serious, but not yet advanced."

He pressed his lips into a thin, colorless line, then continued briskly, as if reciting from a well-rehearsed memory. "Laudanum for the cough and nerves. Calomel to purge the system. And we must commence bleeding without delay to balance the humors."

Mr. Anderton nodded gravely, but a leaden dread settled in Victoria's chest.

She drew in a long breath. Her mind flashed first to Annabelle's daughter, Catherine, who had wasted away after being bled and poisoned with mercury. She thought of Cobbett's scathing words on the ruin brought by Jenner's legacy—the very practice that had taken Annabelle's brother and sister. She recalled Dr. Brett's firebrand speech in Market Square, a direct challenge to the establishment. And then, settling her nerves, came the tranquil wisdom of Olivia and Tillie, who spoke of healing not through torment, but through nourishment, nature, and care.

Beyond all of that, a deeper instinct stirred—an unshakable certainty in her gut that what the doctor proposed was not only misguided, but dangerous. The lancet and the purgatives belonged to an age of brutality masquerading as medicine. She couldn't let Mabel be broken by the same cruel hands of tradition. There was another path. A gentler one. And she would see her friend walk it.

Victoria's spine straightened, steel-hard, as she tightened her grip on Mabel's hand. "That won't be necessary, Doctor."

The physician froze, blinking as though he'd misheard. "I beg your pardon?"

"This is not the course we'll be taking," Victoria said calmly with unshakable resolve.

The doctor's brow furrowed. "What are you talking about? This is not a matter for emotional women to interfere with. These are medical decisions, grounded in science."

Victoria's eyes never wavered. She looked down at Mabel as she extended her hand for her to grasp. "Do you trust me?"

Though pale and exhausted from sorrow and sickness, Mabel clasped Victoria's hand, nodding faintly. "Yes. Completely."

Victoria turned back to the doctor, her voice like flint. "Then you are dismissed, sir. We will not be requiring your services."

The physician's face reddened with indignation; his pride pricked as sharply as if she had slapped him. "This is outrageous!" he blustered, his words puffed with outrage.

He snapped his bag shut with a loud, punctuating click and stormed from the room, his parting shot spat like venom over his shoulder. "You'll regret this. She'll be dead within the month without calomel and bleeding!"

His angry footsteps echoed down the hall, with Mabel's mortified father giving chase. "Doctor, please— wait!" he called out.

Victoria squeezed Mabel's hand. "Rest now. We'll see you well again."

Mabel smiled weakly before closing her eyes, drifting into a shallow, fevered sleep.

A few moments later, Annabelle entered the room in silence, her face composed but watchful. "I saw the doctor was a bit... perturbed... as he left."

Victoria, without turning from Mabel's side, defended her decision, "I wasn't going to let what happened to your daughter happen to her. Not while I still had the strength to say no."

Annabelle placed a steady palm on Victoria's shoulder. "I'm glad I told you Catherine's story. And I'm proud of you—for standing firm. That takes more courage than most realize."

Victoria looked up at Annabelle, eyes moist with gratitude. "You gave me the resilience. You've been guiding me all along... even when I didn't realize it."

Annabelle's lips curved into a knowing smile as she looked from Victoria to the sleeping Mabel. "I remember telling you once that life can harden us or break us. You, my dear, have grown into a woman far stronger than I ever imagined."

Victoria was resolute. Mabel had to be removed from London—with its soot-choked air and commotion—for the sake of her health and that of the child growing within her. Only in the clean countryside, with nourishing food, rest, and the gentle rhythms of the farm, could true healing begin. That evening, she gently broached the subject with Mabel, who, fragile but lucid, listened with glistening eyes and gave a quiet, grateful nod.

Mabel's parents were far from pleased. Mr. Anderton, in particular, bristled at the idea of his daughter leaving their care. "We can summon the finest physicians in London!" he argued, his voice tight with frustration. But Victoria held her ground, reassuring them she would write regularly and keep them informed of Mabel's progress. After tense deliberation, they gave their reluctant blessing.

By morning, with essentials hastily packed into satchels, Victoria and Mabel departed the city. The journey north—by carriage through crowded, busy streets and then by train along the soot-streaked rails—was grueling. At every stop, passengers eyed Mabel warily as she coughed discreetly into her handkerchief, her pallor and weariness unmistakable.

At the train station, Emmett met them with a tender embrace and a waiting cart. They rode the final miles in the crisp winter dusk, the wheels crunching over frozen ruts, until Barrington Farms came into view—a peaceful haven nestled amid snow-dusted fields.

Olivia and Tillie greeted them at the door, their arms open and their faces lit with welcome. They led Mabel to her room, where a fire crackled gently in the hearth, fresh white linens dressed the bed, and a small window, left purposefully ajar, let in the clean, bracing country air.

Mabel sat down slowly, her body worn and trembling, yet something about the surroundings—the stillness, the kindness—gave her a flicker of peace. Olivia brought over a steaming cup and set it in her hands.

"This is mullein, licorice, and elderberry tea, sweetened with our own farm honey," Olivia said, her voice soothing. "It will ease your cough and strengthen you." She added with a wink, "And it's quite delicious, if I do say so myself."

Mabel sipped, her eyes scanning the circle of gentle women—strangers, save for Victoria—whose faces radiated warmth and quiet resolve. Overwhelmed, she managed a soft smile and whispered, "Thank you. You're all so kind."

From the back of the room, another woman stepped forward—a steady presence with keen eyes and calloused hands. "This," Olivia said, "is Florence Bennett, a midwife from two farms over. She'll see you and the babe safely through."

The first night at the farm was perhaps the most harrowing. Mabel's hacking deepened, and with every strained breath, streaks of red stained her linen handkerchief. Her voice was hollow, her body fragile; the slightest exertion left her trembling with exhaustion. Her limbs were gaunt, her complexion a ghastly pallor—yet

340

A Breath of Brimstone

paradoxically, her cheeks held an unnatural flush, a telltale sign of illness. By nightfall, a low-grade fever set in, and by dawn, the bedclothes were soaked through with sweat.

A careful, restorative regimen was begun—one aimed at healing both body and spirit. Each morning, she was gently wrapped in blankets and brought outside to sit beneath the open sky. If the weather permitted, they bared her arms and face to the sunlight, allowing its golden rays to nourish her as best they could. For breakfast, she was given fresh eggs and thick slices of rustic bread slathered in garlic and honey—the former a natural curative, the latter a soothing balm for her raw throat. Shortly after came a pressed tonic of carrots, beets, and other root vegetables, strained carefully through muslin.

Though fatigued, Mabel was urged to move about, however slowly. Fresh air was as vital as any broth, and they encouraged even the smallest walks in the open fields. She often protested, claiming she didn't have the strength, but her companions—gentle, firm, and ever encouraging—would not relent.

Lunches and suppers were hearty affairs: steaming bowls of chicken broth rich with herbs, soft root vegetables, mashed turnips, oatcakes spread with creamy farm butter, and warm stews made with whatever the season provided. Herbal remedies were never far— syrups infused with garlic, elderberry, licorice root, and mullein were administered throughout the day with reassuring frequency.

Gone were the smog-choked days of London—the stifling sickrooms with their sealed windows, the endless rounds of bleeding and mercury, the grim routines imposed by men in black coats. In their place: sun and soil, clean air, whole food, and—perhaps most curative of all—a circle of kind, attentive women who treated her not as a patient, but as family.

On the third day at Barrington Farms, Mabel rallied. Her strength, though modest, was enough. In the early hours of February fifteenth, under a canopy of stars and breathless anticipation, she gave birth to a baby boy. At first, he was silent—but after a brisk smack to his backside, he let out a cry with all the force of new life.

Spent but glowing, Mabel cradled him to her chest, whispering through eyes brimming, "Charles Terrance Hawthorne." With that, she wept freely—tears of grief and joy—her heart echoing with love for the husband who could not be there to witness their son's arrival.

That night, after another nightmare, Victoria sat beside her friend, cradling her gently as Mabel gasped awake. It took her a moment to recognize where she was, to feel the comfort of the firelight and the soft creak of the wooden room. All around her were the hushed sounds of the farmhouse at rest, and beside her, nestled in a carved wooden cradle, was her newborn son.

This wasn't the future she had imagined without Terrance—but it was hers. And she knew, for Charles' sake, she must go on.

Mabel turned her head, weak but clear-eyed, and gave a faint smile as the last of her tears slipped down her cheek. "Thank you."

Victoria smiled back, brushing a strand of damp hair from Mabel's forehead. "We're always here for each other... Nothing will change that."

With her friend's hand in hers, Mabel's eyelids wavered shut, and she drifted into the first restful sleep she'd had in weeks.

36. Interwoven Souls

Poetry is that crystal river of the soul which runs through all the avenues of life, and after purifying the affections of the heart, empties itself into the Sea of God.
—Thomas Holley Chivers, *Nacoochee*, 1837

Mabel's nose wrinkled as she squinted against the early June midday sun. Her delicate fingers moved deftly to split another pea pod, sending its emerald pearls clattering into the porcelain bowl in the middle of the picnic table. Mabel paused, bringing a hand beneath her chin and pursing her lips as she tilted her head slightly to the right, gazing thoughtfully up at the clear azure sky.

Victoria cocked an eyebrow, her sunhat casting a lace-fringed shadow over her amused smile as she popped a fresh pea into her mouth. "That's your thinking face. Out with it—what's rattling around in that head of yours?"

Mabel grinned, a pea pod splitting with a soft snap under her thumbs. "I've sat on this for weeks... umm... I wasn't sure if I'd ever tell this to another living soul... but if anyone would understand, it's you."

Victoria's brow furrowed in interest, her own pea-shelling slowing as she leaned in, the wooden table creaking beneath her. "Oh, hush, you dramatic thing. After all we've been through, you know you can trust me."

Mabel snickered. "I know. I trust you with my life... obviously. You saved me."

343

Victoria's smile softened. "And you saved me. That's just what we do for each other. Right?"

"Well, of course... It's just that... I don't want you to think I'm going mad."

Victoria let out a hearty giggle. "Me? I'm the one who was nearly dragged off to the asylum, if you remember."

Mabel took a steadying breath. "Well... one night I had... an experience. Not a dream, not exactly—"

Mabel twisted her mouth again, trying to find the words. "Umm... I was..."

Victoria waited patiently for her friend to find her footing.

The wooden bowl between them wobbled slightly as Mabel added another handful of shelled peas. "I was in this radiant meadow, bathed in this amazing golden light. There were colors that I had never seen before. It was like here—" she gestured with her hand at the world around her. "—but a thousand times more. The air shimmered, and every blade of grass, every tree, every flower seemed alive."

Victoria smirked, tossing a pod at her friend. "That's a dream, you goose."

Mabel caught the pod with a laugh, but her eyes remained serious. "No. You don't understand. It was more real than here right now. It's hard to put into words."

She put her hand to her chin as if to steady herself. "As I stood there, someone came toward me. At first, just a silhouette in the light, then... it transformed into Terrance. But not as he was at the end. This was the Terrance from our courting days, his smile as bright as the day he first kissed me. He looked perfect, so vibrant."

Victoria's hands stilled completely now, a forgotten pea rolling across the table.

"He didn't speak," Mabel continued, "but I heard him all the same—right here." She touched her chest. "He said Charles needed me. That I had to go back."

Victoria frowned softly, "Go back where?"

"Here," Mabel said, tapping the table with her index finger. "Then he hugged me. The warmth was overwhelming. I felt him. I smelled him. It wasn't just physical—it was like our souls touched. I could hear his heart beating in time with mine. Then, as we embraced, he slowly melted in my arms like a snowman in an August heatwave. Then I felt pulled back... and I snapped awake in bed." She finished as if reliving the moment.

A long hush settled between them, broken only by the wind rustling the oak leaves overhead.

Victoria reached across the pea pods to squeeze Mabel's hand. "You're sure it wasn't just—"

Mabel turned her palm up to clasp Victoria's fingers, her grip surprisingly strong. "Feel that? It was real, Victoria. More real than this table. More real than these peas. More real than the sun on our backs."

A yellow butterfly fluttered between them. Victoria studied her friend's face, noting the soft lines around her eyes and the subtle fatigue still lingering from her long illness. She twisted her mouth in thought, wondering.

Mabel released her hand with a quiet laugh and picked up another pea pod. "I know it sounds mad. I just needed you to know."

Victoria remained silent for a moment longer and then softly asked, "Do you think it was heaven?"

"I don't know," Mabel whispered. "But it felt... sacred... It is not like the heaven depicted in books, with clouds and angels playing harps. It felt like home."

"Do you think you'll see him again?"

Mabel's eyes shimmered. "Yes. I do. And I think he'll be waiting. Just beyond the edge of whatever this is. I don't know how I know that. I just do."

Victoria pursed her lips thoughtfully. "It's hard to believe something like that... It's so... well, not something one hears every day. And I certainly wouldn't tell anyone else—they'd have you packed off to an asylum before you could blink, and melt the key for good measure."

Mabel, with her eyes swelling slightly with moisture, added, "I believe it. I believe that love doesn't just end. That Terrance... that he can see Charles."

Victoria reached across and took her friend's hand again, her fingers warm and steady, "Then believe it. There's more to this world than medicine and markets and men with ledgers. There's spirit. And memory. And love— love seems to be the one thread that doesn't snap, even when everything else does. That's something men like Simon or Dr. Ashford could never understand."

Mabel smiled softly. "I remember sitting in church and thinking all that was just to comfort the weak. But now... it feels like the only thing worth holding on to."

Victoria reached for another pod, her hands now moving slowly, reverently. The bowl between them was now half-filled. Sunlight dappled through the leaves, casting shifting patterns on their skin. The moment hung, heavy with meaning, a hush between two women who had faced down death and come back changed.

Breaking the quiet lull between them, Mabel began softly. "I can't believe I feel so much better...almost normal. I hardly cough anymore... just the occasional fit in the evenings."

Victoria listened with a warm smile, her hands deftly splitting pods.

Mabel slowly continued, "Perhaps it's…" She faltered and restarted, "When you come that close to… vanishing… something changes. You stop taking time for granted. If I don't make it through the coming winter—"

Victoria looked up sharply, her smile fading. She stared at her friend with quiet intensity and interrupted, "—You'll see him grow, Mabel. You're mending."

Mabel continued, "Still… if I don't…"

"You will. I didn't go through all this work to have you up and—"

Mabel reached out suddenly, halting Victoria's steady work, her fingers clasping her friend's with urgency, "But if I don't. I want you to… I hope you will raise Charles."

Victoria's eyes glistened, but she nodded without hesitation. "Of course. And the same if anything ever happened to me—you'd help raise Mary."

"Of course," Mabel whispered, her voice catching slightly

They sat silently for a moment, eyes locked, the air heavy with unspoken promises and a profound understanding that sometimes passed between souls bound by love and suffering.

Victoria broke the tender quiet with a bright shift in tone. "Next week is Mary's eighth birthday! Can you believe we've been here nearly a year?"

Mabel smiled, brushing a few peas into the bowl. "That's wonderful. I'm so glad you adopted that little angel."

Victoria hesitated, her fingers slowing on the pods. "There's something I've been meaning to tell you. I didn't want to say anything while you were so unwell—or after what happened with—" Her voice faltered.

Mabel glanced over, her expression gently inquisitive. "Is it Emmett?"

Victoria's face flushed as she smiled shyly. "He proposed. On Christmas evening."

Mabel's eyes widened, then softened into a glowing warmth. "Oh, Victoria... I could tell." She reached for her hand, squeezing it with affection.

"We decided to wait until you were more... settled. So, we're marrying in the autumn." Her voice was cautious but hopeful.

Mabel's gaze didn't waver. "Thank you for waiting... and for telling me. I'm so glad. Truly—I'm happy for you."

Victoria looked down, brushing a few pea shells aside before speaking again. "I wasn't sure it would ever feel right... after everything. But now, I just want to build something real. Something rooted in peace and love. And I want you there."

Mabel smiled through a veil of fresh tears. "I'll be there. No matter what. Even if I have to be carried in a wheelbarrow."

They both laughed—a rich, honest sound, tinged with both joy and the ache of everything they had endured.

Victoria wiped a tear from the corner of her eye, then added with a touch of nervous excitement, "Oh, and... I'm trying to arrange for my mother to be here by then."

Mabel lit up. "Oh, that's wonderful news! Is she doing well?"

"She's so much better... She's always improving since she left that dungeon."

Victoria leaned back, the sunshine warming her face. "Fingers crossed."

With the last pod shelled, the two friends stood, stretching their limbs in quiet contentment. Victoria picked up the bowl, now heaped with bright green peas, glinting in the sun like little gems. They walked side by side toward the farmhouse, a gentle breeze weaving through their hair, sunshine warm on their shoulders, their steps unhurried, their silence easy. A bond forged in the shared furnace of hardship now settled into a deep, quiet understanding.

37. Taking the Reins

I am the master of my fate, I am the captain of my soul.
—William Ernest Henley, *Invictus*, 1875

*T*he chestnut mare's sweat-slicked, muscle-rippled flanks gleamed as she galloped across the sunlit morning field—her long mane whipping side to side with the rhythm of a metronome. The horse's nostrils flared as air rushed in and out of her mighty lungs, each thunderous heartbeat visible beneath her sleek hide. Hooves threw dirt and grass into the air, leaving behind a dusty trail of soiled clouds.

Victoria urged the mighty beast onward, her auburn hair a tangled mass that spilled behind like a wild, fiery banner against the azure sky. With practiced hands on the reins and a secure grip of her thighs against the mare's ribs, she looked as if she'd been born to the saddle. She felt not just astride the horse, but part of it—her pulse synced with the drumming hooves. She was unchained, free, and vibrating with energy.

Last October, as the trees transformed into a cascade of russet, amber, and gold, she reflected on how she had finally settled into the rhythm of farm life. Like many mornings, after finishing the haying, she leaned against the weathered split-rail fence at the edge of the paddock, the scent of sun-warmed cut grass and distant woodsmoke lingering in the air. She wiped her brow with the back of her dirt-streaked hand, flinging her locks away from her eyes while watching a young chestnut mare nicker at the fence rails. The horse looked back at her with curious, deep brown eyes.

As she took in the moment, Emmett came up behind her, his shadow long in the slanting autumn light, holding a halter and wearing a smile that crinkled the corners of his eyes. "You've been eyeing Nutmeg all week. Time you stopped admiring and got on."

Victoria looked down nervously at the bridle. "I've never ridden before. I don't have the foggiest—"

Emmett chuckled, "Vic. That doesn't matter. I can tell you can do this. She's gentle, and you've done harder things." He held out the bridle, its bit gleaming in the morning light.

Moments later, Victoria stood in the stirrups, unsure and wobbling, but upright. The mare, sensing her uncertainty, snorted and sidestepped, but calmed at Emmett's low whistle.

The first circuit around the enclosure was more bouncing than riding, but Victoria clung on. Then—like a key turning in a secret lock—she adjusted her posture and leaned into the rhythm. The horse responded and surged forward with new confidence. She let out a laugh—sharp, surprised, and joyful. "I'm doing it!"

Emmett braced his arms on the fence, grinning, "It's in your blood."

That week, Victoria worked with the relentless energy of someone determined to prove herself. She cleaned the stalls until her shoulders burned, hauled water until her palms blistered, and helped Samuel mend fences, their hammers ringing a syncopated rhythm across the hills. With each task, she felt less like a fugitive and more like a farmer—her skin browned by the sun, her laughter easier.

At night, after singing Mary to sleep with half-remembered lullabies, she'd sit on the porch with Emmett, their fingers laced together over the shared ache of honest labor. The stars overhead no longer looked distant—they looked like the kind of map one might use to chart a new life.

Now, after a winter of riding through frost-rimmed fields and a spring of dawn gallops, she guided the mare back to the paddock with a gentle pressure of her legs. Emmett waited, his grin wide with pride. In his eyes, she saw the reflection of the woman she'd become—wind-brushed and radiant.

Victoria swung her right leg over Nutmeg's back, her skirts brushing the mare's sweat-dampened flank as she slid into Emmett's waiting arms. He lowered her down with ease, her boots landing with a satisfying thud onto the sun-warmed earth below.

He looked down at her with a smile. "Vic, remember last autumn, you were so hesitant, and now look at you."

Victoria's cheeks bloomed with a mix of satisfaction and joy. "I had a wonderful guide." She brushed a stray bit of straw from his shirt collar, her fingers lingering against the faded red checkered cotton.

They embraced and shared a gentle, heartfelt kiss.

Then, with a slight start, Victoria said, "Oh, I truly must get back to the house and get ready for Mary's birthday party."

But before she could take a step, he spun her back again, one work-roughened hand cradling the nape of her neck, and kissed her—honey-slow, lingering—before letting her go. "And I've got three more fence posts to wrestle into the ground. See you at the party."

Taking the Reins

Mary, her sun-bleached hair pinned back with an azure ribbon Victoria had saved from her own girlhood, darted from one game to the next—all nimble limbs and wind-swept joy. She was all scraped knees and gap-toothed grins, eight years old today, a number she'd been anticipating for weeks, as if it would change everything. Between breaths, she showered Victoria with questions like a little barrister cross-examining a witness.

"Mama, will I feel different when I'm eight?"

"Do you remember what you did when you turned eight?"

"Do I look older, Mama? Can you tell?" She stood suddenly very straight, chin lifted as if waiting for inspection.

Feigning mock exhaustion and with an equally dramatic huff, Victoria replied. "My word, girl! Do you ever run out of questions?"

Mary giggled, and she crinkled her nose.

"Do other children ask this many questions?"

"What happens if I run out of questions, Mama?"

"That's impossible, you goose!" Victoria laughed, jabbing her fingers into Mary's sides and sending her into a helpless fit of giggles.

It turned out to be a warm, sunny summer afternoon on the farm. Wildflowers bloomed along the edge of the hayfield. Checkered linen cloth draped the tables beneath a cluster of elms for Mary's small birthday gathering—simple but heartfelt. A few children from the local school attended and chased each other through the grass, their laughter carried on the breeze.

Victoria and Mabel watched from beneath the speckled shade of an oak tree, baby Charles nestled in Mabel's arms, a faint smile on her lips. For all the shadows they had come through, today felt as if it were lit from within.

Mabel thoughtfully commented, "She's growing into herself, that one. Quick as a sparrow, and nearly as fearless."

Victoria plucked a blade of grass, twirling it between her fingers. "She's endured more than any child ever should. Maybe that's what gives her wings."

Just then, a shriek of giggles erupted from the children. Mary came running, her braids coming undone, cheeks rosy as crabapples. Half-laughing, half-scandalized, Mary exclaimed, "Mama! Henry kissed me!"

Victoria raised an eyebrow, her mouth wide open in mock amazement, blinking in surprise, "Mercy! He did?"

Mary scuffed her boot in the grass, grinning but feigning outrage, "On the cheek! And then he ran off like a coward!"

Laughter followed. Samuel, overhearing from the porch, chuckled as he carved a slice of apple tart. "A bold lad. Might want to teach him the art of subtlety."

Victoria suppressed a smile, adopting an exaggerated stern expression. "And what did you do?"

Mary, folding her arms in mock seriousness, declared, "I threw an acorn at him. Missed, though."

Mabel snorted into Charles' blanket, sparking another round of laughter.

The moment was small, almost silly, and yet it marked something important. Mary was no longer just a survivor of hardship. She was becoming a girl with her own stories, little heartbreaks and triumphs, adventures and indignities. Victoria felt her throat tighten with something like gratitude for sunlight, fresh air, laughter, and her daughter's joy.

As the laughter dissipated, Olivia eased the back screen door open with a protesting creak. "Samuel!" she called, waving a flour-dusted hand as her voice cut clean through the chatter. "There are two men here who insist on speaking to the head of the household."

Samuel looked over, placed the half-eaten apple tart on the broad oak-plank picnic table, and followed Olivia inside. The door slapped shut after he passed through with a loud thwack.

Mabel arched an eyebrow at Victoria and, in a curious whisper, said, "I wonder what that's all about."

"Hmm..." Victoria pondered out loud. "That's odd. I don't remember anyone coming to the farm except local farmers, and they wouldn't be so formal as to ask for the head of the household."

They rose, Mabel holding the sleeping Charles, and passed through the back door, with the ever-curious Mary trailing close behind.

As they approached the front door, they could see Samuel standing in the open doorway. Just beyond stood a man in a silk top hat next to another man who was unmistakably a constable.

They could see that Samuel was not his usual relaxed and hospitable self. "—as I said. No, thank you, gentlemen. As Christian men, you'll respect our home—"

The man in the silk top hat emphatically interrupted. "Sir, it is the law. We must verify that all children and infants on the premises are up to date with—"

Samuel stepped forward calmly, "We're aware. We also know the harm it can do. We've seen it in some of our neighbors, so—"

The man in the top hat's expression soured. He began flipping through papers. "I'll need the names and birthdates of any children here. Infants, especially—" He interrupted himself as he noticed Mabel holding Charles, Victoria, and Mary standing several feet behind Samuel.

His eyes narrowed. "You two women. I see you have children. Step forward."

He and the constable quickly pushed past Samuel. The narrow-cheeked man in the top hat snapped open a leather-bound ledger. "The 1867 Vaccination Act gives us full authority. That child—" his quill jabbed toward Mary "—lacks the arm scar. And the babe's never been lymph-treated."

By this point, Emmett and the rest of the farm family, curious as to what the commotion was, had entered the house through the back door.

For the first time she had ever known, Samuel, his face red with anger, yelled at the men. "How dare you invade our home! Get out!" Samuel barely moved his lips. "Patrick. The pitchfork."

The constable touched his truncheon. "Now see here—"

Victoria swept forward, her shadow falling across the inspector's ledger. "I've dealt with men like you who push their fanciful nostrums. We will not allow you to touch our children."

As the burly farm men moved forward, both the man in the top hat and the constable backed toward the door. As the inspector fumbled over the threshold, he stumbled over the doorstop, his hat flying off to reveal a balding crown slick with sweat.

The top hat man's eyes flashed. "You understand the consequences? This is defiance of the law."

Victoria firmly locked eyes with his, "I understand your law," emphasizing with venom, "your." She continued, "I also understand my duty as a mother."

The top hat man's pencil-thin mustache twitched. "Ungovernable women." He thrust a summons at her chest. "You'll both—" pointing to Mabel, "—report to the magistrate's court. Tenth of July. Refusal of compulsory vaccination."

The constable added, "You'll need to answer formally. If not, the fine escalates—and the law permits removal of the children."

A heavy silence settled over the group. Then Olivia stepped forward, voice steely. "You've made your point. You can go now."

Mary, who had stood by Victoria's side observing the exchange, added as her nose wrinkled, "Your head looks like a cow's rump."

A few sharp laughs escaped the farmhands before silence clamped down again. The top-hatted man hesitated, but sensing he was outnumbered and had delivered his message, he continued to walk away without uttering another word. The constable reluctantly tipped his cap and followed. After a few minutes, the men in their carriage rattled away over the hill. Mabel's arms tightened around the baby. Samuel placed a hand on Victoria's shoulder. Olivia pulled Mary close.

She stared down the dusty road. "Damn them all," she murmured. "I thought we'd left these charlatans behind."

38. Deep Wounds

Tears, idle tears, I know not what they mean,
Tears from the depth of some divine despair
Rise in the heart, and gather to the eyes,
In looking on the happy autumn-fields,
And thinking of the days that are no more.
—Lord Tennyson, *The Princess*, 1847

*T*he carriage wheels bit into the farm's gravel drive, the sound like teeth grinding bone. Sarah Jane pressed her forehead to the sun-warmed glass—six years since she'd seen Samuel, over a year since the men at Earlswood had last restrained her in Room 18. Her wrists bore only faint scars now, having largely recovered under the progressive and humane treatment at Hanwell—at least where the eye could see.

Yet, her spine still remembered the way the straw-stuffed mattress had creaked under his weight, the sour tang of his breath as he'd hissed, "Quiet, now. You're mad—who'd believe you?" Every time she closed her eyes, she saw in excruciating detail that orderly's face—Buckland—those narrow black eyes, the pockmarked cheeks, the slight zigzag scar on the tip of his nose, his widely spaced teeth in his lecherous grin. It was that breath that really clung to her memory—an acrid mixture of cheap whiskey and decay.

Victoria's fingers tightened around hers, pulling her back. Her daughter—her fierce, impossible savior—who had dragged her from Earlswood's hell to Hanwell's lush gardens and weekly concerts. Now, thanks to a sharp-minded solicitor and Victoria's stubbornness, she had been granted three months' convalescent leave under family care. Although she felt fortunate, she was also nervous—terrified really, as if her sanity sat at the edge of the White Cliffs of Dover, where a moderate gust of wind could send her plummeting back over the edge into a mad despair.

The door of the carriage they had taken from the Leicester Midland Railway Station yawned open, unleashing a furnace blast of July air. Sunlight seared her face, unfiltered by the soot-stained skies of London.

Samuel stood frozen at the edge of the yard, his old oak-handled pitchfork slack in his hands. Time had etched streaks of silver into his brown sideburns and stolen the fullness from his cheeks, but his eyes were unchanged— dark and deep as the quarry pool where they'd skinned their knees as children.

"Sarah?" His voice cracked like ice dropped into a glass of water while he steadied his smile.

She meant to step down gracefully, but instead, her knees buckled.

The gravel dug into her palms. She focused on that pain—welcome pain—while Samuel's work-roughened hands hovered just above her shoulders. No restraints. No one dragging her upright by the hair. Just her brother's shuddering breath as he rasped, "Christ. What did they do to you?"

Above them, a lark trilled—the sound obscenely bright.

Victoria and Samuel lifted her gently, letting her collapse into her brother's linen-clad shoulder. For three heartbeats, the world held its breath. Then the dam broke—great, heaving sobs wrenched from someplace deeper than grief.

Samuel cradled her face, his thumbs brushing away tears that tasted of salt and years of anguish. "Hush now, little sister," he spoke softly, kissing the crown of her head exactly as he had when she was seven and afraid of thunderstorms. "You're home."

Arm in arm, they turned toward the whitewashed farmhouse, its open doorway spilling the aromas of baking bread and dried lavender.

Hearing the carriage's arrival, Mary met them at the door, joy written across her features, her grin wide enough to cut through the summer heat. In her grasp, she clutched a lopsided, tangled bouquet of cornflowers, meadow buttercup, and crimson clover—plucked with more enthusiasm than skill from the nearby meadow.

"Hello, Gramma!" she chirruped, thrusting the blossoms toward Sarah Jane.

Sarah Jane stared down at the offering, her fingers twitching at her sides, puzzled and lost in her inner battle.

Victoria's hand settled on Mary's shoulder, her thumb brushing the freckles there in silent apology. "Grandma's a mite tired from her journey, my little goose. Let's give her—"

A shuddering breath. Then, like a candle guttering back to life, Sarah Jane's face softened. She emerged from her stupor and managed a flicker of warmth, taking the bouquet in her quivering fingers. "Hello. That... that is very nice of you."

Mary, blissfully unaware of the tectonic shift she had caused, beamed. "You're welcome!" She spun away and vanished toward the kitchen.

Samuel's smile deepened as he watched Mary's wildflowers melt a little of Sarah Jane's frosted wounds. "Lunch is almost—"

"Might I... might I rest first?" Sarah Jane's voice was feather-soft, the words shaped by years of asking permission for every act.

Victoria curled her fingers around her mother's—those hands that had once braided her hair and now trembled. "This way, Mama." She guided her up the oak staircase, its tread-worn steps singing familiar creaks, past the landing where childhood pencil marks still recorded giggling children's growth.

The bedroom door stood open, afternoon sunlight pooling like liquid gold on the wide-plank floor. A dancing breeze made the lace curtains billow—ghostly lungs inhaling the scent of hay and clover. The bedroom, like all of them in the house, was plainly furnished, yet welcoming in its simplicity—a washstand with a blue enamel pitcher with hairline cracks, a small pine bedside table, a pine chest, and the narrow bed covered with a hand-sewn patchwork quilt made up of scraps of worn-out cotton dresses, shirts, and aprons.

Sarah Jane lowered herself onto the blanket's sun-warmed surface, setting Mary's welcoming bunch of flowers next to her, a buttercup and a few cornflowers falling silently unnoticed down to the floor. She traced her finger along a portion of the quilt while her other hand kneaded the softness of the bedding's wool batting.

"This was my room... before it was yours."

Victoria smiled. "I remember, Mama." Then, looking out of the window and deep into her memories, "Those picnics with Papa were some of my favorite memories. That red-and-white checkered blanket, like a chessboard, that you used to spread out with that old wicker basket on top? I remember he would act out a sword fight..." Noticing her mother's forlorn expression, she uttered a faded last word, "...laughing—"

Sarah Jane stared down at a washed-out indigo patch on the quilt and confessed, "I was weak."

Victoria sat next to her mother, taking her fragile hand in hers. "No, Mama. You were my lantern in the dark... along with father, who was... amazing."

They looked into each other's eyes, sharing a moment of perfect, painful knowledge. "Then he was killed, we both... we both didn't know how to handle it. I still had nightmares for a long time... so I understand."

Their grief-twinned gazes held the unspoken truth— how swiftly light could be snuffed out.

Sarah Jane's knuckles whitened. "Still... I failed you."

"No!" Victoria's voice splintered the quiet. Victoria gently stroked her mother's hair as her face shifted to disgust mixed with anger. "No, you did not. You suffered a tragedy and... instead of offering support, those butchers in white coats—they took a wounded soul and called it madness!"

Her thumb stroked the raised welt along her mother's wrist. "They took my beautiful mother and put her in that... that dungeon... where they tortured you and abused you. Their failure, Mama. Never yours."

Outside, a bird's song threaded through the silence— three clear notes, repeating.

Streams of tears etched well-worn salt trails down Sarah Jane's face, landing in splashes on her lap. "You... don't blame me?"

Staring deep into her mother's eyes, she assured her, "Never!" in a clear and firm voice—a daughter's love as unyielding as prison bars.

"You raised me, which helped me become the woman I am today... I love you."

Sarah Jane put her arms around her daughter, holding each other in an embrace that lightened some of the pain of the last many years.

After what felt like an eternity wrapped in silence, Olivia entered the room quietly, her footsteps muffled by the braided rug. In her hands, she carried a small wooden tray with a steaming bowl of savory chicken soup, a slice of still-warm bread, and a small crock of golden butter. She placed the tray on the bedside table and knelt beside the two women, her kind eyes shimmering in the soft afternoon light.

"I'm so glad to see you again, Sarah," she said, her voice gentle, her eyes glistening with warmth.

Moments later, Mary bounded into the room, cradling her handmade castle in both arms. Its crooked turrets and painted flags fluttered slightly from the breeze drifting in through the open window.

"Look, Grandma! You can borrow Queen Victoria's castle to make you feel better."

And just then, something stirred within Sarah Jane—something so unfamiliar it felt like a forgotten song remembered. A smile. And not just a polite one, but a true, radiant smile, followed by a laugh—small, yes, but unforced, bubbling up from someplace that had long been sealed shut.

It was, to her, a warmth spreading through her chest, so sudden and fierce it stole her breath.

A few quiet drops slipped from her eyes, but she didn't wipe them away. She only let her face brighten and whispered, her voice rough but sincere, "Thank you. I'm so glad to be home."

39. The Immovable Law

If the law supposes that... the law is a ass —an idiot.
—Charles Dickens, *Oliver Twist*, 1838

 *rack! Crack!* The judge's gavel struck with the force of twin cannon blasts, their echoes ricocheting off the paneled walls of Leicester's courtroom.

The magistrate—a jowly man in a black satin robe, his skin ruddy beneath a wilting powdered wig—took a labored breath, dabbing moisture from his brow with a linen handkerchief. Despite his efforts, sweat coursed in rivulets down his flushed cheeks, soaking into the unruly gray muttonchops bracketing his face. Setting the gavel down on the ink-stained bench, he reached for a glass tumbler, gulping the tepid water, which did little to douse the stifling July heat.

With an air of tedium and authority, he barked, "Next case!"—his jowls trembling with exertion.

A thin clerk rose, wire-framed spectacles perched on the tip of his nose—the perspiration on his forehead and fogged glasses evidence of the intense July humidity. He began reading from a ledger with an equally dispassionate posture. "Case 227: Arthur and Mary Ward of Wharf Street. Refusal to comply with the Vaccination Act of 1867."

The magistrate leaned forward, eyes narrowing at the trembling figure before him—a swollen-bellied, thin-boned woman, her dress clinging damply to her petite frame. Her underarms were dark with perspiration, her cheeks sunken and pale.

"Your husband, Mrs. Ward?"

"He is at work at the mill..." she answered, barely above a whisper, then added with effort, "Your Honor."

The magistrate sniffed. "Very well. The issue is simple—you must vaccinate your child as required by law or pay a fine of twenty shillings."

Mrs. Ward looked up, raw desperation etched upon her face. "Your Honor... if you please... my husband makes far less than twenty shillings in a week... and my two previous children, Randal and Michael, were injured and—"

The magistrate cut her off without looking up. "Twenty shillings or the lancet."

Crack! Crack!

Mrs. Ward's eyes welled with tears. "My husband will be furious. Your—"

"Next case!" he thundered, already turning his attention to the clerk, ignoring Mrs. Ward as if she had ceased to exist. Mrs. Ward shuffled toward the bailiff, her head hung low.

The clerk's ink-stained finger slid methodically down the docket. "Case 228: Victoria Barrington and Mabel Hawthorne. Defiance of the compulsory Vaccination Act of 1867."

A tall, austere man in black robes escorted the two women forward.

The judge's stare hardened. "Ah... Dr. Brett." He leaned back, waving his hand like brushing off a fly. "Say your peace."

The Immovable Law

Dr. Brett stepped forward, his smooth and precise voice shaped by years of public speaking. "Your Honor," he said, gesturing toward Victoria and Mabel, "these two respectable and conscientious women have retained my services."

Turning back to the bench, he continued: "As a physician with many decades of experience, I must inform the court that this so-called 'glycerinated calf lymph'—now peddled throughout the Empire—is a vile concoction of calf pus, equine grease, and in some batches, syphilitic material—all forcibly inserted into the arms of innocent children—"

The judge groaned, cutting him off. "Spare me the hysterics. Twenty shillings per child or—"

Victoria stepped forward, her tone firm and unwavering. "Your Honor, are we not a free people? If so, why are we compelled—"

"Mrs.—" the judge interrupted, motioning dismissively.

"Mrs. Barrington. Victoria Barrington."

The judge's bloodshot eyes gleamed with recognition and disdain. "Ah... Yes. Mrs. Pembroke." He spat out the name like spoiled milk. "I read of your little... performance in London. Nearly ruined a fine gentleman's bid for Parliament."

Victoria blinked. *Simon is in Parliament?*

Standing firm, Victoria responded, "I don't know what you read, sir, but my former husband's associate kidnapped me and intended to sell me into slavery."

The judge narrowed his gaze, scoffing. "Wasn't your mother confined for madness?"

"My mother," Victoria said evenly, "was committed after the death of her husband, for mourning too openly. A

367

court of law—much like this one—found Mr. Wilby guilty of kidnapping and attempted trafficking. And yet here we stand, still at the mercy of tyrannical—"

The judge slammed his glass down, causing water to splash across the bench. "You'll address this court with proper respect, madam, or I'll have you in irons for contempt!"

Victoria held her ground. "Sir, I mean no disrespect to your... *delicate sensibilities.* But we are endowed by God with free will. Many of us refuse to take part in this state-mandated experiment."

The Judge's face turned crimson. "You women have already sown enough chaos in this Empire—with your National Society for Women's Suffrage—" He sneered. "And your pamphlets and protests. I'll not have trouble-makers like you in my court—or my city."

Victoria's mouth curved into a frost-edged smile. "I wasn't aware this was your city... your Honor."

The judge's nostrils flared. "One more word, Mrs. Barrington, and I will have you removed. You will pay your fines or face legal consequences."

Mabel stepped forward quietly, her arms wrapped protectively around Charles. "Your Honor, I've nearly died once already. I won't risk my baby. I won't let them cut his arm and push that filth into his veins. I won't."

Dr. Brett raised a hand to interject. "Let the record show, Your Honor, that both women act not out of defiance, but conscience and medical concern. Something with which I have a great deal of experience."

Ignoring Dr. Brett, the judge, eyes narrowed, waved his hand again. "Both women are hereby fined twenty shillings per child. If payment is not received within ten days, a summons will be issued for further proceedings—

including removal of the children into state custody or imprisonment."

Victoria's fists clenched at her sides. "Then I suppose I will see you again."

The judge jeered, "You'd do well to hold your tongue, madam. My patience is at its end."

Mabel's voice was quieter, but firmer. "You can try to take him. You'll have to kill me first."

There was a long, taut silence—then a few voices in the stifling hot courtroom murmured "Hear, hear," followed by soft clapping.

The judge slammed the gavel down. Crack! "Enough! This is a court of law, not a stage for emotional theatrics. Take your summons and leave. Bailiff, escort them out."

The bailiff—a younger man who'd clearly heard enough for one afternoon—shuffled forward and handed them each a folded slip of parchment. "The date is at the top. July twentieth. Don't be late."

Victoria gave him and the Judge a withering look. "Don't worry. I wouldn't miss it. It's time for mothers to stand up to men who blindly follow rules that send little ones to their graves."

The judge proffered no reaction as he was absorbed in filling his tumbler and mopping his plump cheeks.

As the two women turned to go, Mabel clutched Charles close, and Victoria refused to lower her head, meeting the stares of the courtroom with a level challenge. Dr. Brett followed behind them, pausing only to give the judge a final, curt nod.

The magistrate muttered something under his breath, something that sounded suspiciously like "Ungovernable women and their damned pamphlets."

Outside, the sun was still bright, too bright for the heaviness of the moment.

Victoria unfolded the court order. "July twentieth," she repeated. "They'll try to make examples of us."

Mabel glanced down at Charles, his cheeks pink with sleep. "Then let's give them something to remember."

40. Iron Bars

Moved earth and heaven, that which we are, we are;
One equal temper of heroic hearts,
Made weak by time and fate, but strong in will
To strive, to seek, to find, and not to yield.
—Alfred, Lord Tennyson, *Ulysses*, 1842

*V*ictoria lay sprawled on a scratchy, straw-stuffed, vermin-chewed mattress, staring up at the cracked, time-stained ceiling. Her nightdress—once a fine powder-blue cotton—clung to her sweat-slicked skin, now sullied with the grime of prison life. The stench of lye-soaked floors, unemptied chamber pots, and human despair hung thick in the air, occasionally stirred by sporadic light gusts from beyond her confinement. Her unbound auburn hair spilled over the bed's edge like a jumbled cascade of copper and shadow against the grime, her bare feet planted resolutely on the mattress as if bracing for another day of defiance.

Beyond the thick walls, the Leicester clock tower struck five. First light crept through the narrow slit of a barred window, casting zebra stripes of shadow across the crumbling limewash walls and dirt floor worn smooth by decades of pacing inmates. The rising sun glinted off something metallic in the corner—a discarded spoon used to scratch tally marks by some previous prisoner. Dead cockroaches lay like relics, their upturned legs occasionally twitching in the draft.

Iron Bars

Day five of twelve.

They had made a spectacle of her sentencing. Tuesday, 20 July 1880—a date now etched into Leicester's collective memory. She could still hear the roar of the crowd that had followed her and Mabel to the courthouse, their boots pounding like war drums on the cobblestones. The flyers had done their work.

A GREAT INJUSTICE!
Mothers of England!
Are your children to be POISONED BY LAW?
The Compulsory Vaccination Act forces government
lancets into tender arms!
Join Mrs. Victoria Barrington
July 20, 10 AM
Leicester Courthouse
Witness the Tyranny—
Defend Our Liberties!

The courtroom had been a furnace of sweat and fury. Magistrate Horace Sedgwick's purple-veined face distorted, his hand white-knuckled as he clutched his gavel like a weapon while a wave of townspeople poured in—women in worn shawls clutching babies, factory men with rolled-up sleeves, even a few preachers in somber black.

Victoria had insisted that Mabel pay the fine—she had to return to nurse baby Charles—but someone had to stand firm. That someone was Victoria.

When her name was called, she approached the bench with the deliberate grace of a duchess entering a ballroom, her smile sharp and bright as a surgeon's scalpel.

She wore a graceful gown with a bronze-colored bodice and a rich scarlet skirt that flowed in stylish folds, complemented by bright, polished black leather boots. Her rich auburn hair tumbled over her shoulders, and a vibrant sapphire pendant caught the light at her throat. The ensemble was complete—a vision of cultivated elegance. Paired with Victoria's years of finishing school and hard-won experience, it lent her an air of quiet sophistication. The gathering was visibly mesmerized. Even the Judge, for a fleeting moment, seemed entranced by the poised and composed beauty she so effortlessly projected, his lips parting slightly in unconscious awe.

"Good morning, Your Honor." Her voice carried to the gallery's farthest corners, her hands firmly clasped in front. "I come not to negotiate, but to declare that no law forged by men shall override my God-given duty as a mother."

A roar exploded from the crowd.

Sedgwick's gavel had nearly splintered on its own block with his first strike. "This is a court of law, not a suffragette rally!"

Victoria's sparkling pendant caught the daylight—a blue flame of resistance at her throat. "I respect justice," Victoria fired back. "But this is an unjust law."

The magistrate licked his dry lips and barked, "Then pay the twenty shillings. You can clearly afford it, madam."

Her voice smooth as silk, she declared with an authoritative tone, "I will not pay this exorbitant fine—not if it were a single penny! This onerous law destroys the very families it claims to protect, and I stand with them."

Another explosion of cheers.

The Judge smashed his gavel repeatedly. "Order!" He yelled, turning increasingly crimson.

Still partially stunned by Victoria, Sedgwick spoke in a half-pleading tone, "Madam, you can afford this fine. Simply pay it and be on your way."

Victoria's smile shone with the defiance and stead-fastness of Joan of Arc. "Simply tell me and the court that I have the right to choose, and I will be on my way."

Sedgwick and the entire court paused in enthralled silence.

Then, as if shaking off a spell, he barked, "Bah!" and pronounced, "Then you have the next twelve days to learn respect for the law! Bailiff, take her away!"

As the bailiff gripped her elbow, she turned to the hushed assembly. "Mark this day—when England jailed mothers for loving too fiercely!"

The townsfolk exploded in thunderous applause. Sedgwick thumped his gavel repeatedly, shouting himself hoarse in a futile attempt to restore order.

She was escorted down the staircase to the jail cells. Behind them, the crowd's roar shifted into a wordless hymn of rebellion, its echoes bouncing off the ceiling.

Then—the sickening finality of iron meeting iron. Her cell door slammed with the sound of a coffin lid sealing, the metal bars trembling in the frame.

That was only day one of twelve—five weary days behind her, seven more still to endure.

She had received visitors most days—Emmett, Mabel, Olivia, Samuel, and even young Mary. She wanted her daughter to know there were moments in life when one must rise and defend what is right, no matter the cost. Dr. Brett would occasionally call in, offering what little comfort he could. Strangers, too, had come—farmers, seamstresses, clerks—offering gratitude, or trembling with resolve to resist.

Today would be yet another long, meandering stretch of time, broken only by the rhythm of footsteps and familiar voices beyond the threshold of her imprisonment. Even so, this was a gentler confinement than the torment she'd endured under Wilby's authority.

She stood, moved to the narrow slit of a window, and tilted her face toward the thread of breeze that slipped through. Eyes closed, she let her thoughts drift to the farm—to Emmett's steadfast presence and the sparkle of joy in Mary's laughter. She could almost hear her now, a burst of giggles echoing like birdsong across the fields. She felt Nutmeg's powerful thighs flexing beneath her as the wind swept through her unconstrained hair.

A voice broke through the stillness of her cell, shattering her trance. "What a situation you've landed yourself in, Victoria."

She quickly spun around. A tall figure stood in silhouette, looming just beyond the cell door—a top hat catching the dim corridor light.

Simon.

Victoria's fingers curled around the rusted iron bars as she stared at the man who once held her marriage vows—now gripping a silver-topped cane worth more than a Leicester mill worker's yearly wage. She found her voice, "Simon. I can't say I expected to see you."

Simon's cane struck each bar with the precision of a metronome—*clunk, clunk*—the sound echoing in the stone corridor. "I heard you'd taken up residence in Leicester's finest institution," he mused.

Victoria allowed herself a sardonic grin. "And yet you didn't bring flowers."

Simon let out a dry laugh.

Their eyes met, and for a heartbeat, there was something of the old Simon peering back—perhaps, just a smidge. Then it seemed to fade.

Victoria settled back on her bed, back against the damp limestone wall. "I hear you're now a Member of Parliament. Congratulations are in order. It's what you always wanted."

Simon executed a practiced half-bow, his top hat's silk brim catching the light. "Thank you. Merely serving the Empire's interests."

Victoria's eyes narrowed. "To what do I owe this honor?"

He reached into his coat and produced a crumpled flyer. "Well, I caught wind of your current predicament." He smirked. "You've become quite the... rabblerouser. A far cry from that shy girl I married."

Victoria grinned, "Well, life has a way of... changing you... A great deal happened, as you well know."

Simon resumed his bar-tapping rhythm. Again, he smirked, "While I'm not sure I agree with your stance on this topic, I have to say I do admire your conviction and tenacity."

Victoria stood and scrutinized Simon through the barred opening. "I still don't know why you are here... are you here to gloat?"

Simon chuckled. "No. Well, perhaps a bit... how your position has changed."

He paused as she continued to evaluate him. "Why are you here is perhaps the more appropriate question."

Victoria let out a slight exhale. "I'm here fighting for the freedom to choose and not have something that has injured and killed be forced onto us by—" She paused, looking Simon up and down. "—men with top hats."

Simon nodded with a smile as he held up the flyer. "So, your colorful flyer indicated."

"And... what are you doing here?"

Simon sighed. "A preliminary commission is reviewing the Vaccination Acts. Brett's testimony was... illuminating." He watched her carefully. "Don't celebrate—it's mere political theater for now."

Victoria's chapped lips parted, but Simon raised a hand—that familiar dismissive gesture she'd grown to loathe. "But I didn't come to debate public health."

Victoria remained motionless, raising her eyebrows. "I still don't understand why you are here."

"I knew you were here because Dr. Brett handed me your flyer."

Simon hesitated before he continued, and for the first time, his polished veneer cracked. "I wanted to apologize, Victoria."

Victoria blinked, her mouth twisted in astonishment. The atmosphere thickened between them.

"Wilby." The name landed like a chill wind through a graveyard. "My lack of judgment put you in grave danger. His words were... convincing... and that's not an excuse as I take full blame... for believing you were mad."

He stopped before the dumbstruck Victoria, his eyes locking onto hers. The confession hung between them, thick as fog.

"I was wrong. About a great many things. I just wanted to tell you that."

The silence between them stood for several seconds.

"My God, Simon. I don't know what to say."

"There is nothing to say. I simply wanted you to know... I wanted to remove that from my ledger."

He turned to leave, then, with half a turn, stepped back. He added, "Oh... the Judge owes me a favor. So, you can leave your... accommodations today. Unless you like living like a pauper."

From behind the cell door, Victoria called softly, "Thank you." She wasn't sure whether the thanks was for the apology or the release. Perhaps both.

Simon paused, glanced back—but said nothing. His polished boots echoed down the corridor.

41. Crossroads

Love is like the wild rose-briar,
Friendship like the holly-tree—
The holly is dark when the rose-briar blooms
But which will bloom most constantly?
—Emily Brontë, *Love and Friendship*, 1850

*I*t was an unseasonably warm September morning at Barrington Farm. Mabel and Sarah Jane strode side by side along the banks of the nearby River Soar, the channel winding lazily through the meadow, their skirts brushing against patches of late-blooming meadow flowers and tufts of wiry riverside grass. Around them, the world seemed to hold its breath—no wind stirred the willow branches, and even the river's current moved sluggishly, as if fatigued by the insistent heat. The usual rustle of foliage was replaced by the rasping of grasshoppers in the fields, the droning buzz of horseflies, the chatter of birdsong, and the faint rumble of cattle from nearby pastures.

In the distance, near the riverbank, where the water shallowly flowed into a ford, Victoria stood with Emmett, who held a hand-carved fishing rod, its line glinting as it arced over the water. Near them, Mary and Lizzy—the latter a freckle-faced farmer's daughter from the neighboring farm—were knee-deep in the shallows, their striped cotton overalls hitched up and dripping. They shrieked with delight as they chased minnows through the reeds, their bare feet sending up sprays of silver droplets that seemed to hang suspended in the thick air before vanishing back into the current. They ran in and out of the slowly meandering waterway, engrossed in some imaginary adventure—laughing, jumping, and splashing with spontaneous joy—their mirth carrying clearly across the stillness.

Sarah Jane paused beneath the gnarled branches of an old oak, its shade dense with coolness. "I remember Victoria at that age," she murmured, her expression rough with emotion. "She raced through these very shallows... like it was just yesterday." Her fingers traced the oval brooch around her neck, within which rested a portrait of the late Mr. Barrington.

Mabel's fingers tightened around Terrance's silver watch, which she frequently carried in her pocket—the watch gears having long ground to a stop, now utterly silent, screaming "2:07". "Six months," she whispered. "Six months since the fog took him, and yet sometimes I still turn to share some trifling thought—only to find..." Her voice somberly trailed off.

Sarah Jane studied the younger woman's profile—the flutter of her lashes as she fought back tears. It was a look she knew all too well—the same haunted expression that had stared back at her from her bedroom mirror after her husband's death. "So much tragedy in life..." she said at last. "I understand, my dear. I lost myself in sorrow... and it's... It's still hard."

Mabel nodded, her expression brimming with sorrowful remembrance.

Sarah Jane turned fully to her now, taking Mabel's hands between her own. The scars on her wrists—pale against her sun-browned skin—were plainly visible.

"When I lost my husband," she said, her tone low but urgent, "I let sorrow brick me up inside. I thought it was strength, that stiff upper lip nonsense they preach. But it's not strength—it's slow suffocation. And when the cracks finally showed…" Her thumb brushed the raised line on her left wrist. "They called it madness and dragged me to Earlswood. Where the doctors…" Her jaw stiffened, a lump forming in her throat.

Mabel stood still as if she had sprouted roots and been anchored to the earth. The water babbled over stones. Somewhere downstream, Mary squealed as Lizzy splashed her with a handful of water.

Sarah Jane cupped Mabel's cheek. "Don't make my mistakes, dear heart. The world already takes too much from women like us. Don't do what I did and shut it all in…"

The hush between the two matched the stillness of the windless trees.

And then the tide she'd held back for too long finally surged free. Mabel crumpled forward, her body wracked with sobs. "It's not right!" she gasped into Sarah Jane's shoulder, the words torn from some deep, wounded place. "He should be here… to see Charles take his first steps… to…"

Sarah Jane held her as the torrent of grief poured out, her own tears slipping free to disappear into Mabel's dark hair. She rocked them both slightly, as she'd once done with a young Victoria after nightmares. "I know," she soothed. "Oh, my dear girl, I know."

Overhead, the first wind of morning finally moved the leaves—a sound like a symphony of whispered comforts. Along the soft bank, wildflowers nodded in the breeze.

"Life isn't always fair," Sarah Jane uttered softly over Mabel's bowed head, "but we stagger forward as best as we can."

They held each other in a deep, shared silence, steeped in remembered tragedy.

Emmett had asked to speak in private, someplace quiet—away from the noise and eyes of others. Now, along the bank of the waterway, Victoria studied Emmett's profile—the way his sun-weathered brow furrowed, and the unfamiliar tension in his jaw made him look almost like a shadow of himself. This was the first time since she'd known him that his usual easy humor had deserted him, leaving behind this grave, restless energy.

The willow's sweeping branches enclosed them in a green hush, his fishing rod now resting limply across his palms. Upstream, the girls' joyful cries carried over the water. Farther still, the silhouettes of Mabel and Sarah Jane stood like sentries beneath the ancient oak, their dark skirts brushing the meadow grass.

Victoria fixed her eyes on the children as she patiently waited for Emmett to find his courage. Mary was attempting to balance on a flat creek rock, arms windmilling wildly, while Lizzy clutched something in her grasp and giggled. The sight sent a pang through her—how quickly childhood's careless joy was tempered by life's relentless anvil, hammered thin by loss until only resilience remained. *Was the secret of life to gather up those shattered fragments of innocence and piece them into something new—to make stained glass windows from broken bottles?*

"Vic." Emmett finally began, his voice slightly rougher than usual, startling her. "I've had this on my mind for... well, since you were locked away."

Victoria narrowed her eyes subtly and turned toward Emmett, her expression wordlessly urging him to continue.

After a thoughtful pause, he continued. "Life on the farm is simple and peaceful. This is my fourth summer here, and well, I want it to stay that way—simple and peaceful."

A dragonfly hovered between them, its shimmering wings catching the light like miniature cathedral windows before darting away.

Her mouth twisted slightly in confusion, with her quickened breath, "I don't understand... and?"

With a slight look of displeasure and a sharp exhale, he continued as he stared off into the distance, "I care about you and, of course, Mary, but... You voluntarily went to jail... and for—" His work-roughened hands clenched around the fishing rod, finishing with an emphatic "—twelve days."

Victoria frowned slightly as Emmett's words sank in, her grip tightening on her skirt. The burbling of the water filled the quiet between them.

Now facing her, his eyes the stormy grey of slate, he added, "That wasn't fair to me. It wasn't fair to Mary. It wasn't fair to anyone on the farm."

Victoria stood quiet and motionless as a realization hit her in the pit of her stomach. She had, of course, informed the family of what she intended to do in court. They'd nodded over supper—Samuel even called it "Christian fortitude"—but had she mistaken resigned acceptance for support?

Now, rather emphatically with an unexpectedly commanding demeanor, Emmett firmly said, "I don't want you doing this kind of thing again."

A skylark's song trilled mockingly from the meadow. Victoria's chest tightened with a range of mixed emotions surging. Surprise, confusion, regret, and righteous anger all bubbled together in a cauldron of emotion. "I only did what I thought—"

Then a transformation—his sun-weathered face hardened into lines she'd never seen, the ghost of Simon passing through his stance. "You thought? Who are you to make that decision? What about—"

Suddenly, one from that froth of emotions burst to the surface—outrage—lips pursed, face scowling, heat flared up her neck. "Who are you to tell me what to do?"

"No, Victoria. I'm not going to—"

Victoria stepped forward, "I was doing this for all of us! These men—"

Emmett scoffed, the sound scraping like a shovel on gravel, "So, all men are evil? Is that it?"

Victoria gaped at him, quickly retorting, "I didn't say that. You're putting words in my mouth."

Emmett went cold as a November frost. "We are not all your former husband."

Her hands found her hips, facing Emmett with a deep scowl. "You indeed are sounding that way now."

His tone dropped to a tight whisper, carrying a quiet intensity. "I see we're all Simons and Doctor So-and-so from the asylum?"

Victoria turned away, her vision blurring as she watched the girls blithely continuing to play at the water's edge. The sun was still warm on her skin, but the peace had shattered. A single glistening drop rolled down her cheek. Am I wrong about everything? *My God, is this the true Emmett? Why didn't I see this earlier?*

She turned back to face Emmett, taking in a deep, calming breath. "I was only doing what I thought was right." The words were barely a whisper, snatched away by a sudden breeze. "Don't you see that?"

Still hard as flint, he shot back. "That's not your job."

"Can't you see what's happening. If someone doesn't—"

"And that is you?" With a brief pause, he added, "You could have afforded to pay from your Wilby money."

A caustic laugh bubbled up, bitter as black tea left to steep too long. "That wasn't right! These—"

"But it was right to abandon us!"

The accusation hung between them like gun smoke. Victoria's fists trembled at her sides. "I didn't abandon anyone! My God!"

A wordless pause again. Heavy and unforgiving.

Emmett stated evenly and quietly, as if saying an unquestionable prayer, "You put family first."

The river's silver current continued its unabated, relentless flow, a low roar that filled the punishing silence between them.

Neither spoke.

With the same tone, she slowly replied, "I was. I am."

The wind whispered, but neither of them did. A single yellowing willow leaf drifted down between them, catching briefly on Victoria's sleeve before floating to the ground.

Again, he said slowly and steadily with a quiet certainty. "You're calling attention to our way of life. You put us all in jeopardy."

Victoria felt the words land like a stone in her belly. She turned toward the children, where Mary's peals of joy rang bright as a chapel bell across the water. Lizzy crouched at the murmuring shallows as she hunted for tadpoles.

Was that true? The doubt uncoiled in her chest like a slow-spreading poison. Her dress suddenly felt too tight, each breath came shallow. *Perhaps it was.*

"I need some time to think," Victoria whispered, her breath barely louder than the rustling grass along the shoreline.

"There is nothing to think about. No more... rabble-rousing." Emmett uttered with a note of finality in his tone.

A memory flashed—Simon's polished boots clicking across the jail floor as he sneered, "*You've become quite the rabblerouser.*" The echo made her stomach churn.

Victoria studied the quiet storm written across his features—the way his sunburnt forehead creased like a furrowed field, the unfamiliar hardness around his mouth that erased his usual dimples. Slowly, she shook her head.

The still stretched on for what felt like an eternity. She stared at him for three heartbeats—five—ten, feeling the hollow ache of emptiness expand beneath her ribs. "We're done here," she said, her breath steady, her expression flat.

Turning, she walked toward Mary with measured steps. "Girls," she called, her tone stripped of all warmth, "we need to go."

Behind her, Emmett's resolve cracked. "Vic... wait." His voice raw and splintered.

Victoria heard him as she had once heard church bells through thick fog—distant, muffled. She took the children's hands, their small fingers wet with cool water and mud, and began the journey across the sun-soaked pasture.

Barrington Farm's visage wavered in the shimmering air ahead—its white walls and smoking chimney no longer symbols of home, but of another shattered fragment of hope.

Mary tugged at her sleeve: "Mama, why's your face wet?"

Victoria wiped her cheeks with the edge of her palm, smearing sorrow and dry dust together. "Just the heat, darling," she lied.

And so, they traveled in silence—three figures moving through the pastoral landscape, their shadows stretching long and thin behind them like wraiths who had lost their way.

42. A Wise Bird

It is the folly of the world, constantly, which confounds its wisdom. Not only out of the mouths of babes and sucklings, but out of the mouths of fools and cheats, we may often get our truest lessons.
—Oliver Wendell Holmes, *The Professor at the Breakfast Table*, 1859

*H*eaven knows we need never be ashamed of shedding tears, for they are rain upon the blinding dust of earth, overlying our hard hearts.

Victoria had read that phrase dozens of times before from her beloved leather-bound copy of *Great Expectations*, its once-gilded edges now dulled by years of adoring use. She shifted in the ladder-back chair, its oak joints groaning, the sound echoing softly through the candlelit bedchamber. Mary looked up from beneath the hand-stitched quilt, her wide hazel eyes fixed on her mother with the singular focus only children possess.

Victoria ran her tongue over her wind-chapped lips from the day's labor before continuing, "I was better after I had cried than before—"

"—Mama," Mary interrupted, her sun-kissed nose wrinkling like crumpled parchment beneath its constellation of summer freckles. "What does that mean?"

Victoria's fingers stilled on the yellowed, slightly fraying page.

"Well, my little one," she said, her voice softening into the warm cadence reserved only for bedtime stories, "Mr. Dickens means tears are like spring rain—they wash away the dust that gathers on our hearts when we try too hard to be strong. Crying is something that helps us heal and reminds us we're still able to feel deeply, and we need that —to truly be ourselves in a world that can sometimes be very hard."

Mary scrunched her face further, her mind whirling with thought.

Victoria bit her lower lip, tucking a stray chestnut curl behind Mary's ear, then said gently, "Real strength isn't about never crying. It's about feeling everything deeply and still choosing kindness."

Seeing her daughter's still-puzzled expression, Victoria leaned closer.

"It means if you don't cry when you're sad and laugh when you're happy, you'll turn into..." She lowered her tone like someone revealing a dire secret, "...an old fuddy-duddy."

Mary's giggle burst forth, her freckled nose wrinkling with delight.

A comfortable silence settled over the room. Victoria looked back down at the novel to find her place, ready to continue reading.

"Is that what happened to Grandma?" Mary asked, gently pulling at a loose thread in the quilt.

Victoria straightened so abruptly that the chair skidded slightly on the wide-plank floor.

"Well... in a way. The world tells women they must be like porcelain figurines—pretty but never showing their fragility. But we're not figurines, we're..." She gestured to the cracked but sturdy washbasin in the corner, "Like that old pitcher—meant to hold living water."

"That's stupid," Mary declared, with all the solemn finality of an eight-year-old judge pronouncing sentence.

Victoria's laughter fluttered against the low ceiling. "I quite agree."

After a moment, Mary asked in a barely audible voice, "Is that why you aren't marrying Emmett?"

Victoria's hands froze on the Dickens novel, "It's complicated, my little—"

"I still love Emmett," Mary blurted out, clutching the quilt to her chin.

Victoria stroked Mary's hair, her fingertips catching on tangles from the day's adventures. "Oh, darling heart, that's..." Emotion caught in her throat. "That's beautiful— "

Mary interrupted again, her eyes fixed on her mother with a look far too wise for her years, "Do you?"

Victoria closed the book with a *thump* and placed it on the bedside table. She cradled her chin in her palm, elbow propped on her knee. "I suppose... It's just... well complicated."

"Grownups are stupid," Mary pronounced with the weary air of one who has solved the world's great mysteries.

Victoria chuckled lightly, "On that, my wise little bird, we are in perfect agreement."

The room held its breath, broken by the slight late September breeze and the distant hoot of a barn owl.

Finally, Mary asked in a voice suddenly small and vulnerable, "If we ever fight, will you stop loving me?"

Victoria felt the question strike with the weight of a blacksmith's hammer—her breath caught as a shimmering drop escaped, tracing a glistening path down her wind-chapped cheek. "Of course I'll always love you..." She swallowed hard, infusing her words with forced cheer as she lightly tapped Mary's nose with her fingertip, "...you goose."

With the mercurial shift only children can manage, Mary stretched like a sun-warmed kitten, her eyelids growing heavy. "Mama, can I stay at Lizzy's tomorrow night?" she asked, as though the weighty conversation had evaporated like morning mist.

"Of course—" Victoria began, only to notice Mary's jaw had gone slack, her breathing deepened into the rhythmic cadence of sleep.

In the honeyed glow of the candles, her face softened into a private vulnerability no waking soul would ever see. "Of course... I love you..." she whispered to the sleeping child, her thumb brushing a stray curl from Mary's forehead with infinite tenderness. "You silly goose... Why would a fight change that?"

The question hung in the still bedroom air like dust particles caught in sunlight. *Why would a fight change that?* Victoria watched the rise and fall of the quilt over the girl she'd rescued from the orphanage, now safe and rosy-cheeked in this sanctuary of patchwork blankets and wildflower-scented sheets.

Mary's innocent words had slipped past her defenses, exposing raw questions beneath: *Had the ghosts of Simon's betrayal, Wilby's cruelty, and Ashford's cold calculations made me see specters where none existed? Had I, in my righteous fury, thrown away something precious? Did I really push away a man I really loved and who loved me?*

Her fingers continued their gentle, rhythmic stroking of Mary's hair—the same soothing motion she'd used when nightmares woke the child screaming in those first fragile weeks.

"Out of the mouths of babes," she quietly murmured, quoting Psalms with a bittersweet twist of her lips.

Outside, the barn owl called once more across moonlit fields. In this quiet room, heavy with lavender and childhood dreams, its cry seemed to echo through her very soul.

Victoria rose from her chair, leaning over the oak side table, sending a blast of air from her puckered mouth toward the candle. The flame danced wildly before surrendering with a soft hiss, leaving a thin, erratic, smoky trail curling toward the ceiling. The moonlight and gentle breeze from the open window filled the room with a perfect nighttime calm, yet an uneasiness kept spreading through her chest.

She moved to the window, the lace curtains quietly fluttering. The moon's glow painted the farmyard in grays and shadow, but her thoughts churned with echoed memories of the riverbank quarrel—Emmett's voice, usually warm as summer earth, gone hard as flint.

"*You voluntarily went to jail for twelve days.*"

"*No more rabblerousing.*"

"*I don't want you doing this kind of thing again.*"

She now realized the way his hands had clenched was not in anger but in fear—fear for her, fear for their fragile peace.

A shiver ran through her despite the warm night as she recalled ending their engagement—the way Emmett's broad shoulders had sagged like a bridge bearing too much weight before he turned wordlessly toward the barn, his work boots kicking up little clouds of dust.

A cold uneasiness grew throughout her entire being.

She drew in a deep breath, turned, glanced down at Mary for a few moments, and pressed her lips gently on the forehead. She pondered, *who had rescued whom?*

The door creaked shut behind her, its familiar groan echoing loudly in the hallway's stillness.

She whirled with a gasp, nearly colliding with the solid warmth of Emmett's chest. His homespun shirt carried the scents of sweat and hay from the barn loft where he'd clearly been sleeping these past weeks.

"Oh!" Her hand flew to her throat, where her pulse fluttered like an imprisoned sparrow. "Emmett. I'm terribly—"

His smile was a fragile thing in the silver light, but his tone held its old gentleness as he raised a hand toward Mary's door. "That's alright... mind if I say good night to our girl?"

Without waiting for a response, Emmett eased the door open with care. Through the cracked doorway, Victoria watched him bend like a willow branch to kiss Mary's forehead—*our girl.* After three heartbeats—long enough to pull the covers up to her neck—he exited the bedroom, the door creaking as he closed it.

In the narrow hallway lit only by moonlight filtering through the stairwell window, Victoria looked up at him with eyes gone liquid in the dimness, whispering, "Emmett... I've been miserable these past weeks. I'm truly sorry—"

Emmett caught her words with two fingers, gently resting softly against her mouth. "Hush now, Vic," he countered, his Leicester brogue thickening with emotion. "I'm the one owes apologies. I came at you like a bull, I did."

Victoria's smile bloomed—tentative but true. "You were frightened... weren't you?"

The pale lunar glow caught the moisture in his eyes as his expression folded into grief. "Lost my whole world once—Da in the pit, Ma and the littl'uns to the mill." His thumb brushed her wrist where her pulse fluttered, as if reassuring himself she was real. "Couldn't bear to lose you and Mary... and our good life."

Victoria cradled his jaw, her fingers tracing the scar from last winter's ice storm. "You won't lose us," she vowed, her voice steady as the old oak by the creek.

"It could happen..." Emmett's voice cracked like dry kindling, his calloused hands trembling against her waist.

"If I don't stand up to them, who will?" Victoria pressed her palm over his pounding chest. "If I teach Mary to stay silent... what kind of mother am I?"

"I understand, but..." His protest died as her thumb brushed the old goat-scar above his eyebrow.

Holding Emmett's cheek, her touch as gentle as the candlelight flickering across their joined shadows, she murmured, "I understand, too... You're the kindest man I've ever known. Nothing like Simon or those other devils."

Victoria continued, "I've learned you have to stand firm against these men... Did you hear about Mrs. Ward?" Her voice dropped to a haunted whisper. "She and her husband had two little ones injured from that vile procedure and refused to risk another. I saw her in court. The poor woman was so distressed." Victoria's nails bit into her own palms. "While her husband was at market, two brutes in uniform came demanding payment." A warm droplet traced her cheek before falling onto their clasped hands. "When they kicked in her door and threatened prison, the shock sent her into labor. The baby came too soon—blue and still. She faded by degrees after that and then died."

Emmett swallowed hard, his throat working against the memory. "I heard... What a horrible tragedy."

Moonlight pooled around them as Victoria lifted their intertwined fingers. "Life is risk." She pressed his knuckles to her lips. "But if we hold fast to each other through the storm, we can weather any tempest. I believe that with every fiber of my being."

Emmett stood motionless, their hands still clasped between them, his breath shallow. For a long beat, he searched her eyes as though trying to believe what he saw there. Then, with a choked sound that was part laugh, part sob, he pulled her into his arms.

Victoria melted against him, burying her face in the curve of his neck. He smelled of hay, sweat, and something warm and honest—like earth after a summer rain. His arms closed around her with quiet desperation, one hand pressing gently to the small of her back as though afraid she might vanish.

"I missed you so damn much," he whispered into her hair.

"I know," she confessed. "Me too."

They stayed like that, rocking slightly, as if swaying could keep the past from slipping back to divide them. The wordless space between them was no longer hollow, but full—full of all the things they hadn't said, all the tenderness they hadn't dared to show.

At last, Victoria leaned back just enough to see his face, her palm resting lightly on his chest. "Emmett?"

"Hmm?" he breathed, his forehead pressed to hers.

She hesitated, feeling the tremor of her heartbeat in her throat. "Will you marry me?"

He blinked. A stunned silence fell between them. His brow knit, lips parting, but no words came.

"I mean it," she said, more firmly now, a flicker of mischief lighting her eyes through the sheen of emotion. "I know you asked me last Christmas. And I said yes. But I broke it. I ended it. So, if it's to be again, it has to come from me. Because I want you. I want this. Not just as a companion or comfort. I want to build a life together. On purpose."

Emmett blinked, stunned. "Are you sure? You're serious?"

"Deadly." Her voice dropped, teasing. "Unless you've gone off the idea."

A rough chuckle escaped him—raw, disbelieving. "Gone off—? Lord help me." He kissed her then. Not with urgency, but with a fierce reverence, as if each second had to be carved into memory. When their lips parted, his forehead rested against hers again. "Yes. Yes, Victoria— yes. I'll marry you a thousand times over."

She laughed through her tears, the sound muffled against his shirt.

Outside, the owl gave one last cry before taking wing across the moonlit fields. And inside the quiet farmhouse, two hearts found their rhythm again, beating not in fear or flight, but in steadfast promise.

As they stood wrapped in each other's arms, the wind shifted, carrying with it the faintest scent of damp earth from the river below the orchard—the one that looked like the stream where Victoria had first dared to dream of freedom a lifetime ago. Now, that dream felt real. Tangible. She could almost feel the water bubble and froth around her ankles, and the pebbles and sand beneath her feet.

A brisk wind stirred the air from the hallway window, punctuating that the dream was no longer a wish, but all too real.

A Wise Bird

As Emmett touched his lips to her brow, Victoria thought again of Dickens's words: *rain upon the blinding dust of earth*. Tears, like love, had softened the hard crust that once shielded her heart.

She smiled, her eyes twin pools reflecting the pale kiss of the moon and hard-won joy. This—this was the rain.

43. Newly Minted Junior Sleuths

She was unlike most girls of her age, in this—that she had ideas of her own, and was stiff-necked enough to set the fashions themselves at defiance, if the fashions didn't suit her views.
—Wilkie Collins, *The Moonstone*, 1868

Mary lay face down on her familiar, faded patchwork comforter, her freckled face cradled in her palms near the footboard. Her elbows dug into the feather mattress as she lost herself in a freshly cracked, leather-bound edition of Wilkie Collins' latest novel. A parade of expressions marched across her face—eyebrows knitting at a twist in the plot, lips quivering at each provocative line—all dappled by the dancing maple-leaf shadows from her bedroom window. Grass-stained knees anchored her as bare feet scissored the air—restless, as if independently conscious—their summer-soiled soles flashing with each cross and uncross of her ankles, a frantic, wordless language all their own. With an impatient exhale, she puffed away a copper-streaked strand—her honey-brown ponytail beginning to escape its ribbon.

Just beyond Mary's restless feet, Lizzy lay mirrored in the same belly-down posture but utterly still, her toes dangling over the edge, legs motionless as marble. Her chin rested on her folded arm, the other limb trailing toward the floor where fingertips absently traced the braided rug. Corkscrew curls—black as printer's ink— spilled across the quilt, forming silken puddles around her face. Every so often, she hummed tunelessly, a quiet soundtrack to the rustle of pages turning at her feet. Occasionally, she would mindlessly twirl her dark, curly hair as she read a book she had propped up against the bed's headboard.

A crisp September breeze, carrying the scent of early apples, set the maple branches outside to clattering against the glass like anxious intruders. Spotted light and ever-shifting shades played across the girls' backs, drenching them in liquid spots of gold, while they lay oblivious—each absorbed in her own world.

When Lizzy's thin finger traced the jagged scar on Mary's left ankle, Mary instinctively flinched as if touched by an icicle, though her eyes never left the page.

Shifting up to her elbows, Lizzy focused more intently on Mary's retreating foot. "Does it still hurt?"

Absent-mindedly, Mary murmured, "No… Shush! I want to finish."

The silence that followed was the comfortable sort, broken only by the occasional sound of an ax splitting wood in the distance and the gentle fussing of hens drifting from the distant coop.

Lizzy studied the scar's raised topography, her voice soft. "I know it hurt when that cow kicked you while you were milking… it looks like a broken tree branch."

"'Tis a lightning bolt," Mary corrected without glancing up, her nose now mere inches from the page.

Curiosity overriding caution of disturbing Mary, Lizzy touched the mark again, this time mapping its contours with the precision of a junior scientist.

Mary let out an exasperated groan. "Cease your poking!" she groaned, finally meeting Lizzy's gaze with mock severity. "And quiet! I only have a few pages left."

The next few minutes were only disturbed by the continued sounds of the industrious woodchopper, the cluck of chickens, the trill of birds, and the distant mooing of cows.

Mary finally closed her novel with a happy thump. She ran her fingers over the gilded cover of The Moonstone. "What a marvelous tale!" she declared, her legs nearly knocking into Lizzy's head as she suddenly sprang upright into a sitting position at the foot of the bed.

With a glow of excitement, her words began tumbling forth from her mouth like apples from an overturned basket. "The Moonstone is a great yellow diamond stolen from an Indian temple. They say it's cursed... A young lady named Rachel inherits it on her eighteenth birthday. But that very night, the diamond vanishes from her room... Then Sergeant Cuff, a detective from Scotland Yard, comes to solve the mystery!"

Finishing with a confident smirk, she added, "I won't spoil the ending. You'll have to read it yourself."

Then a spark of delight passed over Mary's face, as glowing as if she'd just uncovered a map to Blackbeard's treasure. "We're going to be detectives!" she proclaimed, flinging her arms wide.

Lizzy furrowed her brow, her nose scrunching in puzzlement. "Why detectives?"

"Because it's an adventure! Mysteries to solve, crimes to unravel!" Mary responded, her voice brimming with theatrical flair.

Lizzy let out a soft giggle. "Last week, you wanted to be a Contorty-thingy after wedging yourself into that barn cabinet."

"A contortionist, you goose." Mary corrected, rolling her eyes.

Continuing her excited outburst, Mary said, "And I still want to! But I'll also be a solo trapeze artist. Imagine flying through the air, defying gravity! I'll be a true aerial queen!

Lizzy's dark eyes glittered. "I want to see lions, giraffes, and elephants—"

Mary quickly interjected, "Did you know an elephant in India killed my grandfather? And my mother nearly got sold into slavery there by a brute named Wilby—but she beat him in court!"

Her friend could only nod as Mary continued her frenetic pace. "But first, we'll solve mysteries—Hartford and Bennington, H & B! The finest detectives in England!"

Lizzy giggled. "Why's your name first?"

"Because it was my idea, of course!"

"We'll start in New York City!" Mary barreled on. "They've got electricity there—no more candles or gas lamps! Can you imagine? So marvelous!"

Lizzy, attempting to get in a word edgewise, said, "But—"

Mary barreled on, "We will start here!"

Mary launched herself off the bed, landing light-footed as a cat, and darted to the towering bookcase crowned with the Emmett-carved Queen Victoria's castle. Marmalade, sprawled in a sunbeam beneath the bedroom window with Biscuit half-buried beneath her ginger fur, cracked one eye open as Mary went airborne. By the time Mary's fingers brushed the leather spines, Marmalade had closed her eye and returned to her siesta. She slid The Moonstone onto the bottom shelf, its gilt-edged spine gleaming—Wilkie Collins' name bold against the leather.

Collapsing cross-legged on the floor, Mary shot a glance at the door. "Remember," she cautioned, "Father built this secret drawer in my library for me. Never tell a soul."

Lizzy nodded solemnly as Mary tugged open the hidden compartment at the base of the bookcase. After shuffling through various artifacts for a few moments, she lifted a scrap of linen, its edges frayed, the embroidered 'Mary H.' faded but legible.

"Our first case," Mary announced, holding it aloft like a sacred relic. "This is from the dress I wore when I was left at the orphanage. I was five—or so they believed. Mother gave me a birthday: June 19, 1872. But who knows if it's real? Am I now truly twelve?"

She bounced up again, landing cross-legged beside the motionless Lizzy, who merely shrugged.

Thrusting the cloth under Lizzy's nose, Mary demanded, "See the H? Odd, isn't it? I became Hartford after mother married, and this was well before. Could it mean something?"

Lizzy opened her mouth—

"Of course not! That'd be absurd, wouldn't it be?!" Mary cut in. "But who were my parents? Was my mother locked away like Grandmother? I must find out!"

"Or maybe..." She lowered her voice to a conspiratorial murmur, "We should investigate that old wishing well down by the abandoned mill."

Lizzy's ink-dark eyes widened with a blend of curiosity and worry.

Newly Minted Junior Sleuths

Mary leaned closer, her summer-freckled nose nearly touching Lizzy's as her whispers rapidly continued, "Old Mrs. Potts claims a girl who escaped from a workhouse drowned there when grandmother was a girl."

Holding her hand to her own throat, her voice dropped even lower, "They say if you peer in at night, a ghost steals your voice clean away... just like what happened to poor Clara Smithson."

With Mary momentarily catching her breath, Lizzy interjected, "Can we go to the river now? I want to keep working on—"

"—the dam. Yes, obviously." Mary cut in, bouncing up on her toes. "But you know we can't slip away until Mother and Father return from town. Grandmother will need my help with Autumn when she wakes from her nap."

Lizzy let out a dramatic sigh, flopping backward onto the mattress, "Your sister has a ridiculous name."

Mary fixed her with a sharp look, suddenly solemn. "It's unique. She was named for Mother's favorite season. I think it's... poetic." The words came out more defensive than she intended, her fingers tightening around the linen scrap.

A deep silence fell between them—the first uncomfortable pause in their afternoon. Outside, the ax blows had ceased, leaving only the contented clucking of hens and the maple branches' restless tapping against the glass.

Lizzy propped herself up on one elbow, studying Mary's face. "I only meant—"

"I know what you meant." Mary tossed the scrap back into the hidden drawer with more force than necessary. The hidden compartment clicked shut like a sealed secret.

Suddenly restless, she paced to the window, leaning over the two old canines, pressing her palms against the cool glass. The September sun gilded the orchard beyond, where early apples hung like rubies among the leaves and branches. "When I'm a detective," she declared, her voice regaining its usual fervor, "I'll solve all the big mysteries of the world."

Lizzy rolled onto her side, chin in hands. "And when I see the elephants in India," she countered, a sly grin creeping across her face, "I'll ask them why they're so rude as to go about killing grandfathers."

Mary snorted, the tension dissolving like sugar in tea. "Deal. But first—" She whirled from the window, eyes alight. "Help me practice my contortionist act in the barn! If I can fit in that cabinet, perhaps I can—"

A piercing wail sliced through the house from down the hall. Both girls froze.

"Autumn's awake," Mary groaned, her sleuthing and other future dreams momentarily forgotten.

Lizzy burst into giggles as Mary trudged toward the door, but paused when her friend called after her.

"Meet me at the river the moment your parents return!"

Mary spun back abruptly, her copper-streaked ponytail whipping like a pennant in a storm, giving her friend a heartfelt hug, "Of course!"

Before Lizzy could reply, Mary sprinted down the hallway, her bare feet slapping against the old oak floors. Suddenly animated, the two farm dogs followed in hot pursuit.

She skidded to a stop in Grandmother's doorway, where Autumn's tears had already transformed into hiccupping giggles as Sarah Jane bounced the toddler on her knee.

"Quick as a bunny, as usual," Sarah Jane remarked, her wrinkled face crinkling into a smile as Mary bounded into the room—Biscuit and Marmalade, tails wagging, close behind.

"Bickee! Marmee!" Autumn exclaimed with delight as she clapped her hands together.

Mary wrapped her arms around her grandmother's neck, planting a smacking kiss on her papery cheek. "Quick as a fox, I think," she corrected with a grin.

Sarah Jane chuckled, patting Mary's freckled cheek. "Clever girl. Though foxes don't usually leave grass stains on their grandmother's quilts." She nodded pointedly at Mary's knees.

Before Mary could retort, Sarah Jane deftly spun her granddaughter around and began reworking the defiant strands into a tamed ponytail. "Now then, my little whirl-wind," she murmured, her knotted yet nimble fingers moving with surprising dexterity, "are you still reading that novel I gave you?"

"Oh, yes, Grandmother!" Mary wriggled excitedly in her grasp, sending a shower of loose copper strands danc-ing across her back. "I've just finished! It was marvelous— full of clues and cunning sleuthing!"

Sarah Jane's hands stilled for just a moment as she chuckled. "Mercy me! You devour stories faster than hogs gobble up table scraps." She secured the ribbon with a practiced tug and tapped Mary's nose. "Though I daresay even Sergeant Cuff needed naps between cases."

Mary bounced on her toes, causing the floorboards to creak. "But I shan't rest until I'm the world's greatest investigator! Mother says I can be anything—"

"—and heaven help anyone who tells you otherwise," Sarah Jane finished, her faded blue eyes crinkling at the corners. She adjusted the cameo brooch at her throat. "Your mother's a rare one indeed. To think she fought her way from..." Her voice trailed off, her face glowing with pride.

Mary, suddenly thoughtful, her grass-stained fingers brushing her grandmother's sleeve. "I'm ever so glad she saved you from that awful place, and you live with us."

The old woman gathered the toddler closer, her embrace tightening for just a heartbeat before she schooled her features into their usual gentle amusement. "As am I, my fierce little sleuth."

From the front porch came the unmistakable creak of the homestead door—her parents were home. Mary lit up like a gas lamp, already darting toward the noise as Sarah Jane's laughter followed her down the hall, mingling with the dogs' joyful barks as they scrambled after her.

Mary half-stumbled, half-leaped down the stairs to the front door. "Mother! Father!" With a last leap —arms spread wider than seemed possible for a young lady—she warmly hugged the two.

As they both lightly patted Mary's back, Victoria smiled, asking, "Well, my busy bee, did you finish your chores? And the book? How is your sister?"

Mary fired off her replies like a Gatling gun, "Yes! Of course! All done! Marvelous read! And yes, yes, Autumn just woke up—Grandmother's with her now."

Her father raised an eyebrow. "You finished the bo—"

Mary feverishly interjected, "—Naturally! Grandmother says I read faster than hogs gobble up table scraps!" She bounced up and down on her toes, "Can I go to the river to meet Lizzy?"

The two lightly chuckled as Emmett ruffled her sun-warmed hair, "Sure enough—"

Before Emmett had fully finished, Mary zipped through the front door. Emmett yelled after her, "Mind you're back before sundown!"

Emmett looked at Victoria, his voice rich with delight, "I can't believe you found this living jack-in-the-box."

Victoria wrapped her arms around Emmett's shoulders, "And I found you, too," she teased as she gave him a warm, heartfelt kiss.

44. Civilization's Castoffs

*From the beginning of their life they are utterly neglected;
their bodies and rags are alive with vermin; they are
subjected to the most cruel treatment; many of them have
never seen a green field, and do not know what it is to go
beyond the streets immediately around them, and they
often pass the whole day without a morsel of food. Here is
one of three years old picking up some dirty pieces of bread
and eating them.*
—Andrew Mearns and William C. Preston, *The Bitter Cry
of Outcast London: An Inquiry into the Condition of the
Abject Poor*, 1883

A crisp, golden autumn morning on London
Road in Leicester bustled with activity—well-
dressed people rushing past, horses and
carriages rattling to and fro. A brisk wind tugged at bonnet
ribbons and coattails as a crowd gathered before the
imposing stone-pillared doors of the *Leicester Orphan
Asylum*. From nearby, the piercing whistle of a locomotive
stabbed the air, its steam hissing like a serpent, while the
rhythmic huffing of engines echoed down the soot-
blackened street.

A wine-red silk banner, trimmed with gold fringe,
stretched across the entrance, its ends fluttering from the
newly installed gas lamps on either side. The lamps—
proud symbols of Leicester's industrial progress—stood

unlit in the daylight, their glass panes polished to a shine, reflecting the organized chaos of the assemblage.

Among the gathered crowd, several women in corseted walking suits and plumed hats stood conversing near the orphanage doors. Victoria Hartford, poised as ever, exchanged words with her dear friend Mabel, whose lavender skirts swished with each animated gesture.

Victoria looked at her friend with a glimmer in her eyes. "How are things at your new home?" she asked, her voice warm yet measured, as befitted a woman of her station.

Mabel adjusted her parasol slightly before responding, the morning light catching the delicate lace of her gloves. "I love it. Not that I didn't love the farm—don't get me wrong—but life in Leicester is..." She paused, searching for the proper phrase, "...far more diverting. It may be smaller than London, but the social season provides just the right amount of amusement."

Victoria's eyes crinkled at the corners as she leaned in slightly. "And how are the first few months with Daniel?"

A soft blush colored Mabel's cheeks as she smoothed her lavender skirts. "He's a good man. As a Quaker schoolmaster, he's not away for months at a time like..." Her voice trailed off momentarily before recovering. "I find myself... quite content with our... arrangement."

Victoria smiled gently as she watched her friend, happy yet still wrestling with grief.

Mabel took in a shallow breath of acceptance. She quietly added, "Just last week, we attended a showing of *The Pirates of Penzance*, and given that Mabel—the heroine—is the daughter of a Major-General, the military references were... rather bittersweet. I suppose I still miss him more than I expected."

Victoria drew her friend into a brief but firm embrace. When she pulled back, she kept her hands resting lightly on Mabel's shoulders—a socially acceptable display of affection that nonetheless conveyed deep understanding. "We never truly let go of those we've loved," she said quietly, her thumbs giving the slightest pressure against Mabel's shoulders. "Their presence stays with us—always."

Mabel nodded quietly, her eyelashes fluttering as she fought to maintain her composure. The brim of her hat cast delicate shadows across her face, concealing the moisture gathering at the corners of her eyes.

From behind, Victoria heard the crisp, cultured tones and cadence of a familiar voice, "Good heavens. I see you at least arrived on schedule."

Victoria whirled around, her face already blooming with a wide grin, "Annabelle! I'm so glad you could make the trip!"

Annabelle's lips curved into her characteristic, reserved smile, "Indeed. It's only proper for—"

Victoria swept her into a tight embrace that was both unexpected and brimming with impropriety. As Victoria pulled back, she kept her hands resting on Annabelle's shoulders, both women's faces alight with genuine affection.

With a faint smirk, Annabelle feigned distress, smoothing her skirt, "Still inappropriate as ever, I see."

"Of course... Ma'am." Victoria said, her eyes twinkling with mischief, "You know us old meandering donkeys."

They both giggled.

Victoria moderated slightly, adding in a softer tone, "I've missed you."

Annabelle replied with uncharacteristic warmth, "And I you." Adding with a modicum of faux pomposity, "Despite your scandalous conduct."

"Oh, and where are my manners?" Victoria said, executing a perfect half-turn to give Annabelle a clear line of sight to Mabel.

"Hello, Annabelle," Mabel said, extending her hand in greeting. "How was the train ride?"

"Quite… unforgivably rickety, actually," Annabelle replied, accepting the extended hand with a brief but firm clasp. "I hear you are recently wed? My sincerest congratulations."

"Thank you. It was so… startlingly unexpected."

Annabelle gave a wry chuckle, "My dear, since when has life ever proceeded according to expectation?"

Victoria asked, leaning closer to maintain discretion, "Do you think you will attend the Anti-Compulsory Vaccination demonstration next spring? They say delegates are coming from every corner of the kingdom—even American reformers are crossing the Atlantic."

Annabelle's gloved fingers tightened for a moment around her parasol handle. "I dare say I will. One must show solidarity against this governmental overreach."

"What does Simon think—" Victoria began, but her question was cut off mid-word.

A short distance away, the great clock of St. Stephen's interrupted—its iron voice tolling noon with twelve thunderous strikes.

A thin man, smartly dressed in a well-tailored dark suit and polished top hat, ascended the small, makeshift wooden stage that had been erected to the right of the

411

orphanage doors. He raised his hands to quiet the crowd and loudly spoke, "Ladies and gentlemen of Leicester!" He paused a moment for the din of the crowd to die down.

"Ladies and gentlemen!" He repeated, his voice carrying the authoritative tone of a man accustomed to public address. "I shall be brief, for though I despise long speeches, duty compels me to deliver one today!"

A slight laugh rippled through the crowd.

"I am John Biggs, J.P., and I have been privileged to oversee the restoration of this orphanage since the devastating fire that ravaged it nearly a year ago. Today—" he motioned with a sweeping gesture to the crowd, "—thanks to your generosity and the tireless efforts of our craftsmen, we restore this beacon of hope to our city."

Polite applause broke out, as many in the crowd nodded in approval.

"Within these walls," he continued, "fatherless and motherless children shall not merely be housed—they shall be educated. Children will learn to read and write, as well as skills such as sewing for girls and trades for boys. This is no grim workhouse, but a foundation for brighter futures!"

More applause rolled through the throng.

After a deliberate pause, he added, "With that, hopefully mercifully short speech," and with a smile, "I am honored to introduce Mr. Andrew Mearns of the London Congregational Union to say a few words."

With that, Biggs descended the stage with a courteous bow, as a cheerful Mr. Mearns rose to replace him.

"Friends and benefactors," he began, his voice carrying the measured gravity of a preacher. "While our empire spans continents, we must not overlook the suffering at our own doorstep."

The crowd stood in respectful silence as he continued.

"Though England leads the world in industry and invention, tens of thousands of children wake each morning to hunger and despair in our slums." He paused, letting the weight of his words settle. "This orphanage represents more than brick and mortar—it is a covenant with the future."

Reaching into his coat, he produced a small pamphlet. "For those unacquainted with the depths of urban poverty, I bring copies of my work—*The Bitter Cry of Outcast London*—authored by myself and Mr. William C. Preston."

A hum of recognition passed through the crowd; the pamphlet had indeed sparked national outrage since its publication the previous year.

"This humble document has already moved Parliament to debate housing reforms," he said, tapping the book for emphasis. "Each shilling spent here today will both enlighten and sustain these children's education."

With that, John Biggs replaced Mearns on the stage. Biggs looked to the side of the stage, "And now, a woman whose philanthropic efforts have been instrumental to this cause—Mrs. Victoria Hartford."

A smattering of applause arose from the crowd.

"Thank you, Mr. Biggs," Victoria said as she took the stage, adjusting her skirts.

A cool gust sent bonnet ribbons fluttering through the street as if on cue.

A lone female voice pierced the air, "Victoria!"—prompting a knowing smile from the speaker.

Standing tall in her leather boots, Victoria began. "My fellow citizens of Leicester..." She paused as a newsboy's cart rattled past.

She continued with the cadence of a seasoned reform speaker, her voice gaining strength with each word. "Our children are our future. Yet here in this year of 1884, in this age of steam and electricity, we still condemn babes to coal dust and the loom! What manner of civilization permits this?"

The crowd stirred, a few breaths of agreement rising like steam.

"Not only is this a moral abomination, it steals prosperity from us all. While enlightened men like Mr. Biggs and Mr. Mearns build institutions of hope, others clutch their ledgers and look away!"

She leaned forward. "They claim we common men and women don't understand practical economics. But we understand greed when we see it! We recognize the stench of child labor beneath their perfumed excuses!"

A roar of approval surged through the crowd.

"Today, we plant our flag with this orphanage! At Barrington Farms, we will bring children from soot-blackened alleys to breathe clean air, to learn that life need not be all grime and grinding toil! To learn how life can be— not living in muck and mire working until their poor little bodies break, but living a life of learning, of living, of love."

A man in the front row shouted "Hear, hear!" as his wife fanned herself vigorously.

She raised her voice to a clarion call, "And when spring comes, we'll show those bureaucrats that Leicester men and women won't be cut and scraped by their vaccination lancets any more than we'll tolerate their

414

factory inspectors looking the other way while infants toil!"

The crowd erupted with women waving handkerchiefs and men stomping in approval.

From the periphery, a uniformed nurse from the isolation hospital shook her head but remained silent.

"Take these pamphlets!" Victoria thrust a bundle toward the front row. "Spread word through every market square and chapel hall! We refuse to be governed by men who value shillings over souls!"

"Join us next spring when thousands shall march," Victoria's voice soared above the din. "We will demand the freedom to make our own choices and that English mothers still rule their own households!"

The chant began near the gas lamps and spread like wildfire, "Victoria! Victoria! Victoria!" Soon, all of London Road echoed with a chant of "Liberty and Conscience!"

45. Beneath the Streets

*Those who have intelligently watched the course of
zymotic outbreaks, and noted the localities where they
have arisen and the causes by which they are engendered,
are convinced that it is within the power of Governments
by means of scientific sanitary appliances and methods to
stamp out small-pox altogether. Supposing vaccination to
be abandoned, this revolution would be brought about, for
it is the opinion of many of the ablest opponents of
vaccination laws in England that one of the causes of the
perpetuation of small-pox in our midst is the application of
this alleged remedy of vaccination.*
—William Tebb, *Sanitation, Not Vaccination, the True
Protection Against Small-pox*, 1882

*O*n the unseasonably sultry last day of September 1884, the sun filtered through drifting cumulus clouds that filled a vast stretch of the sky. Victoria and Mabel strode down the cobbled center of Leicester's High Street with a large, like-minded group of reformers and townsfolk on their way to view the progress being made by the sanitation engineers north of Wharf Street. Their leather-heeled boots thumped along the uneven cobblestones as their conversations mixed with the din of horse-drawn carts and street vendors hawking wares.

Along the way, they stopped at *Silverdale's Ice Cream Emporium*, a newly fashionable establishment with frosted glass windows and a striped awning, to cool their parched throats. Inside the narrow, marble-countered shop, a white-aproned ice cream jack—a vendor of the frosty delight—stood behind the counter.

He paddled the frozen concoction into thick, hobnail-bottomed goblets—their dimpled bases clinking against the counter as he slid the "penny lick" delights across the polished surface. The raised dots under each glass caught the light, designed for durability—sturdy enough to withstand a hundred careless thumps onto tabletops, while their curved sides magnified the "penny lick" into a deceptively generous mound.

The large group sat amongst wrought-iron bistro tables, enjoying the novelty of the cold treat. Toward the back of the shop, Victoria and Mabel sat with longtime resident Annie Ensworth—a lace-gloved widow known for her charity work—and Mr. Elias Crouch, a whiskered member of the town council renowned for promoting public sanitation reforms, his fingers rhythmically drumming against one of the dimpled goblets as he listened.

Annie leaned forward, her lace gloves tightening around her cup as she vividly described how, years earlier, the stench of the open sewers used to curl up through the floorboards. Despite what they had seen over their years of reform work, both Mabel and Victoria grimaced as she told how, during the heatwaves of '78 the reek of human waste and rotting offal—chamber pots left to fester, fish-gut runoff from the canal—seeped in through every crack in the warped pine boards of their tenement on Wharf Street. How it clung to the cheap paint on the walls, and how youngsters woke themselves coughing, their small fists pressed to their mouths. Fearless rats and large cockroaches scuttled with impunity, their droppings peppering the nooks and crannies of the residence.

Annie said in a low voice, her fingers tracing the rim of her glass, "The vile conditions we endured would seem nigh unimaginable. 'Twas all like some fevered nightmare."

Victoria and Mabel both nodded in solemn agreement. Mabel pursed her lips as she shook her head, her silver brooch catching the light, "The filth and despair we witnessed in London's East End rookeries—whole families living in single cellars..." Her voice trailed off before rallying. "Yet what astonishes me most is how long society has tolerated such conditions."

"Engineering," Mr. Crouch interjected, wiping his wire-rimmed spectacles with a handkerchief pulled from his waistcoat pocket. "The sewers carry the muck westward to the treatment. Away from the water supply. No more seeping into the River Soar."

Annie exhaled softly, her smile crinkling the parchment-thin skin around her eyes. "Now, when I draw my morning water from the pump, it runs clear as crystal. And the courts no longer flood with every summer storm—no more floating refuse or foul pools at our doorsteps."

Mr. Crouch's mutton-chop whiskers bristled with pride. "A Herculean undertaking—miles of glazed brick tunnels laid by men working day and night. We've essentially built an underground river to replace the open channels." He tapped his goblet for emphasis. "Some called it folly, but when you've seen the cesspits we uncovered— the veritable strata of waste accumulated under Leicester's streets—you understand this is true medical progress. Not bleeding or mercury, but proper civil engineering."

Annie nodded vigorously, her bonnet ribbons trembling. "The change in the children's health! My granddaughter hasn't had the summer cholera once, and her teeth stay firm in her gums now." Her joy illuminated her careworn face like gaslight chasing shadows from a room. "'Tis as if we've been transported to a cleaner, brighter world."

Victoria let out an uncharacteristically inelegant huff. "The simplicity of it galls me—how many generations suffered and died while physicians clung to bloodletting and purging instead of demanding clean water and working drains."

Mr. Crouch cleared his throat, adjusting his cravat. "The 1875 *Public Health Act* gave us the tools, but it required men willing to wield them—and people willing to fund the work." He glanced meaningfully at the frosted shop window where two merchants stood arguing over potato prices.

Annie continued grinning, "Well, I am grateful for the progress—quiet, invisible progress."

"All this vaccination controversy," Mabel said suddenly, turning her spoon in the melted dessert, "when simple sanitation has done more for Leicester's health than all the lancets in England."

Mr. Crouch removed his glasses entirely, polishing them with renewed vigor. "You'd have smallpox run rampant like in '71?"

"I'd have clean water and fair wages before compulsory jabs," Mabel countered, her sleeves brushing against the tablecloth. "Our isolation hospital and disinfectors have kept Leicester free of major outbreaks for a decade—without dragging mothers before magistrates."

Victoria nodded, quoting from memory with precision. "Since 1873, not a single significant epidemic has gripped Leicester. Surveillance, quarantine, and proper sanitation—these break the chain of infection far more effectively than coercion ever could."

Mr. Crouch replaced his spectacles with deliberate slowness, the frames settling into grooves worn by years of similar gestures. "The statistics... do bear you out," he conceded. "Can't argue with success."

Four empty cups sat between them, the faceted patterns casting tiny starburst rainbows on the marble tabletop where the last amber droplets of melted delicacy clung like memories of sweetness.

After a weighted pause in the conversation, Mr. Crouch adjusted his tie once more before noting, "And let us not forget the *Dwellings Act* of '82—those new brick tenements with cross-ventilation windows and proper drainage gullies. Finally replaced those pestilential basement warrens where families huddled twelve to a room!" His knuckles rapped the table for emphasis, making the empty goblets tremble.

Mabel's spoon clinked sharply against her glass as she set it down. "To think mothers once swaddled babes in dirty rags," she complained, her dark eyes fixed on some middle distance where memory and horror intertwined. "No wonder the infant mortality registers ran longer than the census rolls. How anyone endured those conditions is beyond belief. Who could possibly be of any health living in sewage?"

Victoria's chin lifted with quiet triumph, the September light catching the silver threads in her bonnet. "Every child playing in a sunlit courtyard instead of a fetid alley proves our work matters." She touched Annie's wrist

420

lightly, feeling the birdlike bones beneath. "This is how civilization progresses—one clean cobblestone, one fresh pump, one child's breath free of stench at a time."

As the group stirred from their seats, the ice cream jack began clearing goblets with experienced efficiency, his rag wiping away the last traces of their discussion along with the melted confection. Outside, the argument between the potato merchants had escalated, their cries carrying over the clatter of cart wheels.

"Same row every Tuesday," muttered one of the crowd, glancing toward the window.

"Aye," said another, shrugging on her shawl. "And not a single potato cheaper for it."

The jack smirked without looking up. "At least they're entertaining. Makes the day go faster."

The reformers reassembled on the pavement, their boots scuffing through fresh horse droppings as they formed a loose procession. Victoria took Mabel's arm, and Mr. Crouch fell into step beside them, his walking stick tapping measured, almost military against the paving stones. "Progress moves forward slowly," he remarked, "but it does move forward, ladies."

As they turned onto Wharf Street, the sharp scent of fresh-cut timber mingled with the river's damp breath. Ahead, the public works crew relentlessly worked in front of the yawning mouth of a new sewer tunnel—its brick arch a monument to modernity, poised to swallow another stream of Leicester's waste forever.

As the afternoon shadows lengthened across Leicester's smoke-blackened buildings, the crowd of observers gradually dispersed, their bonnets and top hats bobbing away down the newly paved lanes. The crew continued their relentless work, their picks and shovels ringing against stone in a rhythmic counterpoint to the distant whistle of a Midland Railway locomotive.

Annie, Mabel, and Victoria made their leisurely way back toward the bustling heart of town. They paused before the Midland Dining Rooms—a modest but respectable establishment tucked beside the railway station's arches, where the mingled scents of roasting mutton and coal smoke created a peculiar Victorian perfume.

The dining room hummed with activity as they entered—clerks in ink-stained cuffs debated coal prices over steak-and-kidney pies, factory girls in faded calico sipped weak tea between shifts, and a pair of commercial travelers argued about the new sewer rates. The clatter of steel cutlery against china provided a constant metallic undercurrent to conversations about vaccination summonses and the shocking price of butter.

"Mind the step, ladies," cautioned the aproned waiter as he guided them to a corner table draped in crisp white linen. Victoria smoothed her skirts beneath the tablecloth, her back instinctively straightening as she took in the room's lively atmosphere.

"Quite satisfying indeed," Victoria remarked, accepting a steaming cup of tea. She stirred in a precise spoonful of sugar, the silver clinking rhythmically against the porcelain. "To see theory made tangible—those sewer arches will endure long after we're gone."

Annie's hands cradled her own cup like a precious relic. "When I think how my daughter nearly perished in the '78 typhoid outbreak..." Her words caught momentarily before brightening. "Now she's bearing healthy children in a proper home with a water closet! Sometimes I pinch myself—it's like living in one of Jules Verne's amazing novels. Twenty Thousand Leagues Under the Seas! Simply—"

She was interrupted by the sudden arrival of their food—plates of mutton stew with dumplings fixed like islands in a rich gravy sea, accompanied by roasted parsnips glistening with beef dripping. The savory aroma momentarily hushed the entire table.

Between delicate bites, Annie's eyes sparkled with newfound excitement. "But nothing compares to the telephone demonstration at the Guildhall! That brass speaking funnel looked like something from a sorcerer's workshop. The operator called loudly into it. There was a pause—" She pressed a hand to her chest. "—and then, astonishingly, a voice answered from two streets away! Muffled, distant, like it had passed through a tunnel from another world!"

Victoria arched an eyebrow. "Practical applications remain limited, of course. Though I daresay it might—"

"Electric lighting!" Mabel interjected with her old enthusiasm, her teaspoon trembling against her saucer. "The Committee's already approved trials. Imagine—no more sooty mantles or foggy streets! Imagine!"

Outside, the shriek of a train whistle pierced the air, its steam curling past the window like the ghost of industry and progress.

After finishing their meal, the trio stepped out into the crisp autumn air, where Leicester lay transformed by the fading light. Gas lamps flickered to life along Granby Street, their yellow flames battling the encroaching dusk as darkness pooled in the cobblestone grooves. The town hall loomed ahead, its neo-classical columns framing a cluster of posters that fluttered like protest banners in the evening breeze. One broadsheet stood out—its bold black lettering proclaiming: *"Join the Leicester Anti-Compulsory Vaccination League. Defend Your Children. Demand Your Liberty!"* The paper's lower edge curled and snapped against its paste, revealing earlier layers of political notices beneath—a tapestry of civic unrest.

The crowd buzzed and pressed through the arched doors. Inside, the scent of woolens damp with dew mingled with sweat and the faint metallic tang of fresh ink from hastily printed pamphlets. The hall's vaulted ceiling amplified the shuffling of boots and rustling of skirts as attendees found seats among the rows of varnished pine benches. The air hummed with the particular tension of a rally where personal anxieties blended with political consequence.

Alderman John Biggs, J.P., stood from his seat at the front row and walked to the polished oak lectern, standing before the sea of faces in Leicester's Town Hall. Clad in a well-cut but deliberately unpretentious brown frock coat—its woolen weave marking him as a self-made man rather than gentry—he adjusted his modest blue silk cravat before taking out a sheaf of papers from his brown leather satchel. He tapped the sheets against the lectern, then brought his closed fist to his lips as if to steady himself before clearing his throat.

The gaslights wavered as he placed his hands on either side of the stand. A hush fell over the hundred-strong crowd as Biggs lowered his papers and leaned forward, his voice booming beneath the hall's ceiling.

"Friends of Leicester," he began, his baritone carrying throughout the hall, "we gather tonight at a crossroads between old fears and new science." He held up a pamphlet whose title page declared it *The Bitter Cry of Outcast London*. "This account of child suffering in our

424

capital's slums sold fifty thousand copies last year—not because it reveals anything new, but because it forces us to see what we've long tolerated."

A buzz of recognition rippled through the crowd as Biggs let the pamphlet fall open to a marked passage. *"In one cellar a sanitary inspector reports finding a father, mother, three children and four pigs! In another room a missionary found a man ill with small pox, his wife just recovering from her eighth confinement, and the children running about half naked and covered with dirt."* He slapped the pamphlet closed, challenging, "Parliament debates the cost of iron pipes, we must ask—what manner of civilization have we built?"

From the benches, a woman's voice called out, "One that jails mothers who refuse the vaccinator's blade!" The outburst sparked a flurry of approving nods and gestures.

Biggs acknowledged the interruption with a slow nod. "Mrs. Thornton speaks truth. The same *Public Health Act* that empowered our sewer works also gave magistrates power to fine objectors twenty shillings per missed vaccination—a week's wages for many here." He removed his spectacles, polishing the lenses with deliberate care. "But I ask you—does medical liberty matter if children still play in cesspools?"

The room erupted in competing voices until Biggs raised both hands. "Tonight, we chart a third course—one where clean water and bodily autonomy flow together." He gestured to a large map unfurled behind him, its inked lines tracing Leicester's expanding sewer network. "These tunnels represent more than brick and mortar; they're proof that when citizens unite, we manifest the future!"

"The Leicester Anti-Vaccination League—" He paused as a chorus of cheers erupted from the gallery, where

425

working-class mothers waved handkerchiefs. "—was formed in 1869 by nineteen men and women who dared question physicians and their silver lancets!"

The scrape of oak benches echoed as artisans and shopkeepers rose to their feet. A dissenting voice barked, "Heresy!" from a top-hatted physician near the back of the room, but was drowned out by stomping work boots and thunderous applause.

Biggs slammed his palm on the lectern, sending up a puff of dust. "In 1867, ninety-four out of every one hundred babes were vaccinated. Today?" He leaned into the silence, veins standing on his temple. "Thirty-six!" The number hung in the air like a jail sentence. "Little more than a third of what it used to be! Why? Because Leicester mothers saw their so-called protected children break out in pustules in '71, '72, and '73!"

He continued, his voice dropping to a hush that forced the crowd to strain forward, "Several hundred vaccinated souls perished as the result of the alleged protection—having lamentably failed in its hour of trial—" he paused as a woman's sob echoed through the hall, "—produced in the minds of Leicester's working men and women pronounced hostility against this government-sanctioned blood-poisoning, which—" he slammed his fist down "—has proven more deadly than the disease it pretends to prevent!"

A woman in mourning black screamed, "My Alice died sweating pus!" triggering a wave of shouts. "Blood poisoners! Freedom!"

He snatched up a ledger, its pages fluttering like wounded birds. "Seventeen smallpox importations since '77 were all contained by sanitation, not vaccination!"

Biggs rolled up his sleeves. "They call us dirty? I say the filth is on their hands!"

The hall erupted. A shoemaker's apprentice hurled his cap at the ceiling; Quakers clutched Bibles to their chests; reporters scribbled furiously. Biggs raised both arms, sleeves straining.

"Next spring, we march for freedom! Let London politicians explain why Leicester's unvaccinated poor outlive their vaccinated aristocrats, and tell them—"

The crowd finished his sentence in a roar. "—To burn their vaccination acts!"

The demands came in waves; a thunderous tide of human will that shook the portrait of Queen Victoria hanging askew above the mayor's empty chair. Dust motes, disturbed from the gilded frame, danced in the lamplight around her stern, youthful face, which seemed to look upon the tumult not with disapproval, but with a ghost of imperial endorsement. The dissenting doctors, their arguments drowned by the rising chant of "No Compulsion! No Tyranny!" were now edging toward the committee room's oak-paneled doors, their black coats and silk cravats a mark of the besieged establishment retreating before the people's wrath.

"No jab! No court! No jail!"

46. The Ghost in the Well

Let us take it easy, and let us take it short; we shall be in
the thick of the mystery soon, I promise you!
—Wilkie Collins, *The Moonstone*, 1868

As clouds drifted across the night sky, inter-mittent moonbeams filtered through the tree branches and into the partially open window of the farmhouse bedroom, the silver light diffused by the lacework curtains that delicately fluttered in the October night breeze. The gnarled limbs of the old maple outside gently tapped rhythmically against the wavy glass panes, a counterpoint to the distant somber-sounding hoot of a barn owl on its last patrol of the fields. The girls lay nestled in their bed, their faces motionless and pale as porcelain dolls in the moonlight, their shared patchwork quilt rising and falling with each steady breath.

Without warning, Mary's fingers twitched as she bubbled up from a deep slumber. Her cornflower-blue eyes blinked open, adjusting to the predawn dimness where darkness pooled in the corners of the room. With a deep inhale that carried the autumn scent of ripening apples from the orchard, she stretched her arms overhead and pointed her toes toward the footboard, hearing her joints pop like green kindling crackling in a fire.

"Lizzy-bean," Mary whispered, nudging her friend's shoulder through the thin nightdress. "The rooster'll crow soon, and we've mysteries afoot."

Lizzy merely tunneled deeper under the quilt, one dark-lashed eye cracking open, peeking at Mary before closing it again. "Five minuets more," she pleaded, her voice thick with sleep.

Mary chuckled, "Minutes, you sleepy dog."

Mary planted her bare feet on the cold pine floorboards and shook Lizzy with the determination of Marmalade gnawing a hambone. "Up! We agreed that today we'd tackle our first case!" She yanked her gray woolen stockings over scuffed knees before stepping into sturdy leather boots still crusted with yesterday's mud.

Lizzy groaned like a rusty pump handle as she pushed herself upright, a revolt of black curls escaping their nighttime braids. She grumbled, fumbling for her homespun overalls draped over a ladder-backed wooden chair. "Tomorrow I'm sl—" the end of the word replaced with a cavernous yawn.

Outside, the first crow of a rooster split the morning calm, soon answered by the mooing of the milking cows in the barn. Mary tossed Lizzy her faded red wool shawl as she exited the bedroom door, Lizzy reluctantly in tow.

Mary's boots thundered down the steep back staircase, her soles occasionally slipping slightly on the worn oak treads polished smooth by generations of feet. She burst into the low-ceilinged kitchen, where the aroma of sunrise tea—a stirring mix of black tea, ginger, peppermint, rosemary, and honey—filled the air.

Victoria and Emmett sat at the pine table, their faces illuminated by the wavering light of a kerosene lamp that supplemented the weak dawn sunlight filtering through the kitchen window. Victoria's work-reddened hands cradled her cup, while Emmett's calloused fingers tapped an absent rhythm against the blue Asiatic Pheasants pattern of his saucer.

"Top of the morning to you, firebrand!" Emmett chuckled as he took in the determined glint in Mary's eye that always preceded mischief.

Before either parent could say anything further, Mary planted her hands on her hips, speaking with all the seriousness of an inquisitor. "Might we have leave to call upon Widow Potts this morning?" she half demanded, then—unable to contain her excitement—blurted, "Hartford and Bennington mean to commence our first professional inquiry into the spectral phenomena at the haunted well!"

Victoria's teaspoon clinked sharply against her cup as she exchanged glances with Emmett—the silent communication of parents long accustomed to their daughter's machinations. "Mind you're back before dinner."

Victoria then added, her tone carrying the unspoken warning that no amount of 'spectral phenomena' would excuse missed chores, "Make sure you collect every last egg from those Rhode Island Reds before you leave, and take this jar of blackberry preserves and a loaf of bread for Mrs. Potts." She then assembled a bundle, pressing it into Mary's already outstretched hands. The scent of fresh bread and summer berries wafted from the opening.

Mary's grin divided her freckled face like a harvest moon, "That's why we got up extra early!" She was half out the door as she uttered a "Thank you!"

Emmett hid a smile behind his newspaper—*The Leicester Chronicle*—its front page dominated by debates over the new *Representation of the People Act*, extending the right to vote in parliamentary elections to more rural laborers. He yelled as Mary exited, "Mind you're careful

430

skulking around the old mill. Wouldn't want our junior detectives becoming someone else's ghost story."

Behind her, Lizzy stumbled out of the house like a sleepwalking specter, rubbing her eyes with bent fingers. "I ain't even sure my feet are awake yet," she mumbled through a yawn wide enough to swallow a turnip whole.

The screen door's spring screeched in protest as Mary bounded and Lizzy lurched onto the gravel path, their boots kicking up puffs of dust that glowed in the slanting dawn light. Lizzy followed at a drowsy shuffle, her braided hair further unraveling into dark storm clouds about her shoulders.

After quickly finishing their morning chores—Mary scattering grain for the hens while Lizzy collected warm eggs into wire baskets—the two girls delivered the eggs to the farmhouse and then raced to the barn, their boots kicking up dew from the early autumn grass. Lizzy's earlier drowsiness had vanished like morning mist, replaced by the exhilaration of their first official investigation.

The barn smelled of dry hay and horse manure, its shadows retreating before the advancing sunbeams that slipped through cracks in the weathered boards. They gathered their investigatory equipment—a fifty-foot coil of Manila hemp rope, a lantern freshly filled with kerosene, and Lizzy's treasured brass-handled penknife—a birthday gift from her mother this past June. The gear, along with the still-warm loaf wrapped in muslin and the jar of preserves, went into the faded suntanned saddlebags.

Nutmeg, one of the farm's chestnut mares, snorted in recognition as they approached her stall. The girls boosted each other onto the mare's broad back using an old apple crate worn with years of similar use. Mary took the reins wrapped in soft leather, while Lizzy settled sidesaddle behind her.

The mare's steady trot carried them past fields where men already labored, their chatter and songs blending with the creak of well pumps and animal pronouncements. The fall sun warmed the wool of their jackets, and the breeze carried the earthy scent of turned soil and woodsmoke from morning cookfires.

As they rounded the final bend, Mrs. Potts' farmhouse came into view—a sagging but tidy structure with trim curling like apple shavings. There sat the widow herself in a faded blue paisley dress that had seen better decades, rocking steadily in a Boston rocker worn smooth by generations of Potts family members. The teacup in her gnarled hands steamed faintly, its faded design barely visible beneath a spiderweb of hairline cracks. She paused mid-sip, her sharp hazel eyes tracking their approach like a barn cat watching sparrows.

"Good mornin', Mrs. Potts!" Mary announced as they dismounted in unison, their leather boots hitting the hard-packed earth with twin thuds that sent chickens scattering. Dust rose around their ankles like brown smoke.

Lizzy's softer greeting came half a beat later, her voice still husky with sleep. "Mornin', ma'am."

The widow's round face creased into a wide smile of delight at the unexpected visit. "Bless my stars if it ain't the Hartford girl and her shadow!" she exclaimed, setting her chipped teacup on a piecrust table beside a basket of darning.

Lizzy's nose scrunched up like a rabbit smelling vinegar. "I ain't nobody's shadow," she muttered under her breath.

432

Mary marched forward, thrusting the bundle forward. "Compliments of mother," she declared. "She thought you might enjoy some preserves and fresh bread."

Mrs. Potts' sausage-like fingers made quick work of the knot, her eyes glinting at the sight of the blackberry preserves. "You tell your mama she's a saint for remembering old Bess Potts."

Mary drew herself up to her full stature of four-foot-ten. "Madam," she intoned, executing a courtroom-worthy half-turn toward Lizzy, "may I present the investigative firm of Hartford and Bennington, undertaking our inaugural inquiry into the supernatural manifestations at the abandoned mill well." Pausing, she corrected herself, "Allegedly supernatural manifestations."

The widow stared in surprise at the two girls, "Lord have Mercy!" she gasped, clutching her face with both pudgy hands. "Ain't no business for young ladies, poking about that cursed mill!"

Mary's grin widened, her freckles dancing on her cheeks. "On the contrary, ma'am. Unexplained mysteries are precisely our business. So, if you would please, tell us what you know about this case."

Mrs. Potts sighed, the rocker loudly screeching as she leaned forward. "That mill's stood empty since my girlhood," she began, her voice dropping to a faint whisper. "Clara Smithson—poor girl—fled a workhouse in '59. They say she hid in the well shaft..." A dramatic pause. "And never came out."

Lizzy's hands crept to her throat, her summer complexion fading to the color of fresh milk.

"Even now," Mrs. Potts continued, tapping the arm of her rocker, "children dare each other to peek in... Them what does..." She brought her hand to her well-creased neck. "The ghost pilfers their voices…" Lowering her tone still further, "Some never speak again."

Mary's eyes glittered with investigative fervor. "Marvelous!" she breathed, completely missing Lizzy's frantic head-shaking.

The widow sat back, her rocking chair protesting the sudden movement. "Mark me, girls—some secrets ought to stay buried. That well's claimed enough young 'uns."

Disregarding the widow's warning, Mary executed a theatrical bow, "Thank you, Mrs. Potts. We'll be on our way."

Using the porch rail for an impromptu mounting, the girls scrambled onto Nutmeg's back, the mare flicking her ears as the girls settled into place. Mary urged her forward with a click of her tongue against her teeth, waving farewell as Lizzy clutched around her Mary's waist, desperately pleading that they should return home.

"Don't be an old worry wart…" Mary chuckled, adjusting her grip on the reins.

Despite Lizzy's protests, the two girls pressed on—down the road, across Miller's field, and along Thatcher's stream, the mare's hooves splashing through the shallow current. After about half an hour, the mill loomed before them—its broken waterwheel jutting at a slight angle, the paddles rotting like skeletal fingers. The well lay nearby, its mossy stones sweating in the sun, the wood-planked cover warped by decades of weather.

Mary dismounted with a purposeful grace, her boots kicking up dirt and century-old mill dust that smelled of damp rot. Lizzy lingered by Nutmeg, holding onto the reins as if they were an amulet.

"Come on, Lizzy-bean!" Mary called, striking a match against her boot heel. The lantern flared to life, casting leaping shadows on the well's surface. With one heave of her arms, she slid the cover aside—the wood screaming against stone and landing on the ground with a thud.

Lizzy edged backward, her shadow stretching long and thin across the ground. Mary leaned over the moss-crusted rim, the lamp light licking at the darkness below.

From the depths came a sound—not a ghost's moan, but the distinct dripping of water falling onto stone. Mary's eyes reflected the flame as she turned, her cry vibrating with discovery, "There's a ladder! Someone's been down there... maybe recently!"

Without a moment's hesitation, Mary turned, facing the stone wall of the well, and planted her right boot on the first rung. The iron ladder groaned like a tired old man but held firm beneath her weight. Lizzy's fingers twisted in her overalls as she watched her friend's braids disappear into the yawning darkness.

After a moment's hesitancy, with her heart beating out of her chest, Lizzy ran and knelt at the well's lip, her knees pressing into the damp moss as she peered downward. Far below, Mary's upturned face shone pale in the trembling light, her eyes bright with adventure.

Mary looked up momentarily and saw her friend's head looking down at her, and then continued her descent —the air growing increasingly cold and clammy. As she peered down, she saw a shimmering surface beneath a layer of dust and leaves. Yelling up at Mary, "I think I'm at the bottom!"

She reached the surface, dipped her boot into it, and lowered her foot deeper, one hand holding tight to the lamp and the other to the rung. As the water level reached her thigh, it felt as if she had hit the ground—one made of dirt and muck. She slowly lowered her other leg and then stood.

Again, she yelled up at the face peering down from above, "I'm on solid ground!" Mary's voice bounced strangely off the curved walls, distorting into something not quite human. She sloshed forward, the black water sucking at her boots like hungry mouths. "It's only thigh-deep here!"

As she walked around the confined circular stone-lined space, a sudden crunch came from beneath her foot. She lifted the lantern, its wavering flame guttering in the moist air, to reveal a broken teacup that was half-buried in the silt, its faded blue Willow Pattern still visible beneath the grime.

"There isn't much down here; just this old—"

Without warning, a low, drawn-out moan, like a dying man's last breath, filled the hollow space of the well. Mary froze, her fingers turning bone-white around the rusted ladder rung. Her breath hitched, but the scream died in her throat—silent as the grave itself.

Lizzy's call tumbled down the shaft, thin and reedy with panic. "Mary Hartford, get back up here this instant!"

In her panic, Mary dropped the lamp. It clattered against the stones, hissing as the flame drowned in the stagnant water, plunging her into inky darkness. Her whole body shuddered, her mouth working soundlessly like a landed trout.

The groan drifted on, swallowed by the gloomy blackness. Her voice refused to materialize—it had been snuffed out like the light in the lantern.

Steady now, Mary. She thought to herself. As her racing heart slowed, she noticed a draft—cool air breathing from her right. Squinting through the gloom, she saw

436

the end of a corroded pipe, weeping droplets into the well. With each gust, the narrow opening wailed like a kneeling widow at a wake.

Mary exhaled, the terror melting from her limbs. Setting free the voice fear had snatched, she yelled up at Lizzy, her words echoing queerly off the mossy stones, "It's just the wind from an old drainpipe!"

Kneeling in the muck, she fished for the lantern, her fingers closing over its dented metal frame. As she climbed, the ladder groaned under her weight, the wrought-iron rungs screeching in protest. At the top, she hauled herself over the well's lip and flopped onto the sun-warmed ground beside Lizzy—her stockings ruined, her arms streaked with algae-green slime.

Lizzy seized her shoulders, eyes wide as harvest moons. "You scared me to death!"

Then the fear broke like a fever, and both of them collapsed into giggles, rolling onto their backs. Above them, a V of migrating geese arrowed across the sky, their cries fading into the rustling symphony of autumn leaves —gilt-edged oak, fiery maple, deep mahogany chestnut, and golden-yellow aspen.

Wiping tears of laughter, Mary turned her head toward Lizzy. "I swear on Grandmother's Bible, I thought Clara Smithson's spirit had cut my tongue clean out!" She flapped a muddy hand dismissively. "No ghost. Just a rusty old pipe singing in the wind."

Lizzy folded her arms across her homespun overalls, her grin widening. "The first case solved by Hartford & Bennington."

"The first of many," Mary declared.

Above them, the October sky stretched like faded denim blue patched with tufts of cotton, the hues of white and gray. Both girls smiled up at that endless sky. For a moment, the world seemed full of nothing but possibilities —as endless as the road ahead of them.

47. Effigy

With bristling mane and grinning teeth, the obscene monster glares at you, and warns you to secure a timely retreat.
—Philip Henry Gosse, *Romance of Natural History*, 1861

A thick cluster of late Michaelmas daisies and goldenrod rested against the whitewashed stone of the farmhouse wall. Bees droned diligently over the last blooms, collecting their final harvest before the first frost. The late-afternoon sun, pale and golden, cast long shadows across the yard where sparrows and chaffinches chirped and squabbled amongst the thistles. A gentle breeze stirred the air, carrying the scent of woodsmoke and turned earth.

Nearby, the remains of the harvest supper lay across several checkered tables, their red-and-white coverings still sprinkled with crumbs, half-eaten meat pies, ginger biscuits, and pitchers of cider. The occasional gust stirred the flowers arranged in jam jars, causing them to wobble.

At one end of the table, Samuel and Olivia watched, their laughter mingling with the din of the children's chaotic games. At the other end, Victoria, Mabel, and Mrs. Eve Bennington—Lizzy's mother—looked on as Mr. Daniel Lorrington—Mabel's husband—and Emmett debated the gruesome case that had dominated the papers since early October.

Effigy

"Better to perish with a clear conscience than to live with blood on one's hands," Daniel declared, his brawny arms crossed over his rough woolen waistcoat, his whisk-ered face flushed with conviction.

Emmett stroked his rough chin thoughtfully. "When a man's adrift and starving, philosophy won't fill his belly," he countered. "The *Mignonette* survivors had been nine-teen days in open waters without provisions—the boy, Richard Parker, was dying of thirst—"

"We're talking about cannibalism!" Daniel's fist struck the table, making the china rattle and the flower arrangements shudder. "By what Christian measure can butchering that ship's boy, a lad of seventeen, be justified? Dudley, Stephens, and Brooks should be jailed for life, I say for their crime!"

"They were going to draw lots—" Emmett countered, "—as is the custom of the sea. But the boy was sick from drinking seawater. He was dying."

"They wouldn't know with certainty he was going to perish, and even if they did, to murder someone like they did—stabbing the poor fellow in the neck—is against God's law. If we don't have moral standards, then we are not better than heathens. We cannot—"

Eve interjected, wrinkling her nose in distaste. "Must we dwell on this ghastly business at this harvest supper and Autumn's birthday celebration?"

With a gentle pressure on her husband's sleeve, Mabel persuaded, "My love, let's not darken such a joyful day with these... horrors."

Daniel exhaled sharply through his nose, his shoul-ders lowering as he took his wife's hand. "You're quite right, my dear. My apologies for becoming too passionate."

Emmett smiled, gently nodding his agreement to end the macabre discussion. "Well debated, sir. Perhaps we can continue another time."

Daniel grinned and politely nodded.

Eve turned her attention to Victoria. "As one of the principals of the protest committee, how are things proceeding with the march next spring?"

After taking a sip of cider, Victoria responded, "We've settled on a date when it seems most can attend, March twenty-third, which is a Monday. We're still lobbying the town council to make it a general holiday for the event so that as many people as possible can attend."

Mabel added, "We're still dispatching notices throughout all of England and beyond. People are quite excited, and we expect tens of thousands to attend."

Victoria continued, "Many have promised to make floats and banners." She motioned with her hand to her left to the farmhouse. "We've almost finished stitching our banner that says 'They that are whole need not a physician.' It just needs some finishing touches."

As they were talking, Sarah Jane made her way to the table with a large sponge cake iced with a thin layer of white sugar frosting. "Time to have some birthday cake."

The adults called and gathered the children to enjoy this special treat. Autumn, now three years old, Charles, Mary, Lizzy, and two children—Louis and Francine—from the orphanage, who had been invited to spend the day, were present.

The cake was sliced and quickly devoured by eager, young faces, adding still more crumbs to the checkered mess.

Effigy

As the cake was vanishing, Mary walked over to Autumn, carrying a large object covered with a tablecloth. "Happy birthday, sister! I have a surprise for you."

She laid the bundle on the table in front of Autumn. The little girl stared, her eyes wide with anticipation.

Mary beamed, watching her sister. "I've had this for five years, and now that I'm quite a bit older and too old for toys like this, I thought you would enjoy—" With a flourish, she whipped off the cloth. "—Queen Victoria and her castle!"

Autumn's face lit up with glee, "Oh! For me?"

"Who else would it be for, you silly goose!"

Autumn said, her words softened by a child's lisp, "Fank 'oo, Sissie!" as she threw her arms around Mary's neck.

Mary knelt, her own smile widening as she watched Autumn's small, reverent hands trace the painted wooden turrets of the castle. "See? And the queen's throne room is here," she explained, pointing.

Their moment was interrupted by a low, amused chuckle. Emmett had wandered over, placing a warm hand on Mary's shoulder. "Passing on the crown, are we?"

Mary nodded. "Yes, Father. I'm happy to share what you made me years ago with my sister. I'll be off soon, solving mysteries, I'm sure."

Victoria looked on from across the table, smiling. "That was a very thoughtful idea, my little sleuth."

As Autumn began arranging the objects in a procession toward the castle gates, Mary felt a swell of contentment. The late sun gilded the scene, casting a warm glow on the happy faces of her family, both old and new. She looked at the castle, then at her sister, and finally

442

at her parents, a new, unshakeable feeling settling in her chest.

After playing with Autumn for a while longer, Mary looked at her two parents, who were now sitting side by side, in a gentle embrace. "May Lizzy and I go to the barn? We have a new act to practice."

Her parents both smiled as Emmett ruffled her hair, "Aye, off you go—"

Before Emmett had fully finished, Mary grabbed Lizzy's hand and they bounded off toward the barn. Emmett yelled after her, "—and mind you're back before full dark!"

Emmett looked over at Victoria, gently laughing, "I don't think she'll ever let me finish a sentence."

Victoria smirked, "Our Mary? Seems unlikely." Slowly getting up from her chair, she added, "Well, it's good timing. We need to get the youngsters to bed."

The two girls entered the great, timber-framed structure and began setting up their act, which they had been practicing over the last few weeks. Moving around apple crates, placing rough-sawn wooden beams between them, and setting up hemp rope over the rafters, they quickly organized their makeshift acrobat workspace. Once everything was in place, they both began practicing—jumping from crate to crate, balancing on the narrow beams, and swinging from one spot in the space to the other.

As the sunlight began to fade, Lizzy lit a few of the kerosene lanterns. The new light flared, then steadied, casting long, dancing shadows over the interior. The sweet smell of hay and old wood grew stronger in the cool evening air, and the world outside the barn doors faded to indigo.

Effigy

In the middle of a particularly ambitious swing from one high crate to another, Mary misjudged the distance entirely. She collided with Lizzy mid-air, and the two tumbled down in a whirl of limbs, landing with a soft, resounding thump in a loose pile of hay. They came to rest in a twisted heap, both their heads buried at the bottom of the pile and their legs sticking up toward the rafters. The peculiar, crumpled position and the sudden shock of it set both of them off laughing hysterically, their muffled giggles swallowed by the straw.

"Capital fun!" Mary gasped, her voice choked with laughter and the dryness of the grass. "Shall we try it again?"

"You're a proper clumsy oaf!" Lizzy sputtered, kicking her legs in the air as she tried to right herself.

As they giggled, brushing themselves off and picking stray pieces of yellow straw from their hair, Mary suddenly fell dead quiet.

Lizzy, still giggling, looked at her friend, "What?"

"Shhh!" Mary admonished, her face frozen in concentration.

In the sudden stillness, they both heard the muffled thud of horse hooves on the soft earth, the sound of riders approaching the barn.

Mary scrambled over to the two wooden doors, peeking through the narrow gap between them. Under a moon that slipped in and out of the speeding clouds, she saw the shadowy figures of three riders on horseback drawing near.

Her eyes grew wide as she saw them slow to a stop near the large oak barely a hundred feet from where they were. She turned and darted toward one of the lanterns. "Quick, extinguish the lamps!"

Effigy

The two swiftly snuffed out the kerosene lamps, plunging the building into a dimness that smelled of hot metal and doused wicks. Both girls scampered back to the barn doors. Mary stood, while Lizzy kneeled, their noses pressed into the gap, peering out in a breathless gaze.

The men had dismounted, their horses standing patiently to the side. One man tossed a rope over one of the lower branches while the other two manhandled a limp, sack-like form from off one of the horses' backs.

Terror struck the two as Lizzy let out a shuddering breath, "Sweet heavens... They're going to hang someone!"

Mary swallowed against a dry throat, her whisper barely audible. "We must get to the farmhouse. Now!"

Mary gradually pushed one of the doors open just enough so they could sneak out into the night. They soundlessly edged through the gap and slid along the barn wall toward a small pile of hay bales, their eyes fixated on the men.

Seemingly unnoticed, Mary whispered to Lizzy as they looked over the top of the bales. "They didn't see us. Let's make a break for it... through the corn field... to the house."

Mary began the count, her voice a tense whisper, "One... Two... Go!" The two sprinted toward their home as fast as their legs could carry them, their hearts thundering against their ribs as they panted from both fear and exertion. Looking over their shoulders as they arrived at the back door of their farmhouse, the men seemed not to have noticed their departure, their focus entirely on the grim task of suspending the ghastly bundle by a rope.

Mary and Lizzy burst into the kitchen, their faces pale with terror.

Emmett, sitting at the old, long kitchen table with Victoria, Samuel, and Olivia, chuckled, "Good heavens, girls, you two see a ghost?"

As the two girls caught their breath, they began to talk over each other, their words tumbling out in panicked fragments.

"There are men..."

"They rode up..."

"On horses..."

"They're..."

"Hanging someone..."

"At the old oak..."

"Near the barn!"

As the two completed their muddled message, the expressions of the four at the table shifted from amusement to grave apprehension. Without a word, they launched themselves from the table.

Rushing into the parlor, the two men each grabbed one of the double-barreled shotguns that sat in the rack over the mantel. Samuel looked at Olivia, "You women, bar the door. Don't open it for anyone but us," as he, Emmett, and the other farmhands who had been sitting bolted from the farmhouse through the squeaking front door, which slammed shut with a sharp crack as the last of them exited.

They all froze on the porch, their breath catching in their throats as they saw the silhouette of a body twisting from the tree, backlit by the great timber-framed building that was now consumed by a raging inferno.

Victoria pushed through the door after them, holding it open as she stared at the horrifying scene. "My God," she breathed, the words a choked whisper.

They all sprinted toward the building, the men with the shotguns in the lead, the other men and Victoria trailing behind.

By the time they reached the oak, the barn was completely engulfed in flames—the heat a physical wall growing in intensity, the acrid smell of coal oil and burning wood permeating the air.

The men who had done this were nowhere to be seen as the group stood before the tree in a moment of shock. From a lower branch, a crude effigy twisted and swayed from a rope, clad in a faded satin gown of bronze and red—stuffed with bunches of straw that protruded to form arms and legs. The burlap sackcloth head wore a bent tin crown, with coarsely stitched Xs for eyes, and the mouth formed by a jagged zigzag of smaller Xs, creating a gruesome twisted sneer.

Around the neck was a rope attached to a rough wooden sign, with a single name painted on it in haphazard bold white letters—"VICTORIA."

48. Shattered Peace

We must meet reverses boldly, and not suffer them to frighten us, my dear. We must learn to act the play out. We must live misfortune down.
—Charles Dickens, *David Copperfield*,1850

While the barn burned unabated, the men quickly formed a ragged bucket brigade, a desperate, hopeless rhythm of throwing one bucket of cool water after another onto the scorching flames. They continued at a frantic pace until a deep, shuddering groan—a long, agonized shriek of nails pulling from the joists—made it clear the structure was about to collapse. As they backed away, the center of the barn roof gave way and fell into itself, sending a whirlwind of crackling sparks and flames higher into the night sky, forcing them to abandon their efforts to save the building.

The family looked on, helpless, at the burning beams that had crumpled into a fiery maelstrom. Emmett, his face grim and soot-streaked, half climbed up the tree, cut the effigy down with his well-used pocket knife, and lowered it to the ground, where it lay looking up at the onlookers with its crudely stitched, blank, twisted smirk.

Victoria looked down at her malicious likeness, her own deep scowl etched on her face. "Who would do something like this? What manner of coward does such a thing?"

With his arms folded tightly in front of himself, Samuel exhaled, a sharp, angry sound. "Seems someone doesn't like what you've been doing in town. This is the work of men who mean to frighten us into silence."

Victoria mouthed just above a whisper, "So it would seem."

A grim silence enveloped the group standing in a solemn circle around the hay-stuffed representation, the only sound the hungry crackle of the fire. Oppressive heat and a ghostly glow from the burning mass played with eerie shadows across their horrified faces.

Emmett shouted over the roaring snaps and crackles, "We knew something like this might happen... but knowing and standing in the ashes of it are two different things." His clenched fists tightened at his sides as his stance shifted to a posture of raw, unvarnished fury, "Someone not only threatened us, but they dared to torch our livelihood and hang this foulness on our land. Cowardly ruffians, the lot of them!"

Victoria picked up her tin-crowned likeness from the ground, crushing the rough burlap and straw in her hands, and began to walk back toward the farmhouse. "Craven bastards," she hissed, her voice low and venomous. "They endangered our children. That I will not forgive."

As she and Emmett approached the farmhouse, the flickering flames behind them made their distorted silhouettes dance fitfully along the white planked walls. Upon entering the farmhouse, the fire's angry light stretched their shadows into grotesque, elongated shapes on the floorboards.

They saw the girls huddled quietly with Olivia at the table—their eyes wide and fixed on them, their lower lids brimming with unshed tears.

"Girls, are you alright?" Victoria asked, her voice softening as she knelt before them and gave them both a reassuring hug. "You are safe now. You were both so very brave."

"We're fine, mother," Mary said with a distinct subcurrent of nervousness, while Lizzy sat quietly, her eyes wide, holding a silence that was louder than any scream.

Victoria took both their hands in hers. "Girls. It's ok to be frightened. Being scared means you understand what's at stake. Now we need to use that understanding."

She stared into their eyes and sensed the tightness in their small faces ease, if only a fraction. "Now... take a deep breath and tell me everything you saw. No detail is too small."

Mary quickly launched into her typical rapid-fire account. "First, I thought I heard hooves outside, so I ran to the barn doors and peeked out. I saw the three riders coming up toward us from the east track."

"Men? Could you tell anything about them? Their size? Their hats?"

"I think so. Yes. They wore dark coats and Bowler hats. It all happened so fast."

"What color were the horses?"

Mary looked up and to the right, searching for the answer. "Not white. It was getting dark... The lead horse was a bay, I think, with a white sock on its right foreleg. The others were darker... perhaps chestnut or dark bay."

"That's excellent, Mary. What else did you notice? The saddles? Their voices?"

"It was getting dark... so nothing else. They didn't speak above a whisper."

Lizzy's eyes widened, "Then they brought out the... the body. Someone they were going to hang."

Victoria gently half held up the effigy, "No, dear. It was only ever this vile scarecrow. Not a person. It was just done to scare me... scare us. It's just a wretched pile of straw... nothing more."

A small, shaky sigh escaped Lizzy's lips as she stared at the dummy, the tension draining from her small frame until her shoulders slumped.

After a few more moments of silence, Victoria continued. "You girls had a terrible fright, but you are safe within these walls. Let's get you to bed early. I'll check on you shortly."

Both girls quietly nodded. Victoria gave them both a long, tight hug, and then they headed for the stairs, their footsteps heavy with weariness.

As the children were making their way up the stairs, the other farmhands trudged back into the house, their faces blackened with soot and etched with fatigue, the open door framing the still-raging fire like a portal to some other, hellish world.

Benjamin sat down with a huff at the dining table, the old wood creaking under his weight. "There were definitely three horses. Shod, all of them. I followed their tracks to the bank of the Soar." Running his hands through his tousled hair, he added in a tone of frustration, "But that's when the trail went cold. They likely rode upstream or downstream to throw off any pursuit."

Victoria added, her voice tight, "Mary says the lead horse was a bay with a white sock on its foreleg. The others were darker bays or chestnuts... that's not much to go on in a county full of working horses."

The room fell into a heavy silence as everyone pondered the grim new reality on the farm, the reek of woodsmoke and defeat clinging to the air. The crude scarecrow propped up against the wall appeared as if it were mocking the family with its stitched mouth, a lipless gash of triumph.

Samuel broke the silence, his voice a low rumble. "It's not likely we'll ever find out who perpetrated this vile act. The law has little reach for this sort of cowardly work. That's something we will have to accept." He took in a shallow breath. "But we'll also have to accept that we need to be more vigilant. We must be our own watchmen now."

Emmett added, his jaw set, "I doubt anyone would be foolish enough to do something tonight, but I'll take the first watch. I'll be on the porch with the shotgun."

Benjamin nodded, his expression grim. "I'll take the second."

Samuel added, "At first light, I'll meet with the men from the local farms to let them know what happened tonight—although I'm sure half the county saw the flames—and see how we can work together to keep a united watch."

Victoria looked over at her malicious likeness, her own expression hardening into one of resolve. "We might be shaken, but this only shows that those who oppose us are getting desperate. They resort to terror because they fear the power of our numbers. We will not be cowed."

Samuel added, his voice heavy with practical concern, "The barn wasn't just a building. It stored over half our winter hay, the seed oats, the tools, and the harnesses. That puts us in a precarious position for the winter, with this happening so late in the season."

Olivia added, placing a reassuring hand on his arm, "We will make it work. We are not without friends. I'll speak to the other farms at first light. The Hodges at Winter Oak Farm are good people; they've got three strong sons, and I'm sure they'll be able to pitch in to get us back on track."

Victoria rose and picked up the rough scarecrow, firmly securing it against the wall near the door. She stared into its lifeless face, its mocking tin crown on a skewed angle.

"At first, I wanted to tear this thing apart... to cast it into the flames... but now I think we should keep this. Let it stand as our reminder of what we are fighting against, and the lengths to which our enemies will go."

She then turned toward the kitchen. "I'll put the kettle on for tea."

In the kitchen, Victoria filled the heavy, soot-blackened kettle with water and placed it onto the hob of the range. While she waited, she looked at her reflection in the cold, darkened windowpane, the pulsating orange glow of the barn's ruin painting her likeness in the glass— a pale, spectral image superimposed over the heart of the devastation. Her hair was disheveled and clung in damp tendrils to her soot-stained face. As she raised her hand to brush the strands from her eyes, she saw the tremor in her fingers, a fine, uncontrollable vibration of shock and rage.

A cold dread tightened in her chest. *Oh my God. Was this all worth it?* She gulped down a deep sniffle, forcing the tears not to fall. *Maybe Emmett was right. I've brought this upon us. I've shattered the sanctuary of the farm.* In her mind, she could see her effigy in the other room, the stitches of its mouth seeming to curl in silent laughter.

49. The Grin in the Corner

*Apprehension, uncertainty, waiting, expectation, fear of
surprise, do a patient more harm than any exertion.
Remember, he is face to face with his enemy all the time,
internally wrestling with him, having long imaginary
conversations with him.*
—Florence Nightingale, *Notes on Nursing: What It Is, and
What It Is Not*, 1860

*T*he shockwave from the fire at Barrington
Farm had reverberated through the local
community for over a week, fueled by little
more than rumor and dread. Then, the *Leicester Mercury*
gave the horror a concrete shape, publishing an article
that announced the full, chilling details of the crime.

THE LEICESTER MERCURY
Tuesday, 4th November 1884
Price One Penny

OUTRAGE AT BARRINGTON FARM
— ANTI-VACCINATION CRUSADER TARGETED
BY NIGHT RIDERS —

Barn Burned to the Ground—Effigy of Lady Activist
Left Hanging

LEICESTER— This paper has learned of a most
dastardly and alarming act of intimidation which
occurred on the evening of the 26th of last month at
Barrington Farm, on the outskirts of our borough. A

party of three unidentified horsemen set upon the property, intentionally setting fire to and utterly destroying one of the farm's principal barns. In a final act of macabre theatre, the criminal gang left a calling card in the form of a crudely-fashioned scarecrow, hanged from an oak tree, made in the likeness of Mrs. Victoria Hartford (née Barrington), a well-known champion of the impoverished children of our fair city and a tireless crusader against the tyrannical compulsory vaccination laws.

When contacted by this correspondent, Mrs. Hartford commented on the incident, her resolve evidently steeled by the event: "The intent was to terrify all those who support liberty and eschew unwarranted government interference in the sacred sanctity of the family and the health of its citizens. However, this cowardly action will not dissuade us, but shall only strengthen our resolve to see this unjust Act consigned to the fire, as our barn has been."

The Leicestershire Constabulary confirms that an investigation is underway, although sources indicate that the perpetrators, having fled under cover of darkness, left few clues. If any person has information regarding this matter, please contact your local constabulary or a Mercury representative at our offices on Gallowtree Gate.

Two constables were summoned to the scene of the crime the day following the fire, the site still acrid and smoldering with a few hot coals beneath the charred remnants of the barn. The two spent several hours conducting a perfunctory examination of the scene, vainly examining the trail leading to the river, and asking questions of the witnesses. Afterwards, they informed the residents of the farm that an investigation would be opened; however, due to the "absence of any significant material evidence," they would have to rely almost entirely on the public to provide leads in the case, a prognosis which offered the victims little solace.

That first week, the community's response was both immediate and heartening. Local farms rallied to the aid of the Barringtons, and through a collective effort of donated labor and timber, the frame of a new barn already stood erected a hundred feet from the ghastly ruins of the former. Furthermore, the local farmers had organized themselves into rotating nightly patrols along the parish lanes as a deterrent against future violence. Adding to this show of solidarity, they also received a letter from Mr. William Young, secretary of the London Society for the Abolition of Compulsory Vaccination, promising to send trusted volunteers to help with security on the farm and at the League's offices in Leicester.

Now, five days after the article had been published in the *Leicester Mercury*, the farm was returning to a fragile semblance of order as Victoria and Emmett finally stole a moment to take a private walk along one of the rutted country roads near the farm, the November chill biting at their cheeks.

After walking side by side for a few minutes, Emmett broke the silence, "Well, the new barn frame is up. Things seem to be coming along."

Victoria seemed tense, her arms crossed tightly against the cold, as she continued to silently look at the dirty, rocky road before her. Somewhere far off, a crow let out its harsh, lonely caw.

"Vic... talk to me. What's weighing on you?"

"I…" she looked for the words in the tiny dust puffs kicked up by their boots, "I'm sorry for getting us into this mess…. You were right to worry."

Emmett studied her with a half-puzzled look. He stopped and held Victoria firmly by the shoulders, forcing her to meet his gaze. "Listen to me. The fire was not your fault. You know that, don't you?"

"If I had just paid the fine… this nightmare—"

"Vic," Emmett interrupted, "Didn't you yourself say we have to stand firm against these… these bloody injustices? And what about all the poor devils who couldn't pay the fines? Who speaks for them if we retreat?"

He gave her a slight, reassuring shake, "You were right. Just because we got a little bloody nose doesn't mean we should go hide under our beds like frightened children."

"I just… I know… but I was scared… What if Mary and Lizzy had been in the barn? They could have been killed."

"I know, my love. It's a deep and abiding terror that sits in my own belly," He continued as he wiped a tear running down Victoria's face with his calloused thumb, "but you were right, we need to stand strong. If we don't, who will? We're all they have."

She managed a weak smile and then wrapped her arms around his broad shoulders, "Thank you… you wonderful, steady man. I didn't want to lose you."

"You didn't. You won't. We're facing this thing head on and you… my fierce, brilliant wife… will make a difference."

She hugged him tight, drawing strength from his solid presence, and then pulled back slightly to look up into his face, "I needed to hear that… I was feeling a little lost at sea."

"Aye... It's a heavy burden you carry. I understand. But you don't carry it alone."

They resumed their quiet stroll, and though the landscape was the same, the November countryside looked a little less desolate, the road a little less dusty and harsh.

Emmett added, "We're going to live our lives and not fall victim to that vile grinning sack of straw. If we don't, then they didn't just burn down our barn... they burned our freedom to cinders."

Her hand tightened around his. "I know. I just needed a little reminder from you." She finished with a gentle kiss on his wind-chapped cheek.

As they rounded the bend, they could see the farmhouse nestled among the ancient elms and oaks, a thin, white wisp of smoke rising from the chimney. Just a short distance away, they could see and hear the rhythmic clatter of men nailing up the clapboards on the side of the new barn.

"I'd better go and join them. We want to get the roof on before the first snow." Emmett kissed Victoria one last time before heading off toward the sound of hammers and saws, the sweet, fresh scent of sawn pine cutting through the persistent smell of ash.

Victoria entered the warm, bustling kitchen. Olivia, Charlotte, and Tillie were peeling potatoes and chopping turnips for a hearty mutton stew simmering in the black pot over the fire.

Victoria slid off her coat and hung it on one of the many wooden coat hooks by the door. "Where is Mary? Lizzy? Those two are joined at the waist."

Olivia smiled, wiping her hands on her apron, "That they are. They went down to the riverbank to investigate

God knows what... You know those two and their mysteries."

"Don't I?" Victoria chuckled.

Charlotte paused her chopping and excitedly leaned in, "Did you hear about the quite extraordinary goings on in town yesterday?"

Victoria looked over, "No. I don't believe so. We've been rather cut off lately."

"Well, it's the talk of the market! That *Mercury* article has got everyone in a proper state. First, there was a great spontaneous march down Granby Street to the Corn Exchange... My cousin said there were hundreds of people carrying scarecrows dressed in top hats and banners saying 'We Stand With Victoria' and 'Liberty or Death'."

Victoria's eyes widened. "Truly? A march?"

Charlotte smiled and nodded vigorously.

"And... more shockingly... Word came by the afternoon train that in Birmingham, a mob broke into the public vaccinator's office and smashed it to bits... or so they say."

Victoria's flicker of pleasure turned into a deep, uncomfortable gulp. "Oh my God. That's not what I intended..."

Charlotte continued, her voice dropping to a hushed, dramatic tone, "The whole front of the office was torn out with crowbars. Quarantine notices and bags of sulphur for disinfecting houses were piled up in the middle of the street and set ablaze."

"Oh, lord in Heaven! Ours is a law-abiding, peaceful movement... this is lawlessness. This is so very wrong."

Charlotte let out a huff, "Not everyone has your patience, it seems. Some folk's anger runs hotter."

The Grin in the Corner

Oh no. This has gotten out of hand, Victoria thought as her hands involuntarily clenched into fists at her sides. She whispered to herself, more to herself than anyone, "The embers from our blaze have been carried with the wind. And now I fear we cannot control the fire."

50. A Shared Humanity

Ah! when shall all men's good
Be each man's rule, and universal Peace
Lie like a shaft of light across the land,
And like a lane of beams athwart the sea,
Thro' all the circle of the golden year?
—Alfred, Lord Tennyson, *The Golden Year*, 1846

A raw and biting December wind whistled down the streets of Leicester as four souls, tightly bundled against the cold, made their way along Oxford Street to a modest, weathered red brick house. Daniel reached into his coat pocket, retrieved a key, and inserted it into the lock. The door swung open, and he hurriedly ushered his wife, Emmett, and Victoria into the chill, drafty front room. Fighting against a powerful gust, he pushed the door firmly shut and strode to the hearth to coax a flame from the banked embers.

"My goodness, this winter bites deep—colder than any I can remember in years," Mabel exclaimed as she rubbed her gloved hands together.

"The almanac says it's going to be a harsh one all through until March," Emmett added as he knelt to assist Daniel in nursing the fire back to life.

"I hope that it warms ahead of our demonstration at the end of March," Victoria wished aloud.

"'Twill be what God wills," Daniel muttered, his breath misting in the frigid air as the fire sputtered and finally flared into a steady, warming glow.

"Still, despite the cold," Victoria said as she began to remove her thick wool coat, "it was worth braving the weather to watch that young man win the roller-skating race at Floral Hall. It was quite exciting. I believe they said he was only fifteen years of age."

Emmett added, "Aye. Young Master Blakesley is an impressive lad."

As the fire took hold and started chasing the shadows from the interior, the four of them settled into the well-worn chairs in the sitting room. They sat back and began to unwind, the whipping winter wind outside occasionally rattling the window sashes.

Victoria sighed softly. "It is lovely to have a quiet, ordinary evening once more."

Daniel leaned back in his leather wingback chair. "Is the farm back to where it was before that wretched business with the barn fire?"

"The new barn is up, thanks to our neighbors, although we did lose a fair bit of feed and a few tools. We will certainly get by," Emmett responded, leaning forward as he continued warming his hands.

"God be praised," Daniel said.

"We were blessed with our wonderful neighbors and friends to rebuild quickly," Emmett added.

"Thankfully, Mary and her friend seem to be back to themselves. It was a hard time for them… for all of us. It is a pity those who set the blaze were never caught." Victoria added with a wry grin and then finished with a strong smile, "But we are all living our lives and moving forward."

A Shared Humanity

Mabel's gaze hardened as she stared into the dancing flames. "Living forward, yes—but the air is thick with unrest. Only a few years ago, in Dewsbury, an effigy of a vaccination officer was hurled to a crowd of ten thousand, and they tore it to pieces as though it were flesh and blood. That kind of fury does not die. It smolders beneath the ashes of complacency. And mark my words—here in Leicester, it will not be long before that anger bursts into the streets for all the world to see."

She shook her head, a shadow of despair crossing her features. "Civilization is a thin veneer. Our grand society can disappear if the people rise up for want of food or feel they can no longer trust those in Westminster."

"As it is written in Proverbs 29:4," Daniel intoned with solemn gravity. "By justice a king giveth a country stability, but he that receiveth gifts teareth it down."

A heavy silence fell upon the room, broken only by the crackle of the fire. Victoria's hands stilled in her lap, her eyes flicking uneasily toward the window as though the dark street outside might already be stirring with the footfalls of an agitated future.

Pursing her lips, Victoria began, "That recent newspaper editorial tried to paint our entire movement as a violent mob. As you say, there has been fury smoldering for so many years; it's ready to combust. Still, I believe most people want to effect change through peaceful means. That's why I wrote that letter in response to call for peace on all sides."

"As it is written in Matthew 26:52," Daniel spoke again with equal seriousness. "Then said Jesus unto him, 'Put up again thy sword into his place, for all they that take the sword shall perish with the sword.'"

Nodding, Victoria continued, "I understand the frustration and rage on our side," her voice low. "When they cut us with their lancet, it's as if they are branding us, almost like we are cattle, slaves, or criminals. They violate the sanctity of our bodies."

Again, Daniel quietly recited, "First Corinthians, 6:19 to 20. 'Know ye not that your body is the temple of the Holy Ghost which is in you, which ye have of God, and ye are not your own? For ye are bought with a price: therefore, glorify God in your body, and in your spirit, which are God's.'"

Victoria smiled, "Thank you, Daniel. That is the very heart of our argument." Then she added, "But they are afraid. They fear smallpox and tell us an unvaccinated child is like a bag of gunpowder, which might blow up the whole school, and ought not, therefore, to be admitted to a school unless he is vaccinated. So, I understand their terror, if not their reasoning."

Her hand clenched into a fist upon her thigh, her voice rising with passionate intensity, "But what they willfully ignore are the injuries, the diseases, the little graves from it. They also ignore the success of the last ten years here in Leicester without it. They refuse to see it—any of it!"

She sat back, her hands coming together with fingertips pointing skyward in a prayerful pose. "We all have an interest in preventing violence, and that's why I had several people on both sides sign my response that called for peace and reason to prevail."

Mabel's face softened, a sigh escaping her lips. "Perhaps you're correct, my dear friend. Things have been calm as of late, and God willing, they will hold until the spring demonstration."

"A few nights ago, I—" Victoria paused, reaching for Emmett's hand and gripping it tightly— "we threw that cursed effigy into the fire. I'm done with the fear and hate. We are going to make changes—that I have no doubt—but it will be through peaceful and lawful means, through the sheer weight of our numbers and the rightness of our cause."

"What if those marauders strike again?" Mabel gently queried.

Victoria sat forward again. "They may, but... we are living our lives. If we give in to fear, they win. We must remain strong, but peaceful."

Emmett added, "We are staying vigilant... as perhaps we should have been in the first place."

"In the spirit of living life, we are taking Mary to her first performance at the Theatre Royal to see Mr. Dickens' *A Christmas Carol*." Victoria's eyes sparkled, "You know how much I love Dickens."

For an instant, Victoria's mind drifted to a distant memory of pretending to read *Great Expectations* in bed so many years ago. A ghost of that girl flickered in her mind—so distant from the woman she now was, separated by a chasm of experience and loss. The memory felt borrowed, the life of a stranger.

She gently shook her head to snap herself back into the present. "Mary doesn't know a thing. It will be a complete surprise for her."

"That's wonderful! My apologies for becoming so morose. It is so unlike me. I let a bit too much of the darkness in." Mabel added with a growing smile.

Daniel took her hand in his, "There is no need for apology amongst family. Your heart feels the weight of the world; it is a testament to your character."

A Shared Humanity

Mabel stood up and, her customary effervescence returning, smiled broadly, "Come now, let us move to the dining room. The kettle must be singing by now, and I have a fresh batch of crumpets I baked this morning that will do us all good."

51. Christmas Blessings

*He went to church, and walked about the streets, and
watched the people hurrying to and fro, and patted the
children on the head, and questioned beggars, and looked
down into the kitchens of houses, and up to the windows;
and found that everything could yield him pleasure. He had
never dreamed that any walk—that anything—could give
him so much happiness.*
—Charles Dickens, *A Christmas Carol*, 1843

Mary was barely able to contain herself as she sat on the plush velvet chair, eagerly awaiting the curtain to rise on her first theater performance—her heart hammering as if it could leap out of her chest. It was not only a theatrical premiere but the first time she was dressed in garments suitable for a special occasion, her customary farm attire of plain homespun overalls banished in favor of elegant finery they had recently purchased at a city boutique.

Tonight, she was uncomfortably resplendent in a pale lavender gown, adorned with raspberry silk ribbons, white stockings, and agonizingly tight patent leather shoes that made her toes scream for escape from their unnatural leather-bound imprisonment.

Yet, she tolerated the discomfort and pinching with the endurance of a martyr, for she felt every inch a princess in a fantasy tale plucked straight from one of her beloved novels.

Her tailored miseries were further pushed into the background as she drank in the sight of the Theatre Royal, jammed to its utmost capacity. The bitter chill of the December night vanished the moment they'd crossed the threshold into the warm and glittering interior.

She tilted her head back, mesmerized by the great gas chandelier whose hundred flames were caught and multiplied by the gilt cherubs and the polished balcony woodwork. Ladies in rustling silks and fur-trimmed winter mantles whirred their painted fans amidst a low hum of conversation, while the gentlemen, stiff in their black evening tailcoats, studied their playbills with an air of anticipation.

She again glanced down at her own playbill, which she held so tightly as if it were a sacred ticket that kept her anchored to this fantasy—its edges already soft and frayed from her clammy, nervous grip.

🎭 THEATRE ROYAL, LEICESTER 🎭
Grand Christmas Entertainment

For Three Nights Only—*Monday 22nd, Tuesday 23rd, & Christmas Eve, Wednesday 24th December*

CHARLES DICKENS'
IMMORTAL & BELOVED TALE
A CHRISTMAS CAROL

Faithfully adapted from the immortal story of Ebenezer Scrooge, Tiny Tim, and the Spirits of Christmas Past, Present, and Yet To Come. A moral and moving drama, interspersed with music and scenes, suitable for all ages.

☞ *Mr. Henry Mordaunt* as Ebenezer Scrooge
☞ *Miss Clara Fairleigh* as Belle
☞ *Master Tom Ellison* as Tiny Tim

With a full supporting cast, festive choruses, and special scenic effects, including the transformation of Scrooge's chamber and the Vision of the Christmas Feast.

Let all who cherish the true spirit of Christmas be present at this heart-warming entertainment, which has delighted audiences across the kingdom.

Here they were on opening night, an occasion to which Mary had repeatedly gushed to the parents sitting on either side of her, "This is simply too marvelous! Positively marvelous!" For once, her boundless energy was entirely consumed by awe; she continued to look around in wide-eyed astonishment, her head swiveling like an owl to take in every gilt angel and painted ceiling panel.

Emmett leaned forward to look at Victoria, chuckling, "Well, I'll be. Our daughter is actually speechless."

Victoria too leaned forward, her expression soft with amusement, "A Christmas miracle, it seems."

When the orchestra struck its opening notes, a hush fell, and the gathered company, high and low alike, leaned forward to partake once more in Mr. Dickens's immortal Christmas story. The gas jets in the theater were turned down until they were mere pinpricks of light, plunging the auditorium into a velvety darkness.

The painted canvas backdrop suggested a dank, narrow London street. A painted sign read "Scrooge & Marley." Snow, fashioned from bits of white cloth and paper, was scattered about the stage. The orchestra played a quiet, mournful air that created a solemn mood.

469

As the lights rose, the figure of Scrooge was seen at his desk, counting coins by the flickering light of a single candle. A clerk—Bob Cratchit—crouched at a smaller desk, shivering and blowing upon his hands.

Scrooge, stacking sovereigns, grumpily uttered, "Cold! Bah! The world grows no warmer for all its noise and folly. Christmas!—A humbug, I say! A mere excuse for idleness and beggary."

Blowing warm air into his hands, Bob Cratchit looked up from his desk and ventured timidly, "If you please, sir, the day is near upon us, and but a morsel of coal in the grate would bring cheer to our labor."

Scrooge snapped, "Coal? Do you think I am made of money? Out with your nonsense, Cratchit, and mind your work! Christmas indeed—be off with it!"

The play continued, with the audience spell-bound, their reactions marked by a few audible gasps and muffled sobs of surprise, fear, and joy.

After over two hours of a riveting performance, the play reached the final scene. The stage was ablaze with festal cheer—a large table groaned under the weight of a roast goose and plum pudding. The orchestra played a sprightly Christmas carol in the background

The Cratchit family gathered around, and Scrooge, now transformed, raised a glass of punch. "My friends! My dear family! This day, and all the days to come, I shall keep Christmas in my heart, and never again be the miser you once knew. Bob, you shall have more coal for your fire, and Tiny Tim—"

Tiny Tim stepped forward, grinning ear to ear, "God bless us—everyone!"

The cast gathered close, hands linked. The orchestra swelled into 'God Rest Ye Merry, Gentlemen' as the curtain began to fall slowly. As the curtain halted mid-fall, it rose again to thunderous applause. The cast stepped forward in turn, bowing deeply to the audience, starting with Tiny Tim, then Bob and Mrs. Cratchit, followed by the spirits. At last, the actor portraying Scrooge took center stage. He bowed low, then straightened, standing tall and lifting his arms in a cheerful acknowledgement. The company joined hands once more and bowed together.

The audience, seated in the ornate, crimson interior of the Theatre Royal, broke into rapturous applause, and many leaped to their feet. Gentlemen waved their hats; ladies clapped with gloved hands. The gaslights brightened as the orchestra struck a final triumphant chord.

Mary jumped to her feet, applauding until her hands stung. She turned to her parents, her eyes shining brighter than the gaslights. "Thank you," she said, her voice thick with an emotion too big for words. "It was perfect."

The trio slowly merged into the throng spilling toward the gas-lit lobby. Murmurs of approval for the performance buzzed among the crowd, snippets of praise for Mr. Mordaunt's Scrooge and Master Ellison's Tiny Tim floated on the warm air. While many exited the theater directly, Victoria and Emmett were intercepted by several portly members of the Leicester town council and soon engrossed in conversation.

Mary, still in joyous rapture from the evening, drifted a few paces to stand in quiet contemplation before a large oil portrait of a young Queen Victoria—her mother's namesake—painted to commemorate her coronation in 1838. The Queen sat dazzling in her parliamentary robes of crimson velvet and ermine, the faintest hint of a smile touching her lips. Mary wondered how she felt all those years ago, posed in her dazzling robes, wearing a diamond-encrusted crown with the weight of an Empire on her young shoulders. *Was she nervous? Terrified? Or already possessed of the formidable resolve that would define her reign?*

A voice cut through the air from behind her. "Mary!"

She broke from the unblinking eyes of Queen Victoria's portrait and spun around. Her mother was beckoning her to come over. Victoria now stood alone with Emmett and a rather tall, sharply dressed gentleman of late middle age. His defining feature was his magnificent white mutton-chop whiskers that flowed well below his chin—giving Mary the distinct impression he was part walrus.

Victoria looked down at her daughter, "Mary, this is our good friend Mr. James Eddington."

Mary immediately stuck her arm out, executing a small but correct curtsy as she did so. "How do you do, sir. I am very pleased to make your acquaintance."

Somewhat taken aback by the forwardness and poise with which Mary had addressed him, he recovered with gentlemanly grace, momentarily bowing before taking her small hand and giving it a single, formal shake. "The pleasure is entirely mine. I've heard many remarkable things about you, young lady."

He continued, "Your parents have done a great deal for our fair city, and they speak most highly of you."

Mary confidently responded, "Thank you, sir. I'm sure it's all overstated, seeing as they are my parents."

James let out a hearty, rumbling chuckle that made his magnificent whiskers quiver, "You're only twelve, hmm? Only twelve? Your parents did not exaggerate. Well then," he said, leaning down slightly, "I have a proposition for you."

Mary stood poised and quiet.

I am the proprietor of 'Eddington's Private Inquiry Office' located on Oxford Street," he announced with a touch of pride, "and I find myself quite in need of a junior assistant. Would you be at all interested?"

Mary's eyes widened to the size of dinner plates. For the first time in her life, she found herself slightly stuttering, "A...a... a real detective?"

"In the professional sense, that is correct," he replied, a smile playing beneath his magnificent whiskers.

Mary stood somewhat less poised, utterly stunned into silence.

"Of course, the role would primarily involve menial office tasks—the prompt delivering of confidential, time-sensitive correspondence about the town, organizing case files, keeping the office in good order—and as such, there would be no interaction with clients. But, since your dear parents have informed me of your keen interest and your rather intrepid local investigations, I thought it might interest you."

Recovering her voice, her stunned expression was replaced with an enormous, beaming smile. "Yes! Oh, yes, Sir!" She seized his hand and began to shake it vigorously with both of her own.

Victoria could not suppress a smile, watching her daughter's reaction. "Now, mind, it's only to be one day a week, Mary. Saturdays, from nine until four."

Mary, now positively ecstatic, said, "Yes, of course!"

Victoria continued, "And young lady, you must keep up with your chores and your schoolwor—"

Mary burst in, "Yes, Mother! I shall! Thank you! Thank you both!"

James let out a hearty laugh that made his formidable whiskers quiver. "Well then... It is settled. Welcome to the firm, Miss Hartford."

52. The Great Demonstration

If there is no struggle there is no progress. Those who profess to favor freedom and yet deprecate agitation are men who want crops without plowing up the ground.
—Frederick Douglass, *If There Is No Struggle, There Is No Progress*, 1857

*T*he dawn cracked open a splinter of light along the horizon, and Victoria's eyes—weary from a long, largely sleepless night—slowly adjusted. She had stared into the darkness for hours, her mind preoccupied with the details of the day ahead, a day so many had planned for the last year.

Leicester had been humming with palpable excitement for weeks in anticipation of the march, with thousands of people—trade unionists, socialists, and reformers from across the country—already having arrived to participate, many of whom hoped it would be a historic event.

"This is it," she whispered to herself. *March 23, 1885, will be a day the world will never forget*, Victoria thought as she stretched her arms above her head, touching the worn oak headboard with the tips of her chilled fingers.

Two days ago, Annabelle had arrived from London and was happily—and unexpectedly—accompanied by Clara, whom she had not seen in years. The two behaved more like old friends to each other than their former positions of mistress and housemaid would have suggested. Clara still tended to the house as she had, but things were apparently more informal as Annabelle had mellowed over the years, particularly after Simon's move to his own household after marrying Elizabeth Chesterfield. In Annabelle's telling, while Simon was often occupied with matters in Parliament, Elizabeth lovingly took care of the household and their two children.

Annabelle noted with her oft-impartial tone, "Both seem content. Since that unfortunate Wilby affair, Simon has turned his life around. Well, as much as I think he ever will, I'm afraid. Still, she is happy raising their children. For all that, I'm quite gratified."

Victoria nodded with a smile. "I'm happy he has found someone. Please relay my sincerest good wishes to both."

Annabelle also pressed a letter into Victoria's hand, its script elegant and flowing. "From Gaston," she explained. "He has written to say that, with his financial situation now secure, he feels he can at long last return to his family in France."

Félicitations, ma vaillante lionne.

I am returning to my homeland and will be reunited with my loved ones. It is to your generous help and your great kindness that I owe this happiness. Perhaps you will honor me one day with a visit here. In that hope, I beg you to accept the expression of my eternal gratitude.

Votre dévoué et reconnaissant serviteur.

Pierre Gaston

Clara had also given her notice. She was to sail to New York City this summer to join her sister and take a position as a shop girl at a relatively new and exciting department store named Macy's.

Clara smiled with an effervescence Victoria had never seen from her before, "I can't tell you how exciting New York City sounds! They say the buildings touch the clouds and the streets are lit by electric arc lamps! It sounds magical!"

After getting dressed and having a hearty breakfast of fried eggs and oatcakes washed down with strong, sweet tea, the ladies, Mary, Emmett, and Benjamin, climbed into the farm wagon. It had been decorated with two colorful banners—'They that are whole need not a physician,' and 'Liberty is our birthright, and liberty we demand.' The others, including Sarah Jane, stayed behind to look after the farm and Autumn.

The sun was well over the horizon as they began their ride toward town. After weeks of bitter wind, the day promised sunshine and a mild south-westerly breeze—a welcome change, for a cold rain would have dampened both spirits and turnout for the demonstration.

In a remarkable show of solidarity, factories and warehouses had shuttered their doors, granting a general holiday so that the townspeople could flood the streets in a massive show of support. The air, usually thick with industrial smoke, was clear and vibrated with a palpable sense of anticipation. By the time they were approaching the Leicester Midland Railway Station, the scene was one of controlled bedlam; the streets were already humming with people and excitement. A river of humanity—comprising men in flat caps, women in shawls, and even children perched on shoulders—flowed from the station, where special excursion trains had been disgorging thousands of demonstrators since dawn.

They made their way down Granby Street to Temperance Hall, which served as the headquarters for the demonstration. The Hall was a hive of activity with hundreds of people buzzing about—organizers marshalling groups, orators reviewing their notes, and flustered delegations searching for their places. Hundreds of colorful banners and flags from Trade Unions, Reform Societies, towns, and parishes from all over Britain were already hanging along the walls and draped from the ornate balconies, a kaleidoscope of defiance.

From Brighton, a simple, elegant banner proclaimed, "Truth conquers."

The joined contingents of Finsbury and Banbury advised, "Stand up for liberty!"

Keighley stated in gilt bold letters, "We fight for our homes and freedom."

Southwark called for "Entire repeal and no compromise," a popular and uncompromising slogan that drew cheers.

Most poignant of all, St. Pancras sent a banner with the inscription 'Cordial greeting and sympathy to the heroic martyrs of Leicester,' a clear reference to the imprisonments of local leaders that had galvanized the movement.

One banner stopped Victoria short. It showed a skeletal figure in a doctor's coat, its bony finger pressing a lancet into the plump arm of a baby. A policeman held back the child's mother, her face a mask of silent horror. The crude, powerful art made her stomach clench.

As they made their way through this vibrant sea of humanity, Victoria was intercepted by a flustered Ms.

Ensworth, who was holding a great stack of leaflets so high it obscured her view. "Victoria... dear... We still have piles to hand out before the procession forms..." she huffed out, her voice strained with urgency.

Victoria calmly replied, "Of course, Annie. Between us all, we'll make sure they're all distributed." She took a portion of the stack to ease the woman's burden.

Turning to her companions, she doled out smaller packets from the large stack to her family members. "Please, make your way outside and pass these out to anyone who will take one. A leaflet in every hand is a blow struck for our cause!"

They each took their flyers and eagerly left Temperance Hall to distribute them to the ever-growing crowd, as Victoria attended to a seemingly endless number of other pressing details.

A BIRTHDAY For LIBERTY!
~ A Call to the People of England ~

Mothers! Fathers! Free Men and Women!

Are you and your family being

forcibly POISONED in your very blood BY LAW?

The State dares to lay its hands upon your

children! The tyrannical Compulsory Vaccination Act

is not merely a law; it is a personal affront to Liberty!

It violates the sanctity of your home and dictates to

you the care of your own flesh and blood.

RISE AND BE COUNTED!

Join the fearless citizens of Leicester, the vanguard of this

great cause, and the voices of conscience from across the

World in a Grand Demonstration of the People's Will!

ON THE TWENTY-THIRD OF MARCH, 1885

Let our numbers be our argument!

The Great Demonstration

THE GRAND PROCESSION:

The procession begins at 2:00 from Market Place
Follow the route of righteous protest through the heart of
our town:

Market Place→ Belgrave Gate→ Junction Road→ Russell
Square→ Wharf Street→ Rutland Street→
Belvoir Street→ Welford Road→ Carlton Street→
Oxford Street→ Southgate Street→ High Cross Street→
Northgate→ Sanvey Gate→ Church Gate→ Gallowtree
Gate → Return to Market Place
For a Great Meeting of the People, featuring addresses by
renowned champions of liberty.
WE ARE THE PEOPLE.
OUR WILL SHALL PREVAIL.
Liberty is our birthright, and liberty we demand!
We will not be trampled in the dust by the hoof of
tyranny!
NO COMPULSION! NO MEDICAL TYRANNY!
ABSOLUTE REPEAL!

By late morning, a massive crowd, numbering in the tens of thousands, had gathered at Market Square. Flags and banners were distributed, and a dozen bands of musicians played stirring marches and popular tunes at different locations. The general mood of the crowd was jubilant and punctuated by laughter—a perfect carnival of common merriment and common sense, all converging toward the great market-place of the fine old stalwart town.

A crude effigy of Edward Jenner, dressed in a parody of a doctor's attire and sporting a grotesque, leering mask, was being hoisted up and dropped from a makeshift gallows by a group of boisterous men. With every drop,

480

the crowd roared its approval, a raw, angry sound that was both thrilling and unsettling.

At the center of Market Square, the mayor stood on the raised speaker's platform, a hastily constructed dais of wooden planks, overlooking the thousands that had congregated.

As the clock struck two, the crowd's chatter reduced to a respectful simmer as the head of the procession, holding a magnificent banner with 'Stand up for Liberty' emblazoned in gold on a rich burgundy background, began marching toward Belgrave Gate.

A solemn group formed to accompany a young mother and two men, all of whom had resolved to give themselves up to the police and endure imprisonment in preference to having their children vaccinated. At Gallowtree Gate, the three were formally taken into custody. The mother turned to the crowd, her voice clear and defiant, "I vow to go to prison over and over again rather than give up my child to the 'tender mercies' of a public vaccinator!" As the three were led through the police station doors, the crowd yelled out hearty cheers of support and promises to care for their families.

An important feature was the presence of a large contingent of men and women, wearing badges and ribbons of honor, who had undergone the extreme process of imprisonment rather than submit to the law. Next came a larger detachment, consisting of men whose household goods—chairs, tables, clocks, and bedding—had been seized and sold by public auction. Samples of the goods that had been seized and sold were conveyed in wagons as grim trophies of state persecution. The subsequent detachment consisted of an open-topped conveyance filled with rosy-cheeked and content unvaccinated children, presented as living proof of their parents' sound judgment. This was followed by a large number of delegates, many of whom were from London, Leeds, Manchester, Halifax, Blackburn, Keighley, Bedford, Birmingham, Lincoln, and Norwich.

Among other features in the procession were a horse and a cow, drawn in wagons and exhibited as the living sources of the much-reviled vaccine lymph; a hearse bearing a child's coffin inscribed with the words 'Another Victim of Vaccination'; carts displaying furniture 'Seized for Blood Money'; a model prison cell on a flatbed wagon; and floats depicting doctors astride cows. The entire spectacle, a bizarre carnival of protest, was met with a mixture of jeers and jubilant cheers from the vast crowd, creating an atmosphere that was at once grimly serious and strangely festive.

The large, two-mile-long procession marched around the town for about two hours, receiving enthusiastic cheering and showers of flower petals at various points along the route. The townspeople showed their support by waving from windows and balconies, flapping handkerchiefs and streamers with flags and sayings along the route. The procession finally returned to Market Square, its purpose declared and its strength displayed to the entire nation.

At the Market Square, Mr. J. T. Biggs produced a copy of the compulsory Vaccination Acts, which was fastened to iron rods and ceremoniously consigned to the flames, the ashes scattered to the wind amid loud acclaim. The detested Acts of Parliament were likewise cast into several blazing bonfires before the Corn Exchange, the flames leaping skyward to the accompaniment of thunderous cheers from the multitude.

On a platform before the Corn Exchange, the leading representatives of the movement sat. Councillor Butcher of Leicester rose, raised his hands to quiet the crowd, and addressed the immense audience.

"Many present had been sufferers under the Acts, and all they asked was that in the future they and their children might be let alone. They lived for something else in this world than to be experimented upon for the stamping out of a particular disease. A large and increasing portion of the public was of the opinion that the best way to get rid of smallpox and similar diseases was to use plenty of water, eat good food, live in light and airy houses, and see that the Corporation kept the streets clean and the drains in order. If such sanitary details were attended to, there was no need to fear smallpox, or any of its kindred; and if they were neglected, neither vaccination nor any other prescription by Act of Parliament could save them."

The crowd cheered its fervent agreement. Mr. William Young, secretary of the London Society, followed with a formally written resolution. "That the principle of the Compulsory Vaccination Acts is subversive of that personal liberty which is the birthright of every free-born Briton; that they are destructive of parental rights, tyrannical and unjust in operation, and ought therefore to be resisted by every constitutional means."

Dr. Hycheman, a veteran physician, quietly climbed the stage and stood on the speaker's platform. His mere presence alone seemed to hush the crowd. "The good people of Leicester. My name is Dr. William Hycheman. I have over forty years of experience as a medical doctor. So, no one can question my credentials or expertise. What I will tell you today will freeze your souls in terror."

The crowd went profoundly silent, with scarcely a murmur, as he continued, his voice a scalpel of cold reason.

"Since this state-sanctioned blood-poisoning of our children was enforced by Act of Parliament, smallpox has increased both in extent and frequency. Now, vaccination—be it by horse pox, cow pox, or humanized pox, whatever the multiplicity of lymph... and the term 'pure vaccine' is but a rhetorical euphemism for filth and corruption—is itself a sickness that breaks out upon the skin. It begins with fever, followed by papule, vesicle, and pustule, in about eight days. And what else is smallpox? They are kin—one poison merely exchanged for another!"

"I have laid open on the mortuary slab more than a dozen children whose deaths were directly caused by vaccination, and no smallpox, however black, could have left more hideous traces of its malignant work—the sores, foul sloughing, hearts empty or congested with clots, than did some of these little victims. Shame! A thousand times shame! Indeed, scarcely a day elapses but I am called upon to witness the sufferings of vaccinated children in the form of cerebral and gastric complications, persistent vomiting, bronchitis, and diarrhea. Some suffer with pustules in the mouth or throat, on the eyelids, and ulceration of the cornea, which remains opaque and may lead to blindness for life."

He finished as quietly as he had begun, "God bless you all for standing against this abomination."

A moment of stunned silence was followed by a thunderous, angry roar of approval from the crowd.

Numerous other speakers ascended the platform and gave vigorous, inspiring speeches throughout the afternoon into the early evening. The bonfires were stoked anew, and the resolve of the people was forged in the fiery oratory.

Then, a hush fell over the crowd as Dr. Spencer T. Hall, a 73-year-old veteran of the cause from Blackpool, slowly mounted the stage, overcome with emotion. "Friends," he began, his voice thick with feeling. "My tears are tears of joy. I never thought I would see the day when vaccination was being so challenged." He cleared his throat and continued, his words gaining strength, "I was made seriously ill after being vaccinated at two years of age. And then at fourteen, I had a severe attack of smallpox. I would far rather have smallpox than be vaccinated. I paid fines for all my children. In my long and wide experience, I have never seen such evil results from smallpox as I have seen from vaccination."

As the lengthening shadows of the late afternoon grew longer, casting a golden hue over the square, Victoria took the stage, her figure silhouetted against the fading light.

"Friends! Brethren! Fellow sufferers and champions of liberty! Thank you all for attending this momentous occasion. Many of us have sacrificed a great deal—our comforts, our fortunes, our very liberty—to make this moment possible, but it was all worth it to protect not only our children but also to push back against this government tyranny. For if we are not secure in our own bodies, if the state can force its will upon our very blood, then we are not free, but mere chattel of the men in top hats in London! Are we slaves? Never!" Victoria emphasized by slamming her palms on the wooden platform railing.

"What say you?" she cried, her voice ringing out across the multitude.

The Great Demonstration

A mighty chorus of "NO!" erupted, a single thunderous voice from ten thousand throats.

"Then I ask you again! Are you slaves?" she yelled, her voice straining with passion.

A veritable earthquake of "NO!" exploded from the crowd, a wave of sound that seemed to shake the very foundations of the buildings surrounding the square.

Victoria stood tall, raising her hands to heaven, "Today is not the end! It is but the beginning! We must continue to push, organize, and agitate until we have compelled a new government. One that respects its citizens! One that does what is right! A government that believes in the God-given right of freedom!"

The tens of thousands of cheers filled the square, echoing down the canyon-like streets and rising into the darkening, star-dusted sky, a testament to a people united and unyielding.

53. Landslide

The only purpose for which power can be rightfully exercised over any member of a civilized community, against his will, is to prevent harm to others. His own good, either physical or moral, is not a sufficient warrant.
—John Stuart Mill, *On Liberty*, 1859

Victoria sat at her plain wood desk in a small basement office of Temperance Hall. Through the grime-specked window just above street level, she heard the passing crowd and felt the gentle, warm breeze of the bright, sunny 5th of May. A large stack of correspondence and other papers sat on the top of the desk, with a pen lying across a half-finished letter that she had been writing.

Alderman Arthur Simmons stood in the doorway, having just entered, silhouetted against the gaslight of the corridor. He was a man of medium build whose most prominent feature was a long, straggly mustache and whiskers that flowed into a veritable, equally sprawling beard, almost completely obscuring his mouth.

"Of course, as you are aware, yesterday was the big vote, but we already knew we had the cat in the bag, as they say. The compulsionists were soundly defeated, and notice was given to rescind the order for prosecutions. Compulsion is a thing of the past starting today!"

Victoria leaned back in her chair, a slow, triumphant grin spreading across her face. "After that landslide in the

Guardians' election last month... it certainly isn't surprising, but by God, it's still so hard to believe. We won. We really have won." She finished, gently shaking her head in disbelief.

"That we have. The fruit of last year's protest—all 100,000 protestors—has proven momentous. It is certainly a watershed moment for civic liberty and public health; the tyrannical regime of compulsory vaccination is no more." The Alderman announced, his voice muffled slightly by his whiskered barrier.

Victoria sat forward, picking up a letter off her desk, "I have word from our allies in Keighley and Gloucester. People are saying our movement is spreading across England!" She met Simmons's gaze, her eyes alight with conviction. "We are not just winning a vote, Alderman. We are ending a delusion. As Mr. Wallace said, vaccination will soon be regarded as a medical curiosity. The Leicester Method will be our legacy."

"Stupendous. Simply stupendous." Simmons uttered while absently scratching his whiskers.

After a few moments basking in the glow of accomplishment, Simmons cleared his throat, the sound returning them both to the practicalities of the day. "Well... I must return to Town Hall. The new sanitary protocols won't formalize themselves, and the town's other business waits for no man." He paused at the door, a gleam of future triumphs in his eye. "And I've a committee meeting this afternoon to discuss the prospect of electric light for our city. Imagine that! Good day, Mrs. Hartford."

"Good day, Alderman."

Victoria picked up her pen, the familiar weight a comfort in her hand. She took a deep, contented breath, the scent of ink and old paper filling her senses as she reread her half-finished letter, tapping the pen absently against her lips.

She had managed only a few more words before the office door burst open. An ecstatic Mabel stood there, her face alight, brandishing a newspaper. "It's here! The Mercury!"

Victoria looked up, a smile already breaking through her feigned concentration. She laid the pen down with a resigned click. "At this rate, I'll never get this letter done," she said, her tone thick with mock exasperation. She rose and met her friend in the middle of the room, where they shared a prolonged, wordless hug that spoke volumes about their shared struggle and ultimate victory.

Finally breaking their embrace, but not the electric energy between them, Victoria took the extended paper. Her eyes fell immediately to the column Mabel had so pointedly folded open, the print still fresh with the scent of the press.

A New Dawn for Public Health — Compulsory Vaccination Falls

LEICESTER— In a historic vote, the newly elected Leicester Board of Guardians has ended the policy of compulsory vaccination. The decision, passed by a margin of twenty-seven to eight, halts all prosecutions against citizens who refused the procedure.

This bold decision is founded upon a decade of remarkable local evidence. The last ten years have witnessed an extraordinary decrease in vaccination, and yet, the town has enjoyed an almost entire immunity from small-pox, there never having been more than two or three cases in the town at one time. In its place, a new method, for which great practical utility is claimed, has been enforced by the Sanitary Committee for the stamping out of small-pox. The chairman of the Committee has gone so far as to declare that small-pox is "one of the least troublesome and most manageable diseases" with which they have to deal.

The Leicester Method, as it is now known, is a marvel of modern efficiency. The method of treatment, in a word, is this: as soon as small-pox breaks out, the medical man and the householder are compelled under penalty to at once report the outbreak.

The special small-pox van is at once ordered to proceed to the house in question; the hospital authorities are also instructed to make all arrangements. Thus, within a few hours, the sufferer is safely isolated in the hospital. The family and inmates of the house are placed in quarantine in comfortable quarters, and the house is thoroughly disinfected and fumigated. The result is that in every instance the disease has been promptly and completely stamped out at a paltry expense.

Under such a triumphant system, the Guardians have expressed their opinion that vaccination is unnecessary, as they claim to deal with the disease in a more direct and much more efficacious manner. This, and a widespread and deeply-held belief that death and disease have resulted from the operation of vaccination, may be said to be the foundation upon which the existing opposition to the Acts rests.

"I'm still quite flabbergasted," Mabel declared, her grin impossibly wide. "To think, this time last year, over 5,000 summonses were clogging the courts! And now... not a single one. Can you fathom it? It's over."

Victoria beamed, a feeling of profound vindication swelling in her chest. "The people of Leicester," she added, her voice thick with emotion, "through determined resolve and peaceful protest, have won their liberty back from an oppressive law."

With the care of an archivist preserving a sacred relic, she took a pair of scissors from her desk and carefully cut the article from the broadsheet. She then brought forth her scrapbook—that weighty tome, its leather cover scarred and softened by years of handling. Her fingers traced the yellowed edges of past headlines before finding a blank page.

THE PALL MALL GAZETTE
White Slavery Scandal Shocks London! Respected Businessman on Trial!
May 5, 1879

THE TIMES
Businessman James Reginald Wilby Sentenced to Twenty Years' Hard Labor for Assault, Kidnapping, and False Imprisonment
May 7, 1879

THE LEICESTER MERCURY
Vaccine Resister Victoria Hartford, Jailed for Twelve Days for Refusing to Comply with the Vaccination Act of 1867
July 20, 1880

THE LEICESTER HERALD
First Telephone Exchange Opened in Leicester
1881

THE LEICESTER CHRONICLE

Midland Railway Experiments with Electric Lighting
in Carriages and Stations
1883

THE LEICESTER HERALD
Leicester Orphan Asylum Reopens After Last Year's
Devastating Fire
September 15, 1884

THE MIDLAND COUNTIES GAZETTE
Outrage at Barrington Farm — Anti-Vaccination
Crusader Targeted by Night Riders
November 4, 1884

THE LEICESTER CHRONICLE
Leicester Historic Protest of 80,000 to 100,000 Against
Compulsory Vaccination Laws
March 23, 1885

She applied a dab of glue to the back and pressed the article onto the page. Taking her pen, she carefully inscribed "May 5, 1886" in the margin beside the article, her script a neat, flowing cursive that contrasted with the stark print of the headline.

THE LEICESTER MERCURY
A New Dawn for Public Health — Compulsory
Vaccination Falls
May 5, 1886

A gentle smile touched her lips as she ran her palm over the pasted article, the newsprint smooth and final beneath her touch. With a weight that felt like every bit of the last seven years, she began to close the heavy book. Its spine groaned a soft accompaniment to the cascade of memories that arose not from the page, but from the scrapbook of her mind: the remembered stench of the asylum; the fleeting taste of justice after Wilby's sentencing; the profound cold of her own cell; the smoke that had clung to her clothes for days after the farm was attacked; the thunder of 100,000 voices raised as one.

"So many battles," she whispered. "So many triumphs. But this is perhaps the sweetest... this is the one I pray history remembers."

54. The Path Remembered

For forty years, corresponding roughly with the advent of the "sanitary era," smallpox has gradually but steadily been leaving this country. For the past ten years the disease has ceased to have any appreciable effect upon our mortality statistics. For most of that period it has been entirely absent except for a few isolated outbreaks here and there. It is reasonable to believe that with the perfecting and more general adoption of modern methods of control and with improved sanitation (using the term in its widest sense) smallpox will be as completely banished from this country as has been the case with plague, cholera, or typhus fever.
—C. Killick Millard, *The Vaccination Question in the Light of Modern Experience: An Appeal for Reconsideration,* 1914

A gentle April breeze, sweet with the scent of freshly cut alfalfa, rippled through the fields of Barrington Farms, the earth warming beneath a sky of pale blue and wispy white cirrus clouds. Bees buzzed, birds chirped, and cows lowed as tractors rattled and hummed between rows of crops, their steel grilles flashing in the light, while overall-clad farmhands called to one another over the growl of machinery.

Mingling with the farm's usual sounds came the lively chatter of more than fifty guests gathered for the farm's first picnic of the year near the newly built white-clap-board farmhouse. Six trestle tables, their red-checkered cloths anchored against the breeze with Mason jars of goldenrod and black-eyed Susans, were laden with heaping platters of abundance—barbecued chicken basted with thick, sweet sauce, Boston baked beans glazed and bubbling, Ball Jars stuffed with pickles preserved the previous fall, loaves of bread still warm from the oven, and other savory dishes reflecting the bounty of the postwar years.

Victoria sat at the head of one of those tables. Her hair—a striking blend of silver and streaks of fiery chestnut, echoes of her youth—was tied back in a practical ponytail beneath a wide-brimmed hat woven from corn straw, its shadow dappling her face like sunlight through an orchard. Though her years showed in the fine lines around her eyes, the fire of her youth still burned in their dark brown depths, flecked faintly with emerald.

Flanking her were several children—ranging from five to twelve years old—their shorts and overalls pressed and clean, some with mouths slightly agape, hanging on her every word.

"Then I realized—plaster dust could be my weapon. Plain old dust!" She demonstrated by crumbling an imaginary handful, her work-roughened hands painting the scene. "I scraped that prison wall until I had a good pile and hid it in a scrap of cloth."

She grabbed the nearly empty, sun-warmed pitcher of lemonade, its sweating glass slick in her grip. "The only thing in that wretched room was a dented pewter pitcher—I practiced my swing until it was perfect. It had to be perfect. One chance was all I'd get!"

Leaning forward, she held the children in rapt attention, her voice dropping to a whisper. "Then I waited... and waited... and..."

Her tone grew even softer, like narrating a Dickens' ghost story, "Finally, he came in."

One little chestnut-haired girl bit her lip. A jet-black-haired boy blurted out, "Weren't you scared stiff?"

"Terrified! Scared as a mouse in a cat factory!" Victoria admitted, eyes wide. "But I played weak, lured him closer... and when he was near enough—"

She paused, letting the tension build—then raised her voice as she flung her hand open, "Whoosh! The dust hit his face!" The children gasped, some jerking back in their seats.

"He staggered and coughed. Blinded him good! Then—wham!—I cracked him in his temple with the pitcher!" She swung the glass pitcher sideways for emphasis, lemonade sloshing out. "Again!—wham!—Down he went like a sack of turnips—thud!—flat on the floor!"

A collective gasp rose as she mimed searching the fallen man. "I fumbled through his pockets, praying... My fingers touched... cold metal. Keys! One click—" she made a twisting motion with her fingers. "—and that lock popped open and I was free!"

One blonde girl breathed, "You're so brave."

Victoria's voice softened. "Bravery's just fear that didn't back down," she said. "If I hadn't fought, I'd have been sold—or worse..." She trailed off, her gaze drifting to the distant fields. The children followed her look, sensing the unspoken horrors of another time, another world.

While Victoria was recounting her story, a man in his forties wearing a soft, well-worn tweed flat cap and holding a rolled-up magazine approached the table. He remained respectfully silent as she continued.

"Then what happened?" questioned the dark-haired boy.

Victoria smoothed her flower-print dress.

"Well, I had to go to trial to prove what he had done. I stood before twelve stuffy old men and told the truth. I had to hold firm and be fearless. And because I did, that villain went to jail for a very long time for what he did to me, and for the other crimes they discovered."

All the children sat there quietly for a few moments.

"He died in jail?" The same jet-black-haired boy inquired.

"Yes. Perished in the jail of his own making. He did worse to many innocent women." Victoria grinned with a slight snarl of satisfaction.

"Children, it was a dreadful experience, but it taught me how much I could do and helped me realize that my own strength was greater than I knew."

She paused again, watching the children as they pondered her words.

She added, "It takes courage to walk a path of your own making, especially when the world urges you to follow theirs."

The chestnut-haired girl crinkled her nose, reminding her of how Mary looked so many decades ago, and asked, "What does that mean?"

Victoria smiled, "Be brave and don't let anyone tell you how to live your life."

The blonde girl—her pigtails bouncing with enthusiasm—clapped her hands together. "Please, tell us about the time you—"

Victoria chuckled, "All stories have their hour, you goose," Victoria interrupted gently, tapping the child's nose with the tip of her finger. "Now, help clear the table and go enjoy playing. It's a beautiful day."

As the children scattered like sparrows, their chatter and laughter slowly fading as they made their way towards the farmhouse, Victoria finally looked up at Nathan. His tweed cap bore the faint sweat marks of a man who'd hurried across fields to share news, his face alight with the particular joy of vindication.

"Out with it then, Nathan. You look fit to burst," Victoria said, accepting the journal with hands that still bore the calluses of six decades of labor. Her fingernails—short and practical—traced the *British Medical Journal*'s cover before flipping to the dog-eared page.

Nathan's finger jabbed at the text, leaving a faint smudge on the thin, postwar paper. "It's official! Compulsory vaccination is finally dead! After sixty-two years of our Leicester Method—isolation and sanitation—only fifty-three smallpox deaths total. Two in the last forty years!"

Victoria adjusted her wire-rimmed spectacles, the afternoon light catching the bifocal line as she scanned Dr. Millard's article. A slow smile spread across her face—the same smile she'd worn in 1885 when they had pushed back on those compulsory laws in Leicester. "Killick. I know him. He's a good man who looks for the truth of things."

Nathan leaned in, his voice barely audible over the clatter of dishes. "The article says medical men confused correlation for causation. All those textbooks giving credit to vaccination..." He snorted. "Turns out clean water and decent housing did the heavy lifting!"

With a smirk, she read out loud a portion of the article, "Looking back it is interesting to consider why medical experts were so mistaken in their prophecies of disaster to come if universal vaccination of infants was abandoned… That this was clearly a case of cause and effect was reiterated in every textbook and in every course on public health. It was hailed, indeed, as the outstanding triumph of preventative medicine. No wonder that medical students accepted it as an incontrovertible scientific fact."

She paused a moment, her eyes scanning the page, then read on. "As for smallpox, no one can foretell the future… et cetera… I suggest, however, that in view of the experience of the unvaccinated town of Leicester, and indeed of the whole country, during the past 60 years, there is no real cause for alarm."

Victoria snapped the journal shut with finality. "Science always catches up to common sense eventually." She handed it back, her attention drifting to where the chestnut-haired girl was helping stack plates. "That one's great-grandmother marched with me in '85. Carried a sign saying 'Mothers Know Best.'" A wistful note entered her voice, "Now little Lily will grow up never fearing the vaccinator's knife."

Victoria exhaled slowly, the decades of struggle etched in the deepening lines around her mouth as she smiled. "Sixty-four years ago," she pronounced, her voice carrying the weight of history. "Sixty-four." She straightened her spine, the faded floral cotton of her dress whispering against the wood. "We resisted and we beat those smug, know-it-all bastards in their top hats. We fought for our free choice and we were right!"

Nathan squeezed her hand gently, feeling Victoria's strong yet bony hand beneath his fingers—a lifetime of labor and protest made tangible. "You've outlasted every one of them—The magistrates, the medical officers... You're still filled with fire, aren't you?"

Victoria sat in quiet reflection, absently turning the silver, bronze, and copper-leaf ring that circled her slender fourth finger.

A single cumulus cloud slowly passed in front of the sun, as if the world itself was issuing a warning. The shadow of the transitory cloud darkened her face momentarily before sunlight reclaimed it, glinting off her spectacles.

She scowled slightly, "There will always be arrogant bastards... like that dreadful dictator so many fought against and died."

Nathan's sudden burst of song that had circulated through Allied ranks cut through the tension like a scythe. "Ven Der Führer says 've is der Master Race'..." He paused, then suddenly thrust his arm forward in a mocking Nazi salute. "Ve heil...pfft... Heil ...pfft..., right in Der Führer's face!" He stuck out his tongue with theatrical flair on each "pfft." His raspberry reverberated so loudly that several nearby picnickers turned to stare.

"You ridiculous man!" Victoria swatted his arm, with laughter bubbling beneath her reproach.

"But accurate," Nathan countered, his grin fading into solemnity. He nodded toward the magazine. "Another tyranny defeated by stubborn men and women and their will to overcome."

Beyond them, the postwar world carried on in all its contrasts—the drone of a newly bought tractor blending with the *clip-clop* of a horse-drawn milk cart; children playing tag around the same oak tree that had shaded their great-grandparents' protests. The scent of victory garden roses blended uneasily with the acrid tang of DDT being sprayed on the far fields—new dangers replacing old.

Victoria's face followed a V-formation of geese crossing the sky. "The battles change, but there's always another smug bastard waiting in the wings," she said quietly. Then, with sudden fierceness. "But by God, we showed them what Leicester women were made of."

Nathan raised a glass of lemonade. "To the troublesome women—may there never be a shortage."

"Hear, hear," Victoria concurred, watching as the chestnut-haired girl twirled in the sunshine, her laughter as bright and relentless as the truth itself.

Around them, the picnic continued—the clink of forks on plates, the distant chatter about the new National Health Service, the hum of a neighbor's radio playing *Some Enchanted Evening*.

Victoria's stare drifted across the sun-streaked lawn, taking in the scene with a quiet intensity. "So many miracles in one lifetime," she contemplated, her fingers tracing along the picnic table. "Electricity flowing like magic through the walls. Motorcars that could outrace the fastest stallion." She shook her head slightly. "I held my breath the first time I saw an airplane—that was something I could never have imagined."

She nodded toward a group of children who were playing a game of tag.

"No more boys and girls working in the cotton mills," she added quietly. "No more six-year-olds hauling coal carts."

"Clean water." Victoria's voice caught on the words, her throat tightening with memory. "You'll never understand the miracle of turning a tap and seeing it run clear." She pressed her palms flat against the table, as if steadying herself against the past. "We've scrubbed the old filth from this world, inch by stubborn inch. That alone was a miracle—I know you can't really understand unless you experienced that disgusting sewage and despair."

Nathan studied her profile—the way the sunlight caught the silver strands in her hair, the stubborn set of her jawline that hadn't softened with age. "No, I'm sure I can't." He paused for a moment, then said softly, "You've lived through such an amazing time."

Staring at one of the far tables, Nathan stood up, "We should celebrate with a piece of that blueberry pie!"

Victoria sat motionless for a few moments longer before she looked up at Nathan with a gentle smile, quietly saying, "No. No... You enjoy. I feel like taking a walk alone."

Nathan hesitated. "You're certain?"

Her eyes glistened with a wordless reply that he fully understood.

He bent over and kissed her gently on her papery cheek before making his way toward one of the other tables. He half-turned and, with a smile, said, "I'll make sure we save you a slice."

Victoria pushed back her chair and made her way toward the stream, unhurried and thoughtful. The breeze caught at her skirt, pressing the floral cotton against legs that had carried her through ninety-three years.

Nathan watched her go, her figure slowly receding into the vastness of the fields. Then, with a quiet chortle, he turned toward the dessert table where two farm wives were arguing good-naturedly over the last piece of rhubarb pie. The postwar world spun on, its wonders now ordinary, its clashes passed into stories. But for one tenacious woman walking alone across a country meadow, the past would always be as present as the wild roses blooming by the fence—sweet-smelling, sharp, and impossible to ignore.

At the bank of the stream, Victoria sat on the trunk of the old fallen oak she had rested on hundreds of times before. She took off her straw hat and dropped it onto the ground, and then reached back and undid the ribbon holding her ponytail in place. She shook her head from side to side, sending her long, silvery strands dancing across her cheeks and brushing along the back of her neck. She slipped off her well-worn black leather shoes, placing them neatly beside the old fallen tree before lowering her bare feet onto the damp grass.

She slowly walked to the water's edge and stepped in. She glanced at her feet—small and pale—disappearing just beneath the rippling, glassy water. A chill curled upward through her calves, making her draw a sharp breath. Around her ankles, the current swirled and fizzed, teasing her skin, while the sand and smooth pebbles shifted restlessly under each careful step. She pressed her toes deeper, wiggling them in the rough, grainy touch of the riverbed.

A playful gust swept past, setting her hair adrift in the breeze. She tilted her head back, taking in the endless sweep of blue above. Wisps of white clouds wandered slowly across the sky. Beyond the stream, the meadow unfurled like a green sea, its grasses swaying in harmony with the scattered trees that stood like watchers in the beams of sunlight. She closed her eyes and lifted her face to the sun, letting its warmth sink deep into her skin.

She thought back to the time when she would daydream—a time both only moments ago and yet a lifetime past—a contradiction she could never fully reconcile in her mind.

The forest itself seemed to whisper, "Victoria!"

She opened her eyes and let out a soft, knowing laugh to herself. This was no daydream. This was a tangible, precious moment. All the challenges, tragedies, triumphs, losses, and loves were vivid and real. They were part of a life she had painstakingly woven, each a delicate thread in the rich tapestry of an existence well lived and deeply cherished.

She stood there, a woman of ninety-three summers, feeling the cool water on her skin and the warm sun on her face. A playful gust swept past, setting her silver hair adrift in the breeze. She closed her eyes, and a slow, deep contentment settled in her bones. Every hard-won battle, every moment of love and loss, had led her here, to this free and unchained life.

Historical Echoes Quotes & Images

The more extensive a man's knowledge of what has been done, the greater will be his power of knowing what to do.
—Benjamin Disraeli

History is not merely a collection of dates and events—it is a living tapestry woven from the lives of those who came before us. The following section illuminates a past that has largely receded into the shadows. It is from these shadows that I have gathered the knowledge which helped inspire and shape this novel—fragments of a lost world, offered here for you to rediscover.

Within the following pages are fully referenced historical quotes that let the people of the past speak for themselves, their testimonies echoing with a clarity that no modern summary can match. To allow for a deeper exploration, they are arranged by chapter, serving as a guide to the factual foundation beneath the fiction. Following and complementing these voices, rare photographs capture vanished visions of the past, providing a haunting visual context to the world they describe.

1. The Dream

ARSENIC IN WALLPAPERS AND TEXTILE FABRICS. The dangers of arsenical wallpapers have long been known; in fact, so far back as the eighties there existed in London a society, numbering among its members many sociologists and leading physicians, one of whose special objects was the suppression of the use of arsenic in wallpapers, textile fabrics, etc. Many forms of chronic illness, coryza, sore throat, intestinal troubles, etc., were proved to result from the continued inhalation of arsenic from sources such as those above named. though death was only occasionally traceable thereto. A report comes from Evansville. Ind.., of the death of the third wife of a farmer from symptoms resembling those of, and supposed to be due to. spinal meningitis. His two previous wives, it is said. died, like the third. soon after the spring cleaning, in which a wallpaper, now said to be thickly charged with arsenic, was vigorously brushed. Scheele's Green. which used to be largely employed, is a particularly virulent poison.[1]

2. Chamber of Solitude

* * *

3. A Nightmare's Grin

* * *

4. Chicken Soup

* * *

---

[1] St. Louis Medical Review, May 18, 1907, p. 508.

5. The Deal

* * *

6. Solace in Sisterhood

A London fog is brown, reddish-yellow, or greenish, darkens more than a white fog, has a smoky or sulfurous smell... and produces, when thick, a choking sensation."[2]

* * *

Goerck and Delancy Streets in New York City. The condition of the streets, with the masses of mud, manure, and other monstrous agglomeration of everything dangerous, unsightly, and offensive, is plainly indicated... Barrels and pails overladen with material, mingled in a foul mess of garbage and ashes, beset the sidewalks. In many cases these have been upset, and the unsavory contents emptied on the curbstone and into the gutter.[3]

* * *

If anyone wants to realize, as the phrase goes, the little army of crossing-sweepers we have in London, let him take a walk – say for a mile or two – on a muddy day, and give a penny to every one who touches hat, makes a bob, as if shutting up like a spy-glass, or trots after him, trailing broom in one hand, and tugging at tangled forelock with the other. I remember when it would have cost anyone, disposed to give in this way, between a shilling and eighteen-pence to walk from the Archway Tavern, Highgate Hill, to Highbury Cock and back. For anyone of a

---

[2] Francis Albert Rollo Russell, FMS, *London Fogs*, 1880.
[3] *Harper's Weekly*, February 18, 1893, pp. 161, 166.

squeezable temperament, therefore, it was decidedly cheaper to take the bus.[4]

* * *

As more women entered the middle class in the 1800s, a widespread market developed for bird feathers used in haute couture [high fashion], fueled by magazines such as Harper's Bazaar. Great snowy egrets, with their long feathery plumes known as "aigrettes," were most prized, but roseate spoonbills and shore birds were also routinely killed by plume hunters, the former for their colored feathers, the later for their long billed carcasses, which, stuffed whole, adorned women's hats.[5]

* * *

At the start of the fad, plumes brought a few dollars an ounce, but at the height, an ounce of feathers was worth more than an ounce of gold.[6]

7. Whispers in the Waltz

Parents whose children are three months old or upwards when a periodical vaccination begins, or who attain three months of age during its progress, must be very careful to get them vaccinated before it concludes or they will be liable to the penalty; the gist of the matter is that parents must have their children vaccinated within three months of birth, or as soon afterwards as the public arrangements

---

[4] Richard Rowe, *Picked Up in the Streets, Or, Struggles for Life Amongst the London Poor*, W. H. Allen and Co., 1880, p. 148.
[5] Sharon Guynup, State of the Wild 2006: A Global Portrait of Wildlife, Wildlands, and Oceans, 2005, Island Press, p. 102.
[6] Grunwald, Michael. *The Swamp: The Everglades, Florida, and the Politics of Paradise*. New York: Simon & Schuster, 2006, p. 120.

of their district afford an opportunity for gratuitous vaccination. The registrar's notice should inform parents of the times when public vaccination will be performed, and public notices will also no doubt be given by the local authorities.[7]

8. Innocence Unraveled

From experience I have seen more evils result from vaccination than I ever saw result from small-pox. In the first place, I have seen direct fatal results from vaccination. In the second place, I have seen chronic-incurably chronic-disease the result of vaccination, and death after the lapse of many years; and, in the third place, I have see introduced into the system, through vaccination, diseases of a destructive character, especially syphilis.

I was vaccinated when a boy, and a few years afterwards I took small-pox. I vaccinated my first four children. One of them died certainly from vaccination, and another was never strong after he was vaccinated. I would rather be shot than have anyone of my family vaccinated.[8]

* * *

Health Commissioner George Michels of this city will be arraigned in the police court to-morrow on a technical charge of disorderly conduct. The complaint is brought by the Board of Education, which accuses Mr. Michels of

---

[7] Edward C. Seaton, A Handbook of Vaccination, Macmillan and Co., 1868, p. 378.
[8] "John Le Gay Bereton, Esq., MD, MRCS, LAC," New South Wales, Compulsory Vaccination, Presented to the Parliament by Command, September 20, 1881, Sydney: Thomas Richards, Government Printer, pp. 1043-1046.

refusing to allow his daughter, Dorothy, a school girl, to be vaccinated. Mr. Michels was placed under arrest to-day. "I would move out of the State rather than be compelled to vaccinate my child," said Mr. Michels to-day. "My father died of smallpox after being vaccinated and my sister was crippled through being vaccinated, and there are many cases on record in and out of the city of great harm and even death caused by vaccination." Two weeks ago Dorothy Michels was sent home from School 9 because she was not vaccinated. She is 11 years old.[9]

* * *

That vaccination leaves scrofula behind—that the lymph lays the foundation for tubercular diseases—that affections of the eyes, ears, throat and mind, have increased with vaccination—that syphilis is propagated by the lancet of the vaccinators; that it increased scrofula, consumption and infant mortality; that it caused ulcerous sores of the most painful and dangerous character, etc., etc.[10]

9. The Road to Redhill

Two murders linked together. The story goes that Catherine Foster was a simple-minded woman who poisoned her husband with arsenic in November 1846, just three weeks after their marriage at All Saints, Acton, near Sudbury. The crime was discovered when he vomited in the garden and the hens mysteriously died. She readily

---

[9] "Fights Vaccination Law, Passaic Health Commissioner Arrested for Refusing to Obey It," *New York Times*, March 8, 1912.
[10] Joe Shelby Riley, MD, MS, PhD, *Conquering Units: Or The Mastery of Disease*, 1921.

confessed to the crime; she had married him to please her mother, and loved another man, so she cooked his suet dumplings in arsenic. Curiously, her father, William Morley, was strongly suspected of robbery and murder just a few years previously. She was hanged before a crowd of 10,000 people on the Market Hill at Bury, the last woman to be executed in Suffolk. She was just 18 years old.[11]

10. Behind the Iron Gates

There was no doubt whatever that among the 50,000 female patients now secluded in lunatic asylums...[12]

* * *

Cages, iron chains, handcuffs, hobbles, straps, crib beds, and fixed chairs, are common modes of restraint of patients, who, being afforded no means of occupation, or diversion for mind or body, naturally become noisy and troublesome. The bath, either shower or immersion, is a favorite means of tranquilizing excited patients. In the cupboard shower bath the patient is subjected to a continuous downpour of water, and this, in some cases as a punishment at the option of the attendants, without the sanction of the medical officer. In the covered hot bath, the head alone protruding, the patient is confined, unable to move, from one to twelve hours at a time, and in many instances unattended, at a temperature of 34 degrees centigrade [93° F], often with cold water dripping on the

---

[11] The Hanging of Catherine Foster, Foxearth & District Local History Society
[12] "The Nervous Diseases of Women," The Dublin Journal of Medical Science, August 1, 1883, p. 156.

head... In one institution I saw 215 women in various modes of restraint – camisoles, wristlets, straps, etc. – secured upright in racks round the day rooms. In another there were 43 women in box beds, ironed hand and foot, and extended in spread-eagle fashion, at three in the afternoon.[13]

* * *

The bath of immersion consists of plunging the patient into cold water and immediately withdrawing him, a process which may be repeated three to six times, while the bath of affusion, following the method of Currie, is administered by placing the patient in an empty tub and pouring water of progressively reduced temperature upon his head. These baths are particularly useful for subjects enfeebled by masturbation or prolonged grief, where the goal is to produce a reaction by withdrawing nervous power from the center and calling it to the circumference. They differ from the bath of surprise, which consists of plunging the patient into a reservoir, river, or sea when he least expects it; it is the fright and the vivid impression of falling unexpectedly into the water with the fear of drowning that renders this means efficacious in overcoming sensibility.[14]

11. Veils of Despair

Spitalfields, the region of Bethnal Green, and Whitechapel, all centre together, making a vast area wholly occupied by the poor people. The first-mentioned quarter, Spitalfields,

---

[13] The Medico-legal Journal, New York, 1885, Vol. III, No. 1, p. 123.
[14] Étienne Esquirol, Mental Maladies; a Treatise on Insanity, Lea and Blanchard, 1845, p. 84.

is the residence of the poorest of the poor. In it the buildings are low and black – the interior walls, ill-ventilated, but crowded; and the streets almost too disgusting to describe. In traversing them, one is assailed by the most noxious stenches, and the most disagreeable sights. This region is no small part of London – not a mere Five Points which occupies a small space – it is the residence of the laboring population of London; there are hundreds of thousands of men, women and children in it; - some just raised about utter wretchedness; others utterly wretched. That many of these people are without principle and virtue, must be evident from the fact that, in London there is an immense number of thieves and prostitutes – the later unfortunate class alone numbering about 80,000.

In some streets there are almost only thieves, robbers and prostitutes; in others there are mechanics and laboring men; and in some perhaps a majority, the thieves, prostitutes, and laboring poor, are herded together in about equal numbers...[15]

12. The Wheels of Justice

In winter, more than a million chimneys breathe forth simultaneously smoke, soot, sulphurous acid, vapour of water, and carbonic acid gas, and the whole town fumes like a vast crater, at the bottom of which its unhappy citizens must creep and live as best they can.[16]

* * *

---

[15] What I Saw in London: Or, Men and Things in the Great Metropolis, David W. Bartlett, 1861, pp. 111-113.
[16] Francis Albert Rollo Russell, FMS, *London Fogs*, 1880.

...the refuse which we thrust up our chimneys simply descends upon our heads and into our houses.[17]

* * *

A London fog is a thick mist... London has so many mechanised wagons and factories, and in winter, every home spews smoke out of its chimneys so that on particular days the smoke becomes heavier than the air, cannot rise up and therefore settles over the city and sometimes engulfs large areas and darkens almost everything... Darkness more horrible than that at night has descended at noon, and no artificial light can really illuminate the blackness created by a fog. It is difficult to breathe; one is suffocated by tiny black, oily particles that clog the nose.[18]

* * *

The smoke pall that formed the sky of Widnes in Leblanc times [1850s to 1890s.] At the highest development of the Leblanc system more than a million tons of coal were consumed annually in the chemical works of the town.[19]

* * *

In 1854, with the appointment of Mr. Denne as resident superintendent of the Hanwell asylum, the non-restraint system was fully implemented; in his first report, he stated

---

[17] "London Fog," *The Illustrated Scientific News*, December 1902, p. 43.
[18] Jayati Gupta, "London Through Alien Eyes," *Literary London Interdisciplinary Studies in the Representation of London*, vol. 1 no. 1, March 2003.
[19] Hardie, D. W. F, "A History of the Chemical Industry in Widnes," 1950, p. 125.

that despite numerous difficulties and the building's poor design, he had wholly abolished mechanical restraint, a change for which the patients had expressed gratitude and which had resulted in "immeasurably less" clothing being destroyed. This banishment of restraints was part of a broader reformation that included an improved diet, more land for patient cultivation, better clothing, and the integration of all compatible elements of the modern system, which would soon be fully realized with the replacement of the old building by a new one constructed according to more enlightened principles.[20]

13. Forging Friendship

* * *

14. Phoenix Rising

* * *

15. The Bitter Cry

This day, the inquest held on the body of the infant that was eaten by rats in Bellevue Hospital, New York, was concluded. The evidence of Mary O'Connor, the mother of the child, and that of numerous other witnesses, was taken... and recommended that proper means be taken to rid the hospital of the rats that now infest the institution.[21]

* * *

---

[20] John Conolly, *The Treatment of the Insane Without Mechanical Restraints*, Smith Elder, & Co., 1856, pp. 310-311.
[21] *Vincent's Semi-Annual United States Register*, 1860, p. 346.

Few who will read these pages have any conception of what these pestilential human rookeries are, where tens of thousands are crowded together amidst horrors which call to mind what we have heard of the middle passage of the slave ship. To get to them you have to penetrate courts reeking with poisonous gases arising from accumulation of sewage and refuse scattered in all directions and often flowing beneath your feet; courts, many of them which the sun never penetrates, which are never visited by a breath of fresh air, and which rarely know the virtues of a drop of cleansing water. You have to ascend rotten staircases, which threaten to give way beneath every step, leaving gaps that imperil the limbs and lives of the unwary. You have to grope your way along dark and filthy passages swarming with vermin. Then, if the intolerable stench does not drive you back, you may gain admittance to the dens in which these thousands of beings who belong, as much as you, to the race for whom Christ died, herd together.[22]

16. Unexpected Developments

* * *

17. Christmas Eve Reflections

* * *

18. Shattered Illusions

Hysteria is a condition in which especially the higher nervous centres are at fault. Chacot calls it a psychic

---

[22] Andrew Mearns and William C. Preston, *The Bitter Cry of Outcast London: An Inquiry into the Condition of the Abject Poor*, 1883, James Clarke & Co., London, p. 4.

disease. According to Havelock Ellis, the general character of the mental phenomena in hysteria may be summed up in the word suggestibility. There is an abnormal degree of response to suggestion in the nervous system... Judgment, accuracy, and power of concentration are weakened. The emotions are easily excited and badly controlled. There is a morbid desire for the sympathy of others; she craves attention continually, is full of caprices, and makes excessive demands about her. As Wendell Holmes says, 'she is a vampire who sucks the blood of the healthy people about her.' If she is checked or chided in any way, she takes offence, gets irritated, bursts into tears, or has an attack of pain, paralysis, or some other manifestation of the hysterical condition. There is often a tendency to tell untruths and to practice deceptions. Clouston has pointed out particularly the changes due to the loss of inhibitory influence on the reproductive and sexual instincts. There may be various perversions of sexual emotion, e.g. abnormal yearning for love.[23]

19. Picking Up the Pieces

In the midst of all this mad work, to which the doctors, after having found it in vain to resist, had yielded, the real small-pox, in its worst form, broke out in the town of Ringwood, in Hampshire, and carried off, I believe, more than a hundred persons, young and old, every one of whom had had the cow-pox "so nicely!" And what was now said? Was the quackery exploded, and the granters of the twenty thousand pounds ashamed of what they had done?

---

[23] John Clarence Webster BA., MD., *Diseases of Women – A Text-Book for Students and Practitioners*, The Macmillan Company, 1898, pp. 137-138

Not at all: the failure was imputed to unskillful operators; to the staleness of the matter; to its not being of genuine quality... what do we know now? Why, that in hundreds of instances, persons cow-poxed by JENNER HIMSELF [Cobbett's emphasis], have taken the real small-pox afterwards, and have either died from the disorder, or narrowly escaped with their lives![24]

20. How the Other Half Lives

In consequence of the fearful description given to me by the ever-active Secretary of this Society, relative to the dwellings of the poor, more especially those situated in Field-Lane, Holborn-Hill, I resolved to visit them myself, in order that I might be better enabled to judge of their condition. Accompanied by the Secretary, I went to Field-Lane at half past eight o'clock this evening, and proceeded upon an inspection...

The first house which I went into, was tenanted entirely Irish, and very entrance was from its dirt and effluvia, both sickening and disgusting. I was taken first into the cellar, into which I descended by some dilapidated stairs, but with no ordinary difficulty. The truly offensive state of this place beggars all description. I scarcely know whether the sense of seeing or the sense of smelling was the most shocked and offended. On all sides I was surrounded by the most filthy abominations, and the smell was so truly overpowering, that I thought I should have been

---

[24] William Cobbett, *Advice to Young Men and (Incidentally) to Young Women*, W Cobbett, London, 1829, pp. 224–225.

compelled for my own preservation to have immediately retired.[25]

* * *

In New York City alone there were seventy-five thousand women workers who lived on the ragged edge of misery. In the first year of peace [after the Civil War], with prices rising to an unprecedented height, fifteen thousand or more of them, employed in shops and factories, earned only from two dollars and fifty cents to four dollars a week. Yet they were far more fortunate than the wretched stratum of women employed as pieceworkers on cheap garments.[26]

* * *

Susan B. Anthony became the head of the Working Women's Protective Association. Women's labor organizations fought to make improvements for those caught in a life of virtual slavery in sweatshops. The labor movement was born out of the desperation of the working masses.

Industries such as dressmaking comprised what was known as the "sweated industries." Those who sewed in the workshops of London endured harsh working conditions. For several months a year, workers were expected to work 18 to 20 hours a day. Because of the seasonal nature of the work, women often turned to prostitution to

---

[25] *The Poor Man's Guardian*, November 20, 1847, pp. 17-18.
[26] Allan Nevins, *The Emergence of Modern America 1865–1878: A History of American Life Volume VIII*, 1927, Macmillan, New York, p. 324.

survive. Activist groups, unions, and the press slowly forced changes in these working conditions.

...the splendor and magnificence of carriages of the aristocracy... you conclude the wealth of London is almost boundless... Charing Cross you see private carriages of great beauty and costliness... from Downing-street away towards Piccadilly and Hyde Park...

...the Great parks... tread upon soft green grass; birds sing melodiously over your heat in the branches of lofty trees; children gambol in the sunshine before you, and you conclude that Englishmen have a care for health as well as wealth.

...wander a little back from Westminster Abbey into old Pye street, or Duck Lane... You see wretchedness the most bitter, destitution the most utter, and vice the most terrible... It was but a step from your former paradise to this unsightly hell... within a stone's throw from the glorious old Abbey!

...everything in this world has its dark, as well as bright side... truly London has one side which is too painfully dark and horrible to gaze at with complacent nerves."[27]

* * *

London... it is upon the whole a smoky, gloomy town, but three buildings it may justly glory in – the new House of Parliament, Westminster Abbey, and Saint Paul's... adds great dignity to the metropolis of the British Empire.

---

[27] What I Saw in London: Or, Men and Things in the Great Metropolis, David W. Bartlett, 1861, p. 18.

...east, into that wild wilderness of misery and suffering called Spitalfields. You traverse street after street, and see nothing but the most disgusting, the most beseeching poverty. There are thousands of men and women there who never have known what plenty is, what pure joy is, but are herded together, thieves, prostitutes, robbers and working-men, in frightful masses. You meet beggars at every step; at night the streets are crowded with wretched women, called in mockery "women of pleasure." And you are horror-struck when you learn from reliable sources, that many of these are but children in age – but fourteen years old, some of them, and the fear of starvation is what has driven them to vice. Upon their faces there is a look of wan despair which tells the story of their infamy... London... enormous wealth and terrible poverty; great virtue and frightful vice... London is the wealthiest and the most wretched city in the world – the city of extremes![28]

* * *

Smithfield... market was full of cattle. The place was exceedingly noxious, and it struck us that it must be prejudicial to the health of the inhabitants who reside in the streets in its vicinity.

In one quarter there were hundreds of small enclosures for sheep, pigs, and calves...There were that morning about ten thousand head of cattle in the market, and perhaps twenty thousand head of sheep. The noise and confusion of the place was indescribable... redolent of traffic and wild bulls and unpleasant odors.

---

[28] What I Saw in London: Or, Men and Things in the Great Metropolis, David W. Bartlett, 1861, pp. 19-20.

Heads of cattle are constantly driven to and from the market through the principal streets of the city, to the constant danger of the people. Many lives have been sacrifices – women have been gored to death on public side-walks.

Victoria Park away in the eastern part of London; amid beggars and poor people, mechanics and small trades-men... it is too vulgar, too plebeian ground!... splendid carriages are never to be seen in it, nor people of wealth and respectable standing in society...

Green Park spreads out in front of Piccadilly... Poor men's children are fond of coming there to catch a sight of the blue skies, and to play in the free breezes which sweep across it. The stomachs of the elite are altogether too delicate to bear the sight of the ragged and dirty-faced children...[29]

* * *

Victoria Park... emphatically the park of the poor. No fashion enters it; wealth and so-styled respectability shun it... It is situated north-east of London, and immediately adjoins Bethnal Green and Spitalfields those great rendez-vous for the wretched, vile, and suffering.

Our walk lay through a portion of Spitalfields and Bethnal Green, and was not pleasant.

The streets were crowded with a filthy set of vagabonds – very likely so because they were unable to obtain work... the gin-shops especially appearing to be driving a heavy

---

[29] What I Saw in London: Or, Men and Things in the Great Metropolis, David W. Bartlett, 1861, pp. 29-31.

business. Some of the streets through which we walked were very low and dirty, and sometimes it was with difficulty that we faced our way through them, the odors the greeted us at every step were so nauseating.[30]

* * *

In some streets there are almost only thieves, robbers and prostitutes; in others there are mechanics and laboring men; and in some perhaps a majority, the thieves, prostitutes, and laboring poor, are herded together in about equal numbers...

Bread is tolerably cheap, but everything else is dear; the price is about twelve cents the quarter loaf; butter is from twenty to twenty-eight cents per pound...

... a mechanic locates in a region of Spitalfields – he is forced to do so because he cannot pay the rents of wholesome neighborhoods – he has a wife and six children depending on his labor. Say he is so fortunate to earn five dollars a week... – how well, how sumptuously can he live on that? Can he eat meat every day? Not oftener than every Sunday. Can he pay to send his children to school? No. He pays his rent – lives upon plain bread and cheese and beer – and rejoices if he is able to keep his children off the parish.

He is taken ill – is there any income then? No. He dies – and where goes the mother with her six children? To the poor-

---

[30] What I Saw in London: Or, Men and Things in the Great Metropolis, David W. Bartlett, 1861, pp. 39-40.

house! How happy can a man be with such a prospect forever staring him in the face?[31]

* * *

Be a little careful, please! The hall is dark and you might stumble over the children pitching pennies back there. Not that it would hurt them; kicks and cuffs are their daily diet. They have little else. Here where the hall turns and dives into utter darkness is a step, and another, another. A flight of stairs. You can feel your way, if you cannot see it. Close? Yes! What would you have? All the fresh air that ever enters these stairs comes from the hall-door that is forever slamming, and from the windows of dark bedrooms that in turn receive from the stairs their sole supply of the elements God meant to be free... That was a woman filling her pail by the hydrant you just bumped against. The sinks are in the hallway, that all the tenants may have access--and all be poisoned alike by their summer stenches. Hear the pump squeak! It is the lullaby of tenement-house babes. In summer, when a thousand thirsty throats pant for a cooling drink in this block, it is worked in vain. But the saloon, whose open door you passed in the hall, is always there. The smell of it has followed you up. Here is a door. Listen! That short hacking cough, that tiny, helpless wail--what do they mean?... The child is dying with measles. With half a chance it might have lived; but it had none. That dark bedroom killed it.[32]

---

[31] What I Saw in London: Or, Men and Things in the Great Metropolis, David W. Bartlett, 1861, pp. 111-113.

[32] Jacob August Riis, *How the Other Half Lives: Studies Among the Tenements of New York*, Charles Scribner's Sons, 1914, pp. 43-44.

21. Silencing Sparrows

* * *

22. Taken

* * *

23. Imprisoned

* * *

24. Prisoner's Aftermath

* * *

25. Trial and Tribulation

* * *

26. Wilby Strikes Back

* * *

27. An Unforeseen Meeting

* * *

28. Simon Says

In discussing the hysterical constitution or temperament, it is incumbent upon us to ask whether hysteria is a hereditary disease; from both personal observation and the works of medical authors, I have no doubt the question must be answered affirmatively, as the malady is in some instances directly transmitted from mother to child. Regarding nervous diseases in general, however, the all but universal law of parental transmission may be expressed thus: if one, or more so both, parents are affected by almost any disease of the nervous system, their offspring—whether one or more—is, with rare exceptions, extremely liable to suffer from some form of nervous disease, although the particular ailment may not be exactly the same disease as that affecting the parent or parents.[33]

29. The Nineteenth of June

* * *

30. New Beginnings

* * *

31. The Good Life

Children from seven years of age upward, were engaged by hundreds from London and other large cities, and set to work in the cotton spinning factories of the north. Since there were no other facilities for boarding them, "apprentice houses" were built for them, in the vicinity of the factories, where they were placed under the care of the superintendents or matrons... They were remotely situated, apart from the observation of the community, left to the burdens of unrelieved labor under the harshness of small masters or foremen. Their hours of labor were excessive. When the demands of the trade were active they were often arranged in two shifts, each shift working twelve hours, one in the day and another in the night, so that it was a common saying in the north that "their beds

---

[33] William Camps, MD, *Hysteria: the Hysterical Constitution or Temperament: with Suggestions as to its Pathology and Treatment*, John Churchill, 1866, p. 19.

never got cold," one set climbing into bed as the other got out. When there was no night work the day work was the longer. They were driven at their work and often abused.[34]

32. Market Square

After fifty years' experience, I arrived at the conclusion that vaccination was not only useless as a preventative, but dangerous. I decline the risk of vaccination, and would not vaccinate my bitterest enemy.[35] — Thomas Brett, MD, London, England, in a speech given on April 17, 1883.

* * *

It is a convenient habit of vaccinators to speak of vaccinations as uniform, as if the virus of the rite were as definite as a drop of water, a pinch of salt, or a grain of gold. Nothing could be further from the truth. The virus called vaccine is not one but various, not uniform but multiform, not certain but uncertain with an uncertainty which in transit from body to body, ad infinitum, can be predicted nor ascertained... The matter of his lancet he cannot define and its effects he cannot foresee... To these Jennerian stocks have been added Smallpox Cowpox obtained by inoculating cows with the virus or pus of human smallpox. Thus we have virus derived from horse grease cowpox, from natural or spontaneous cowpox, from horsepox, and from smallpox cowpox, plus the constitutional taints of the generations of vaccinifers through which these diverse

---

[34] Edward P. Cheyney, *An Introduction to the Industrial and Social History of England*, 1920, Macmillan, New York, p. 233.

[35] *Terrible Results of Vaccination: TESTIMONIES concerning Vaccination and its Enforcement: by Scientists, Statisticians, Philosophers, Publicists, and Vaccine Physicians*, 1892, Providence, Snow & Farnham, Printers, pp. 14–33.

poxes have been passed; and which is which, and how modified for better or for worse in the course of travel none can tell.[36] — Dr. T. V. Gifford

* * *

What is called 'pure glycerinated calf lymph' is the lineal descendant, for vaccination purposes, of cow-pox, horse grease, swine-pox, donkey-pox, goat-pox, buffalo-pox, humanized lymph, chloroformed calf lymph and a few other beastly poisons. The above photo shows how calves are outraged in order to obtain it. The abdomen is shaved, and then stabbed from 100 to 120 times with a spear-headed lancet blade. The wretched animal, thus mutilated, is thrust back into its stall, and its head and legs tied to prevent it licking or scratching its wounds. After six days agony, the poor calf is subjected to another revolting piece of barbarism. The healing scabs are scraped from its wounds and the filthy exuding matter collected into a gruelly mass. It is then mixed with glycerine, which is a nutritive medium for the growth of petrifactive and other germs which invade the whole of the fluid. This dangerous concoction is then put into tubes and injected into the bodies of babies, and adults who wish to enter the military, naval, civil, railway, and other services. The calves are sold to butchers at a cheap rate, and afterwards eaten by the public. In the above photo workmen are seen scraping the calf's sores open to collect the poison.[37]

---

[36] Dr. T. V. Gifford, "What is Vaccination," *Journal of Hygeio-therapy*, vol. II, no. 8, August 1888, p. 178.
[37] "Vaccination the Foul Invention of Hell," *Leaves of Healing*, vol. XXXV, No. 14, January 2, 1915, p. 316

33. Harvest of the Heart

* * *

34. A Friend in Need

Some of the great fogs of the end of January and beginning of February, 1880, were uncommon in their character and development. On the 27th of January there was a sudden great increase in the intensity of the frost, almost absolute calm prevailed, and the easterly current gave way on the ground to a westerly air, with which it became intimately mixed. The east wind apparently continued at a moderate elevation. In many parts of London the fog was exceedingly dark, being mixed with a great volume of smoke, and the sun was invisible. At Hammersmith, at midday, the sun was just visible, at Richmond shining dimly, and at Willesden very brightly. The fog was not inconveniently thick outside London till the evening, when it greatly increased in density. At Richmond, at 2.45 P.M., the thermometer stood at 22, an extremely low temperature. More or less fog occurred here and there on the following days, and the sky remained clear above it. On the 30th and 31st an exceedingly light lower current from the south moved over southern England, greatly augmenting the temperature. Radiation, however, was not arrested by clouds, and the ground being chilled to a temperature much below the freezing- point by the previous severe frosts, did not thaw even when the thermometer stood at 45 in the open air. Thus, in certain localities, especially those least exposed to sunshine, very dense clouds were formed upon the ground by the reduction of the temperature of this slow warm current below the dew-point. On the 31st, at 10 A.M., a ground fog of extraordinary density, little discoloured by smoke, lay over parts of the south-western district of London. I measured the distance at which objects became visible, and found it to be four and a half yards. In some places the fog did not extend as high as the tops of the houses, and the smoke thus escaped into the upper air. In central London, great darkness accompanied the fog during the morning. This fog differed from most others in being entirely due to the chilling of a single atmospheric current by contact with the earth; and for this reason it extended in its intensity only a few feet above the ground. The day was extremely fine in some of the suburbs. In the evening, with a rapid fall of temperature, the fog returned and caused the greatest difficulty to locomotion. On the 1st of February the atmosphere was less foggy in most districts, but again became almost impenetrable for traffic in the early morning of the 2nd. On the 4th the fog was again exceedingly thick. The fog had thus lasted eight days, on and off, with very great intensity. They were remarkable for their local character, the shady side of a square being several times plunged in a dense mist, while the opposite side rejoiced in sunshine; one end of Piccadilly in thick darkness, while the other remained bright and clear.[38]

35. A Breath of Brimstone

I may say that I have lived with numbers of these con-sumptives in the large hotel which I have always inhabited, and have attended shoals [many] of them living in other hotels, or in small boarding-houses, or in villas. Often these consumptives passed their lives, especially the Continental ones, notwithstanding my persistent advice,

---

[38] Francis Albert Rollo Russell, FMS, *London Fogs*, 1880.

in badly ventilated rooms, surrounded by relations and servants, who lived with them for many months consecutively for half the year, and yet I cannot recollect a single case of evident contagion occurring... amongst them.[39]— Dr. Henry Bennett

* * *

The great Hospital for Consumption at Brompton, London, in existence for over sixty years, is the largest hospital for lung diseases in the world. It has a large staff of physicians, with scores of nurses and other hospital attendants. If consumption [tuberculosis] was infectious it certainly would show itself among those in such close and constant contact with it, in all its worst and most advanced stages; and yet Dr. Williams, the senior physician, says: 'Infection in the wards of the hospital between consumptives and non-consumptives is unknown.'...[40]

* * *

Dr. Sweetser, in his work on consumption, states that calomel or mercury has been often ranked among the causes of consumption. That it may act as an exciting cause of the tubercles, hardly admits of a question. Mercury saps the constitution, creates the very diseases for which it is given to remove, and lays the foundation for infirmity, suffering, and premature decay. If mothers or doctors deal

---

[39] Duncan Turner, *Is Consumption Contagious?* 1894, Melbourne, pp. 20–21.
[40] Robert Hunter, MD, "Consumption Not Contagious," *The Canadian Magazine*, vol IX., 1897, Ontario Publishing Company, Limited, p. 540.

out calomel to children or others, we can only commend them to the mercy of heaven.[41]

* * *

In all its [mercury] preparations, or different modes of giving it, salivation [caused by mercury] in some states of the lungs is as certainly fatal as the dagger or pistol; in some sections of our country, calomel, as it is given, is a most dreadful scourge. In many parts of the United States, cities, towns, villages, and country, are strewn with the wrecks of living men, women, and children; whilst the graveyards conceal the decaying remains of thousands killed by mercury...

Every consumptive should understand, that when he takes calomel, uncombined blue pills, &c. [etc.], he does it at the risk of his life. There is no doubt that mercury will remain in the system years after it is taken, and produces injurious effects even twenty years after it has been swallowed or rubbed into the skin. If tubercles exist in the lungs, calomel softens and inflames them, and thus develops consumption.[42]

* * *

Pulmonary Tuberculosis is a disease of malnutrition. The plan of treatment is based upon what is universally accepted as the most rational method for the relief of the

---

[41] Wooster Beach, MD, *The American Practice Condensed: Or, The Family Physician*, 1850, New York, p. 122.
[42] Samuel Sheldon Fitch, AM, MD, *Six Discourses on the Functions of the Lungs; and Causes, Prevention, and Cure of Pulmonary Consumption, Asthma, and Diseases of the Heart*, 1853, New York, pp. 60–61.

disease, viz.: fresh air and sunlight in abundance, good food, plenty of sleep, regulated exercise, care of sputum and attention to the small things of daily life which are known to influence nutrition favorably... The coming of the patients to the dispensary twice each day gives the opportunity to educate them how best to live according to their means. They come ostensibly only to drink emulsion and vegetable juice...[43]

* * *

I have known deplorable consequences to ensue from a want of ventilation. I was once called to a young man in consumption, whom I found in a small room not more than eight feet square, into which the fresh air had no access, excepting when the door was casually opened. On entering the apartment, I was almost suffocated from the closeness of the atmosphere. I ordered the patient to be removed to a large room, where the air could circulate freely, and he soon recovered from the stupid and almost exhausted condition in which I found him.[44]

* * *

He had suffered from a cough for more than thirty years and raised a great deal from his lungs; at one time, after a bad influenza joined to his old cough, he presented strong symptoms of rapid consumption. It was in March, a very cold, windy month, and he was attended by two extremely

---

[43] John F. Russell, MD, *Report of Fifty-Five Apparent Cures of Pulmonary Tuberculosis Occurring in Working People Who Were Treated at a Dispensary Without Interruption to Their Work*, New York, February 1906, p. 9.
[44] Dr. Morris Mattson, *The American Vegetable Practice or a New and Improved Guide to Health*, vol 1, 1841, p. 400.

well-educated physicians, both professors, teachers, and practitioners of medicine. They adopted the usual practice—a very warm room, as if cold were a mortal enemy to the lungs, and emetic tartar, confinement to his bed, and all accessible remedies to reduce the strength of the patient and thus drive off his disease. Under this treatment his strength rapidly declined; cough and expectoration became profuse, and every symptom of rapid consumption appeared. In this state his two physicians, knowing the extent of his business, felt it to be their duty to make known to him that he was near his end. On this announcement, he said at once, "If that is the case, why have you kept me so long in bed? I should have much preferred to have been up." He immediately had an arm chair brought to him that had wheels on its feet, caused himself to be dressed, and was wheeled into his parlor—a large, well-aired room. This was on Thursday; on the Saturday after, his physicians called; he told them that the next Monday morning he should start for Montreal, capital of Canada, about eighty miles north from Burlington— "For," said he, "as you say, I have a great deal to do, and but a short time to do it in." They remonstrated against this unheard-of temerity, as a species of suicide, insisting his death must be the result in a very short time, but their entreaties and positive advice had no effect upon his resolution. He went to Montreal and returned nearly well; I saw him eighteen years after this transaction in vigorous health, although still subject to his old cough and expectoration.[45]

---

[45] Samuel Sheldon Fitch, AM, MD, *Six Discourses on the Functions of the Lungs; and Causes, Prevention, and Cure of Pulmonary*

* * *

"[Dr. Carrazzani] believes that a sufficiently generous use of garlic in tuberculosis will produce immunity against infection. Of a group of guinea pigs kept in an atmosphere charged with tubercle bacilli, those whose daily diet had contained one gm. of garlic were found at the end of three months to be free from tuberculosis, while the others were badly infected... The views of Dr. Carrazzani include a hint at an explanation for the comparatively low death rate from pulmonary tuberculosis among the Italians, both in their own country, and in America."[46]

* * *

William Charles Minchin writing in the Medical Press and Circular for June 13, 1917, gives the results of years of special study of the therapeutic action of oil of garlic. This oil is composed of allylsulphide with volatile terpenes, and would appear to be Nature's antiseptic for internal use, destroying many pathogenic germs within the body, and being at the same time harmless to the tissues... In the treatment of whooping cough Minchin has found garlic to be most efficacious. In the case of adults an inhalation of fresh succusallii sativa, rapidly relieves the distressing symptoms. It must be used, however, continuously from three to five hours for two or three days in order to produce the best results. In the case of infants and young children 20 minims to half a dram of the juice of garlic taken internally every four hours in a little syrup gives speedy relief in the early stages. The author lays special

---

Consumption, Asthma, and Diseases of the Heart, 1853, New York, p. 72.
[46] "Garlic," *The Medical Council*, vol. IX, 1904, p. 420.

emphasis upon the beneficial effects of garlic in the treatment of tuberculosis, and he quotes the results obtained by the staff of the Metropolitan Hospital, New York, in the treatment of 1082 cases of tuberculosis according to fifty-six different methods, out of which garlic gave the best results.[47]

* * *

Dr. Russell says he has found a combination of foods which seems effective in the destruction of the bacilli of tuberculosis. The most beneficial item in the food combination—consisting of butter, bread, eggs, milk, and emulsion—is, he says, vegetable juices. Since the introduction of this juice the report records remarkable results among the tuberculosis patients. The fluid, which Dr. Russell and his colleagues at the Post-Graduate believe to have beneficial properties, is the combined juice of every kind of vegetable to be had in the market. It has been in regular use at the hospital along with the regular diet since Jan. 7. It is now recorded that in the first five months of this year eleven patients were discharged "apparently cured," against a record number of thirteen cures effected during the whole of 1904. This sudden increase, and the fact that the patients are still thriving upon the vegetable-juice treatment, lead the examiners to believe that Dr. Russell has discovered a fluid, the properties of which are fatal to the progress of tuberculosis... The vegetables first used were potato, onion, beet, turnip, cabbage, and celery. Later were added sweet potato, apple, pineapple, carrot, parsnip, and later still rhubarb, (pieplant), summer

---

[47] "The Therapeutic Uses of Garlic," *Medical Record—A Weekly Journal of Medicine and Surgery*, September 1, 1917, p. 376.

squash, tomato, spinach, radishes, string beans, and green peas with the pods.[48]

36. Interwoven Souls

* * *

37. Taking the Reins

In 1854, an outraged John Gibbs, a hydropathic practitioner and anti-vaccinationist, directly attacked the Compulsory Vaccination Act of 1853—which mandated vaccination for all infants in England and Wales—by arguing, "Are we to be leeched, bled, blistered, burned, douched, frozen, pilled, potioned, lotioned, salivated... by Act of Parliament?" However, his opposition, and that of his followers, also reveals a larger concern with the expansion of the state into the previously private realm of medical practice and bodily care, a trend already apparent since the passage of the Anatomy Act and the New Poor Law in the 1830s.[49]

* * *

The technology of vaccination in and of itself provoked significant anxiety amongst Victorian parents. Not only could the resulting scars be painful and disfiguring, but parents feared the arm-to-arm method could spread human afflictions such as cancer, syphilis, scrofula, or

---

[48] "Vegetable Juice a New Consumption Remedy, Tried with Success at Post-Graduate Hospital, 11 Believed to be Cured," *New York Times*, August 25, 1905.

[49] Nadja Durbach, "'They Might As Well Brand Us': Working-Class Resistance to Compulsory Vaccination in Victorian England, *The Society for the Social History of Medicine*, 2000, p. 45.

mental illness, leading to debility or even death. Equally troubling was the nature of the vaccine matter itself; many maintained that cow-pox could contaminate their children with animal diseases, disrupting both physical and spiritual health. Indeed, opponents denounced vaccination as un-Christian, proclaiming it 'the mark of the beast'. The fact that what many considered 'blood pollution' was made mandatory gave rise to a fervent anti-vaccination movement.[50]

38. Deep Wounds

* * *

39. The Immovable Law

A man named Arthur Ward had two children injured through vaccination and refused to submit another one to the operation. A fine was imposed and on 24th November two police officers called for the penalty, or in default to ticket the goods. The husband was out at the market, and the poor woman had no money to pay. The goods downstairs were considered insufficient to cover the amount, and the officers demanded to go upstairs. The woman refused to allow this, and an altercation took place, and harsh language was used by the officers, who threatened to take her husband to prison, terrifying Mrs. Ward. At that time she was pregnant, and the shock to the system, and the fright, were of such a character that symptoms ensued which ultimately led to a premature confinement, and on 26th December she gave birth to a

---

[50] Nadja Durbach, "'They Might As Well Brand Us': Working-Class Resistance to Compulsory Vaccination in Victorian England, *The Society for the Social History of Medicine*, 2000, p. 47.

still-born child. She never recovered and last week she expired. The doctor who had attended Mrs. Ward said that although he believed in vaccination he did not think it was the duty of any professional man to carry out the laws in the outrageous and brutal manner in which they were enforced.[51]

* * *

The Vaccination Acts themselves also imposed a severe economic burden that disproportionately targeted the working class. The penalty for non-compliance was a fine of 20 shillings plus court costs, which could range from a penny to a full pound. This was a crushing sum for a labourer earning only 15 to 20 shillings for an entire week's work. The Vaccination Officer's Birth Books for Enfield in the 1880s and 1890s confirm that most defaulters were factory workers and journeymen whose meager salaries could not withstand such a penalty, and who could ill afford to lose a day's wages by appearing in court. Furthermore, the punitive nature of the 1867 and 1871 Acts allowed for repeated fines for the same child, creating a devastating 'cat and mouse' game that could push penniless parents into debtors' prison.[52]

* * *

Edward Irons was summoned for neglecting to comply with an order for the vaccination of his son, aged two years. He said he had a conscientious objection to

---

[51] Stanley Williamson, "Anti-Vaccination Leagues," *Archives of Disease in Childhood*, vol. 59, 1984, pp. 1195–1196.
[52] Nadja Durbach, "'They Might As Well Brand Us': Working-Class Resistance to Compulsory Vaccination in Victorian England, *The Society for the Social History of Medicine*, 2000, p. 53.

conforming to the Vaccination Act, and he was also acting under the advice of his doctor, who stated that vaccination was not conducive to the child's health, nor would it benefit him. One of his children had been vaccinated, and she had suffered considerably from the effects of it, and he could not allow the boy to undertake the same risk. He then gave the opinions of several medical gentlemen on the evils of vaccination, and said he thought it would be inadvisable for the Bench to enforce the law upon a conscientious objection. The Chairman said there were few questions which had given rise to more varied opinions than the subject of vaccination. It had been proved beyond doubt that vaccination had caused smallpox to show itself in a much milder form. The Bench were unanimous in their opinions upon the question. They acted upon public grounds, and decided that the order should be enforced within a fortnight. If the order were not complied with, defendant would be liable to a penalty of twenty shillings. That course would be taken with all cases that came before them.[53]

40. Iron Bars

After the serious smallpox epidemic of 1870-1, part of the pandemic which swept over Europe, the appointment of vaccination officers was made compulsory, and the authorities in Leicester, as elsewhere, attempted to enforce vaccination more rigorously. Prosecutions in the town increased from two in 1869 to over 1,100 in 1881, the total for the twelve years being over 6,000. Of these, 64 had involved imprisonment and 193 distraints [seizure of

---

[53] Stanley Williamson, "Anti-Vaccination Leagues," *Archives of Disease in Childhood*, vol. 59, 1984, p. 1195.

property to obtain money owed] upon goods, the latter often being effected with much difficulty owing to popular sympathy with the defendants. All classes of the community were represented—among those who set the law at defiance, and those who were prosecuted were regarded as martyrs.[54]

* * *

Smallpox vaccination in the nineteenth and early twentieth centuries was neither a painless nor a minor intervention. Victorian public vaccinators used a lancet to score lines into the flesh of the arm, typically in at least four places. They then smeared matter, or 'lymph,' directly from a blister on another infant vaccinated eight days earlier into these cuts. Although preserved human lymph or lymph from calves was sometimes available, public vaccinators were urged to use the arm-to-arm method to maintain the community's supply. Indeed, after 1871, parents could be fined for refusing to allow lymph to be taken from their child, a policy that transformed infants into not just recipients of the vaccine, but also its essential incubators.[55]

41. Crossroads

* * *

---

[54] C. Killick Millard, MD, DSc, "The End of Compulsory Vaccination," *British Medical Journal*, December 18, 1948, p. 1073.

[55] Nadja Durbach, "'They Might As Well Brand Us': Working-Class Resistance to Compulsory Vaccination in Victorian England, *The Society for the Social History of Medicine*, 2000, p. 47.

42. A Wise Bird

Heaven knows we need never be ashamed of shedding tears, for they are rain upon the blinding dust of earth, overlying our hard hearts.[56]

Children began their life in the coal mines at five, six, or seven years of age. Girls and women worked like boys and men; they were less than half clothed, and worked alongside men who were stark naked. There were from twelve to fourteen working hours in the twenty-four, and these were often at night. Little girls of six or eight years of age made ten to twelve trips a day up steep ladders to the surface, carrying half a hundred weight of coal in wooden buckets on their backs at each journey. Young women appeared before the commissioners when summoned from their work, dressed merely in a pair of trousers, dripping wet from the water of the mine, and already weary with the labor of the day scarcely more than begun. A common form of labor consisted of drawing on hands and knees over the inequalities of a passageway not more than two feet or twenty-eight inches high a car or tub filled with three or four hundred weight of coal, attached by a chain and hooked to a leather band around the waist.[57]

...a majority of the workers in the cotton mills are under 16, and that the ages of them run down to 6 and 7. The girls are used as "spinners" and for the most part—walking up and down between the spinning frames and knotting

---

[56] Charles Dickens, *Great Expectations*, Chapman & Hall, 1861, p. 185

[57] Edward P. Cheyney, *An Introduction to the Industrial and Social History of England*, 1920, Macmillan, New York, pp. 243–244.

threads that break; and the boys are employed as "doffers"— for the replacement of the empty bobbins with full ones. The hours that these children work is well nigh incredible. Either they toil from six in the morning until six at night, or from six at night until six in the morning ...It is also the truth that the day-shift is frequently asked to work two and three nights a week, so that there are days when the child works for seventeen hours at a stretch.[58]

43. Newly Minted Junior Sleuths

* * *

44. Civilization's Castoffs

To describe the other two localities where our work is to be commenced, in Ratcliff and Shadwell, would, in the main, be but to repeat the same heart-sickening story. Heart-sickening but soul-stirring. We have opened but a little way the door that leads into this plague-house of sin and misery and corruption, where men and women and little children starve and suffer and perish, body and soul. But even the glance we have got is a sight to make one weep. We shall not wonder if some, shuddering at the revolting spectacle, try to persuade themselves that such things cannot be in Christian England, and that what they have looked upon is some dark vision conjured by a morbid pity and a desponding faith. To such we can only say, Will you venture to come with us and see for yourselves the ghastly reality? Others, looking on, will believe, and pity, and despair. But another vision will be

---

[58] Judge Benjamin B. Lindsey and George Creel, "Children in Bondage: The Sacrifice of Golden Boys and Girls," *Good Housekeeping*, July 1913, pp. 17–18.

seen by many, and in this lies our hope —a vision of Him who had "compassion upon the multitude because they were as sheep having no shepherd," looking, with Divine pity in His eyes, over this outcast London, and then turning to the consecrated host of His Church with the appeal, "Whom shall we send and who will go for us?"[59]

45. Beneath the Streets

Ice cream began to achieve widespread popularity in England in the mid 1800s. Before the invention of the cone, ice cream vendors, or Jacks, served scoops in cups called penny licks. They hawked ice cream in ha'penny (half penny) and tu'penny (two penny) licks, too. But the standard penny lick was most popular.

These small glasses were designed especially for ice cream. Their bottom-heavy build kept them stable as Jacks paddled peaks of frozen cream on top, and their conical shape and the thick glass obscured the magnitude of their contents. Even the tiniest dollop of ice cream appeared bountiful.

During the penny lick's day, Englishmen had little conception of germs. After finishing their ice cream, customers handed back their well-licked penny lick, and the next customer ate from the same cup. Because of the conical openings, Jacks couldn't keep the narrow point clean if

---

[59] Andrew Mearns and William C. Preston, *The Bitter Cry of Outcast London: An Inquiry into the Condition of the Abject Poor*, 1883, James Clarke & Co., London, pp. 31-32.

they tried. Penny licks became the perfect vessel for transmitting disease.[60]

* * *

In one cellar a sanitary inspector reports finding a father, mother, three children and four pigs! In another room a missionary found a man ill with small pox, his wife just recovering from her eighth confinement, and the children running about half naked and covered with dirt.[61]

* * *

The Leicester Anti-Vaccination League was formed in 1869. The stalwart little band of pioneers, numbering less than twenty persons, laboured on, until they grew numerically to such an extent that, whereas in 1867 over 94 per cent, of the children born were vaccinated, in 1897 only 1.3 per cent, of the infants were subjected to the trying ordeal...

Since 1873 up to the present time, an interval of eleven years, the town has enjoyed an almost complete immunity from the inroads of the disease (small-pox). In the last seven years here have been no fewer than seventeen importations of small-pox into the town. Notwithstanding this large number of importations, the disease has always been stamped out, and the town thus saved from the distress and mortality which have hitherto accompanied its prevalence.'

---

[60] Rachel Rummel, "Penny Lick: This is some deceptive, dirty ice cream ware," *Atlas Obscura*.

[61] Andrew Mearns, *The Bitter Cry of Outcast London*, London, 1883, p. 9.

The Guardians wish to point out that the distress and mortality here referred to were prior to 1873, when vaccination was in full practice, while the means since resorted to with such uniform success have been isolation of patients, disinfection of their homes, with the adoption of general sanitary precautions, and in no case vaccination.

They also wish to state that this success has been attained in the midst of an increasingly unvaccinated population.

The enclosed return shows that the opposition now embraces more than half the population only 1,732 being vaccinated out of 4,819 births for the year 1883."[62]

46. The Ghost in the Well

* * *

47. Effigy

By 17 July all supplies on board the little dinghy had been exhausted. After a further three days, the inexperienced Richard Parker could not resist gulping down sea water in an attempt to allay his thirst. It is now known that small quantities of sea water can help to sustain life in survival situations, but in that period it was widely believed to be fatal. Parker also drank far in excess of modern recommendations and he was soon violently unwell, collapsing in the bottom of the boat with diarrhoea.

Even before Parker fell ill, Tom Dudley had broached the fearful topic of the 'custom of the sea', the practice of

---

[62] J.T. Biggs, *Leicester: Sanitation Versus Vaccination*, 1912, pp. 79, 97-98.

drawing lots to select a sacrificial victim who could be consumed by his crew-mates. Over the coming days, as Parker's condition deteriorated, Dudley raised the idea again. As he insisted to Stephens in the early hours of 25 July, when the men had been adrift for almost three weeks: "The boy is dying. You have a wife and five children, and I have a wife and three children. Human flesh has been eaten before."

According to their subsequent depositions, however, no lots were drawn. Instead, Dudley told Stephens to hold Parker's legs should he struggle, before kneeling and thrusting his penknife into the boy's jugular. A chronometer case was used to catch the oozing blood and this was quickly passed between Parker's three crew-mates, to moisten their parched mouths. Parker's body was then stripped and butchered. The heart and liver were eaten immediately; strips of flesh were cut from his limbs and set aside as future rations. What remained of the young man was heaved overboard.[63]

* * *

"The mayor of the city received the procession, and a member of the municipal council presided. An effigy of Jenner [considered the father of vaccination] was hung from the gallows and given the "long drop" at intervals as the procession advanced. Those men who had suffered the extreme penalty of imprisonment made a prominent figure, and others, whose goods had been seized, displayed samples of the otherwise rather commonplace utensils to admiring eyes. The obnoxious parliamentary

---

[63] Carl Thompson, "Cannibalism at sea: the starving Victorian sailors who ate a cabin boy," *History Extra*, May 2014.

acts were enthusiastically burned. A wagon carrying unvaccinated children bore the motto: 'They that are whole need not a physician.'"[64]

48. Shattered Peace

* * *

49. The Grin in the Corner

The by-law passed by the Provincial Board of Health making vaccination compulsory having appeared in the Official Gazette increased the excitement among the French Canadians to such an extent that a riot broke out in the east end this morning, and before the crowd dispersed they smashed many of the windows of the East End Health Office... some 50 police had meantime arrived and drove the mob down the street, but they immediately gathered on the Champ de Mars in the rear, where a lively hand-to-hand conflict took place, but the rioters, when dispersed at one place, immediately met at another and renewed the stone throwing, and several of the police were wounded... the mob returned to the house of Dr. Laporte, public vaccinator, and set fire to it... the rioters proceeded once more to the East End Health Office, and easily over-powered the five policemen who were on guard. The whole front of the office was torn out and the smallpox placards and sulphur for disinfecting houses were piled up in the middle of the street and set fire to... The police then charged the crowd and drove them out to

---

[64] "A Demonstration Against Vaccination," *Boston Medical and Surgical Journal*, April 16, 1885, p. 380.

the city limits. The clubs were plied with vigor and many of the rioters were badly cut about the head.[65]

50. A Shared Humanity

Blakesley continued to race and try his luck almost every weekend either at the Floral Hall or Rutland Hall, then on 15th December 1884 Blakesley wins his first race. Still only 15 he is victorious in the half mile handicap at the Floral Hall off 163 yards. With 36 entries the event is watched by more than 2000 spectators. The final is close with some good racing but Blakesley takes the victory just ahead of a fast finishing Satchell.[66]

* * *

In Dewsbury in 1880 the effigy of a vaccination officer was thrown to a crowd of 10,000 people and was "torn to pieces." Four years earlier an "anti-vaccination Guy" representing a particularly harsh magistrate was incinerated in a Somerset Guy Fawkes bonfire.[67]

* * *

The movement was also a form of social and political commentary that revealed profound working-class anxieties over bodily control. This sentiment was clearly articulated as early as 1856 by an "intelligent working man" opposed to vaccination, who argued, "they might as well brand us." In this context, the act of branding evoked

---

[65] "French Against English, A Riot in Montreal Caused by Compulsory Vaccination," *New York Times*, September 29, 1885.

[66] Tertius Picton Blakesley, British Skating Legends

[67] Nadja Durbach, "'They Might As Well Brand Us': Working-Class Resistance to Compulsory Vaccination in Victorian England, *The Society for the Social History of Medicine*, 2000, p. 55.

the dehumanizing marking of cattle, slaves, and criminals, framing compulsory vaccination as an oppressive act of ownership and violation.[68]

* * *

Sir Duminie Corrigan, M.D. when acting as one of the committee in 1871, on the Vaccination Act, said: "An unvaccinated child is like a bag of gunpowder which might blow up the whole school, and ought not, therefore to be admitted to a school unless he is vaccinated."[69]

51. Christmas Blessings

Scrooge having no better answer ready on the spur of the moment, said, "Bah!" again; and followed it up with "Humbug."

"Don't be cross, uncle!" said the nephew.

"What else can I be," returned the uncle, "when I live in such a world of fools as this? Merry Christmas! Out upon merry Christmas! What's Christmas time to you but a time for paying bills without money; a time for finding yourself a year older, but not an hour richer; a time for balancing your books and having every item in 'em through a round dozen of months presented dead against you? If I could work my will," said Scrooge indignantly, "every idiot who goes about with 'Merry Christmas' on his lips, should be

---

[68] Nadja Durbach, "'They Might As Well Brand Us': Working-Class Resistance to Compulsory Vaccination in Victorian England, *The Society for the Social History of Medicine*, 2000, p. 58.
[69] J. W. Hodge, MD, "How Small-Pox Was Banished from Leicester," *Twentieth Century Magazine*, vol. III, no. 16, January 1911, p. 340.

boiled with his own pudding, and buried with a stake of holly through his heart. He should!"[70]

52. The Great Demonstration

Anti-vaccinationists were largely drawn from the ranks of labourers, artisans, and small shopkeepers. Their occupational and social identities—as grocers, tailors, factory workers, journeymen, sectarian ministers, and schoolmistresses—closely resembled those involved in contemporary movements for spiritualism, temperance, and alternative medicine. Furthermore, many were also active in the co-operative movement, friendly societies, and trade unionism, with significant numbers identifying as teetotalers, vegetarians, and religious sectarians.[71]

* * *

...a goodly number of anti-vaccinators were present, and an escort was formed, preceded by a banner, to accompany a young mother and two men, all of whom had resolved to give themselves up to the police and undergo imprisonment in preference to having their children vaccinated. The utmost sympathy was expressed for the poor woman, who bore up bravely, and although seeming to feel her position expressed her determination to go to prison again and again rather than give her child over to the "tender mercies" of a public vaccinator. The three were attended by a numerous crowd and in Gallowtreegate three hearty cheers were given for them,

---

[70] Charles Dickens, *A Christmas Carol*, Chapman & Hall, 1843.
[71] Nadja Durbach, "'They Might As Well Brand Us': Working-Class Resistance to Compulsory Vaccination in Victorian England, *The Society for the Social History of Medicine*, 2000, pp. 47-48.

which were renewed with increased vigor as they entered the doors of the police cells.[72]

* * *

The most important feature was a large number of men who had undergone the extreme process of imprisonment rather than submit to the law. Next came a larger detachment, consisting of men who had their household goods seized and sold by public auction, samples of the goods which had been seized and sold being conveyed in wagons. The next detachment consisted of a conveyance filled with unvaccinated children... This was followed by a large number of delegates, many of whom were from London, Leeds, Manchester, Halifax, Blackburn, Keighley, Bedford, Birmingham, Lincoln, and Norwich. Among other features in the procession were a horse and cow, drawn in wagons and exhibited as sources of vaccination.[73]

* * *

Both the devices and mottoes were of the most profuse order. One of the devices was an effigy of Dr. Jenner inscribed "child-slayer"; a second was a complete funeral cortège, consisting of a coffin on open bier, mourners, etc., and inscribed "another victim of vaccination"...[74]

* * *

---

[72] Stanley Williamson, "Anti-Vaccination Leagues," *Archives of Disease in Childhood*, vol. 59, 1984, p. 1195.
[73] "Anti-Vaccination Demonstration at Leicester," *The Times*, March 24, 1885.
[74] "Anti-Vaccination Demonstration at Leicester," *The Leeds Mercury*, March 24, 1885.

The headquarters of the Demonstration were at the Temperance Hall, and long before midday it was a scene of intense activity, most of the banners and flags being fitted up there. Of these there were some 700, large and small. Many were tastefully designed, and the colours were as various as the inscriptions. Northampton bore witness that 'Compulsory vaccination is a usurpation of unjust power,' and Brighton that 'Truth conquers.' Kent, with its rampant horse and legend *Invicta*, set 'Parental affection before despotic law,' and demanded 'The repeal of the Vaccination Acts, the curse of our nation,' clenched with the adjuration, 'Men of Kent, defend your liberty of conscience; better a felon's cell than a poisoned babe.' Kettering pronounced for 'Freedom,' and Halifax that 'Jenner's patent has run out.' Middleton set on high 'The crusade against legalised compulsory medical quackery'; whilst Oldham called for 'Health and liberty,' and exhorted beholders to 'Be just and fear not,' assuring them, truly enough, 'The price of liberty is eternal vigilance.'

Finsbury and Banbury united in the advice, 'Stand up for liberty!' Southwark called for 'Entire repeal and no compromise,' and Barnoldswick for 'Sanitation, not vaccination.' Truro pertinently asked, 'Who can bring a clean thing out of an unclean?' Keighley, ever to the fore, said, 'We fight for our homes and freedom.' Earlstown asked for 'Pure blood and no adulteration,' and Lincoln averred, 'We protect our offspring.' Eastbourne advised, 'Cease to do evil, learn to do well.' St. Pancras sent 'Cordial greeting and sympathy to the heroic martyrs of Leicester.'

There was a well-appointed hearse, with a child's coffin inscribed, 'Another victim of vaccination,' and the observation of Sir Joseph Pease in the House of Commons,

'The President of the Local Government Board cannot deny that children die under the operation of the Vaccination Acts in a wholesale way.' A banner bore the prayer, 'From horse-grease, calf-lymph, cow-pox, and the Local Government Board, good Lord deliver us.' Another had, 'A dead swindle — a vaccination death certificate.' The origin of cow-pox in horse-grease was illustrated by a mangey horse with bandaged heels and a heifer on a dray. The varieties of virus, indifferently and ignorantly used for vaccination, were represented in six labelled jars, the original Jennerian grease being inscribed, "'Tis grease, but living grease no more.'

Mr. Golding, of Leytonstone, marched with a model of Holloway Prison, wherein he had recently suffered incarceration for saving his child from vaccination. There were numerous banners with piquant local allusions, which would require more or less interpretation outside Leicester. A fine banner from Belgium bore the inscription in French, "Neither penalties nor prison can prevent vaccine from being a poison and the vaccination laws an infamy. — Dr. Hubert Boens." On the other side was a babe in a cradle and a doctor with an ass's head vaccinating it."[75]

* * *

The demonstration... drew delegates from all parts of the country, while many letters of sympathy were received not only from England, Scotland, and Ireland, but from Jersey, France, Switzerland, Belgium, Germany, and America. Most of the large towns in the kingdom sent special banners, the Yorkshire, Irish, and Scotch being

---

[75] J.T. Biggs, *Leicester: Sanitation Versus Vaccination*, 1912, pp. 108-110.

very prominent. The anti-vaccinationists in Jersey sent a very elaborate banner setting forth that the Acts had been four times defeated there, while the Belgium banner had this inscription in French— "Neither fines nor imprisonment will prevent vaccine being a poison nor the vaccination laws an infamy."[76]

* * *

Many present had been sufferers under the Acts, and all they asked was that in the future they and their children might be let alone. They lived for something else in this world than to be experimented upon for the stamping out of a particular disease. A large and increasing portion of the public were of opinion that the best way to get rid of smallpox and similar diseases was to use plenty of water, eat good food, live in light and airy houses, and see that the Corporation kept the streets clean and the drains in order. If such details were attended to, there was no need to fear smallpox, or any of its kindred; and if they were neglected, neither vaccination nor any other prescription by Act of Parliament could save them.[77]

* * *

The Leicester Demonstration of March 1885 was a tour de force of anti-vaccination organization and a perfect example of the "carnival of common merriment" that characterized such protests. A giant parade, featuring banners and babies, converged on the marketplace. Its macabre and satirical elements included a hearse bearing

---

[76] "Anti-Vaccination Demonstration at Leicester," *The Times*, March 24, 1885.
[77] J.T. Biggs, *Leicester: Sanitation Versus Vaccination*, 1912, p. 117.

a child's coffin inscribed "Another victim of vaccination," trolleys displaying furniture "seized for blood money," and an effigy of Edward Jenner that was hanged, tossed about, and decapitated before being taken to the police station. The crowd of 80,000 to 100,000 participants conspicuously enjoyed these spectacles, along with a model prison cell and floats depicting doctors riding cows and policemen attempting "legal burglary," treating the entire event with the festive air of a local fair.[78]

* * *

Dr. Spencer T. Hall, of Blackpool, aged seventy-three and infirm, was overcome with emotion when speaking of the events of the preceding day. His tears, he said, were tears of joy and gratitude in having lived to see the vaccination question attain its present position. He had been vaccinated at two years of age, and very seriously injured; but at fourteen he had a severe attack of small-pox, which was followed by improved health. Far rather would he have small-pox than be vaccinated. He had paid fines for all his children. In his long and wide experience he had never seen such evil results from small-pox as he had seen from vaccination.[79]

* * *

...since blood-poisoning of our children was enforced by Act of Parliament, small-pox has increased both in extent and frequency. Now vaccination by calf-pox, cow-pox, or

---

[78] Nadja Durbach, "'They Might As Well Brand Us': Working-Class Resistance to Compulsory Vaccination in Victorian England, *The Society for the Social History of Medicine*, 2000, p. 57.
[79] J.T. Biggs, *Leicester: Sanitation Versus Vaccination*, 1912, pp. 125–126.

humanised pox, whatever may be the multiplicity of lymphs, (and "pure vaccine" is only a rhetorical euphemism for horse-grease) is an eruptive disease, setting in with febrile symptoms, followed by papule, vesicle, and pustule, in about eight days. And what else is small-pox?

I have recently dissected more than a dozen children whose deaths were caused by vaccination, and no small-pox, however black, could have left more hideous traces of its malignant sores, foul sloughing, hearts empty or congested with clots, than did some of these little victims. Shame! Indeed, scarcely a day elapses but I am called upon to witness the sufferings of vaccinated children in the form of cerebral and gastric complications, persistent vomiting, bronchitis, diarrhoea, with pustules in the mouth or throat (pharynx), on the eyelids, and ulceration of the cornea, which remains opaque and may lead to blindness.[80] — William Hycheman, MD, forty years' experience as a Doctor of Medicine, 1879

53. Landslide

The result of this demonstration was momentous. At the next triennial election of Guardians in April 1886, the traitors were dismissed, and an overwhelming majority of members were returned pledged to vote in opposition to compulsion. The subject was very soon introduced to the newly-elected Board, and on 4th May 1886, after a debate, the compulsionists were routed by twenty-seven votes to eight. Thus ended the tyranny initiated by the previous

---

[80] William Hycheman, MD, "Small-pox and Vaccination," The Medical Tribune, February 15, 1879, vol. I, no. 4, pp. 172-175.

Board, which doubtless in the end did more to defeat than to establish compliance with the law.[81]

* * *

At the election of Guardians in 1886, the principal question before the electors was that of enforcing vaccination. A large majority of the candidates expressed themselves against the principle of compulsion, and with few exceptions these were returned. The votes cast for the opponents of compulsion rose from about 41,000 in 1883 to nearly 48,000 in 1886, while the votes for the advocates of prosecutions fell from about 31,000 in 1883 to about 20,000 in 1886. The result of the election was seen in the fact that at the first meeting of the newly-elected Board, notice was given to rescind the order for prosecutions. On 4th May, 1886, this order was rescinded on the motion of Mr. J. T. Biggs after a long debate, by twenty-seven votes against eight.[82]

* * *

The widespread opposition to the enforcement of the compulsory clauses of the Vaccination Acts which exists in Leicester culminated yesterday in a great demonstration, which was carried out very successfully. The position which the inhabitants of the town have assumed with regard to this question is due to a variety of causes. At the present moment there are over 5,000 persons being summoned for refusing to comply with the law.... summonses issued in the year 1884 only reached seven,

---

[81] J.T. Biggs, *Leicester: Sanitation Versus Vaccination*, 1912, p. 130.
[82] J.T. Biggs, *Leicester: Sanitation Versus Vaccination*, 1912, pp. 152-153.

or a little over one summons in every two months, while at the present moment forty-five summonses are being heard and disposed of every week. But even the disposal of forty-five defendants every week is not sufficient to meet the requirements of the case, and the defaulters and the objectors increase faster than the cases can be dealt with. The last decade has witnessed an extraordinary decrease in vaccination, but nevertheless, the town has enjoyed an almost entire immunity from small-pox. There never having been more than two or three cases in the town at one time. A new method, for which great practical utility is claimed, has been enforced by the sanitary committee of the Corporation for the stamping out of small-pox. The chairman of the Committee has gone so far as to declare that small-pox is one of the least troublesome diseases with which they have to deal. The method of treatment, in a word, is this: as soon as small-pox breaks out, the medical man and the householder are compelled under penalty to at once report the outbreak to the Corporation. The small-pox van is at once ordered by telephone to proceed to the house in question; the hospital authorities are also instructed by telephone to make all arrangements. Thus, within a few hours, the sufferer is safely in the hospital. The family and inmates of the house are placed in quarantine in comfortable quarters, and the house is thoroughly disinfected. The result is that in every instance the disease has been promptly and completely stamped out at a paltry expense. Under such a system the Corporation have expressed their opinion that vaccination is unnecessary, as they claim to deal with the disease in a more direct and much more efficacious manner. This, and a widespread belief that death and disease have resulted from the operation of vaccination, may be said to be the foundation upon which the existing opposition to the Acts rests."[83]

* * *

The practice of vaccination will, in the next century, be regarded as one of the most curious of the medical delusions of our time.[84]

54. The Path Remembered

The year 1948 will ever be memorable in the history of vaccination in this country as seeing the end of compulsory vaccination of infants, a measure which has been the subject of such acute and bitter controversy for so many years. Having regard to the great importance attached to universal vaccination of infants as our "first line of defense," and to the firm belief that only by compulsion could this be secured, it is rather surprising that the proposal to abolish compulsion did not arouse more opposition. In the event the opposition was almost negligible.[85]

* * *

...in Leicester during the 62 years since infant vaccination was abandoned there have been only 53 deaths from smallpox, and in the past 40 years only two deaths. Moreover, the experience in Leicester is confirmed, and

---

[83] "Anti-Vaccination Demonstration at Leicester," *The Times*, March 24, 1885.

[84] Alfred Russel Wallace, *Vaccination a Delusion: Its Penal Enforcement a Crime*, E.W. Allen, 1889.

[85] C. Killick Millard, MD, DSc, "The End of Compulsory Vaccination," *British Medical Journal*, December 18, 1948, p. 1073.

strongly confirmed, by that of the whole country. Vaccination has been steadily declining ever since the "conscience clause" was introduced, until now nearly two-thirds of the children born are not vaccinated. Yet smallpox mortality has also declined until now quite negligible. In the fourteen years 1933-1946 there were only 28 deaths in a population of some 40 million, and among those 28 there was not a single death of an infant under 1 year of age...

Looking back it is interesting to consider why medical experts were so mistaken in their prophecies of disaster to come if universal vaccination of infants was abandoned. It was probably due to the belief, then so strongly held, that it was infant vaccination, and that alone, which had brought about the great diminution of smallpox mortality that followed upon an introduction of vaccination. That this was clearly a case of cause and effect was reiterated in every textbook and in every course of lectures on public health. It was hailed, indeed, as the outstanding triumph of preventative medicine. No wonder that medical students accepted it as an incontrovertible scientific fact.[86]

* * *

Ven Der Fuehrer says, "Ve iss der Master Race"
Ve Heil, Heil right in Der Fuehrer's face
Not to luff Der Fuehrer iss a great disgrace
So ve Heil, Heil right in Der Fuehrer's face[87]

---

[86] C. Killick Millard, MD, DSc, "The End of Compulsory Vaccination," *British Medical Journal*, December 18, 1948, p. 1074.
[87] Irving Berlin, "Right in Der Fuehrer's Face," This is the Army, Inc., 1942.

"Box-bed in which a naked woman lived forty-three years."
(1861-1904)

Sixth Biennial Report of the Commissioner, Superintendent, and Treasurer of the Illinois Asylum for the Incurable Insane at Peoria, June 30, 1906, p. 7.

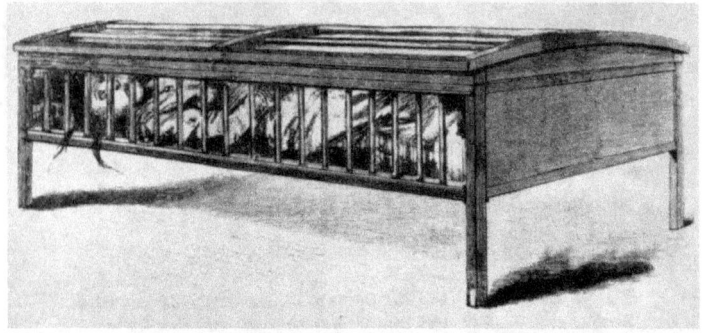

"It is a bed like a child's crib, with slatted sides, eighteen inches deep, 6 feet long, and 3 feet wide. It has a slatted lid which shuts with a spring lock. A lunatic put in it can barely turn over. There is not as much space between the patient's head and the lid as if he were in a coffin. He is kept in the crib at the will of an attendant, the key being in the possession of the latter and not a physician. Patients have sometimes died in these cribs."

Meghan MacRae, Horrifying Psychiatric Treatments from the Age of Reason, CVLT Nation, December 2, 2020.

"So-called "humane" restraint apparatus, consisting of the leather "muff," "mitts," "anklets," "wristlets," and the famous "bed saddle. Wholly abolished in 1905.""

Sixth Biennial Report of the Commissioner, Superintendent, and Treasurer of the Illinois Asylum for the Incurable Insane at Peoria, June 30, 1906, p. 9.

"Surprise Bath" used in colonial times to "restore the distracted to their senses." Original wood engraving by John De Pol.

to restore them to

Less than 200 years ago, the mentally ill were bled, purged, beaten and sometimes nearly drowned in efforts to restore them to their senses.

The treatment of mental illness has progressed far beyond methods such as these. One of the major advances in psychiatry has come through chemotherapy—now an important factor in the treatment of mental illness, pioneered and developed with 'Thorazine'.

The importance of 'Thorazine' in psychiatry is twofold: (1) its continued widespread use has established it as a fundamental drug that can be used with confidence, and (2) it has led S.K.F. to the development of related drugs which offer the psychiatrist opportunities to help an even greater number of patients.

their senses

THORAZINE*
chlorpromazine, S.K.F.

Smith Kline & French Laboratories
*T.M. Reg. U.S. Pat. Off.

"Another treatment that was widely used for the treatment of mental illness in the 17th and 18th centuries was the Bath of Surprise. In its original form, the Bath of Surprise was exactly like the Dunk Tank, except it was ice-cold water and an agitated mentally ill patient being dropped into it without warning. Again, an effective but deranged way of sedating patients."

Meghan MacRae, Horrifying Psychiatric Treatments from the Age of Reason, CVLT Nation, December 2, 2020.

No. 3.   SATURDAY, NOVEMBER 20, 1847.   PRICE ONE PENNY.

FIELD-LANE LODGING-HOUSE.

"Field-Lane Lodging House. The first house which I went into, was tenanted entirely Irish, and very entrance was from its dirt and effluvia, both sickening and disgusting. I was taken first into the cellar, into which I descended by some dilapidated stairs, but with no ordinary difficulty. The truly offensive state of this place beggars all description. I scarcely know whether the sense of seeing or the sense of smelling was the most shocked and offended."

The Poor Man's Guardian, November 20, 1847.

"Types of tenement houses which the city destroys."

Robert W. DeForest and Lawrence Veiller, *The Tenement House Problem*, 1903, p. 180.

"Halfpenny dinners for poor children in East London."

Courtesy of the Wellcome Collection. Public Domain.

"A Thaw in the Streets of London."

The Illustrated London News, February 25, 1865.

"The Beggar Family of Whitechapel."

The Working Man's Friend and Family Instructor, vol. I, no. 20,
February 14, 1852, p. 313.

"Goerck and Delancy Streets in New York City. The condition of the streets, with the masses of mud, manure, and other monstrous agglomeration of everything dangerous, unsightly, and offensive, is plainly indicated... Barrels and pails overladen with material, mingled in a foul mess of garbage and ashes, beset the sidewalks. In many cases these have been upset, and the unsavory contents emptied on the curbstone and into the gutter."

Harper's Weekly, February 18, 1893, pp. 161, 166.

"A photograph of pollution caused by the mass production factories in Widnes. Displays the living conditions of the people in England where the pollutants produced by factories were released into the air and rivers, contaminating water sources and the air. The smoke pall that formed the sky of Widnes in Leblanc times. At the highest development of the Leblanc system more than a million tons of coal were consumed annually in the chemical works of the town."

D. W. F. Hardie, *A History of the Chemical Industry in Widnes*, 1950.

"McDermott-Bunger Dairy Co. is painted on the building in the center of the photograph. As of 1903, this dairy company was located at 527 West 125th Street. There are 10 kids, all but one seem to be barefoot, playing in the street gutter and around puddles of raw sewage, all within a few feet of a dead horse. They seem completely unbothered and disinterested in its existence. They don't even seem slightly out of sorts, caught up in the moment of play and Joseph Byron's lens."

Vintage Photograph of New York City Children Playing Next to a Dead Horse in 1903, Viewing NYC.

"1938 - South Pittston, Pa. Jan. 1911. A view of workers in Ewen Breaker of Pa. Coal Co. Dust so thick that it obscured the view much of the time. The boys were bent over constant streams of broken coal, picking out slate, while a boss, who is a kind of slave driver, stands over them, prodding or kicking the boys into obedience."

Lewis Wickes Hine, A View of Workers in Ewen Breaker of Pennsylvania Coal Company, Art Institute of Chicago.

"Adolescent girls in the Payne Cotton Mill, Macon, Georgia, 'It is a shame for a nation to make its young girls weary.' – Ruskin."

Child Labor in Georgia, National Child Labor Committee, 1911, Pamphlet No. 138, p. 2.

17 Crossing sweepers

"Crossing Sweepers."

Francis Henry Wollaston Sheppard, *London, 1808-1870: The Infernal Wen*, University of California Press, 1971, p. 148.

"Woman with an entire bird in her hat, circa 1890. Late-Victorian and Edwardian fashions led to the deaths of several hundred million birds in the days before state, national, and international laws stepped in to help prevent the extinction of many of them."

Taylor, Stephen, "The 'Bird Bills': A tale of the plume boom," *Hoosier State Chronicles.*

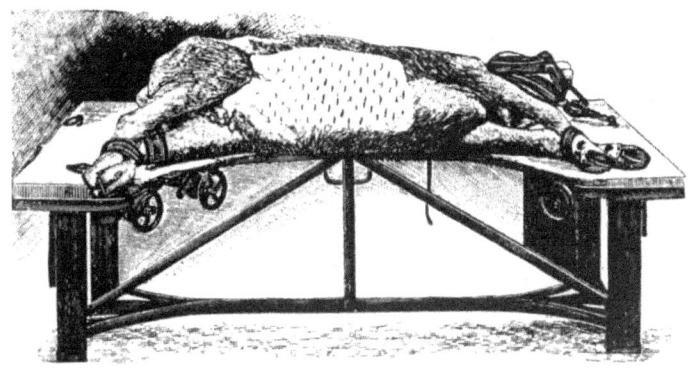

"How cattle are diseased and tortured and Vaccine Virus produced."

Chas M. Higgins, *Horrors of Vaccination Exposed and Illustrated*, 1920, p. 79.

"Mrs. Helen Goates of Bolivar, Missouri was a strong, healthy woman with no skin trouble or chronic disease when she was persuaded, during a vaccination drive, to submit to vaccination. Almost immediately, after the injection, an inflamed swelling started to develop around the vaccination. It continued to increase in size and intensity until it covered her entire arm and hand. After a period of time it spread over her back and breast as is shown in the photograph."

Eleanor McBean, *The Poisoned Needle*, 1957, p. 43.

"The above photographs are of Miss Fannie Lent, of Cincinnati, Ohio. She was vaccinated when a child, and thereafter became a mass of running sores. She visited Zion City a few years ago, and has since died. She suffered the tortures of hell, and was a sight that would melt a heart of stone. These pictures tell the story of what vaccination can do, and has done in thousands of cases. The time has come to down the dirty doctors, and drive vaccination back to hell where it came from."

"Vaccination," Leaves of Healing, January 2, 1915, vol. XXXV, No. 14, p. 313.

"The Great Leicester Demonstration against the Vaccination Acts, 23rd March 1885."

J. T. Biggs, JP, *Sanitation Versus Vaccination*, 1912, p. 64.

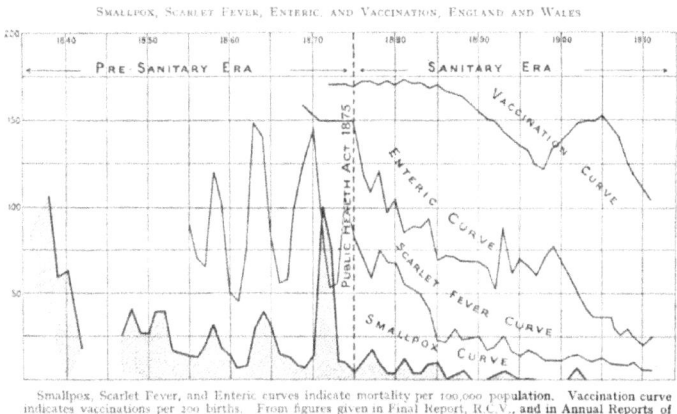

SMALLPOX, SCARLET FEVER, ENTERIC, AND VACCINATION, ENGLAND AND WALES

Smallpox, Scarlet Fever, and Enteric curves indicate mortality per 100,000 population. Vaccination curve indicates vaccinations per 200 births. From figures given in Final Report, R.C.V., and in Annual Reports of Registrar-General.

"England and Wales death rate for scarlet fever, enteric fever, and smallpox 1838-1912. In addition, vaccination rate curve from 1872-1912."

C. Killick Millard, *The Vaccination Question in the Light of Modern Experience: An Appeal for Reconsideration*, 1914, London, p. 16.

About The Author

Roman Bystrianyk is an author and researcher drawn to the crucial, yet often overlooked, intersections of history, science, and society. He co-authored the groundbreaking *Dissolving Illusions: Disease, Vaccines, and the Forgotten History* with Dr. Suzanne Humphries, a work that meticulously re-examines the narrative of disease and medicine. His collaboration with Kathryn Schmutter, *Moving Back from Midnight: Working Together to Save Our Planet*, applies the same rigorous lens to our most pressing environmental crises. It is this same passion for uncovering the past—and the conviction that its lessons are essential for our present—that drives his foray into historical fiction.

www.ingramcontent.com/pod-product-compliance
Lightning Source LLC
Chambersburg PA
CBHW072007020726
47501CB00006B/1721